PRAISE FOR *JANE SLAYRE*

"Erwin displays great affection for Brontë and her characters; the undeniable spark between Erwin's Jane and Rochester is made all the more delightful by Jane's plucky fearlessness in the face of evil. . . . Fans of *Jane Eyre* will find much to love, with moments of laugh-out-loud hilarity; horror fans unfamiliar with the original will also be pleased."

—*Publishers Weekly*

"Unique and gripping revision of a well-loved classic. Enthusiastically recommended."

—*Library Journal* (starred review)

"Not only is Erwin an accomplished writer, but she demonstrates a good appreciation of Brontë's novel, a mastery of its language and its aesthetic. . . . A great way to enjoy the best the genre currently has on offer."

—Science Fiction World

"All of the elements I love about the original are there, with just a little something extra for the supernatural junkie in me. *Jane Slayre* is fun. It is wry. It is an entertaining exercise in 'What If?'"

—Bitten by Books

"What Erwin does well with this book is show how this twist of being a Slayre would effect Jane in her growth and personality. . . . I would definitely recommend this book to anyone who is a fan of the original *Jane Eyre* or anybody who is at all interested in any kind of supernatural stories, especially if you are a fan of *Buffy the Vampire Slayer*. Pretty much if you are interested in a good story, pick this up."

This title is also availa

GRAVE EXPECTATIONS

CHARLES DICKENS
AND SHERRI BROWNING ERWIN

GALLERY BOOKS

New York   London   Toronto   Sydney   New Delhi

Gallery Books
A Division of Simon & Schuster, Inc.
1230 Avenue of the Americas
New York, NY 10020

First Gallery Books trade paperback edition August 2011

For information about special discounts for bulk purchases,
please contact Simon & Schuster Special Sales at
1-866-506-1949 or business@simonandschuster.com.

The Simon & Schuster Speakers Bureau can bring authors
to your live event. For more information or to book an
event contact the Simon & Schuster Speakers Bureau at
1-866-248-3049 or visit our website at www.simonspeakers.com.

Designed by Jaime Putorti

Manufactured in the United States of America

10 9 8 7 6 5 4 3 2 1

Library of Congress Cataloging-in-Publication Data is available.

ISBN 978-1-4516-1724-5
ISBN 978-1-4516-1725-2 (ebook)

ACKNOWLEDGMENTS

I would like to thank Stephany Evans and the entire team at Fine-Print Literary Management for their encouragement and support; my editor, Jennifer Heddle, for her creative insights and brilliant suggestions; everyone at Gallery Books who shared their time and talent to help make *Jane Slayre* and *Grave Expectations* work so well; my Whine Sisters, for their love and for the cuuube; and Charlotte Brontë and Charles Dickens for sharing their words and for being such good sports.

CHAPTER 1

MY FATHER'S FAMILY NAME being Pirrip, and my Christian name Philip, my occasionally altered infant tongue could make of either name nothing longer or more explicit than Pip, sometimes Yip. So I called myself Pip, on occasion Yip, and came to be called Pip.

I give Pirrip as my father's family name on the authority of his tombstone and my sister, Mrs. Joe Gargery, who married the silversmith. As I never saw my father or my mother, and never saw any likeness of either of them, my first fancies regarding what they were like were unreasonably derived from their tombstones. The enormity of my father's stone, the shape of the letters, gave me an odd idea that he was fierce and stout, requiring great effort to hold back even in death, with coarse black hair curling over every inch of him when the moon was full—for he was my sire in the truest sense, responsible for the beast within me, according to Mrs. Joe. From the character and turn of the inscription, "Also Georgiana, Wife of the Above," I drew a childish conclusion that my mother was freckled and sickly, entirely human.

The wolfish nature was passed from male to male down the line, Mrs. Joe said, almost with a grudging air by way of explanation. There had been known to be female werewolves, but only as infected by a bite and never by birth (again with the bitter tone). And birth, or at least infancy, was quite a trial for my kind, or so it seemed by the five little stone lozenges, each about a foot and a half long, which were arranged in a neat row beside my parents' graves, and were sacred to the memory of five little brothers of mine, who gave up exceedingly early in that universal struggle.

I believed that they had all been born as pink gasping babes, unable to cope with the violence of transformation when the first moon came and proved too strong a foe for their inferior infant bodies. I, on the other hand, was born under a full moon as a robust pup, and stronger in wolf form to handle the force of the change when it next came on, for experience had taught me that werewolf to human was a much less traumatic transformation than human to wolf.

Ours was the marsh country, down by the river, within twenty miles of the sea. My first vivid and broad impression of the identity of things seems to have been gained on a memorable raw evening under a full moon. At such a time I found out for certain that this bleak place overgrown with nettles was the churchyard, where Philip Pirrip, late of this parish, and also Georgiana, wife of the above, were buried. And that Alexander, Bartholomew, Abraham, Tobias, and Roger, infant children of the aforesaid, also dead, were buried. And that the small bundle of shivers feeling his bones shift and grind, his skin stretch under a sudden flurry of hair, growing afraid of it all and beginning to cry, was Pip.

"Hold your noise!" cried a terrible voice as a man started up from among the graves at the side of the church porch. "Keep still, you little devil, or I'll bite your throat out!"

A beast of a man, all in coarse grey, with a great silver cuff on his leg, stood suddenly before me. He was missing a hat and shoes, and had an old rag tied round his head. From the looks of him, he had been soaked in water, smothered in mud, lamed by stones, cut by flints, stung by nettles, and torn by briars. He limped, shivered, glared, and growled. His teeth chattered as he seized me by the chin, and he slowly took on wolflike proportions before my eyes.

"Oh! Don't bite me, sir," I pleaded in terror. "Pray don't do it, srrr."

"Tell us your name!" said the man. "Quick! Before the power of human speech forsakes us."

"Pip." It came out more a yip, as I was increasingly more wolf than boy.

"Once more," said the man, staring at me with his hungry yellow eyes. "Give it mouth!"

"Pip. Pip, srrr." The sir turned into an unfortunate snarl. I fought the temptation to roll over on my back, thus demonstrating my vast inferiority and probably sealing my doom.

"Show us where you live," said the man. "Pint out the place!"

With more paw than hand, I pointed to where our village lay, on the flat in-shore among the alder-trees and pollards, a mile or more from the church. I shouldn't have come out so late. On full moon nights, my sister usually had Joe lock me in. She would be in fits trying to find me. But the trouble I faced from Mrs. Joe paled in comparison to the fear of what the stranger might do to me, or what I might do out in the marsh when I was not quite myself, or more myself than usual, as it were, considering I was born a wolf.

The man, after looking at me for a moment, nudged me to the ground and sniffed at me, centering on my pockets and eventually tearing out a piece of bread with his teeth. I remained on the ground, on my back, instinctively submissive, trembling while he, on all fours, ate the bread ravenously.

"You young dog," said the man, licking his lips, "what fat cheeks you ha' got. Darn me if I couldn't eat 'em, and if I haven't half a mind to't!"

I earnestly expressed my hope that he wouldn't, or ended up merely whining as my tongue lolled half out of its own accord as I struggled to roll over to a more defensive posture.

"Now lookee here!" said the man. "Where's your mother?" Being bigger and stronger, even saddled with that band of silver around his leg, he seemed more able than I to hold full transformation at bay. He stood to his full height.

I gestured with a paw.

He started, made a short run, and stopped and looked over his shoulder.

He quickly realised I had pointed at their graves.

"Oh!" he said, coming back. "And is that your father alongside your mother?"

I nodded and forced out the words, relieved to find I was still able. "Him, too. Late of this parish."

"Ha! Who d'ye live with—supposin' you're kindly let to live, which I haven't made up my mind about?"

"My sister, srrr—Mrs. Joe Garrgery—wife of Joe Garrrgery, the silversmith, srrr." It was increasingly difficult not to growl.

"Silversmith, eh?" said he. And looked down at his leg.

After darkly looking at his leg and me several times, he pounced, rolled me onto my back, and stood over me, pinning me to the ground under him. His eyes looked most powerfully down into mine, and mine looked most helplessly up into his.

"Now lookee here," he said. "The question being whether you're to be let to live. You know what a file is?"

I nodded.

"And you know what wittles is?"

I nodded again.

After each question he bared his teeth so as to give me a greater sense of helplessness and danger.

"You get me a file. And you get me wittles. You bring 'em both to me. Or I'll tear your heart and liver out." He took a step away as if to let me up.

I was dreadfully frightened, and so giddy that I struggled to roll back to all fours. I was already nearly in full wolf form and sure to be locked in the moment I returned home. I supposed he was too weak from dragging the silver cuff to hunt his own food, but how was I to do as he bid?

He gave me a knock and I took a most tremendous roll, so that I was under him again. "You bring me, tomorrow morning early, that file and them wittles. You bring the lot to me, at that old battery over yonder. You do it, and you never dare to say a word or dare to make a sign concerning your having seen such a person as me, or any person sumever, and you shall be let to live. You fail, or you go from my words in any partickler, no matter how small it is, and your heart and your liver shall be tore out and ate.

"Now, I ain't alone, as you may think I am. There's a young man hid with me, in comparison with which young man I am a angel. That young man hears the words I speak. That young man has a secret way pecooliar to himself, of getting at a pup, and at his heart, and at his liver, and his blood. It is in wain for a pup or boy to attempt to hide himself from that young man. I am keeping that young man from harming you at the present moment, with great difficulty. He's not like you or I, but something worse, something wicked, and he thirsts for blood. Now, what do you say?"

I tried to say that I would get him the file, and I would get him what broken bits of food I could, and I would come to him at the battery, early in the morning, but all that came out was a low rumble.

"Say Lord strike you dead if you don't!" said the man.

I howled my agreement, and he let me up.

"Now," he pursued, "you remember what you've undertook, pup, and you get home!"

At the same time, he writhed, his body shuddering, and dropped down to all fours as if finally giving in to the change from man to wolf as he made his way towards the low church wall.

As I saw him go, picking his way among the nettles, and among the brambles that bound the green mounds, he looked in my young eyes as if he were eluding the hands of the dead people stretching up cautiously out of their graves to get a twist upon his ankle and pull him in.

When he came to the low church wall, he got over it in a single pounce, one back leg dragging behind him due to the weight of the silver, which still clung to him, unshakeable. When I saw him turning, I set my face towards home.

I was frightened again, and ran home without stopping.

CHAPTER 2

M Y SISTER, MRS. JOE Gargery, was more than twenty years older than I, and had established a great reputation with the neighbours, and in her own mind, because she had brought me, the wolfish terror, up "by hand." Having at that time to find out for myself what the expression "by hand" meant, and knowing her to have a hard and heavy hand, and to be much in the habit of laying it upon her husband as well as upon me, I supposed that Joe Gargery and I were both brought up by hand.

My sister was not a good-looking woman, and I had a general impression that she must have made Joe Gargery marry her by hand. Joe was a fair man, with flaxen curls and with eyes of such a very undecided blue that they seemed to have somehow got mixed with their own whites. He was a mild, good-natured, sweet-tempered, easy-going, foolish, dear fellow—a sort of Hercules in strength, and also in weakness.

Mrs. Joe, with black hair and eyes, had such a prevailing redness of skin that I sometimes used to wonder whether it was possible she washed herself with a nutmeg-grater instead of soap. She was tall and bony, and almost always wore a coarse apron with a square impregnable bib in front that was stuck full of pins and needles. She made it a powerful merit in herself, and a strong reproach against Joe, that she wore this apron so much. Though I really see no reason why she should have worn it at all, or why, if she did wear it at all, she should not have taken it off every day of her life.

Joe's forge adjoined our house, which was a wooden house, as many of the dwellings in our country were at that time. When I ran home from the churchyard, the forge was shut up, and I leapt and peeked in a window of the house to see that Joe was sitting alone in the kitchen. Joe looked after me. When I scratched at the door, he opened and let me in.

"Mrs. Joe has been out a dozen times looking for you, Pip. And she's out now, making it a baker's dozen."

Unable to answer with my thick wolf tongue protruding as I panted, I tilted my head in the way that showed interest.

"Yes, Pip," said Joe. "And what's worse, she's got Tickler with her."

At this dismal intelligence, I bounded across the room and tried to crouch under a chair. Tickler was a silver-tipped piece of cane, worn smooth by collision with my tickled frame. I wasn't a very big wolf yet, not bold enough to rise up against her, and the silver kept me weaker than usual, nearly defenseless.

"She sot down and she got up, and she made a grab at Tickler, and she rampaged out. That's what she did," Joe said, as he slowly cleared the fire between the lower bars with the poker. "She rampaged out, Pip. She's been on the rampage, this last spell, about five minutes. She's a coming! No time to get you locked away safe. Get behind the door, old chap."

I took the advice. My sister, Mrs. Joe, threw the door wide open and, finding an obstruction behind it, immediately divined the cause. She poked behind the door with Tickler. I ducked, but couldn't get away, the silver tip burning like a red-hot poker through my coarse covering of hair right into my skin. She concluded by getting hold of me, wrenching me up by the scruff of my neck, and throwing me at Joe, who, glad to get hold of me on any terms, passed me on into the chimney and quietly fenced me up there with his great leg.

"Where have you been, you young whelp?" said Mrs. Joe, stamping her foot. "And your clothes scattered out from here to the churchyard."

She threw my trousers on the hearth. I vaguely remembered wiggling out of them along the way, my body continuing to change shape as I ran.

"You've worn me out with fret and worry, or I'd have you out of that corner if you was fifty Pips, and he was five hundred Gargerys. Don't know what took you off to the churchyard on a full moon night! If it warn't for me, you'd have been to the churchyard long ago, and stayed there. Who brought you up by hand?"

I could only look at her. I might have whimpered slightly under my breath.

"And why did I do it, I should like to know?" exclaimed my sister, going on without any need of answers from me. "I'd never do it again! I know that. I may truly say I've never had this apron of mine off since you were born. It's bad enough to be a silversmith's wife (and him a Gargery) without being your mother."

My thoughts strayed from that question as I looked disconsolately at the fire. The fugitive out on the marshes with the clamped leg, the mysterious young man, the file, the food, and the dreadful pledge I was under to commit a larceny on those sheltering premises, rose before me in the avenging coals. I had to find a way to make my transformation, get to the pantry, and out by morning.

"Hah!" said Mrs. Joe, restoring Tickler to his station. "Churchyard, indeed! You'll drive me to the churchyard betwixt you, one of these days, and oh, a pr-r-recious pair you'd be without me!"

As she applied herself to set the tea things, Joe peeped down at me over his leg, as if he were calculating what kind of pair we practically should make, under the grievous circumstances foreshadowed. After that, he sat feeling his right-side flaxen curls and whisker, and following Mrs. Joe about with his blue eyes, as his manner always was at squally times.

My sister had an incisive method of cutting our bread and butter that never varied. First, with her left hand, she jammed the loaf hard and fast against her bib, where it sometimes got a pin into it, and sometimes a needle, which we afterwards got into our mouths. Then she took some butter (not too much) on a knife and spread it on the loaf, in an apothecary kind of way, as if she were making a plaster using both sides of the knife with a slapping dexterity, trimming and moulding the butter off round the crust. Then, she gave the knife a final smart wipe on the edge of the plaster, and sawed a very thick round off the loaf, then finally, separated the loaf into two halves, of which Joe got one, and I the other.

On the present occasion, though I was hungry, I dared not eat my slice. I felt that I must have something in reserve for my dreadful acquaintance, and his ally the still more dreadful young man. I knew Mrs. Joe's housekeeping to be of the strictest kind, and that my larcenous researches might find nothing available in the pantry if I could even recover in time to get there and get out. Therefore I resolved to hide the hunk of bread and butter in my heaped-up trousers.

The effort necessary to the achievement of this purpose I found to be quite awful. I had to sniff at the bread, paw around as if I were interested, and wait until Joe was distracted enough with his own meal that I could push it under my rumpled trousers with my snout and dig a bit to cover it up.

Joe was evidently made uncomfortable by what he supposed to be my loss of appetite, and took a thoughtful bite out of his slice, which he didn't seem to enjoy. He turned it about in his mouth much longer than usual, pondering over it a good deal, and after all gulped it down like a pill. He was about to take another bite when his gaze fell on me, and he saw that my bread and butter was gone.

The wonder with which Joe stopped on the threshold of his bite and stared at me was too evident to escape my sister's observation.

"What's the matter now?" she said, as she put down her cup.

"I say, you know!" muttered Joe, shaking his head at me in very serious remonstrance. "Pip, old chap! You'll do yourself a mischief. You can't have chawed it."

"What's the matter now?" repeated my sister, more sharply than before.

"If you can cough any trifle on it up, Pip, I'd recommend you to do it," said Joe, all aghast. "Manners is manners, but still your elth's your elth."

This time, my sister pounced on Joe, and, taking him by the two whiskers, knocked his head for a little while against the wall behind him, while I sat in the corner looking guiltily on.

"Now, perhaps you'll mention what's the matter," said my sister, out of breath, "you staring great stuck pig."

Joe looked at her in a helpless way, then took a bite, and looked at me again.

"You know, Pip," said Joe, solemnly, with his last bite in his cheek, and speaking in a confidential voice, as if we two were quite alone, "you and me is always friends, and I'd be the last to tell upon you, any time. But such a"—he moved his chair and looked about the floor between us, and then again at me—"such a most uncommon bolt as that!"

"Been bolting his food, has he?" cried my sister.

"You know, old chap," said Joe, looking at me, and not at Mrs. Joe, with his bite still in his cheek, "I bolted when I was your age—frequent—and as a boy I've been among a many bolters, but I never see your bolting equal yet, Pip. It's a mercy you ain't bolted dead."

My sister made a dive at me, and fished me up by the nape, saying nothing more than the awful words, "You come along and be dosed."

Some medical beast had suggested tar water in those days as a suppressant for supernatural urges. Mrs. Joe always kept a supply of it in the cupboard, having a belief in its virtues correspondent to its nastiness. At the best of times, so much of this elixir was administered to me as a choice suppressant that I was conscious of going about smelling like a new fence. On this particular evening, the urgency of my case demanded a pint of this mixture, which was poured down my throat, for my greater comfort, while Mrs. Joe held my head under her arm as a boot would be held in a bootjack. Joe, who didn't have any hint of supernatural in him in the first place, got off with half a pint.

Conscience is a dreadful thing when it accuses man or pup, but when, in the case of a pup, that secret burden cooperates with another secret burden hidden in his trousers, it is (as I can testify) a great punishment. The guilty knowledge that I was going to rob Mrs. Joe—I never thought I was going to rob Joe, for I never thought of any of the housekeeping property as his—made it necessary to always keep one paw on my bread and butter as I sat, and kept my mind wild with fear. As the marsh winds stirred the fire to glow and flare, I thought I heard the howling outside of the wolfman with the silver on his leg. At other times, I thought, what if the young man who was, with so much difficulty, restrained from coming after me should yield to a constitutional impatience, or should mistake the time, and should think himself accredited to my heart and liver tonight instead of tomorrow! My hair stood on end with terror, if it were possible, but one might mistake it for my hackles being raised, more to my detriment.

It was Christmas Eve, and my usual task was to stir the pudding for next day with a copper stick from seven to eight by the Dutch clock. I couldn't do it in wolf form without shedding hair in the pudding, so I watched with regret as Joe was forced to take my place. I could smell the bread hidden in the pile of cloth. Once Joe was occupied in his task and my sister was occupied with watching Joe, I slipped my nose in to retrieve the bread and trotted it to my garret bedroom, nudging it under the bed with my nose.

I returned in time to hear great guns going off and catch Joe's explanation of such.

"Ah!" said Joe. "There's another Scapegrace off."

"Escaped. Escaped from the Hulks. Containment ships, right 'cross the marshes." Mrs. Joe administered the definition like tar water. "The second in two nights."

I wanted to stay to hear more about the escaped Scapegraces, the term for those of a supernatural sort. There were beasts other than werewolves populating England at the time. There were vampires. Vampires, however, were considered civilized and welcome to mix in society, while werewolves were considered a scourge, to be kept in the country and forgotten or ignored. I never understood the distinction afforded vampires, who turned beastly by choice, thrived on human victims, and were generally sneaky and dishonest. Werewolves were simply born different, and only became entirely wolfish once a moon cycle. Of course, there was the occasional human victim, but my kind (not that I had any experience, kept under lock and key during full moon) preferred to roam and hunt livestock or roving beasts for sport, and sometimes food. What harm were we to society?

Of great harm, as the presence of containment ships might suggest. Scapegraces of suspicious nature, which I came to understand was almost any nature at all, were gathered and locked up, usually for little more than feeding on sheep belonging to an unsympathetic farmer. I wondered what these two convict Scapegraces might have done. Murder? Rob? I suspected a bit of both as I recalled the man in the marsh, the man like me. I'd never seen another, but he frightened me more than I could say. I must have whimpered aloud, for Mrs. Joe suddenly recalled my presence and rose.

"I tell you what, young whelp," she said. "You might have put us all in danger rambling 'round the marshes on a night with Scapegraces escaping the hulks. Now, you get along to bed!"

I was never allowed a candle to light me to bed, but tonight I didn't need one. My vision was sharp, even in the dark. All my senses were improved in my wolf form, and I was glad of it. I would be up half the night worrying about the Scapegraces breaking in and robbing me of my heart and liver. I had to do as I was bid, first thing in the morning. I felt fearfully sensible of the great convenience that the containment hulks were handy for me. I was clearly on my way there. Perhaps it's where all of my kind ended up, there or dead.

I'd never considered it before, but having met the convict on the night of visiting my family's graves, it seemed a logical concern. Was it a crime to merely be different? Perhaps the convict was guilty of nothing more than his ability to take the shape of a wolf, in which case I was headed for trouble. I couldn't control who I was or what happened to me when the moon was full. I was in mortal terror of the young man who wanted my heart and liver, of my interlocutor with the silvered leg, and of myself, from my own capricious changing form and for my questionable ability to live up to the awful promise that had been extracted.

If I slept at all that night, it was only to imagine myself drifting down the river on a strong spring-tide, to the Hulks. I was afraid to sleep, even if I had been inclined, for I knew that at the first faint dawn of morning I must rob the pantry. There was no doing it in the night, for I couldn't risk fumbling about with my paws. I must have slept some, for I woke to find my body back to boy form, and the great black velvet pall outside my little window was shot with grey. Changing back to boy was much less pain on the joints than becoming wolf and I often slept right through it.

I got up and pulled on my clothes, deposited outside my door most likely by a thoughtful Joe, and went downstairs. Every board creaked upon the way, and every crack in every board called after me, "Stop thief!" and "Get up, Mrs. Joe!"

In the pantry, which was far more abundantly supplied than usual owing to the season, I had no time for verification, no time for selection, no time for anything, for I had no time to spare. I stole some bread, some rind of cheese, about half a jar of mincemeat (which I tied up in my pocket-handkerchief with my last night's slice), some brandy from a stone bottle (which I decanted into a glass bottle, diluting the stone bottle from a jug in the kitchen cupboard), a meat bone with very little on it, and a beautiful round compact pork pie. I was nearly going away without the pie, but I was tempted to mount upon a shelf, to look what it was that was put away so carefully in a covered earthen ware dish in a corner, and I found it was the pie, and I took it in the hope that it was not intended for early use, and would not be missed for some time.

There was a door in the kitchen that led into the forge. I unlocked and unbolted that door, and got a file from among Joe's tools. Then I put the fastenings as I had found them, opened the door at which I had entered when I ran home last night, shut it, and ran for the misty marshes.

CHAPTER 3

THE MORNING WAS DAMP, as evidenced by the mist coating the window, as if a wolf, or something worse, had been licking the windowpane. Once outside, I saw the damp lying on the bare hedges and grass like a coarser sort of spiders' webs hanging from twig to twig and blade to blade. The marsh mist was so thick that the wooden finger on the post directing people to our village—a direction which they never accepted, for they never came there—was invisible to me until I was quite close under it. Then, as I looked up at it while it dripped, it seemed to my oppressed conscience like a phantom devoting me to the Hulks.

The mist was heavier yet when I got out upon the marshes, so that instead of my running at everything, everything seemed to run at me. The gates and dikes and banks came bursting at me through the mist, as if they cried as plainly as could be, "A wolfboy with somebody's else's pork pie! Stop him!" The cattle came upon me with like suddenness, staring out of their eyes, and steaming out of their nostrils, "Halloa, young thief!" I had a sudden idea that my Scapegrace might have recovered enough to have done some hunting in the night and eaten his fill of something, perhaps one of the cows. I could return home with the pie intact. Though how I would manage to get it back without drawing notice, I hadn't a clue.

I knew my way to the battery pretty straight, for I had been down there on a Sunday with Joe, and Joe, sitting on an old gun, had told me that when I was 'prentice to him, regularly bound, we would have such larks there! However, in the confusion of the mist, I found myself at last too far to the right, and consequently had to try back along the riverside, on the bank of loose stones above the mud and the stakes that staked the tide out.

Making my way along, I had just crossed a ditch I knew to be very near the battery, and had just scrambled up the mound beyond the ditch, when I saw the man sitting before me. His back was towards me, and he had his arms folded, and was nodding forward, heavy with sleep. He was fully clothed, which meant that he had probably been up and about since his change back, perhaps looking for me. My throat closed up, as it sometimes did for a brief moment when I was changing from boy to wolf, making it hard to draw breath.

I thought he would be more agreeable if I came upon him with his breakfast in that unexpected manner, so I went forward softly and touched him on the shoulder. He instantly jumped up, and it was not the same man, but another man!

And yet this man was dressed in coarse grey, too, and had a great silver clamp on his leg, and was lame, and hoarse, and cold, and was everything that the other man was except that he had not the same face, and he had a flat broad-brimmed low-crowned felt hat on. All this I saw in a moment, for I had only a moment to see it in.

"Sunlight!" He swore an oath and made a hit at me. It was a round weak blow that missed me and almost knocked him down, for it made him stumble, and then he ran into the mist, stumbling twice as he went, and I lost him.

"It's the young man!" I thought, feeling my heart shoot as I identified him. I dare say I should have felt a pain in my liver, too, if I had known where it was. I would not have called him young as he looked to be at least as old as Joe, but perhaps he was in comparison to my Scapegrace convict.

I was soon at the battery after that, and there was the right man, hugging himself and limping to and fro as if he had never all night left off hugging and limping, waiting for me. He was awfully cold, to be sure. I half expected to see him drop down before my face and die of deadly cold. His eyes looked so awfully hungry, too, that when I handed him the file and he laid it down on the grass, it occurred to me he would have tried to eat it if he had not seen my bundle. He did not knock me down this time to get at what I had, but left me standing while I opened the bundle and emptied my pockets.

"What's in the bottle, boy?" he said.

"Brandy," I replied.

He was already handing mincemeat down his throat in the most curious manner—more like a man who was putting it away somewhere in a violent hurry, than a man who was eating it—but he left off to take some of the liquor. He shivered all the while so violently that it was quite as much as he could do to keep the neck of the bottle between his teeth without biting it off.

"I think you have got the ague," I said.

"I'm much of your opinion, boy. That, and the silver, kept me too weak to hunt."

"It's bad about here," I told him. "You've been lying out on the marshes, and they're dreadful aguish. Rheumatic, too."

"I'll eat my breakfast afore they're the death of me," he said.

He was gobbling mincemeat, meat bone, bread, cheese, and pork pie, all at once, staring distrustfully while he did so at the mist all round us. He often stopped—even stopping his jaws—to listen. Some real or fancied sound, some clink upon the river or breathing of beast upon the marsh, now gave him a start.

"You're not a deceiving imp?" he said suddenly. "You brought no one with you?"

"No, sir! No!"

"Nor giv' no one the office to follow you?"

"No!"

"Well, I believe you. You'd be but a fierce young hound indeed, if at your time of life you could help to hunt a wretched warmint hunted as near death and dunghill as this poor wretched warmint is!"

Something clicked in his throat as if he had works in him like a clock and was going to strike. He smeared his ragged, rough sleeve over his eyes. Pitying his desolation, and watching him as he gradually settled down upon the pie, I made bold to say, "I am glad you enjoy it."

"Did you speak?"

"I said I was glad you enjoyed it."

"Thankee, my boy. I do."

I had often watched a large dog in our neighborhood eating his food, and I now noticed a decided similarity between the dog's way of eating and the man's. The man took strong sharp sudden bites, just like the dog. He swallowed, or rather snapped up, every mouthful, too soon and too fast. While he ate, he looked sideways here and there, as if he thought there was danger in every direction of somebody's coming to take the pie away. In all of which particulars he was very like the dog. I wondered if I was the same when I ate, if I was like a dog even when I'd changed back to boy.

"I am afraid you won't leave any of it for him," I said timidly, after a silence during which I had hesitated as to the politeness of making the remark. "There's no more to be got where that came from."

"Leave any for him? Who's him?" My friend stopped in his crunching of pie-crust.

"The young man. That you spoke of. That was hid with you."

"Oh ah!" he returned, with something like a gruff laugh. "Him? Yes, yes! He don't want no wittles."

"I thought he looked as if he did," I said.

The man stopped eating, and regarded me with the keenest scrutiny and the greatest surprise.

"Looked? When?"

"Just now."

"Where?"

"Yonder." I pointed. "Over there, where I found him nodding asleep, and thought it was you."

He held me by the collar and stared at me so that I began to think his first idea about tearing my throat out had revived.

"Dressed like you, you know, only with a hat," I explained, trembling. "And—and"—I was very anxious to put this delicately—"and with—the same reason for wanting to borrow a file. Didn't you hear the cannon last night?"

"Then there *was* firing!" he said to himself.

"I wonder you shouldn't have been sure of that," I returned, "for we heard it up at home, and that's further away, and we were shut in besides."

"Why, see now! When a man's alone on these flats, with a light head and a light stomach, perishing of cold and want, he hears nothin' all night, but guns firing, and voices calling. He sees the soldiers, with their red coats lighted up by the torches carried afore, closing in round him. And as to firing! Why, I see the mist shake with the cannon, arter it was broad day. But this man." He had said all the rest as if he had forgotten my being there. "Did you notice anything in him?"

"He had an odd-shaped face," I said, recalling what I hardly knew.

"Not like this?" exclaimed the man, making his brow heavy and sucking in his cheeks.

"Yes, quite like! And he had a very prominent forehead, and such a thin nose." A vampire, I thought. His companion was a vampire!

"Where is he?" He crammed what little food was left into the breast of his grey jacket. "Show me the way he went. I'll pull him down like a bloodhound. Curse this silver on my sore leg! Give us hold of the file, boy."

I indicated in what direction the mist had shrouded the other man, and he looked up at it for an instant.

"Seeking shelter afore the full sunrise." He nodded and ducked down on the rank wet grass, filing at his silver clamp like a madman, and not minding me or minding his own leg, which had an old chafe upon it and was bloody, but which he handled as roughly as if it had no more feeling in it than the file.

I was very much afraid of him again, now that he had worked himself into this fierce hurry, and I was likewise very much afraid of keeping away from home any longer. I told him I must go, but he took no notice. I thought the best thing I could do was to slip off. The last I saw of him, his head was bent over his knee and he was working hard at his fetter, muttering impatient imprecations at it and at his leg. The last I heard of him, I stopped in the mist to listen, and the file was still going.

CHAPTER 4

WHEN I RETURNED HOME, I fully expected to find a constable in the kitchen waiting for me. But not only was there no constable, but no discovery had yet been made of the robbery. Mrs. Joe was prodigiously busy in getting the house ready for the festivities of the day.

"And where the deuce ha' you been?" was Mrs. Joe's Christmas salutation when I showed myself.

"Down to hear the carols," I said.

"Ah! Well!" observed Mrs. Joe. "You might ha' done worse. Perhaps if I had the wolf in me, I'd be free to roam about as the spirit took me instead of being forced to the role of caretaker, a smithy's wife, and (what's the same thing) a slave with her apron never off."

Joe, who had ventured into the kitchen after me as the dustpan had retired before us, drew the back of his hand across his nose with a conciliatory air, when Mrs. Joe darted a look at him. When he saw her look away, he secretly crossed his two forefingers, and exhibited them to me, as our token that Mrs. Joe was in a cross temper. This was so much her normal state that Joe and I would often, for weeks together, cramp our fingers for keeping them crossed days at a time.

We were to have a superb dinner, consisting of a leg of pickled pork and greens, and a pair of roast stuffed fowls. A handsome mince pie had been made yesterday morning (which accounted for the mincemeat not being missed), and the pudding was already on the boil. These extensive arrangements occasioned us to be cut off unceremoniously in respect of breakfast.

"For I ain't a going to have no formal cramming and busting and washing up now, with what I've got before me, I promise you!" Mrs. Joe said.

So, we had our slices served out, as if we were two thousand troops on a forced march instead of a man and boy at home, and we took gulps of milk and water, with apologetic countenances, from a jug on the dresser. In the meantime, Mrs. Joe put clean white curtains up, and tacked a new flowered flounce across the wide chimney to replace the old one, and uncovered the little state parlour across the passage, which was never uncovered at any other time, but passed the rest of the year in a cool haze of silver paper, which even extended to the four little white crockery poodles on the mantel-shelf, each with a black nose and a basket of flowers in his mouth, and each the counterpart of the other. Poodles, to Mrs. Joe, were respectable dogs in contrast perhaps to the wolves in her life.

My sister, having so much to do, was going to church vicariously, that is to say, Joe and I were going. In his working clothes, Joe was a well-knit characteristic-looking smithy. In his holiday clothes, he was more like a scarecrow in good circumstances than anything else.

On the present festive occasion he emerged from his room when the blithe bells were going, the picture of misery in a full Sunday suit. As for me, even when I was taken to have a new suit of clothes, the tailor had orders to make them like a kind of reformatory and on no account to let me have the free use of my limbs. Joe and I going to church, therefore, must have been a moving spectacle for compassionate minds. Yet, what I suffered outside was nothing to what I underwent within.

The terrors that had assailed me whenever Mrs. Joe had gone near the pantry, or out of the room, were only to be equaled by the remorse with which my mind dwelt on what my hands had done. Under the weight of my wicked secret, I pondered whether the church would be powerful enough to shield me from the vengeance of the terrible young vampire if I divulged to that establishment.

Mr. Wopsle, the clerk at church, was to dine with us, along with Mr. Hubble the wheelwright and Mrs. Hubble, and Uncle Pumblechook (Joe's uncle, but Mrs. Joe appropriated him), who was a well-to-do bokor (that is to say, he reanimated corpses into useful zombie servants of society) in the nearest town, and drove his own chaise-cart. The dinner hour was half past one. When Joe and I got home, we found the table set, Mrs. Joe dressed, the dinner dressing, the front door unlocked (it never was at any other time) for the company to enter by, and everything most splendid. And still, not a word of the robbery.

I opened the door to the company, making believe that it was a habit of ours to open that door. First to arrive, Mr. Wopsle, united to a Roman nose and a large shining bald forehead, had a deep voice of which he was uncommonly proud. Indeed, it was understood among his acquaintance that given the chance, he would read the clergyman into fits. Next came Mr. and Mrs. Hubble, and last of all, Uncle Pumblechook. I was not allowed to call him uncle, under the severest penalties.

"Mrs. Joe," said Uncle Pumblechook, a large hard-breathing middle-aged slow man, with a mouth like a fish, dull staring eyes, and sandy hair standing upright on his head, so that he looked as if he had just been all but choked, and had that moment come to. "I have brought you as the compliments of the season—I have brought you, mum, a bottle of sherry wine—and I have brought you, mum, a bottle of port wine."

Every Christmas Day, he presented himself as a profound novelty, with exactly the same words, and carrying the two bottles like dumbbells. Every Christmas Day, Mrs. Joe replied, as she now replied, "O, Un—cle Pum-ble—chook! This is kind!" Every Christmas Day, he answered, "It's no more than your merits. And now are you all bobbish, and how's the little chomper?"

By "little chomper," he meant me.

We dined on these occasions in the kitchen, and adjourned for the nuts and oranges and apples to the parlor, a change very like Joe's change from his working clothes to his Sunday dress. My sister was uncommonly lively on the present occasion, and indeed was generally more gracious in the society of Mrs. Hubble than in other company. I remember Mrs. Hubble as a little curly-haired woman, much younger than Mr. Hubble. I remember Mr. Hubble as a high-shouldered, stooping old man, of a sawdusty fragrance, with his legs extraordinarily wide apart.

Among this good company I should have felt myself, even if I hadn't robbed the pantry, in a false position. They wouldn't leave me alone. They seemed to think the opportunity lost if they failed to point the conversation at me, every now and then, and stick the point into me.

It began the moment we sat down to dinner. Mr. Wopsle said

grace with theatrical declamation and ended with the very proper aspiration that we might be truly grateful. Upon which my sister fixed me with her eye, and said, in a low reproachful voice, "Do you hear that? Be grateful."

"Especially," said Mr. Pumblechook, "be grateful, boy, to them which brought you up by hand."

Mrs. Hubble shook her head, and, contemplating me with a mournful presentiment that I should come to no good, asked, "Why is it that the young are never grateful?"

This moral mystery seemed too much for the company until Mr. Hubble tersely solved it by saying, "Naterally wicious."

Everybody then murmured "True!" and looked at me in a particularly unpleasant and personal manner as if they could imagine the sight of my making a full transformation to wolf before their eyes.

As it was a waning moon, no longer full, I might only get a light fuzzing of hair and some bit of a snout, with sharper teeth.

A little later on, Mr. Wopsle reviewed the day's sermon with some severity, remarking that he considered the subject of the homily ill chosen; which was the less excusable, he added, when there were so many subjects "going about."

"True again," said Uncle Pumblechook. "You've hit it, sir! Plenty of subjects going about, for them that know how to put salt upon their tails. A man needn't go far to find a subject, if he's ready with his salt-box. Look at pork alone. There's a subject! If you want a subject, look at pork!"

"True, sir. Many a moral for the young might be deduced from that text," Mr. Wopsle said.

"You listen to this." My sister nudged me.

"Swine," pursued Mr. Wopsle, in his deepest voice, and pointing his fork at my blushes, as if he were mentioning my Christian name. "Swine were the companions of the prodigal. The gluttony of swine is put before us, as an example to the young." (I thought this pretty well in him who had been praising up the pork for being so plump and juicy.) "What is detestable in a pig is more detestable in a boy."

"Or girl," suggested Mr. Hubble.

"Of course, or girl, Mr. Hubble," assented Mr. Wopsle, rather irritably, "but there is no girl present."

"Or wolf." Mrs. Joe nodded. No one dared answer, all knowing what I was but never speaking of it in company.

"Besides," said Mr. Pumblechook, turning sharp on me, "think what you've got to be grateful for. If you'd been born a Squeaker—"

"He was, if ever a child was," said my sister, most emphatically.

"Well, but I mean, that is to say, a pig instead of—er, well," said Mr. Pumblechook. "If you had been born a pig, would you have been here now? Not you—"

"Unless in that form," said Mr. Wopsle, nodding towards the dish.

"But I don't mean in that form, sir," returned Mr. Pumblechook, who had an objection to being interrupted. "I mean, enjoying himself with his elders and betters, and improving himself with their conversation, and rolling in the lap of luxury. Would he have been doing that? No, he wouldn't. And what would have been your destination, son? You would have been disposed of for so many shillings according to the market price of the article, and Dunstable the butcher would have come up to you as you lay in your straw, and he would have whipped you under his left arm, and with his right he would have tucked up his frock to get a penknife from out of his waistcoat-pocket, and he would have shed your blood and had your life. No bringing up by hand then. Not a bit of it!"

How fortunate then, I thought, that wolves were more likely to do the eating than to be the one eaten. I fought against the urge to gnash my teeth.

Joe offered me more gravy, which I was afraid to take, the taste of meat perhaps urging me toward such wayward thoughts. I'd started having dreams about running after rabbits and tearing them apart, enjoying the coppery taste of fresh blood. I woke with cravings to hunt, but I'd never acted on them.

"He was a world of trouble to you, ma'am," said Mrs. Hubble, commiserating with my sister.

"Trouble?" echoed my sister, and then she entered on a fearful catalogue of all the illnesses I had been guilty of, and all the acts of sleeplessness I had committed, and all the fearful transformations I had made in the many moons of my young life, the escapes from home and resulting injuries from scraping my hairy hide on a fence or leaving my clothes behind and catching a near-deadly chill exposed in the great outdoors, and all the times she had wished me in my grave, and I had contumaciously refused to go there.

"Yet," said Mr. Pumblechook, leading the company gently back to the theme from which they had strayed. "Pork—regarded as biled—is rich, too, ain't it?"

"Have a little brandy, Uncle," said my sister.

Oh heavens, it had come at last! He would find it was weak, he would say it was weak, and I was lost! I held tight to the leg of the table under the cloth, with both hands, and awaited my fate.

My sister went for the stone bottle, came back with the stone bottle, and poured his brandy out, no one else taking any. The wretched man trifled with his glass—took it up, looked at it through the light, put it down—and prolonged my misery. All this time Mrs. Joe and Joe were briskly clearing the table for the pie and pudding.

I couldn't keep my eyes off him. Always holding tight by the leg of the table with my hands and feet, I saw the miserable creature finger his glass playfully, take it up, smile, throw his head back, and drink the brandy off. Instantly afterwards, a hush fell over us, owing to Pumblechook's springing to his feet, turning round several times in an appalling spasmodic whooping-cough dance, and rushing out the door. He then became visible through the window, violently plunging and expectorating, making the most hideous faces, and apparently out of his mind. I feared he was having a transformation of his own, perhaps turning into the pork he'd so artfully described. I wondered if Uncle Pumblechook might indeed be a werepig.

I held on tight, while Mrs. Joe and Joe ran to him. I didn't know how I had done it, but I had no doubt I had murdered him somehow. In my dreadful situation, it was a relief when he was brought back, and surveying the company all round as if they had disagreed with him, sank down into his chair with the one significant gasp, "Tar!"

I had filled up the bottle from the tar water jug.

"Tar!" cried my sister, in amazement. "Why, how ever could tar come there?"

But, Uncle Pumblechook wouldn't hear the word, wouldn't hear of the subject, imperiously waved it all away with his hand, and asked for hot gin and water. My sister, who had become alarmingly meditative, had to get the gin, the hot water, the sugar, and the lemon-peel, and mix them. For the time being at least, I was saved. I held on to the leg of the table, clutching it with the fervor of gratitude now that my fear had passed.

By degrees, I became calm enough to release my grasp and partake of pudding. The course terminated, and Mr. Pumblechook had begun to beam under the genial influence of gin and water. I began to think I should get over the day, when my sister said to Joe, "Clean plates—cold."

I clutched the leg of the table again immediately, and pressed it to my bosom as if it had been the companion of my youth and friend of my soul. I foresaw what was coming, and I felt that this time I really was gone.

"You must taste," said my sister, addressing the guests with her best grace. "Such a delightful and delicious present of Uncle Pumblechook's!"

Must they! Let them not hope to taste it!

"You must know," said my sister, rising. "It's a pie. A savory pork pie."

The company murmured their compliments. Uncle Pumblechook, sensible of having deserved well of his fellow-creatures, said—quite vivaciously, all things considered—"Well, Mrs. Joe, we'll do our best endeavours. Let us have a cut at this same pie."

My sister went out to get it. I heard her steps proceed to the pantry. I saw Mr. Pumblechook balance his knife. I saw reawakening appetite in Mr. Wopsle. I heard Mr. Hubble remark that "a bit of savory pork pie would lay atop of anything you could mention, and do no harm," and I heard Joe say, "You shall have some, Pip."

I have never been absolutely certain whether I uttered a shrill yell of terror, merely in spirit, or in the bodily hearing of the company. I felt that I could bear no more, and that I must run away. I released the leg of the table, and ran for my life.

But I ran no further than the house door, for there I ran headfirst into a party of soldiers with their muskets, one of whom held out a pair of handcuffs to me, saying, "Here you are, look sharp, come on!"

CHAPTER 5

THE DINNER PARTY GUESTS rose from the table in confusion at the sight of a line of soldiers bearing muskets at the door. Mrs. Joe re-entered the kitchen empty-handed and stopped short, cutting off her lament of "Gracious goodness gracious me, what's gone—with the—pie!"

The sergeant and I were in the kitchen when Mrs. Joe stood staring, at which crisis I partially recovered the use of my senses. The sergeant looked round at the company, with his handcuffs invitingly extended towards them in his right hand, and his left on my shoulder.

"Excuse me, ladies and gentlemen," said the sergeant, "but as I have mentioned at the door to this smart young shaver" (which he hadn't), "I am on a chase in the name of the king, and I want the silversmith."

"And pray what might you want with him?" retorted my sister, quick to resent his being wanted at all.

"Missis," returned the gallant sergeant, "speaking for myself, I should reply, the honour and pleasure of his fine wife's acquaintance. Speaking for the king, I answer, a little job done."

This was received as rather neat in the sergeant, insomuch that Mr. Pumblechook cried audibly, "Good again! And welcome, Sergeant."

"You see, silversmith," said the sergeant, who had by this time picked out Joe with his eye, "we have had an accident with these, and I find the lock of one of 'em goes wrong, and the coupling don't act pretty. As they are wanted for immediate service, will you throw your eye over them? I've heard you have the skill."

"The skill to work silver, aye." Joe examined them and pronounced that the job would necessitate the lighting of his forge fire, and would take nearer two hours than one.

"Will it? Then will you set about it at once, smithy?" the sergeant said, "as it's on His Majesty's service. And if my men can bear a hand anywhere, they'll make themselves useful."

With that, he called to his men, who came trooping into the kitchen one after another, and piled their arms in a corner. And by arms, I mean to say both muskets and in a few cases, literally arms. Many of them were of the type known in our area as "Recommissioned" soldiers, a special kind of soldier, better to hunt down Scapegraces, according to Joe. While they had the superhuman strength and endurance required for handling Scapegraces, the Recommissioned moved more slowly than regular soldiers, and they occasionally lost body parts, a foot here, some fingers there, arms on occasion. They were able to reattach them, though, with some effort.

Uncle Pumblechook's business involved creating these special Recommissioned soldiers and providing them for their line of work, for he knew the sergeant and enquired as to how the Recommissioned were serving him.

"Very well. They're serviceable fellows, a bit inconvenient when we have to stop to retrieve the odd hand or leg," the sergeant replied to Mr. Pumblechook. "But overall, quite useful."

"I'm working on a new set of Recommissioneds," Mr. Pumblechook added eagerly. "Not so easy to fall apart. They're getting better all the time. Contact me when you're ready for replacements. Or perhaps you'll want some for your own personal use. I've branched out into domestic service. The Recommissioned make fine workers for the home or shop."

"That I will do," the sergeant said distractedly. "Would you give me the time?"

"It's just gone half past two."

"That's not so bad," said the sergeant, reflecting. "Even if I was forced to halt here nigh two hours, that'll do. How far might you call yourselves from the marshes, hereabouts? Not above a mile, I reckon?"

"Just a mile," said Mrs. Joe.

"That'll do. We begin to close in upon 'em about dusk. A little before dusk, my orders are. That'll do."

"Scapegraces, Sergeant?" asked Mr. Wopsle, in a matter-of-course way. "Werewolf, witch, or demon?"

He didn't even ask about a vampire, I thought, disappointed. Why did no one assume a vampire would be up to no good?

"A werewolf and a vampire!" returned the sergeant. "Two. Of a special sort of evil, those two, thus the need for silver cuffs. Silver, as you know, slows them down and cuts the force of their powers."

A special sort of evil? Mrs. Joe kept silver in prominent places around the house, in my room, and on the tip of Tickler. Did she fear me becoming evil or simply too powerful, I wondered, for the very first time? Did living around silver make me far less strong than I could be? What would happen if I lived far away from the Gargery house? Would I be hated? Feared? So big and sturdy, as I'd fancied my father was, that people would stand in awe of me?

"They're pretty well known to be out on the marshes still, and they won't try to get clear of 'em before dark. Anybody here seen anything of any such game?"

Everybody, myself excepted, said no, with confidence. Nobody thought of me.

"Well!" said the sergeant. "They'll find themselves trapped in a circle, I expect, sooner than they count on. Now, smithy! If you're ready, His Majesty the king is."

Joe had got his coat and waistcoat and cravat off, and his leather apron on, and passed into the forge. One of the soldiers opened its wooden windows, another lighted the fire, another turned to at the bellows, the rest stood round the blaze, which was soon roaring. Then Joe began to work, melting and hammering, and we all looked on.

The interest of the impending pursuit not only absorbed the general attention, but even made my sister liberal. She drew a pitcher of beer from the cask for the soldiers who were not Recommissioned, as the Recommissioned took no food or drink, and she invited the sergeant to take a glass of brandy. But Mr. Pumblechook said, sharply, "Give him wine, mum. I'll engage there's no tar in that."

"My thanks to you," the sergeant said. "I prefer my drink without tar, and I will take wine if it's equally convenient. To your health. May you live a thousand years, and never be a worse judge of the right sort than you are at the present moment of your life!"

The sergeant tossed off his glass and seemed quite ready for another glass. Mr. Pumblechook, in his hospitality, appeared to forget that he had made a present of the wine, but took the bottle from Mrs. Joe and had all the credit of handing it about in a gush of joviality. Even I got some.

At last, Joe's job was done, and the ringing and roaring stopped. As Joe got on his coat, he mustered courage to propose that some of us should go down with the soldiers and see what came of the hunt. Mr. Hubble declined, on the plea of a pipe and ladies' society. Mr. Pumblechook, as delighted as he seemed to see the sergeant again, declined with the explanation that he had witnessed the Recommissioned in action on many past occasions and preferred to keep out of their way. Mr. Wopsle said he would go, if Joe would. Joe said he was agreeable, and would take me, if Mrs. Joe approved. We never should have got leave to go, I am sure, but for Mrs. Joe's curiosity to know all about it and how it ended. As it was, she merely stipulated, "If the boy goes wolf and runs off to the wild, don't look to me to go hunt him down and bring him back."

The sergeant took a polite leave of the ladies, and parted from Mr. Pumblechook as from a comrade. His men resumed their arms, and muskets, and fell in. Mr. Wopsle, Joe, and I received strict charge to keep in the rear, and to speak no word after we reached the marshes. When we were all out in the raw air and were steadily moving towards our business, I treasonably whispered to Joe, "I hope, Joe, we shan't find them." and Joe whispered to me, "I'd give a shilling if they had cut and run, Pip."

The weather was cold and threatening, with darkness coming on. I felt the hair become a slight furring on my arms and back, but I seldom experienced a complete change after the night of a full moon, and indeed my bones and skin felt right as they should, no grinding or stretching to make me fear exposing my nature.

We passed the finger-post, and held straight on to the churchyard. There we were stopped a few minutes by a signal from the sergeant's hand, while two or three of his men dispersed themselves among the graves, and also examined the porch. They came in again without finding anything, and then we struck out on the open marshes. A bitter sleet came rattling against us here on the east wind, and Joe took me on his back.

Now that we were out upon the dismal wilderness, I considered for the first time, with great dread, if we should come upon them, would my particular convict suppose that it was I who had brought the soldiers there? The soldiers were in front of us, extending into a pretty wide line with an interval between man and man. With my heart thumping at Joe's broad shoulder, I looked all about for any sign of the convicts. My senses were wolf-sharp, but I could see none. I could hear none.

The soldiers moved on in the direction of the old battery, and we moved on a little way behind them, when, all of a sudden, we all stopped. For there had reached us on the wings of the wind and rain a long shout. Nay, there seemed to be two or more shouts raised together, one a more distinctive howl while the other was something like a shriek.

To this effect the sergeant and the nearest men were speaking under their breath when Joe and I came up. After another moment's listening, Joe (who was a good judge) agreed, and Mr. Wopsle (who was a bad judge) agreed. The sergeant, a decisive man, ordered that the sound should not be answered, but that the course should be changed, and that his men should make towards it "at the double." So we slanted to the right, heading east, and Joe ran so fast that I had to hold on tight to keep my seat. Many of the soldiers, the Recommissioned, were left behind us to catch up as they could.

Down banks and up banks, and over gates, and splashing into dikes, and breaking among coarse rushes: no man cared where he went. As we came nearer to the noise, it became more and more apparent that it was made by more than one voice. Sometimes, it seemed to stop altogether, and then the soldiers stopped, allowing the Recommissioned to catch up. When it broke out again, the soldiers made for it at a greater rate than ever, and we after them, and the Recommissioned after us.

A mad howling was followed by an inhuman snarl. Finally, voices, one calling, "Murder!" and another voice, "Scapegraces! Runaways! Guard! This way for the runaway convicts!" Then both voices would seem to be stifled in a struggle, and then would break out again. And when it had come to this, the soldiers ran like deer, and Joe, too.

The sergeant ran in first, when we had run the noise quite down, and two of his men ran in close upon him. Their muskets cocked and leveled, we all ran in, except for the Recommissioned, who were still making their way through the rushes, stopping now to retrieve a lost limb.

"Here are both men!" panted the sergeant, struggling at the

bottom of a ditch. "Surrender, you two! And confound you for two wild beasts! Come asunder!"

Beasts! I both anticipated and feared the sight of them.

Water splashed. Mud flew. Oaths were sworn. Blows were struck. Some of the Recommissioned caught up and went down into the ditch to help the sergeant, and dragged out, separately, my convict and the other one. Both were bleeding and panting and struggling; but of course I knew them both directly. The convict like me only had a mild covering of hair, only slightly thicker than what I guessed to be usual for him. I was slightly disappointed to miss the chance to see my convict in his full wolfish glory, to know what a fearsome creature he could be, what I might one day become. As for his friend, he looked like an ordinary man.

"Mind!" said my convict, wiping blood from his face with his ragged sleeves, and shaking torn hair from his fingers. "I took him! I give him up to you! Mind that!"

"It's not much to be particular about," said the sergeant. "It'll do you small good, my man, being in the same plight yourself. Handcuffs there!"

"I don't expect it to do me any good. I don't want it to do me more good than it does now," said my convict, with a greedy laugh. "I took him. He knows it. That's enough for me."

The other convict was livid to look at, and, in addition to the old bruised left side of his face, seemed to be bruised and torn all over. He could not so much as get his breath to speak, until they were both separately handcuffed, but leaned upon a soldier to keep himself from falling.

"Take notice, guard, he tried to murder me," were his first words.

"Tried to murder him?" said my convict, disdainfully. "Try, and not do it? I don't have a stake, then, do I? I took him, and giv' him up; that's what I done. I not only prevented him getting off the marshes, but I dragged him here, dragged him this far on his way back. He's a gentleman wampire, if you please, this villain. Now, the Hulks has got its gentleman wampire again, through me.

Murder him? Worth my while, too, to murder him, when I could do worse and drag him back!"

The other one still gasped, "He tried—he tried—to—murder me. Bear—bear witness."

"Lookee here!" said my convict to the sergeant. "Single-handed I got clear of the containment ship. I made a dash and I done it. I could ha' got clear of these death-cold flats likewise—look at my leg: you won't find silver on it—if I hadn't made the discovery that he was here. Let him go free? Let him profit by the means as I found out? Let him make a tool of me afresh and again? Once more? No, no, no. If I had died at the bottom there," and he made an emphatic swing at the ditch with his manacled hands, "I'd have held to him with that grip, that you should have been safe to find him in my hold."

The other Scapegrace, who was evidently in extreme horror of his companion, repeated, "He tried to murder me. I should have been a dead man if you had not come up."

"He lies!" said my convict, with fierce energy. "He's a liar born, and he'll die a liar. It takes more than brute force to kill the likes of him. Look at his face; ain't it written there? Let him turn those eyes of his on me. I defy him to do it."

The other, with an effort at a scornful smile, looked at the soldiers, and looked about at the marshes and at the sky, but certainly did not look at the speaker.

"Do you see him?" pursued my convict. "Do you see what a villain he is? Do you see those groveling and wandering eyes? That's how he looked when we were tried together. Lord Wampire never looked at me, a lowly werewolf."

The other, always working and working his dry lips and turning his eyes restlessly about him far and near, did at last turn them for a moment on the speaker, with the words, "You are not much to look at," and with a half-taunting glance at the bound hands.

"Indeed! It's not my blood that whets your cravings. You look for a sweeter meal. I'm beginning to wish I'd dragged you into the sunlight when I had the chance!"

"Didn't I tell you," said the other convict then, "that he would murder me, if he could?" He shook with fear.

"Enough of this parley," said the sergeant. "Light those torches."

As one of the soldiers, who carried a basket in lieu of a gun, went down on his knee to open it, my convict looked round him for the first time and saw me. I had alighted from Joe's back on the brink of the ditch when we came up, and had not moved since. I looked at him eagerly when he looked at me. I had been waiting for him to see me that I might try to assure him of my innocence. It was not at all expressed to me that he even comprehended my intention, for he gave me a look that I did not understand, and it all passed in a moment.

The soldier with the basket soon got a light, and lit three or four torches, and took one himself and distributed the others. It had been almost dark before, but now it seemed quite dark, and soon afterwards very dark. Before we departed from that spot, four soldiers standing in a ring fired twice into the air. Presently we saw other torches kindled at some distance behind us, and others on the marshes on the opposite bank of the river.

"All right," said the sergeant. "March." We had not gone far when three cannons were fired ahead of us with a sound that seemed to burst something inside my ear. "You are expected on board," said the sergeant to my convict. "They know you are coming. Don't straggle, my man. Close up here."

The two were kept apart, and each walked surrounded by a separate guard. I had hold of Joe's hand, and Joe carried one of the torches. Mr. Wopsle had been for going back, but Joe was resolved to see it out, so we went on with the party. There was a reasonably good path now, mostly on the edge of the river, with a divergence here and there where a dike came. When I looked round, I could see the other lights coming in after us. We could not go fast because of their lameness, and the naturally slow pace of the Recommissioned guarding them.

After an hour or so of travelling, we came to a rough wooden hut and a landing-place. There was a guard in the hut. He challenged, and the sergeant answered. Then, we went into the hut, where there was a smell of tobacco and whitewash, a bright fire, a lamp, a stand of muskets, a drum, and a low wooden bedstead capable of holding about a dozen soldiers all at once. Three or four soldiers, probably Recommissioned judging from their grey pallor, who lay upon it in their greatcoats were not much interested in us, but just lifted their heads and took a sleepy stare, and then lay down again. The sergeant made some kind of report, and some entry in a book, and then the Scapegrace whom I call the other convict was drafted off with his guard to go on board first.

My convict never looked at me, except that once. While we stood in the hut, he stood before the fire looking thoughtfully at it. Suddenly, he turned to the sergeant, and remarked, "I wish to say something respecting this escape. It may prevent some persons laying under suspicion alonger me."

"You can say what you like," returned the sergeant, standing coolly looking at him with his arms folded, "but you have no call to say it here. You'll have opportunity enough to say about it, and hear about it, before it's done with, you know."

"I know, but this is another pint, a separate matter. A man can't starve. At least, I can't. I took some wittles, up at the willage over yonder, where the church stands a'most out on the marshes."

"You mean stole," said the sergeant.

"And I'll tell you where from. From the silversmith's."

"Halloa!" said the sergeant, staring at Joe.

"Halloa, Pip!" said Joe, staring at me.

"It was some broken wittles—that's what it was—and a dram of liquor, and a pie."

"Have you happened to miss such an article as a pie, silversmith?" asked the sergeant, confidentially.

"My wife did, at the very moment when you came in. Don't you know, Pip?"

"So." My convict turned his eyes on Joe in a moody manner, and without the least glance at me. "You're the smithy, are you? Then I'm sorry to say, I've eaten your pie."

"God knows you're welcome to it, so far as it was ever mine," returned Joe, with a saving remembrance of Mrs. Joe. "We don't know what you have done, but we wouldn't have you starved to death for it, poor miserable fellow-creature. Would us, Pip?"

The something that I had noticed before clicked in the man's throat again, and he turned his back. The boat had returned, and his guard were ready, so we followed him to the landing-place made of rough stakes and stones, and saw him put into the boat, which was rowed by a crew of Scapegrace convicts like himself. No one seemed surprised to see him, or interested in seeing him, or glad to see him, or sorry to see him, or spoke a word, except that somebody in the boat growled as if to dogs, "Give way, you!" which was the signal for the dip of the oars.

By the light of the torches, we saw the black Hulk lying out a little ways from the mud of the shore, like a wicked Noah's ark. Cribbed and barred and moored by massive rusty chains, the containment ship seemed in my young eyes to be silvered like the prisoners. We saw the boat go alongside, and we saw him taken up the side and disappear. Then, the ends of the torches were flung hissing into the water, and went out, as if it were all over with him.

I was glad of my unexpected exoneration from pilfering the pie, but not impelled to tell the truth of the matter, certainly not to my sister and not even to Joe. As much as I loved Joe, I feared he would think me worse than I was.

As I was sleepy before we were far away from the containment ship, Joe took me on his back again and carried me home. He must have had a tiresome journey of it, for Mr. Wopsle was in such a very bad temper.

Once back at home, I came to myself (with the aid of a heavy thump between the shoulders, and the restorative exclamation "Yah! Was there ever such a boy as this!" from my sister) and found Joe telling them about the convict's confession, and all the visitors suggesting different ways by which he had got into the pantry.

This was all I heard that night before my sister clutched me, as a slumberous offence to the company's eyesight, and assisted me up to bed with a strong hand.

CHAPTER 6

WHEN I WAS OLD enough, I was to be apprenticed to Joe. Until I could assume that dignity, I was not to be what Mrs. Joe called "pompeyed," or (as I render it) pampered. Therefore, I was not only odd boy about the forge, but if any neighbour happened to want an extra boy to frighten birds, run off vermin, or do any such job, I was favoured with the employment. In order, however, that our superior position might not be compromised thereby, a moneybox was kept on the kitchen mantel-shelf, in to which it was publicly made known that all my earnings were dropped. I had no hope of any personal participation in the treasure.

Mr. Wopsle's great-aunt kept an evening school in the village. In fact, she was a ridiculous old woman who used to go to sleep from six to seven every evening in the society of youth who paid two pence per week each for the improving opportunity of seeing her do it. She rented a small cottage, and Mr. Wopsle had the room upstairs, where we students used to overhear him reading aloud in a most dignified and terrific manner, and occasionally bumping on the ceiling. There was a fiction that Mr. Wopsle "examined" the scholars once a quarter. What he did on those occasions was to turn up his cuffs, stick up his hair, and give us Mark Antony's oration over the body of Caesar.

Mr. Wopsle's great-aunt, besides keeping this educational institution, kept in the same room a little general shop. She had no idea what stock she had, or what the price of anything in it was, but there was a little greasy memorandum book kept in a drawer, which served as a catalogue of prices. By this oracle, Biddy arranged all the shop transactions. Biddy was Mr. Wopsle's great-aunt's granddaughter. She was an orphan like myself. Like me, she, too, had been brought up by hand. She always drew my notice. Her hair always wanted brushing, her hands always wanted washing, and her shoes always wanted mending and pulling up at the heel.

On my own and with the help of Biddy more than with any effort from Mrs. Wopsle, I struggled through the alphabet as if it had been a silver-walled maze serving to weaken and burn me with every letter. After that, I fell among those thieves, the nine figures, who seemed every evening to change into new sorts of beasts to baffle recognition. But, at last, I began to read, write, and cipher, on the very smallest scale.

One night I was sitting in the chimney corner with my slate expending great efforts on the production of a letter to Joe. I think it must have been a full year after our hunt upon the marshes. With an alphabet on the hearth at my feet for reference, I contrived in an hour or two to print something out and hand it over to Joe.

"I say, Pip, old chap!" cried Joe, opening his blue eyes wide. "What a scholar you are! An't you?"

"I should like to be." I glanced at the slate as he held it, with a misgiving that the writing was rather hilly.

"Why, here's a J," Joe said. "And a O equal to anythink! Here's a J and a O, Pip, and a J-O, Joe."

I had never heard Joe read aloud to any greater extent than this monosyllable. Wishing to embrace the present occasion of finding out whether in teaching Joe, I should have to begin quite at the beginning, I said, "Ah! But read the rest, Joe."

"The rest, eh, Pip?" said Joe, looking at it with a slow, searching eye. "One, two, three. Why, here's three Js, and three Os, and three J-O, Joes in it, Pip!"

I leaned over Joe, and, with the aid of my forefinger read him the whole letter.

"Astonishing!" said Joe, when I had finished. "You ARE a scholar. Tho' I'm uncommon fond of reading, too."

"Are you, Joe?"

"On-common. Give me a good book, or a good newspaper, and sit me down afore a good fire, and I ask no better. Lord!" he continued, after rubbing his knees a little.

"Didn't you ever go to school, Joe, when you were as little as me?"

"No, Pip," said Joe, taking up the poker, and settling himself to his usual occupation when he was thoughtful, of slowly raking the fire between the lower bars. "I'll tell you why. My father, he were given to drink, and when he were overtook with drink, he hammered away at my mother, most onmerciful. It were a'most the only hammering he did, indeed, 'xcepting at myself. You're a listening and understanding, Pip?"

"Yes, Joe."

"'Consequence, my mother and me, we ran away from my father several times. My mother she'd go out to work, and she'd say, "Joe," she'd say, "now, please God, you shall have some schooling, child," and she'd put me to school. But my father were that good in his hart that he couldn't abear to be without us. So, he'd come with a most tremenjous crowd and make such a row at the doors of the houses where we was that they used to be obligated to have no more to do with us and to give us up to him. And then he took us home and hammered us. Which, you see, Pip," said Joe, pausing in his meditative raking of the fire, and looking at me, "were a drawback on my learning."

"Certainly, poor Joe!"

"Consequence, my father didn't make objections to my going to work, so I went to work at my present calling, which were his, too, if he would have followed it. In time I were able to keep him, and I kep him till he went off in a purple leptic fit. And it were my intentions to have had put upon his tombstone that, 'Whatsume'er the failings on his part, Remember reader he were that good in his heart.'"

Joe recited this couplet with such manifest pride and careful perspicuity, that I asked him if he had made it himself.

"I made it," said Joe, "my own self. I made it in a moment. It was like striking out a Scapegrace cuff complete in a single blow. I never was so much surprised in all my life. As I was saying, Pip, it were my intentions to have had it cut over him, but poetry costs money. Not to mention bearers, all the money that could be spared were wanted for my mother. She were in poor elth, and quite broke. She weren't long of following, poor soul, and her share of peace come round at last."

Joe's blue eyes turned a little watery. He rubbed first one of them, and then the other, in a most uncongenial and uncomfortable manner, with the round knob on the top of the poker.

"It were but lonesome then," said Joe, "living here alone, and I got acquainted with your sister. Now, Pip, your sister is a fine figure of a woman."

I could not help looking at the fire, in an obvious state of doubt.

"Whatever family opinions, or whatever the world's opinions, on that subject may be, Pip, your sister is," Joe tapped the top bar with the poker after every word following, "a-fine-figure—of—a—woman!"

I could think of nothing better to say than, "I am glad you think so, Joe."

"So am I," returned Joe, catching me up. "I am glad I think so, Pip. When I got acquainted with your sister, it were the talk how she was bringing you up by hand. Very kind of her, too, all the folks said, and I said, along with all the folks. As to you, if you could have been aware how hairy and gnarly and mean you was, dear me, you'd have formed the most contemptible opinion of yourself!"

Not exactly relishing this, I said, "Never mind me, Joe."

"But I did mind you, Pip," he returned with tender simplicity. "When I offered to your sister to keep company, and to be asked in church at such times as she was willing and ready to come to the forge, I said to her, 'And bring the poor little child. God bless the poor little child,' I said to your sister, 'there's room for him at the forge!'"

I broke out crying and begging pardon, and hugged Joe round the neck. He dropped the poker to hug me, and to say, "Ever the best of friends; ain't us, Pip? Don't cry, old chap!"

When this little interruption was over, Joe resumed. "Well, you see, Pip, and here we are! You ain't gnarly now really, and not so much hairy unless the moon's full. Now, when you take me in hand in my learning, Pip, Mrs. Joe mustn't see too much of what we're up to. It must be done, as I may say, on the sly. And why on the sly? I'll tell you why, Pip. Your sister is given to government. Which I meantersay the government of you and myself."

"Oh!"

"And she an't over partial to having scholars on the premises," Joe continued, "and in partickler would not be over partial to my being a scholar, for fear as I might rise. Like a sort or rebel, don't you see. Well," said Joe, passing the poker into his left hand, that he might feel his whisker. "Your sister's a mastermind. And I ain't a mastermind. And last of all, Pip—and this I want to say very serious to you, old chap—I see so much in my poor mother, of a woman drudging and slaving and breaking her honest hart, that I'm dead afeerd of going wrong in the way of not doing what's right by a woman, and I'd fur rather of the two go wrong the t'other way, and be a little ill-conwenienced myself. I wish it was only me that got put out, Pip. I wish there warn't no Tickler for you, old chap. I wish I could take it all on myself. But this is the up-and-down-and-straight on it, Pip, and I hope you'll overlook shortcomings."

Young as I was, I believe that I fostered a new admiration of Joe from that night.

"However," said Joe, rising to replenish the fire. "Here's the Dutch-clock a working himself up to being equal to strike eight of 'em, and she's not come home yet! I hope Uncle Pumblechook's mare mayn't have set a forefoot on a piece o' ice, and gone down."

Mrs. Joe made occasional trips with Uncle Pumblechook, a bachelor, on market days to assist him in buying such household stuffs and goods as required a woman's judgment. Uncle Pumblechook held no confidence in his Recommissioned domestic servant for trips to market. This was market day, and Mrs. Joe was out on one of these expeditions.

Joe made the fire and swept the hearth, and then we went to the door to listen for the chaise-cart. It was a dry cold night, and the wind blew keenly, and the frost was white and hard. "Here comes the mare," said Joe, "ringing like a peal of bells!"

The sound of her iron shoes upon the hard road was quite musical. We got a chair out, ready for Mrs. Joe's alighting, and stirred up the fire, and took a final survey of the kitchen that nothing might be out of its place. When we had completed these preparations, they drove up, wrapped to the eyes. We were soon all in the kitchen, carrying so much cold air in with us that it seemed to drive all the heat out of the fire.

"Now," said Mrs. Joe, unwrapping herself with haste and excitement, and throwing her bonnet back on her shoulders where it hung by the strings. "If this boy ain't grateful this night, he never will be!"

I looked as grateful as any boy possibly could, who was wholly uninformed why he ought to assume that expression.

"It's only to be hoped," said my sister, "that he won't be pompeyed. But I have my fears."

"She ain't in that line, mum," said Mr. Pumblechook. "She knows better."

She? I looked at Joe, making the motion with my lips and eyebrows, "She?" Joe looked at me, making the motion with his lips and eyebrows, "She?" My sister catching him in the act, he drew the back of his hand across his nose with his usual conciliatory air on such occasions, and looked at her.

"Well?" said my sister, in her snappish way. "What are you staring at? Is the house afire?"

"You mentioned—she?" Joe politely hinted.

"And she is a she, I suppose?" said my sister. "Unless you call Miss Havisham a he. And I doubt if even you'll go so far as that."

"Miss Havisham, uptown?" said Joe.

"Is there any Miss Havisham downtown?" returned my sister. "She wants this boy to go and play there. And of course he's going. And he had better play and not turn wolfish there or I'll work him."

The moon was waxing, two days from full. She knew there was reason for concern.

I had heard of Miss Havisham uptown—everybody for miles round had heard of Miss Havisham uptown—as an immensely rich and grim lady who lived in a large and dismal house barricaded against robbers, and who led a life of seclusion.

"Well, to be sure!" said Joe, astounded. "I wonder how she come to know Pip!"

"Noodle!" cried my sister. "Who said she knew him?"

"She wanted him to go and play there, you said." Joe was still polite.

"And couldn't she ask Uncle Pumblechook if he knew of a boy to go and play there? Isn't it possible that Uncle Pumblechook may be a tenant of hers, and that he may sometimes go there to pay his rent and place a servant or two in her care? Recommissioned, of course." She nodded appreciatively in Mr. Pumblechook's direction. "And couldn't Uncle Pumblechook, being always considerate and thoughtful for us, then mention this boy, panting here"—

which I solemnly declare I was not doing—"that I have for ever been a willing slave to?"

"Good again!" cried Uncle Pumblechook. "Well put! Prettily pointed! Good indeed! Now, Joseph, you know the case."

"No, Joseph," said my sister, still in a reproachful manner, while Joe apologetically drew the back of his hand across and across his nose. "You do not yet know the case. For you do not know that Uncle Pumblechook has offered to take him into town tonight in his own chaise-cart, and to keep him tonight, and to take him with his own hands to Miss Havisham's tomorrow morning. And Lor-a-mussy me!" cried my sister, casting off her bonnet in sudden desperation, "here I stand talking, with Uncle Pumblechook waiting, and the mare catching cold at the door, and the boy grimed with crock and dirt from the hair of his head to the sole of his foot!"

With that, she pounced upon me, like an eagle on a lamb, and my face was squeezed into wooden bowls in sinks, and my head was put under taps of water, and I was soaped, and kneaded, and toweled, plucked (the hair on my face and body was starting to fill in as a downy fuzz in preparation of my wolfishness), and thumped, and harrowed, and rasped, until I really was quite beside myself.

When my ablutions were completed, I was put into clean linen of the stiffest character, like a young penitent into sackcloth, and was trussed up in my tightest and most fearful suit. I was then delivered over to Mr. Pumblechook, who formally received me as if he were the sheriff, and who let off upon me the speech that I knew he had been dying to make all along: "Boy, be forever grateful to all friends, but especially unto them which brought you up by hand!"

"Goodbye, Joe!"

"God bless you, Pip, old chap!"

I had never parted from him before, and what with my feelings and what with soapsuds, I could at first see no stars from the chaise-cart. But they twinkled out one by one, without throwing any light on the questions why on earth I was going to play at Miss Havisham's, how I could keep myself from howling inappropriately, and what on earth I was expected to play.

CHAPTER 7

ON ARRIVAL AT MR. Pumblechook's house, the proper house of a merchant, I had been sent straight to bed in an attic with a sloping roof, which was so low in the corner where the bedstead was that I calculated the tiles as being within a foot of my eyebrows. Of course, my eyebrows were in an alarmingly rapid state of growth with the waxing of the moon.

I didn't sleep as I was up shaking and fighting the pain of my bones as they stretched slowly to take new shape under the furred skin. Uncomfortable as I was, I hungered for meat. I could smell the horses in the yard, hear their pulses beating, and it made me think strange thoughts of their blood and how it might influence the flavour of their flesh. The changes were never so overwhelming in Mrs. Joe's house as they were here at Mr. Pumblechook's, and the moon not yet full. I began to fret that I wouldn't be able to control myself in Miss Havisham's company, until I reassured myself that I would be visiting in full daylight, and I was always mostly entirely human under the sun.

Mr. Pumblechook and I breakfasted at eight o'clock in the parlour behind the shop, while the Recommissioned shopman sat on a sack of peas in the front premises.

"The Recommissioned mustn't partake," Mr. Pumblechook explained. "It's the key to keeping them docile and submissive."

I thought I heard the shopman groan from afar. I didn't understand how the Recommissioned could live if they did not eat, but I wanted nothing less than a profound explanation of Mr. Pumblechook's except perhaps to have anything to do with the Recommissioned. The shopman frightened me, with his gray skin and constant grunting. I could not help remembering the sight of one of the Recommissioned soldiers chasing after his own foot when it got loose as we were running after the convicts. I prayed that Miss Havisham did not keep a number of Recommissioned as servants.

As it was, Mr. Pumblechook was wretched company. From my sister, he got the idea that I required little more sustenance than a Recommissioned to keep me humble and penitent. He gave me as much crumb as possible in combination with as little butter, and put such a quantity of warm water into my milk that it would have been more candid to have left the milk out altogether. Worse than his hospitality, though, was his conversation, which consisted of nothing but arithmetic.

On my politely bidding him good morning, he said, pompously, "Seven times nine, boy?" And how should I answer, dodged in that way, in a strange place, on an empty stomach! I was hungry, but before I had swallowed a morsel, he began a running sum that lasted all through the breakfast. "Seven?" "And four?" "And eight?" "And six?" "And two?" "And ten?" And so on. And after each figure was disposed of, it was as much as I could do to get a bite or a sup, before the next came.

For such reasons, I was very glad when ten o'clock came and we started for Miss Havisham's, though I was not at all at my ease regarding the manner in which I should acquit myself under that lady's roof. As the morning's arithmetic had continued, the bread and butter had become dry as ash in my mouth and the craving for raw meat returned. Never had meat so appealed in the daylight hours, and never with such intensity that my mouth watered with merely thinking of tearing into some poor animal's flesh. What if Miss Havisham kept a pet—a lap dog, or perhaps a tasty little morsel of a kitten? I'd never tried either dog or cat, but who knew what I might do while under the influence of a moon not yet full or even high in the sky?

Within a quarter of an hour we came to Miss Havisham's house, which was of old brick, and dismal, and had a great many iron bars to it. Some of the windows had been walled up. Of those that remained, all the lower were rustily barred. There was a courtyard in front, and that was barred, so we had to wait, after ringing the bell, until some one should come to open it. While we waited at the gate, I peeped in (even then Mr. Pumblechook said, "And fourteen?" but I pretended not to hear him), and saw that at the side of the house there was a large brewery. No brewing was going on in it, and none seemed to have gone on for a long time.

A window was raised, and a clear voice demanded, "What name?" To which my conductor replied, "Pumblechook." The voice returned, "Quite right," and the window was shut again, and a young lady came across the courtyard, with keys in her hand.

"This," said Mr. Pumblechook, "is Pip."

"Come in, Pip," returned the young lady, who was very pretty and seemed very proud.

I wasn't sure what Mr. Pumblechook had told Miss Havisham about me, but I guessed nothing out of the ordinary, as the young lady did not look at me with any apparent hesitation or suspicion.

Mr. Pumblechook was coming in also, when she stopped him with the gate.

"Oh!" she said. "Did you wish to see Miss Havisham?"

"If Miss Havisham wished to see me," returned Mr. Pumblechook, discomfited.

"Ah! But you see, she don't." She said it so finally, and in such an inarguable way, that Mr. Pumblechook, though in a condition of ruffled dignity, could not protest.

Instead, he eyed me severely—as if I had done anything to him!—and departed with the words reproachfully delivered: "Boy!

Let your behaviour here be a credit unto them which brought you up by hand!"

My young conductress locked the gate and we went across the courtyard. It was paved and clean, but grass was growing in every crevice. The brewery buildings had a little lane leading up to the house, and the wooden gates of that lane stood open, and the brewery beyond stood open, away to the high enclosing wall. All was empty and disused. The cold wind seemed to blow colder there than outside the gate, and it made a shrill noise. I couldn't smell the wind for the overpowering fragrance of my companion. She smelled familiar and yet new and strange, sweet, sharp, and pungent. I turned my attention to the brewery buildings to distract from my sniffing in her direction.

She saw me looking at it, and she said, "You could drink without hurt all the strong beer that's brewed there now, boy."

"I should think I could, miss," said I, in a shy way.

"Better not try to brew beer there now, or it would turn out sour, boy. Don't you think so?"

"It looks like it, miss."

"Not that anybody means to try," she added, "for that's all done with, and the place will stand as idle as it is till it falls. As to strong beer, there's enough of it in the cellars to drown the Manor House."

"Is that the name of this house, miss?"

"One of its names, boy."

"It has more than one, then?"

"One more. Its other name was Satis; which is Greek, or Latin, or Hebrew, or all three—or all one to me—for enough."

"Enough House. That's a curious name, miss."

"Yes," she replied. "But it meant more than it said. It meant, when it was given, that whoever had this house could want nothing else. They must have been easily satisfied in those days, I should think. But don't loiter, boy."

Though she called me "boy" so often, and with a carelessness that was far from complimentary, she was of about my own age. She seemed much older than I, of course, being a girl, and beautiful and self-possessed; and she was as scornful of me as if she had been one-and-twenty, and a queen.

We went into the house by a side door. The great front entrance had two chains across it outside, and the first thing I noticed was that the passages were all dark, and that she had left a candle burning there. She took it up, and we went through more passages and up a staircase, and still it was all dark, and only the candle lighted us.

At last we came to the door of a room.

"Go in," she said.

I answered, more in shyness than politeness, "After you, miss."

"Don't be ridiculous, boy. I am not going in." She scornfully walked away, and—what was worse—took the candle with her.

Uncomfortable, and half afraid, I knocked, and was told from within to enter. I entered, therefore, and found myself in a pretty large room, well lit with wax candles. There was no visible glimpse of daylight. It was a dressing room, as I supposed from the furniture, but prominent in it was a draped table with a gilded looking glass, that I made out to be a fine lady's dressing-table.

Whether I should have made out this object so soon if there had been no fine lady sitting at it, I cannot say. In an armchair, with an elbow resting on the table and her head leaning on that hand, sat the strangest lady I have ever seen, or shall ever see. Even stranger, her reflection did not shine back from the looking glass though she was seated in front of it.

She was dressed in rich materials—satins, and lace, and silks—all of white. Her shoes were white. And she had a long white veil over her dark hair, laced with bridal flowers. Some bright jewels sparkled on her neck and on her hands, and some other jewels lay sparkling on the table. Dresses, less splendid than the dress she wore, and half-packed trunks, were scattered about. She had not quite finished dressing, for she had but one shoe on—the other was on the table near her hand—her veil was but half arranged, her watch and chain were not put on, and some lace for her bosom lay with those trinkets, and with her handkerchief, and gloves, and some flowers, and a prayer book all confusedly heaped about the looking glass. Those objects reflected in the glass, though she did not.

It was not in the first few moments that I saw all these things, though I saw more of them in the first moments than might be supposed. But I saw that everything within my view that ought to be white, had been white long ago, and had lost its lustre and was faded and yellow. I saw that the bride within the bridal dress had withered like the dress, and like the flowers, and had no brightness left but the brightness of her sunken eyes. She appeared young, much younger than I expected, and yet she had the brittle, frail appearance of one old beyond her years.

"Who is it?" said the lady at the table.

"Pip, ma'am. Mr. Pumblechook's boy, ma'am. Come—to play."

"Come nearer; let me look at you. Come close."

It was when I stood before her, avoiding her eyes, that I took note of the surrounding objects in detail, and saw that her watch had stopped at twenty minutes to nine, and that a clock in the room had stopped at twenty minutes to nine.

"Look at me," said Miss Havisham. "You are not afraid of a woman who has never seen the sun since you were born?"

I regret to state that I was not afraid of telling the enormous lie comprehended in the answer "No."

"Do you know what I touch here?" she said, laying her hands, one upon the other, on her left side.

"Your heart."

"Broken!" She uttered the word with an eager look, and with strong emphasis, and with a weird smile that had a kind of boast in it. Afterwards she kept her hands there for a little while, and slowly took them away as if they were heavy.

"I am tired," said Miss Havisham. "I want diversion, and I have done with men and women. Play."

She could hardly have directed an unfortunate boy to do anything in the wide world more difficult to be done under the circumstances.

"There, there!" with an impatient movement of the fingers of her right hand. "Play, play, play!"

For a moment, with the fear of my sister's working me before my eyes, I had a desperate idea of starting round the room in the assumed character of Mr. Pumblechook's Recommissioned Shopman. But I felt myself so unequal to the performance that I gave it up, and stood looking at Miss Havisham in what I suppose she took for a dogged manner, inasmuch as she said, when we had taken a good look at each other, "Are you sullen and obstinate?"

"No, ma'am, I am very sorry for you, and very sorry I can't play just now. If you complain of me I shall get into trouble with my sister, so I would do it if I could; but it's so new here, and so strange, and so fine—and melancholy—" I stopped, fearing I might say too much, or had already said it, and we took another look at each other.

Before she spoke again, she turned her eyes from me, and looked at the dress she wore, and at the dressing-table, and finally at the looking glass as if she could see her own reflection in it though I could not see her at all there.

"So new to him," she muttered, "so old to me; so strange to him, so familiar to me; so melancholy to both of us! Call Estella."

As she was still looking at the reflection of herself, or the absence of her reflection, I thought she was still talking to herself, and kept quiet.

"Call Estella," she repeated, flashing a look at me. "You can do that. Call Estella. At the door."

To stand in the dark in a mysterious passage of an unknown house, calling out to a scornful young lady neither visible nor responsive, and feeling it a dreadful liberty so to roar out her name, was almost as bad as playing to order. But she answered at last, and her light came along the dark passage like a star.

Miss Havisham beckoned her to come close, and took up a jewel from the table, and tried its effect upon her fair young bosom and against her pretty brown hair. "Your own, one day, my dear, and you will use it well. Let me see you practice combat with this boy."

"With this boy? Why, he is a common labouring boy!"

I thought I overheard Miss Havisham answer, "Well? You can break him."

"Do you know how to fight, boy?" asked Estella of myself, with the greatest disdain.

"I would not strike you, miss." Besides which, I had no idea how to fight.

"Hit him," said Miss Havisham to Estella. So she did, a stinging slap across my face.

"Ouch." I held my cheek. It was then I began to understand that everything in the room had stopped, like the watch and the clock, a long time ago. I noticed that Miss Havisham put down the jewel exactly on the spot from which she had taken it up. For a moment, I felt my heart had stopped along with the rest of the room. As Estella prepared to deal another blow, I blocked her and sent her tumbling back in surprise.

"He does have some fight in him," she said, with some disbelief, as she jumped back to her feet with feline grace.

"I do not want to play anymore," I said, aware that this would cause some concern with my sister. I preferred to face Tickler than to have to play at combat with Estella for Miss Havisham's amusement.

Miss Havisham sighed. "Play at cards, then, for now. Beggar My Neighbour. Let's see what sort of strategist you are."

Estella laughed as if she didn't think much of my skills. I thought she might be right to laugh. I felt unequal to any game with Estella, but I took my seat at the card table.

I glanced at the dressing-table again, and saw that the shoe upon it, once white, now yellow, had never been worn. I glanced down at the foot from which the shoe was absent, and saw that the silk stocking on it, once white, now yellow, had been trodden ragged.

The withered bridal dress on Miss Havisham's withered form looked so like grave-clothes, the long veil so like a shroud. She was not one of Pumblechook's Recommissioned, though. She could only be a vampire, I thought, with growing alarm.

She sat, corpse-like, as we played at cards; the frillings and trimmings on her bridal dress looking like earthy paper. I knew nothing then of the discoveries that are occasionally made of bodies buried in ancient times, which fall to powder in the moment of being distinctly seen. She looked as if the admission of the natural light of day would have struck her to dust, and this was probably quite true.

"He calls the knaves Jacks, this boy!" said Estella with disdain, before our first game was out. "And what hairy hands he has! And what thick boots!"

I was hairier than usual, being near the change, though in my opinion not offensively so. She could not know what I was, what I could be, and I hadn't thought on it much with the shock of being in a new and odd place taking precedence in my consideration. Now I looked at my hands and the covering of hair. I looked at my clothes and boots. Her contempt for me was so strong that it became infectious, and I caught it.

She won the game, and I dealt. I misdealt, as was only natural, when I knew she was lying in wait for me to do wrong. She denounced me for a stupid, clumsy labouring-boy.

"You say nothing of her," remarked Miss Havisham to me, as she looked on. "She says many hard things of you, but you say nothing of her. What do you think of her?"

"I don't like to say," I stammered.

"Tell me in my ear," said Miss Havisham, bending down.

"I think she smells very proud," I replied, in a whisper.

"Smells?" Miss Havisham seemed to raise a brow, but I could hardly tell with her forehead being so high and her brows so sparse. "Anything else?"

"I think she is very pretty."

"Anything else?"

"I think she is very insulting." (She was looking at me then with a look of supreme aversion.)

"Anything else?" She sniffed my neck as I sometimes sniffed about the kitchen when we had bacon in the house, and as I'd nearly sniffed Estella.

"I think I should like to go home."

"And never see her again, though she is so pretty?"

"I am not sure that I shouldn't like to see her again, but I should like to go home now." I suddenly wondered if I had been brought here not to play, but to be the teatime snack.

"You shall go soon," said Miss Havisham, aloud. "Play the game out."

Saving for the one weird smile at first, I should have felt almost sure that Miss Havisham's face could not smile. Perhaps vampires lacked the ability. She had the appearance of having dropped body and soul, within and without, under the weight of a crushing blow.

I played the game to an end with Estella, and she beggared me. She threw the cards down on the table when she had won them all, as if she despised them for having been won of me.

"When shall I have you here again?" said Miss Havisham. "Let me think."

I was beginning to remind her that today was Wednesday, when she checked me with her former impatient movement of the fingers of her right hand.

"There, there! I know nothing of days of the week; I know nothing of weeks of the year. Come again after six days. You hear?"

"Yes, ma'am." They could not have known what I was, I thought. A werewolf would never be asked back again. I was not about to confess it and risk my sister's wrath, or worse, never be able to come back again. Why I would want to return, I could not say.

"Estella, take him down. Let him have something to eat, and let him roam and look about him while he eats. Go, Pip."

I followed the candle down, as I had followed the candle up, and she stood it in the place where we had found it. Until she opened the side entrance, I had fancied, without thinking about it, that it must necessarily be nighttime. The rush of the daylight quite confounded me, and made me feel as if I had been in the candlelight of the strange room many hours.

"You are to wait here, you boy," Estella said, then disappeared and closed the door.

I took the opportunity of being alone in the courtyard to look at my hairy hands and my common boots. For the first time, I hated what I was. I felt common, vulgar, and entirely wrong. I determined to ask Joe why he had ever taught me to call those picture-cards Jacks, which ought to be called knaves. I wished Joe had been rather more genteelly brought up, and then I should have been so, too. I longed to get my hands on something silver to keep me from the force of the change or at least to help suppress my hair growth.

Estella came back with some bread, meat, and a little mug of beer. She put the mug down on the stones of the yard, and gave me the bread and meat without looking at me, as insolently as if I were a dog in disgrace. Hungry as I was, I would not allow her the satisfaction of watching me pounce on the food and devour it. I was so humiliated, hurt, spurned, offended, angry, sorry—I cannot hit upon the right name for the smart—that tears started to my eyes. The moment they sprang there, the girl looked at me with a quick delight in having been the cause of them. This gave me power to keep them back and to look at her. She gave a contemptuous toss— but with a sense, I thought, of having made too sure that I was so wounded—and left me.

As soon as she was gone, I gobbled up the bread and meat, feeling ashamed to have even wanted it but unable to resist my cravings any longer. Licking up the last of the crumbs, I felt my bones begin to move and stretch. In midday! It was an unusual new circumstance that I attributed to being far from home. I looked about me for a place to hide away and got behind one of the gates in the brewery-lane, leaned my sleeve against the wall there, and cried.

I kicked the wall, and took a hard twist at my hair, wishing I could pull it all out, though knowing it would only grow back as fast as I got rid of it. Fortunately, the grinding under my skin stopped almost as quickly as it came on. I looked down at my body, only slightly hunched but mostly human in appearance, and my hands, not much hairier than they had been. My sense of smell was suddenly more acute. I could smell Estella's unique scent as if she were right upon me, though I had seen her walk away. A brush of my hand across my face revealed that I probably had a slight snout, but nothing much to fear as I still seemed more boy than wolf. I downed the mug of beer, warming and tingling as it went down, and I was soon in spirits to look about me.

To be sure, it was a deserted place, down to the pigeon-house in the brewery yard, which had been blown crooked on its pole by some high wind. But there were no pigeons in the dovecote, no horses in the stable, no pigs in the sty, no malt in the storehouse, no smells of grains and beer in the copper or the vat. All the uses and scents of the brewery might have evaporated with its last reek of smoke.

In a by-yard, there was a wilderness of empty casks. I caught Estella's scent still in the air and looked around for her. Behind the furthest end of the brewery, I pounced on the wall of a rank garden and prowled around the edge of it. On the other side, past tangles of overgrown weeds, there was a track upon the green and yellow paths, as if some one sometimes walked there, and I saw that Estella was walking away from me. But she seemed to be everywhere. For when I jumped down to leap across the casks, Estella was walking on casks at the other end of the yard.

She had her back towards me. She never looked round, and passed out of my view directly. I followed to the brewery itself, by which I mean the large paved lofty place in which they used to make the beer, and where the brewing utensils still were. When I first went into it, I saw her pass among the extinguished fires, and ascend some light iron stairs, and go out by a gallery high overhead, as if she were going out into the sky.

It was in this place, and at this moment, that a strange thing happened to my fancy. I turned my eyes—a little dimmed by looking up at the frosty light—towards a shaded window at the side of the house, an upper story. I could only see in silhouette through the shade what looked like the dark shadow of Miss Havisham in her veil, getting closer to someone, a woman, and taking her in her arms and biting her on the neck until the woman seemed to faint and drop to the floor. In the terror of seeing the silhouette savagery, and in the terror of being certain that it had been quite real, I at first ran from it, and then ran towards it. And my terror was greatest of all when I found no shadows there at all, only a dark-shaded window.

Nothing less than the frosty light of the cheerful sky, the sight of people passing beyond the bars of the courtyard gate, and the reviving influence of the rest of the bread and meat and beer, would have brought me round. Even with those aids, I might not have come to myself as soon as I did, but that I saw Estella approaching with the keys to let me out. She would have some fair reason for looking down upon me, I thought, if she saw me frightened. I would give her no fair reason.

She flashed me a triumphant glance in passing, as if she rejoiced that my hands were so hairy and my boots were so thick, and she opened the gate, and stood holding it. I was passing out without looking at her, when she touched me with a taunting hand.

"Why don't you cry?"

"Because I don't want to."

"You do," she said. "You have been crying till you are half blind, and you are near crying again now."

She laughed contemptuously, pushed me out, and locked the gate upon me. I went straight to Mr. Pumblechook's, and was immensely relieved to find him not at home. So, leaving word with the Recommissioned shopman on what day I was wanted at Miss Havisham's again, I set off on the four miles to our forge. I felt agile, as I normally did when a change was coming on soon, and ran all four miles, pondering as I ran. I was a common labouring boy, but uncommon in a way that would make Estella hate me more. Had she suspected, from the hairy hands? Had she noticed the bit of a snout? It was awful enough that I was much more ignorant than I had considered myself last night, and generally that I was in a low-lived bad way. But if she were to see that I turned wolf as well? Her contempt would know no bounds.

CHAPTER 8

BY THE TIME I reached home, the moon, still not yet full but enough to provoke a more than partial transformation, had risen in the darkening sky. I struggled to hold my pants up over my haunches. My tongue was too thick to allow for speech, but my sister was very curious to know all about Miss Havisham's, and asked a number of questions. I soon found myself getting heavily bumped from behind in the nape of the neck and the small of the back, and having my face ignominiously shoved against the kitchen wall because of my failure to answer. For the first time, I struggled against an intense urge to strike back, to tear at my sister's flesh with my claws, to gnash at her with my sharpening teeth.

Another knock to the head put it out of me. My heart calmed. My pulse slowed. I felt more myself again, a very pounded and bruised self.

Even if I had been able to describe Miss Havisham's as my eyes had seen it, I should not be understood. Not only that, but I felt convinced that Miss Havisham too would not be understood. I'd heard nothing of her being vampire. Although she was perfectly incomprehensible to me, I entertained an impression that there would be something coarse and treacherous in my dragging her as she really was (to say nothing of Miss Estella) before the contemplation of Mrs. Joe. Consequently, I said as little as I could, and had my face shoved against the kitchen wall.

The worst of it was that the bullying old Pumblechook, preyed upon by a devouring curiosity to be informed of all I had seen and heard, came gaping over in his chaise-cart later in the evening to have the details divulged to him. And the mere sight of his fishy eyes and open mouth made me vicious in my reticence and nearly wishing I could transform at will.

"Well, boy," Uncle Pumblechook began, as soon as he was seated in the chair of honour by the fire. "How did you get on uptown?"

I answered, now able to speak. "Pretty well, sir."

"Pretty well?" Mr. Pumblechook repeated. "Tell us what you mean by pretty well, boy?"

My sister with an exclamation of impatience was going to fly at me and I had no shadow of defence, for Joe was busy in the forge.

"No! Don't lose your temper. Leave this lad to me, ma'am." Mr. Pumblechook then turned me towards him. "Boy! What is Miss Havisham like?"

"Very tall and fair," I told him.

"Is she, Uncle?" asked my sister.

Mr. Pumblechook winked assent; from which I at once inferred that he had never seen Miss Havisham, for she was nothing of the kind.

"Good!" said Mr. Pumblechook conceitedly. "Now, boy! What was she a doing of, when you went in today?"

"She was sitting," I answered, "in a black velvet coach."

Mr. Pumblechook and Mrs. Joe stared at one another and both repeated, "In a black velvet coach?"

"Yes. And Miss Estella—that's her niece, I think—handed her in cake and wine at the coach-window, on a gold plate. And we all had cake and wine on gold plates. And I got up behind the coach to eat mine, because she told me to."

"Was anybody else there?" asked Mr. Pumblechook.

"Four dogs," said I.

"Oh, she fancies dogs?" My sister seemed surprised and not quite pleased.

"Large or small?" Mr. Pumblechook prompted.

"Immense," I said. "Black poodles. And they fought for veal-cutlets out of a silver basket."

Mr. Pumblechook and Mrs. Joe stared at one another again, in utter amazement. "Where was this coach, in the name of gracious?" asked my sister.

"In Miss Havisham's room." They stared again. "But there weren't any horses to it." I added this saving clause.

"Can this be possible, Uncle?" asked Mrs. Joe. "What can the boy mean?"

"I'll tell you, mum," said Mr. Pumblechook. "My opinion is, it's a sedan-chair. She's flighty, you know, quite flighty enough to pass her days in a sedan-chair."

"Did you ever see her in it, Uncle?" asked Mrs. Joe.

"How could I," he returned, forced to the admission, "when I never see her in my life? Never clapped eyes upon her!"

"Goodness, Uncle! And yet you have spoken to her?"

"Why, don't you know," Mr. Pumblechook said testily, "that when I have been there, I have been took up to the outside of her door, and the door has stood ajar, and she has spoke to me that way. What did you play at, boy?"

"We played with flags," I said. (I beg to observe that I think of myself with amazement, when I recall the lies I told on this occasion.)

"Flags!" echoed my sister.

"Yes," I said. "Estella waved a blue flag, and I waved a red one, and Miss Havisham waved one sprinkled all over with little gold stars, out at the coach-window. And then we all waved our swords and hurrahed."

"Swords!" repeated my sister. "Where did you get swords from?"

"Out of a cupboard. And I saw pistols in it, and jam, and pills. And there was no daylight in the room, but it was all lighted up with candles."

"That's true, mum," said Mr. Pumblechook, with a grave nod. "That's the state of the case, for that much I've seen myself." And then they both stared at me, and I stared at them, and pawed at the right leg of my trousers.

If they had asked me any more questions, I should undoubtedly have betrayed myself. They were so much occupied, however, in discussing the marvels I had presented for their consideration, that I escaped. The subject still held them when Joe came in from his work to have a cup of tea. To whom my sister, more for the relief of her own mind than for the gratification of his, related my pretended experiences.

Now, when I saw Joe open his blue eyes and roll them all round the kitchen in helpless amazement, I was overtaken by penitence, but only as regarded him, not as regarded the other two. Towards Joe, and Joe only, I considered myself a young monster, while they sat debating what results would come to me from Miss Havisham's acquaintance and favour. They had no doubt that Miss Havisham would "do something" for me. Their doubts related to the form that something would take. My sister stood out for "property." Mr. Pumblechook was in favour of a handsome premium for binding me apprentice to some genteel trade, say, the trade of recommending Recommissioneds to fine homes, for instance. Joe fell into the deepest disgrace with both, for offering the bright suggestion that I might only be presented with one of the dogs who had fought for the veal-cutlets, but I was certain he meant as a companion and not as a future mate.

"If a fool's head can't express better opinions than that," said my sister, "and you have got any work to do, you had better go and do it." So he went.

After Mr. Pumblechook had driven off, and when my sister was washing up, I stole into the forge to Joe, and remained by him until he had done for the night. Then I said, "Before the fire goes out, Joe, I should like to tell you something."

"Should you, Pip?" said Joe, drawing his stool near the forge. "Then tell us. What is it, Pip?"

"Joe," said I, taking hold of his rolled-up sleeve, and twisting it between my finger and thumb, "you remember all that about Miss Havisham's?"

"Remember?" said Joe. "I believe you! Wonderful!"

"It's a terrible thing, Joe. It ain't true."

"What are you telling of, Pip?" cried Joe, falling back in the greatest amazement.

"It's lies, Joe."

"But not all of it? Why sure you don't mean to say that there was no black welwet coach?" I stood shaking my head. "But at least there was dogs, Pip?"

"No, Joe."

"A dog?" said Joe. "A puppy? Come?"

"No, Joe, there was nothing at all of the kind."

Joe contemplated me in dismay. "Pip, old chap! This won't do, old fellow! I say! Where do you expect to go to?"

"It's terrible, Joe. Ain't it?" I sat down in the ashes.

"Terrible?" cried Joe. "Awful! What possessed you?"

"I don't know what possessed me, but I wish you hadn't taught me to call knaves at cards Jacks; and I wish my boots weren't so thick nor my hands so hairy sometimes when the moon is waxing." And I wished I hadn't knocked Estella down when she moved to strike me.

And then I told Joe that I felt very miserable, and that I hadn't been able to explain myself to Mrs. Joe and Pumblechook, who were so rude to me, and that there had been a beautiful young lady at Miss Havisham's who was dreadfully proud, and that she had said I was common, and that I wished I was not common, and I was afraid of turning wolf while there, that it had come on something fierce when I was away from the forge. Somehow, the lies had come of it, though I didn't know how.

"There's one thing you may be sure of, Pip," said Joe, after some rumination, "namely, that lies is lies. Howsever they come, they didn't ought to come, and they come from the father of lies, and work round to the same. Don't you tell no more of 'em, Pip. That ain't the way to get out of being common, old chap. And as to being common, I don't make it out at all clear. You are oncommon in some things. You're oncommon in your abilities to change from boy to wolf under a moon. Some think it odd, no doubt, but it's right amazing when you think on it, Pip. Likewise, you're a oncommon scholar."

"No, I am ignorant and backward, Joe."

"Why, see what a letter you wrote last night! Wrote in print even! I've seen letters—Ah! and from gentlefolks!—that I'll swear weren't wrote in print," said Joe.

"I have learnt next to nothing, Joe. You think much of me. It's only that."

"Well, Pip," said Joe, "be it so or be it son't, you must be a common scholar afore you can be a oncommon one, I should hope! And I know what that is to do, though I can't say I've exactly done it."

There was some hope in this piece of wisdom, and it rather encouraged me.

"Whether common ones as to callings and earnings," pursued Joe, reflectively, "mightn't be the better of continuing for to keep company with common ones, instead of going out to play with oncommon ones, which reminds me to hope that there were a flag, perhaps?"

"No, Joe."

"I'm sorry there weren't a flag, Pip. Whether that might be or mightn't be, is a thing as can't be looked into now, without putting your sister on the rampage and that's a thing not to be thought of as being done intentional. Lookee here, Pip, at what is said to you by a true friend. You'll never be common. If it had been night and the full moon on the rise, all would know."

This was what filled me with dread, not celebration as Joe seemed to believe it should. I nodded.

"You don't need to make up lies when you have an oncommon way about you." Joe went on. "So don't tell no more on 'em, Pip, and live well and die happy."

"You are not angry with me, Joe?"

"No, old chap. But bearing in mind that them were which I meantersay of a stunning and outdacious sort—alluding to them which bordered on weal-cutlets and dog-fighting—a sincere well-wisher would adwise, Pip, their being dropped into your medita-tions, when you go upstairs to bed. That's all, old chap, and don't never do it no more."

When I got up to my little room and said my prayers, I did not forget Joe's recommendation, and yet my young mind was in that disturbed and unthankful state. Long after I laid me down, I thought how common Estella would consider Joe, a mere silversmith; how thick his boots, and how coarse his hands.

I fell asleep recalling what I "used to do" when I was at Miss Hav-isham's, as though I had been there weeks or months, instead of hours, and as though it were quite an old subject of remembrance, instead of one that had arisen only that day. That was a memorable day to me, for it made great changes in me. But it is the same with any life. Imagine one selected day struck out of it, and think how different its course would have been. Pause you who read this, and think for a moment of the long chain of silver or gold, of thorns or flowers, that would never have bound you, but for the formation of the first link on one memorable day.

CHAPTER 9

A MORNING OR TWO LATER when I woke, the idea occurred to me that the best step I could take towards making myself uncommon—not just for my dubious abilities to transform, which seemed impressive only to Joe—was to get out of Biddy everything she knew. In pursuance of this bright idea, I mentioned to Biddy, when I went to Mr. Wopsle's great-aunt's at night, that I had a particular reason for wishing to get on in life, and that I should feel very much obliged to her if she would impart all her learning to me. Biddy, who was the most obliging of girls, immediately said she would, and indeed began to carry out her promise within five minutes. She gave me materials to study, including some information from her little catalogue of prices under the head of moist sugar and print copied from some newspaper.

Of course there was a public house in the village, and of course Joe liked sometimes to smoke his pipe there. I had received strict orders from my sister to call for him at the Three Jolly Bargemen, that evening, on my way from school, and bring him home at my peril. To the Three Jolly Bargemen, therefore, I directed my steps.

It being Saturday night, I wished the landlord good evening, and passed into the common room at the end of the passage, where there was a bright large kitchen fire, and where Joe was smoking his pipe in company with Mr. Wopsle and a stranger.

Joe greeted me as usual with "Halloa, Pip, old chap!"

The stranger turned his head and looked at me.

He was a mysterious-looking man whom I had never seen before. One of his eyes was half shut up, as if he were taking aim at something with an invisible gun. He had a pipe in his mouth, and he took it out, slowly blew all his smoke away, and looking hard at me all the time, nodded. So, I nodded, and then he nodded again, and made room on the settle beside him that I might sit down there.

But as I was used to sit beside Joe whenever I entered that place of resort, I said, "No, thank you, sir," and fell into the space Joe made for me on the opposite settle.

The strange man, after glancing at Joe, and seeing that his attention was otherwise engaged, nodded to me again when I had taken my seat, and then rubbed his leg—in a very odd way, as it struck me.

"You was saying," said the strange man, turning to Joe, "that you was a silversmith."

"Yes. I said it, you know," said Joe. "And I work iron, too, on occasion, to make ends meet."

"What'll you drink, Mr.—? You didn't mention your name, by-the-bye." Joe mentioned it now, and the strange man called him by it. "What'll you drink, Mr. Gargery? At my expense?"

"Well," said Joe, "to tell you the truth, I ain't much in the habit of drinking at anybody's expense but my own."

"Habit? No," returned the stranger, "but once and away, and on a Saturday night, too. Come! Put a name to it, Mr. Gargery."

"I wouldn't wish to be stiff company," said Joe. "Rum."

"Rum," repeated the stranger. "And will the other gentleman have something?"

"Rum," Mr. Wopsle said.

"Three rums!" cried the stranger, calling to the landlord. "Glasses round!"

"This other gentleman," observed Joe, by way of introducing Mr. Wopsle, "is a gentleman that you would like to hear give it out. Our clerk at church."

"Aha!" said the stranger, quickly, and cocking his eye at me. "The lonely church, right out on the marshes, with graves round it!"

"That's it," said Joe.

The stranger, with a comfortable kind of grunt over his pipe, put his legs up on the settle that he had to himself. He wore a flap-

ping broad-brimmed traveller's hat, and under it a handkerchief
tied over his head in the manner of a cap, so that he showed no hair.
As he looked at the fire, I thought I saw a cunning expression, followed by a half-laugh, come into his face.

"I am not acquainted with this country, gentlemen, but it seems
a solitary country towards the river."

"Most marshes is solitary," said Joe.

"No doubt, no doubt. Do you find any gypsies, now, or tramps, or
Scapegraces of any sort, out there?"

"Some," said Joe. "And a runaway convict now and then."

"Seems you have been out after such?" asked the stranger.

"Once," returned Joe. "Not that we wanted to take them, you
understand. We went out as lookers on; me, and Mr. Wopsle, and
Pip. Didn't us, Pip?"

"Yes, Joe."

The stranger looked at me again and said, "He's a likely young
parcel of bones that. What is it you call him?"

"Pip," said Joe.

"Christened Pip?"

"No, not christened Pip. No," said Joe, "it's a kind of family name
what he gave himself when a infant, and is called by."

"Son of yours?"

"Well," said Joe, meditatively, not, of course, that it could be in
anywise necessary to consider about it, but because it was the way
at the Jolly Bargemen to seem to consider deeply about everything
that was discussed over pipes—"well—no. No, he ain't."

"Nevvy?" said the strange man.

"Well," said Joe, with the same appearance of profound cogita-
tion, "he is not—no, not to deceive you, he is not—my nevvy."

"What the blue blazes is he?" asked the stranger.

Mr. Wopsle struck in upon that, as one who knew all about re-
lationships. And here I may remark that when Mr. Wopsle referred
to me, he considered it a necessary part of such reference to rumple
my hair and poke it into my eyes. I cannot conceive why everybody

of his standing who visited at our house should always have put me through the same hair-rumpling process.

All this while, the strange man looked at nobody but me, and looked at me as if he were determined to have a shot at me at last, and bring me down. But he said nothing else until the glasses of rum and water were brought; and then he made his shot, and a most extraordinary shot it was.

It was not a verbal remark, but a proceeding in dumb-show, and was pointedly addressed to me. He stirred his rum and water pointedly at me, and he tasted his rum and water pointedly at me. And he stirred it and he tasted it—not with a spoon that was brought to him, but *with a file*.

He did this so that nobody but I saw the file. When he finished, he wiped the file and put it in a breast-pocket. I knew it to be Joe's file. The moment I saw the instrument, I knew that he knew my convict. I sat gazing at him, spell-bound. But he now reclined on his settle, taking very little notice of me, and talking principally about turnips. The rum and water running out together, Joe got up to go, and took me by the hand.

"Stop half a moment, Mr. Gargery. I think I've got a bright new shilling somewhere in my pocket, and if I have, the boy shall have it." The stranger found it in a handful of small change, folded it in some crumpled paper, and gave it to me. "Yours! Mind! Your own."

I thanked him, staring at him far beyond the bounds of good manners, and holding tight to Joe. He gave Joe goodnight, and he gave Mr. Wopsle goodnight, and he gave me only a look with his aiming eye.

On the way home, if I had been in a humour for talking, the talk must have been all on my side, for Mr. Wopsle parted from us at the door of the Jolly Bargemen, and Joe went all the way home with his mouth wide open, to rinse the rum out with as much air as possible. But I was in a manner stupefied by this turning up of my old misdeed and old acquaintance, and could think of nothing else.

My sister was not in a very bad temper when we presented our-

selves in the kitchen, and Joe was encouraged by that unusual circumstance to tell her about the bright shilling.

"A bad un, I'll be bound," said Mrs. Joe triumphantly, "or he
wouldn't have given it to the boy! Let's look at it."

I took it out of the paper, and it proved to be a good one. "But
what's this?" said Mrs. Joe, throwing down the shilling and catching up the paper. "Two one-pound notes?"

Joe caught up his hat again, and ran with them to the Jolly Bargemen to restore them to their owner. While he was gone, I sat down
on my usual stool and looked vacantly at my sister, feeling pretty
sure that the man would not be there.

Presently, Joe came back, saying that the man was gone, but that
he, Joe, had left word at the Three Jolly Bargemen concerning the
notes. Then my sister sealed them up in a piece of paper, and put
them under some dried rose-leaves in an ornamental teapot on the
top of a press in the state parlour. There they remained, a nightmare
to me many a night and day.

I had sadly broken sleep when I got to bed, through thinking
of the strange man taking aim at me with his invisible gun, and
of the guiltily coarse and common thing it was to be on secret
terms of conspiracy with convicts. I was haunted by the file, too.
A dread possessed me that when I least expected it, the file would
reappear. I coaxed myself to sleep by thinking of Miss Havisham's
next Wednesday, and in my sleep I saw the file coming at me and I
screamed myself awake.

CHAPTER 10

At THE APPOINTED TIME, I returned to Miss Havisham's. Estella answered my hesitating ring and locked the gate after admitting me, as she had done before, and again preceded me into the dark passage where her candle stood. She took no notice of me until she had the candle in her hand, when she looked over her shoulder.

"You are to come this way today," she said, and took me down a path new to me.

The passage was a long one, and seemed to pervade the whole square basement of the Manor House. We traversed but one side, however, and at the end of it she stopped, put her candle down, and opened a door. Here, the daylight reappeared, and we entered the small paved courtyard of a detached dwelling house that looked as if it had once belonged to the manager or head clerk of the extinct brewery. A clock in the outer wall of this house, like the clock in Miss Havisham's room, and like Miss Havisham's watch, had stopped at twenty minutes to nine.

We went through an open door at the back into a gloomy room with a low ceiling. There were some people assembled there, and Estella directed me to go and stand in a corner by the window until I was wanted.

The company, and her demands, made me very uncomfortable and I looked out the window, opened to the ground, to avoid showing it. The view was of a most neglected garden. There had been some light snow overnight, and it had not quite melted from the cold shadow of this bit of garden, and the wind caught it up in little eddies and threw it at the window, as if it pelted me for coming there.

I divined that my coming had stopped conversation in the room, and that its other occupants were looking at me. I could see nothing of the room except the shining of the fire in the window-glass, but I stiffened in all my joints with the consciousness that I was under close inspection.

There were three ladies in the room and one gentleman. They all had a listless and dreary air of waiting somebody's pleasure, and the most talkative of the ladies had to speak quite rigidly to repress a yawn. This lady, whose name was Camilla, very much reminded me of my sister.

"Poor dear soul!" said this lady, with an abruptness of manner quite my sister's. "Nobody's enemy but his own!"

"It would be much more commendable to be somebody else's enemy," said the gentleman. "Far more natural."

"Cousin Raymond," another lady said, "we are to love our neighbour."

"Sarah Pocket," returned Cousin Raymond, "if a man is not his own neighbour, who is?"

The other lady, who had not spoken yet, said gravely and emphatically, "Very true!"

The ringing of a distant bell, combined with the echoing of some cry or call along the passage by which I had come, interrupted the conversation and caused Estella to say to me, "Now, boy!"

On my turning round, they all looked at me with the utmost contempt, and, as I went out, I heard the one called Sarah Pocket say, "Well I am sure! What next!" and Camilla add, with indignation, "Was there ever such a fancy! The i-de-a!"

As we were going with our candle along the dark passage, Estella stopped all of a sudden, and, facing round, said in her taunting manner, with her face quite close to mine, "Well?"

"Well, miss?" I answered, almost falling over her and checking myself.

She stood looking at me, and, of course, I stood looking at her.

"Am I pretty?" she asked.

"Yes." I paused a moment as if considering. "I think you are very pretty."

"Am I insulting?"

"Not so much so as you were last time," I said quite honestly.

She fired when she asked the last question, and she slapped my face with such as much force as she seemed to possess. "Now? You little coarse monster, what do you think of me now?"

"I shall not tell you." I bristled under her contempt, but I was no longer fearful enough to reveal it.

"Because you are going to tell upstairs. Is that it?" she taunted.

"No," said I, "that's not it."

"Why don't you cry again, you little wretch?"

"Because I'll never cry for you again," I said. Which was, I suppose, as false a declaration as ever was made.

We went on our way upstairs after this episode and, as we were going up, we met a gentleman groping his way down.

"Whom have we here?" asked the gentleman, stopping and looking at me.

"A boy," said Estella.

He was a burly man of an exceedingly dark complexion, with an exceedingly large head, and a corresponding large hand. He took my chin in his large hand and turned up my face to have a look at me by the light of the candle. He was prematurely bald on the top of his head, and had bushy black eyebrows that wouldn't lie down but stood up bristling. His eyes were set very deep in his head, and were disagreeably sharp and suspicious. He had a large watch-chain, and strong black dots where his beard and whiskers would have been if he had let them.

"Boy of the neighbourhood? Hey?" said he, sniffing a little in my direction.

"Yes, sir," said I, doing the same, as if catching the scent of him would help me size him up. He smelled right to me somehow, though a bit much of scented soap, so I was not bristly or shy.

"How do you come here?"

"Miss Havisham sent for me, sir," I explained.

"Well! Behave yourself. I have a pretty large experience of boys, and you're a bad set of fellows. Now mind!" said he, biting the side of his great forefinger as he frowned at me, "you behave yourself!"

I wondered if he meant all boys, or if he smelled the bad on me somehow. With those words, he released me and went on his way downstairs. I wondered whether he could be a doctor. There was not much time to consider the subject, for we were soon in Miss Havisham's room, where she and everything else were just as I had left them. Estella left me standing near the door, and I stood there until Miss Havisham cast her eyes upon me from the dressing-table.

"So!" she said, without appearing startled or surprised. "The days have worn away, have they?"

"Yes, ma'am. Today is—"

"There, there, there!" with the impatient movement of her fingers. "I don't want to know. Are you ready to play?"

I was obliged to answer in some confusion, "I don't think I am, ma'am."

"Not up for combat again?" she demanded, with a searching look. "We'll start with cards?"

"Yes, ma'am. I could do that, if I was wanted."

"Since this house strikes you old and grave, boy," said Miss Havisham, impatiently, "and you are unwilling to play, are you willing to work?"

I could answer this enquiry with a better heart than I had been able to find for the other question, and I said I was quite willing.

"Then go into that opposite room," said she, pointing at the door behind me with her withered hand, "and wait there till I come."

I crossed the staircase landing, and entered the room she indicated. From that room, too, the daylight was completely excluded, and it had an airless smell that was oppressive. A fire had been lately kindled in the damp old-fashioned grate, and it was more disposed to go out than to burn up, and the reluctant smoke which hung in the room seemed colder than the clearer air, like our own marsh mist. Certain wintry branches of candles on the high chimneypiece faintly lit the chamber.

It was spacious, and I dare say had once been handsome, but every discernible thing in it was covered with dust and mould, and dropping to pieces. The most prominent object was a long table with a tablecloth spread on it, as if a feast had been in preparation when the house and the clocks all stopped together. A centerpiece of some kind was in the middle of this cloth, but it was so heavily overhung with cobwebs that its form was quite undistinguishable. As I looked along the yellow expanse out of which it seemed to grow, like a black fungus, I saw speckle-legged spiders with blotchy bodies running home to it, and running out from it, as if some circumstances of the greatest public importance had just transpired in the spider community.

I heard the mice, too, rattling behind the panels, as if the same occurrence were important to their interests. But the black beetles took no notice of the agitation, and groped about the hearth in a ponderous elderly way, as if they were short-sighted and hard of hearing, and not on terms with one another.

These crawling things had fascinated my attention, and I was watching them from a distance, when Miss Havisham laid a hand upon my shoulder. In her other hand she had a crutch-headed stick on which she leaned, and she looked like the witch of the place.

"This," said she, pointing to the long table with her stick, "is where I will be laid when I am dead. They shall come and look at me here."

With some vague misgiving that she might get upon the table then and there and die at once, I shrank under her cold touch. Of course, I knew that vampires didn't die, like the rest of us, but lived on and on unless killed by some extraordinary means.

"What do you think that is?" she asked me, again pointing with her stick. "That, where those cobwebs are?"

"I can't guess what it is, ma'am."

"It's a great cake. A bride-cake. Mine!"

She looked all round the room in a glaring manner, and then said, leaning on me while her hand twitched my shoulder,

"Come, come, come! Run for me! Run! Around the table. I shall chase you."

I made out from this, that my work was to run with Miss Havisham chasing, round and round the room. Accordingly, I started at once, and she seemed a little slow to start, so I slowed until we went away at a pace that might have been an imitation of Mr. Pumblechook's chaise-cart.

She was physically stronger than I expected, and after a little time said, "Faster!" I didn't go fast enough, however, and she gripped the hand upon my shoulder, and worked her mouth, as if she was going to take a bite. I dodged her sharp teeth and rolled over, struggling to try and control my urge to transform to wolf as I sprang away. After a few sprints and pounces, she said, "Call Estella!" so I went out on the landing and roared that name as I had done on the previous occasion. When her light appeared, I returned to Miss Havisham, and we started away again round and round the room.

If only Estella had come to be a spectator of our proceedings, I should have felt sufficiently discontented. As she brought with her the three ladies and the gentleman whom I had seen below, I didn't know what to do. In my politeness, I would have stopped, but Miss Havisham brushed my shoulder, and we chased on.

"Dear Miss Havisham," said Miss Sarah Pocket. "How well you look!"

"I do not," returned Miss Havisham, pausing as she trapped me in a corner. "I am pale skin and bone."

Camilla brightened when Miss Pocket met with this rebuff and she murmured, "Poor dear soul! Certainly not to be expected to look well, poor thing. The idea!"

"And how are you?" said Miss Havisham to Camilla. I took advantage of the distraction to leap clear, springing over her head and to the other side of the room. I could feel my hair starting to grow and I reminded myself, again, that I must not allow myself to transform, though Miss Havisham pounced after me with alarming agility and my defences were raised. As we were close to Camilla then, I would have stopped as a matter of course, only Miss Havisham wouldn't stop. We raced on, and I felt that I was highly obnoxious to Camilla.

"Thank you, Miss Havisham. I am as well as can be expected," remarked Camilla, amiably repressing a sob, while a hitch came into her upper lip, and her tears overflowed. "Raymond is a witness to what nervous jerkings I have in my legs. Chokings and nervous jerkings, however, are nothing new to me when I think with anxiety of those I love. If I could be less affectionate and sensitive, I should have a better digestion and an iron set of nerves. I am sure I wish it could be so." Here, a burst of tears.

The Raymond referred to, I understood to be the gentleman present, and him I understood to be Mr. Camilla. He came to the rescue at this point, and said in a consolatory and complimentary voice, "Camilla, my dear, it is well known that your family feelings are gradually undermining you to the extent of making one of your legs shorter than the other."

"I am not aware," observed the grave lady whose voice I had heard but once, "that to think of any person is to make a great claim upon that person, my dear."

Miss Sarah Pocket, whom I now saw to be a little dry, brown, corrugated old woman, with a small face that might have been made of walnut-shells, and a large mouth like a cat's without the whiskers, supported this position by saying, "No, indeed, my dear."

"Oh, yes, yes!" cried Camilla, whose fermenting feelings appeared to rise from her legs to her bosom. "It's all very true! It's a weakness to be so affectionate, but I can't help it." Here another burst of feeling.

Miss Havisham and I had never stopped all this time, but kept going round and round the room, slower now to hear conversation, and faster again, in circles.

"There's Matthew!" said Camilla. "Never mixing with any natural ties, never coming here to see how Miss Havisham is!"

When this same Matthew was mentioned, Miss Havisham

stopped us, and stood looking at the speaker. This change had a great influence in bringing Camilla's chemistry to a sudden end.

"Matthew will come and see me at last," said Miss Havisham, sternly, "when I am laid on that table. That will be his place, there," striking the table with the stick she retrieved from where she had dropped it, "at my head! And yours will be there! And your husband's there! And Sarah Pocket's there! And Georgiana's there! Now you all know where to take your stations when you come to feast upon me. And now go!"

At the mention of each name, she had struck the table with her stick in a new place. She now said, "Run, run!" and we went on again, and paused again when she had trapped me in another corner, her sharp fangs exposed.

"I suppose there's nothing to be done," exclaimed Camilla, "but comply and depart."

Mr. Camilla interposed as Mrs. Camilla kissed her hand to Miss Havisham, and was escorted forth. Sarah Pocket and Georgiana contended who should remain last, but Sarah was too wise to be outdone. She ambled round Georgiana with such artful slipperiness that the latter was obliged to go first. Sarah Pocket then made her separate effect of departing with, "Bless you, Miss Havisham dear!"

Georgiana, the last standing, did not make it out with the others. Miss Havisham's appetite whetted, perhaps, from chasing me around the room, she turned on Georgiana as she stayed to bid her goodbye.

"How generous of you, dear, to volunteer to be my dinner," Miss Havisham said, springing on Georgiana, knocking her to the floor, and sinking her fangs into her neck. On all fours, hunched over her prey, she drank greedily. Georgiana thrashed at first, only for a moment, and then slowed, either from blood loss or the conscious attempt to impress Miss Havisham. Apparently sated, Miss Havisham sprang up again, swiping the back of her hand over her crimson mouth, before helping a dazed Georgiana to her feet. Georgiana swayed, then seemed to find her footing enough to run out after the others.

While Estella was still away lighting them down, Miss Havisham walked with her hand on my shoulder, but more and more slowly. I didn't shy away from her, as I imagined I might. Although I could still smell Georgiana's blood, I seemed to know that I was not at risk, and would manage to hold my own if necessary. At last Miss Havisham stopped before the fire, and said, after muttering and looking at it some seconds, "This is my birthday, Pip."

I was going to wish her many happy returns, when she lifted her hand.

"I don't suffer it to be spoken of. I don't suffer those who were here just now, or any one to speak of it. They come here on the day, but they dare not refer to it."

Of course I made no further effort to refer to it.

"On this day of the year, long before you were born, this heap of decay," she took up her stick again and stabbed at the pile of cobwebs on the table, but not touching it, "was brought here. The mice have gnawed at it, and sharper teeth than teeth of mice have gnawed at me, as I have gnawed at others."

She stroked her neck, as if remembering, as she stood looking at the table; she in her once white dress, all yellow and withered; the once white cloth all yellow and withered; everything around in a state to crumble under a touch.

"When the ruin is complete," said she, with a ghastly look, "and when they lay me dead, in my bride's dress on the bride's table, which shall be done, and which will be the finished curse upon him, so much the better if it is done on this day!"

She stood looking at the table as if she stood looking at her own figure lying there. I remained quiet. Estella returned, and she, too, remained quiet. It seemed to me that we continued thus for a long time. In the heavy air of the room, and the heavy darkness that brooded in its remoter corners, I even had an alarming fancy that Estella and I might presently begin to decay.

At length, not coming out of her distraught state by degrees, but in an instant, Miss Havisham said, "Let me see you two play at cards. Why have you not begun?"

With that, we returned to her room, and sat down. I was beggared, as before, and again, as before, Miss Havisham watched us all the time.

Estella, for her part, likewise treated me as before, except that she did not condescend to speak. When we had played some half-dozen games, a day was appointed for my return, and I was taken down into the yard to be fed in the former dog-like manner. Though the moon was on the wane, I felt the usual effects of the early stages of my transformation and I struggled to control them. I'd tucked a silver spoon and watch chain in my pockets to aid in my holding off any possible changes, and though my hands were somewhat covered in a downy fair fuzz, I managed to avoid pouncing on my repast. Afterwards, like before, I was left to wander about as I liked.

I was spared the necessity of using my strengthened hindquarters to spring up to prowl the garden wall, for I noticed a gate left open. I strolled into the garden. It was quite a wilderness, and there were old melon-frames and cucumber-frames. When I had exhausted the garden and an empty greenhouse, I found myself in the dismal corner upon which I had looked out of the window. Never questioning for a moment that the house was now empty, I looked in at another window, and found myself, to my great surprise, exchanging a broad stare with a young gentleman with red eyelids and light hair.

This young gentleman quickly disappeared, and reappeared beside me. He had been at his books when I had found myself staring at him, and I saw that he was inky.

"Halloa, young fellow!" he said.

Halloa being a general observation, which I had usually observed to be best answered by itself, I said, "Halloa!" politely omitting young fellow.

"Who let you in?" he asked, leaning to sniff in my direction.

"Miss Estella." I said, doing likewise. He had an earthy aroma about him, mixed with something of the homey smell of baking bread.

"Who gave you leave to prowl about?" he asked, circling and looking me up and down.

"Miss Estella." I turned on my heel, keeping my face in his direction as he walked.

"Come and fight," the young gentleman said.

Not until that moment did I realize he was sporting a light fur over his pale skin. So we were alike? Could he be gentleman, and wolf? Or, was he something else entirely? I wanted to ask, but what could I do but follow him? His manner was so final, and I was so astonished, that I followed where he led, as if I had been under a spell.

"Stop a minute, though," he said, wheeling round before we had gone many paces. "I ought to give you a reason for fighting, too. There it is!"

In a most irritating manner he instantly slapped his hands against one another, daintily flung one of his legs up behind him, pulled my hair, slapped his hands again, dipped his head, and butted it into my stomach.

The bull-like proceeding last mentioned, besides that it was unquestionably to be regarded in the light of a liberty, was particularly disagreeable just after bread and meat. I therefore hit out at him and was going to hit out again, when he said, "Aha! Would you?" and began dancing backwards and forwards in a manner quite unparalleled within my limited experience.

I felt myself turning to wolf, slowly gaining fur and tail, sharper teeth, as he appeared to be, and I allowed it. He pounced about, back and forth.

I was secretly afraid of him when I saw him so dexterous, but I felt morally and physically convinced that his light head of fur could have had no business in the pit of my stomach. Therefore, I followed him without a word, to a retired nook of the garden, formed by the junction of two walls and screened by some rubbish. On his asking me if I was satisfied with the ground, and on my replying in the affirmative, he begged my leave to absent himself for a moment, and quickly returned with a bottle of water and a sponge dipped in vinegar.

"Available for both," he said, placing these against the wall. And then fell to pulling off, not only his jacket and waistcoat, but his shirt and trousers, too, in a manner at once light-hearted, business-like, and bloodthirsty. I stripped as well.

Although he did not look very healthy—having pimples on his face visible even under his light furring and a breaking out at his snout, perhaps an effect of stretching from a human nose—these dreadful preparations quite appalled me. I judged him to be about my own age, but he was much taller, and he had a way of spinning himself about that was full of appearance. For the rest, he was a young gentleman in a grey suit (when not denuded for battle), with his elbows, knees, wrists, and heels considerably in advance of the rest of him as to development.

My heart failed me when I saw him entirely wolfish, thick brown fur covering every inch of him as he reared up on his hindquarters, claws and fangs bared, ready to strike. I must have looked somewhat like him, having turned, but I never have been so surprised in my life as I was when I let out the first blow, and saw him lying on his back, looking up at me with a bloody snout and his face exceedingly fore-shortened.

But, he was on his paws directly, and pouncing back at me. The second greatest surprise I have ever had in my life was seeing him on his back again, looking up at me. I gave a sound, an impressive roaring of sorts, and gnashed my teeth as if daring him to get up again.

His spirit inspired me with great respect. He seemed to have no strength, and he never once broke my skin. He was always knocked down, but he would be up again in a moment, and then came at me with an air and a show that made me believe he really was going to do for me at last. He got heavily bruised, for I am sorry to record that the more I hit him, the harder I hit him, but he came up again and again and again, until at last he got a bad fall with the back of his head against the wall.

Even after that crisis in our affairs, he got up and turned round and round confusedly a few times, as if chasing his fluffy tail. Finally he dropped to a crouch and howled loud and long, as if to say, "That means you have won."

He seemed so brave and innocent, that although I had not proposed the contest, I felt but a gloomy satisfaction in my victory. Indeed, I regarded myself a savage wolf in the making. We rested near each other, gradually restored to ourselves, and dressed in haste.

"Good afternoon," I said, as it seemed to be time to part.

"Same to you," he said.

When I got into the courtyard, I found Estella waiting with the keys. But she neither asked me where I had been, nor why I had kept her waiting. There was a bright flush upon her face, as though something had happened to delight her. Instead of going straight to the gate, too, she stepped back into the passage, and beckoned me.

"Come here! You may kiss me, if you like."

I kissed her cheek as she turned it to me. I think I would have gone through a great deal to kiss her cheek, but I felt that the kiss was given to the somewhat hairy common boy as a piece of money might have been, and that it was worth nothing. She must not have seen us fighting or she would never have let a wolfboy kiss her.

What with the birthday visitors, the cards, and the fight, my stay had lasted so long that when I neared home, the light on the spit of sand off the point on the marshes was gleaming against a black night-sky, and Joe's furnace was flinging a path of fire across the road. I had turned full wolf at will, without influence of a full moon. I felt more wild and full of beastly life within me than ever I had in the past. I stopped outside the door and let out a long, satisfying bay at the moon, not even fearing the consequences should my sister hear me, before I took a deep breath and went in.

CHAPTER 11

ONLY AFTER I HAD gone to bed for the night, my mind grew very uneasy on the subject of the furry young gentleman. The more I thought of the fight, the more certain it appeared that something would be done to me. I felt that the furry creature's blood was on my head, and that the law would avenge it. How, I had no idea, but it was clear that wolfish boys could not go stalking about the country, ravaging the houses of gentlefolks, and pitching into each other, without laying themselves open to severe punishment or exposure of their true natures.

For some days, I even kept close at home, and looked out at the kitchen door with the greatest caution before going on an errand, lest the officers of the county jail should pounce upon me. I had cut my paws against the gnasher's teeth, and I twisted my imagination into a thousand tangles, as I devised incredible ways of accounting for that damnatory circumstance when I should be set before the judges.

When the day came round for my return to the scene of the deed of violence, my terrors reached their height. Whether myrmidons of justice, specially sent down from London, would be lying in ambush behind the gate; whether Miss Havisham, preferring to take personal vengeance for an outrage done to her house, might rise in those grave-clothes of hers, draw her fangs, and drink me dead; whether a band of mercenaries might be engaged to fall upon me in the brewery, and cuff me until I was no more; it was high testimony to my confidence in the spirit of the furry young gentleman that I never imagined him accessory to these retaliations.

However, go to Miss Havisham's I must, and go I did. And behold! Nothing came of the late struggle. It was not alluded to in any way, and no furry young gentleman was to be discovered on the premises. I found the same gate open, and I explored the garden, and even looked in at the windows of the detached house. Only in the corner where the combat had taken place could I detect any evidence of the furry gentleman's existence. There were traces of his gore in that spot, and I covered them with garden-mould.

On the broad landing between Miss Havisham's room and that other room in which the long table was laid out, I saw a post with a target attached and Miss Havisham throwing wooden stakes into it, dead center. There was a board behind the target to catch the missed stakes, but Miss Havisham never missed. She began instructing Estella in how to properly throw the stakes and tried to convince me to stand in front of the board to act as the target. I declined, but accepted the offer to try my hand at throwing stakes. I was not as accurate as Miss Havisham or Estella, with over half of my throws ending up stuck in the board behind. Target practise became a regular occupation of my visits, and eventually I did pose as target and discovered I could catch the stakes in my bare hands before they hit me. Over and over and over again, we would practise, and sometimes as long as three hours at a stretch. It was at once settled that I should return every alternate day at noon for these purposes.

I am now going to sum up a period of at least eight or ten months.

As we began to be more used to one another, Miss Havisham talked more to me, and asked me such questions as what had I learnt and what was I going to be? I told her I was going to be apprenticed to Joe, I believed. I professed to my knowing nothing and wanting to know everything, in the hope that she might offer some help towards that desirable end. On the contrary, she seemed to prefer my being ignorant. She never gave me any money, or anything but my daily dinner. She never stipulated that I should be paid for my services.

Estella was always about, and always let me in and out, but never told me I might kiss her again. Sometimes, she would coldly tolerate me. Sometimes, she would condescend to me. Sometimes, she would be quite familiar with me. Sometimes, she would tell me energetically that she hated me.

"Does she grow prettier and prettier, Pip? And yet stronger and stronger?" Miss Havisham would often ask me in a whisper, or when we were alone. And when I said yes to both (for indeed she did, on both counts), the vampire would seem to enjoy it greedily.

Also, when we played at cards to relax after target practise, Miss Havisham would look on with a miserly relish of Estella's moods, whatever they were. And sometimes, when her moods were so many and so contradictory of one another that I was puzzled what to say or do, Miss Havisham would embrace her with lavish fondness, murmuring something in her ear that sounded like, "Break their hearts and limbs, my pride and hope, break them body and soul, and have no mercy!"

"There, there, there! Sing!" Miss Havisham suddenly said to me, with the impatient movement of her fingers, one day soon after the appearance of the target.

There was a song, Old Clem, of which Joe used to hum fragments at the forge. I was surprised into crooning this ditty as I stood in front of the target while Estella tried to hit me and I caught her stakes instead. It happened so to catch her fancy that she took it up in a low brooding voice as if she were singing in her sleep. After that, it became customary with us to have it as we practised, and Estella would often join in. And, to be honest, it was the steady hum of a repeated refrain, along with the small bit of silver I always kept in my pocket, which allowed me a sort of meditation to keep my transformations at bay.

At Miss Havisham's, my wolf side seemed to be always chomping at the bit to appear, full moon or no. Perhaps it was the steady darkness or the eerie feel of the place, or the sense of always being prepared for an attack. Perhaps being away from Joe and the forge. And when confronted by the furry young gentleman, my inner beast jumped to the fore. I was ready to fight, though I'd never fought before, and I was good at it.

Perhaps I might have told Joe about the furry young gentleman, if I had not previously been betrayed into those enormous inventions to which I had confessed. Under the circumstances, I felt that Joe could hardly fail to discern in the furry young gentleman an appropriate passenger to be put into the black velvet coach; therefore, I said nothing of him. I reposed complete confidence in no one but Biddy; but I told poor Biddy everything. Why it came natural to me to do so, and why Biddy had a deep concern in everything I told her, I did not know then, though I think I know now.

That swine Pumblechook used to come over in the evenings to discuss my prospects with my sister. I really do believe (to this hour with less penitence than I ought to feel), that if these hands could have ripped a strip of flesh out of his chest to expose his bare, beating heart and prove that he indeed had one despite his actions, they would have done it. The miserable man could not discuss my prospects without having me before him, and he would drag me up from my stool (usually by the collar) where I was quiet in a corner, and, put me before the fire as if I were going to be cooked.

"Now, mum, here is this boy!" So he would begin. "Here is this boy which you brought up by hand. Hold up your head, boy, and be forever grateful."

Then, he and my sister would pair off in such nonsensical speculations about Miss Havisham, and about what she would do with me and for me, that I used to want—quite painfully—to burst into spiteful tears, fly at Pumblechook, and gnaw him all over like the beef bones that inhabited my dreams.

In these discussions, Joe bore no part. He was often talked at, while they were in progress, by reason of Mrs. Joe's perceiving that he was not favourable to my being taken from the forge. I was fully old enough now to be apprenticed to Joe.

We went on in this way for a long time, when one day Miss Havisham stopped short as I caught a stake thrown quite high and out of range.

"You are growing tall, Pip!" she said with decided displeasure.

I thought it best to hint, through the medium of a meditative look, that this might be occasioned by circumstances over which I had no control.

She said no more at the time, but she looked frowning and moody. On the next day of my attendance, when our usual exercise was over, and she had taken a seat at her dressing-table, she stayed me with a movement of her impatient fingers.

"Tell me the name again of that silversmith of yours."

"Joe Gargery, ma'am."

"You had better be apprenticed at once. Would Gargery come here with you, and bring your indentures, do you think?"

"At any particular time, Miss Havisham?"

"There, there! I know nothing about times. Let him come soon, and come along with you."

When I got home at night, and delivered this message for Joe, my sister "went on the rampage," in a more alarming degree than at any previous period. She asked Joe and me whether we supposed she was a doormat under our feet, and how we dared to use her so, and what company we graciously thought she *was* fit for, and why didn't he just marry a slave? Joe offered no answer, poor fellow, but stood feeling his whisker and looking dejectedly at me, as if he thought it really might have been a better speculation.

CHAPTER 12

TWO DAYS LATER, I struggled with my conflicting emotions as I watched Joe dressing in his Sunday clothes to accompany me to Miss Havisham's. At breakfast, my sister declared her intention of going to town with us, and being left at Uncle Pumblechook's and called for "when we had done with our fine ladies." The forge was shut up for the day.

We walked to town, my sister leading the way in a very large beaver bonnet. When we came to Pumblechook's, my sister bounced in and left us. As it was almost noon, Joe and I went straight to Miss Havisham's house. Estella opened the gate as usual, and, the moment she appeared, Joe took his hat off and stood weighing it by the brim in both his hands.

Estella took no notice of either of us, but led us the way that I knew so well. I followed next to her, and Joe came last. When I looked back at Joe in the long passage, he was still weighing his hat with the greatest care, and was coming after us in long strides on the tips of his toes.

Estella told me we were both to go in, so I took Joe by the coat-cuff and conducted him into Miss Havisham's presence. She was seated at her dressing table, and looked round at us immediately.

"Oh!" said she to Joe. "You are the husband of the sister of this boy?"

I could hardly have imagined dear old Joe looking so unlike himself or standing speechless.

"You are the husband," repeated Miss Havisham, "of the sister of this boy?"

Throughout the interview, Joe persisted in addressing me instead of Miss Havisham, which was very aggravating.

"Which I meantersay, Pip," Joe now observed in a manner that was at once expressive of forcible argumentation, strict confidence, and great politeness, "as I hup and married your sister, and I were at the time what you might call (if you was anyways inclined) a single man."

"Well!" said Miss Havisham. "And you have reared the boy, with the intention of taking him for your apprentice. Is that so, Mr. Gargery?"

"You know, Pip," replied Joe, "as you and me were ever friends, and it were looked for'ard to betwixt us, as being calc'lated to lead to larks."

"Has the boy," said Miss Havisham, "ever made any objection? Does he like the trade?"

"Which it is well beknown to yourself, Pip," returned Joe, strengthening his former mixture of argumentation, confidence, and politeness, "that it were the wish of your own hart."

It was quite in vain for me to endeavour to make him sensible that he ought to speak to Miss Havisham. The more I made faces and gestures to him to do it, the more confidential, argumentative, and polite he persisted in being to me.

"Have you brought his indentures with you?" asked Miss Havisham.

"Well, Pip, you know," replied Joe, as if that were a little unreasonable, "you yourself see me put 'em in my 'at, and therefore you know as they are here." With which he took them out, and gave them, not to Miss Havisham, but to me. I am afraid I was ashamed of the dear good fellow—I know I was ashamed of him—when I saw that Estella stood at the back of Miss Havisham's chair, and that her eyes laughed mischievously. I took the indentures out of his hand and gave them to Miss Havisham.

"You expected," said Miss Havisham, as she looked them over, "no premium with the boy?"

"Joe!" I remonstrated, for he made no reply at all. "Why don't you answer—"

"Pip," returned Joe, cutting me short as if he were hurt, "which I meantersay that were not a question requiring a answer betwixt yourself and me, and which you know the answer to be full well no. You know it to be no, Pip, and wherefore should I say it?"

Miss Havisham took up a little bag from the table beside her.

"Pip has earned a premium here," she said, "and here it is. There are five-and-twenty guineas in this bag. Give it to your master, Pip."

As if he were absolutely out of his mind with the wonder awakened in him by her strange figure and the strange room, Joe, even at this pass, persisted in addressing me.

"This is wery liberal on your part, Pip," said Joe, "and it is as such received and grateful welcome, though never looked for, far nor near, nor nowheres. And now, old chap, may we do our duty!"

"Goodbye, Pip!" said Miss Havisham. "Let them out, Estella."

"Am I to come again, Miss Havisham?" I asked.

"No. Gargery is your master now. Gargery! One word!"

Thus calling him back as I went out of the door, I heard her say to Joe, in a distinct emphatic voice, "The boy has been a good boy here, and that is his reward. Of course, as an honest man, you will expect no other and no more."

How Joe got out of the room, I have never been able to determine. I know that when he did get out he was steadily proceeding upstairs instead of coming down, and I went after him and laid hold of him. In another minute we were outside the gate, and it was locked, and Estella was gone. When we stood in the daylight alone again, Joe backed up against a wall.

"Astonishing!" he said, and there he remained so long saying it again. "Astonishing" at intervals, so often, that I began to think his senses were never coming back. At length he prolonged his remark into "Pip, I do assure you this is as-TON-ishing!" and so, by degrees, became conversational and able to walk away.

I have reason to think that Joe's intellects were brightened by the encounter they had passed through, and that on our way to Pumblechook's he invented a subtle and deep design.

"Well?" cried my sister, addressing us both at once. "And what's happened to you? I wonder you condescend to come back to such poor society as this, I am sure I do!"

"Miss Havisham," said Joe, with a fixed look at me, like an effort of remembrance, "made it wery partick'ler that we should give her—were it compliments or respects, Pip?"

"Compliments," I said.

"Which that were my own belief," answered Joe. "Her compliments to Mrs. J. Gargery—"

"Much good they'll do me!" observed my sister; but rather gratified, too.

"And wishing," pursued Joe, with another fixed look at me, like another effort of remembrance, "that the state of Miss Havisham's elth were sitch as would have—allowed, were it, Pip?"

"Of her having the pleasure," I added.

"Of ladies' company," said Joe. And drew a long breath.

"Well!" cried my sister, with a mollified glance at Mr. Pumblechook. "She might have had the politeness to send that message at first, but it's better late than never. And what did she give young hair ball here?"

"She giv' him," said Joe, "nothing."

Mrs. Joe was going to break out, but Joe went on.

"What she giv'," said Joe, "she giv' to his friends. 'And by his friends,' were her explanation, 'I mean into the hands of his sister Mrs. J. Gargery.' Them were her words; 'Mrs. J. Gargery.' She mayn't have know'd," added Joe, with an appearance of reflection, "whether it were Joe, or Jorge."

My sister looked at Pumblechook, who smoothed the elbows of his wooden arm-chair, and nodded at her and at the fire, as if he had known all about it beforehand.

"And how much have you got?" asked my sister, laughing. Positively laughing!

"It's five-and-twenty pound," said Joe, delightedly handing the bag to my sister.

"It's five-and-twenty pound, mum," echoed that basest of swindlers, Pumblechook, rising to shake hands with her. "And it's no more than your merits (as I said when my opinion was asked), and I wish you joy of the money!"

If the villain had stopped here, his case would have been sufficiently awful, but he blackened his guilt by proceeding to take me into custody, with a right of patronage that left all his former criminality far behind.

"Now you see, Joseph and wife," said Pumblechook, as he took me by the arm above the elbow, "I am one of them that always go right through with what they've begun. This boy must be bound, out of hand. That's my way. Bound out of hand."

"Goodness knows, Uncle Pumblechook," said my sister (grasping the money), "we're deeply beholden to you."

"Never mind me, mum," returned that diabolical flesh-merchant. "A pleasure's a pleasure all the world over. But this boy, you know, we must have him bound. I said I'd see to it—to tell you the truth."

The Justices were sitting in the Town Hall near at hand, and we at once went over to have me bound apprentice to Joe in the Magisterial presence.

The Hall was a queer place, I thought, with higher pews in it than a church, and with people hanging over the pews looking on, and with mighty Justices (one with a powdered head) leaning back in chairs, with folded arms, or taking snuff, or going to sleep, or writing, or reading the newspapers, and with some shining black portraits on the walls. Here, in a corner, my indentures were duly signed and attested, and I was "bound."

When we had come out again, we went back to Pumblechook's. And there my sister became so excited that nothing would serve her but we must have a dinner out of that windfall at the Blue Boar, and that Pumblechook must go over in his chaise-cart, and bring the Hubbles and Mr. Wopsle.

It was miserable for me. And to make it worse, they all asked me from time to time—in short, whenever they had nothing else to do—why I didn't enjoy myself? And what could I possibly do then, but say I was enjoying myself—when I wasn't!

However, they were grown up and had their own way, and they made the most of it. That swindling Pumblechook, exalted into the beneficent contriver of the whole occasion, actually took the top of the table. They wouldn't let me go to sleep, but whenever they saw me dropping off, woke me up and told me to enjoy myself. I remember that when I got into my little bedroom, I was truly wretched, and had a strong conviction on me that I should never like Joe's trade. I had liked it once, but once was not now.

It is a most miserable thing to feel ashamed of home.

Owing to my sister's temper, home had never been a very pleasant place to me. But, Joe had sanctified it, and I had believed in it. I had believed in the best parlour as a most elegant saloon. I had believed in the kitchen as a chaste though not magnificent apartment. I had believed in the forge as the glowing road to manhood and independence. Within a single year all this was changed. Now it was all coarse and common, and I would not have had Miss Havisham and Estella see it on any account. I had learned that though Pip and a werewolf, I could be accepted in fine company. I could be a gentleman, if only I had the means.

Miss Havisham had sent me home to my fate. I would never have the means to be a gentleman, and perhaps I was not so accepted in fine company after all.

Once, it had seemed to me that when I should at last roll up my shirt-sleeves and go into the forge, Joe's 'prentice, I should be distinguished and happy. Now the reality was in my hold, I only felt that I was dusty with the dust of ash and filth from working metal over fire. Never has that curtain dropped so heavy and blank as when my way in life lay stretched out straight before me through the newly entered road of apprenticeship to Joe.

I was quite as dejected on the first working day of my apprenticeship as in that after-time, but I am glad to know that I never breathed a murmur to Joe while my indentures lasted. It is about the only thing I am glad to know of myself in that connection.

What I dreaded was, that in some unlucky hour I, being at my hairiest and commonest, under a full moon, I should lift up my eyes and see Estella looking in at one of the wooden windows of the forge. I was haunted by the fear that she would, sooner or later, find me out, with black brows, furred face and hands, doing the coarsest part of my work, and would exult over me and despise me. Often after dark, when I was pulling the bellows for Joe, and we were singing Old Clem, and when the thought of how we used to sing it at Miss Havisham's would seem to show me Estella's face in the fire, with her pretty hair fluttering as she turned a pirouette before throwing a stake, and her eyes scorning me as I caught the missile instead of letting it pierce me through the heart—often at such a time I would look towards those panels of black night in the wall which the wooden windows then were, and would fancy that I saw her just drawing her face away, and would believe that she had come at last.

After that, I would feel more ashamed of home than ever, in my own ungracious breast.

CHAPTER 13

As I was getting too big for Mr. Wopsle's great-aunt's room, my education under that preposterous female terminated. Not, however, until Biddy had imparted to me everything she knew, from the little catalogue of prices, to a comic song she had once bought for a half-penny. Whatever I acquired, I tried to impart to Joe. I wanted to make Joe less ignorant and common that he might be worthier of my society and less open to Estella's reproach.

The old battery out on the marshes was our place of study, and a broken slate and a short piece of slate-pencil were our educational implements: to which Joe always added a pipe of tobacco. I never knew Joe to remember anything from one Sunday to another, or to acquire, under my tuition, any piece of information whatever. Yet he would smoke his pipe at the battery with a far more sagacious air than anywhere else, even with a learned air, as if he considered himself to be advancing immensely. Dear fellow, I hope he did.

One Sunday when Joe, greatly enjoying his pipe, had so plumed himself on being "most awful dull," that I had given him up for the day, I lay on the earthwork for some time with my chin on my hand, descrying traces of Miss Havisham and Estella all over the sky, until at last I resolved to mention a thought concerning them that had been much in my head.

"Joe," I said. "Don't you think I ought to make Miss Havisham a visit?"

"Well, Pip," returned Joe, slowly considering. "There is some wisits p'r'aps, as for ever remains open to the question, Pip. But in regard to wisiting Miss Havisham. She might think you wanted something—expected something of her."

"Don't you think I might say that I did not, Joe?"

"You might, old chap," said Joe. "And she might credit it. Similarly she mightn't. You see, Pip, when Miss Havisham done the handsome thing by you, she called me back to say to me as that were all."

"Yes, Joe. I heard her."

"ALL," Joe repeated, very emphatically.

"But, Joe. Here am I, getting on in the first year of my time, and, since the day of my being bound, I have never thanked Miss Havisham, or asked after her, or shown that I remember her."

"Well," Joe said, "if I was yourself, Pip, I wouldn't. No, I would not."

"Yes, Joe; but what I wanted to say, was, that as we are rather slack just now, if you would give me a half-holiday tomorrow, I think I would go uptown and make a call on Miss Est—Havisham."

"Which her name," said Joe, gravely, "ain't Estavisham, Pip, unless she have been rechris'ened."

"I know, Joe, I know. It was a slip of mine. What do you think of it, Joe?"

In brief, Joe thought that if I thought well of it, he thought well of it.

Now, Joe kept a vampire journeyman whose name was Orlick. He was a broad-shouldered loose-limbed fellow of surprising strength, never in a hurry, and always slouching. Joe's first choice probably would not have been to hire a vampire, but he needed the help and a vampire was available. Orlick never seemed to come to work on purpose, but would slouch in as if by mere accident after dark, and when he went away towards morning, he would slouch out, as if he had no idea where he was going and no intention of ever coming back. He lodged at a sluice-keeper's out on the marshes, and on working-nights would come slouching from his hermitage, with his hands in his pockets.

This vampire journeyman had no liking for me. When I was very small and timid, he gave me to understand that the Devil lived in a black corner of the forge, and that he knew the fiend very well. Also, that it was necessary to make up the fire, once in seven years, with a live boy, and that I might consider myself fuel. Dolge Orlick was at work and present after dusk, when I re-minded Joe of my half-holiday. He said nothing at the moment, for he and Joe had just got a piece of hot iron between them, and I was at the bellows.

"Now, master!" he said, leaning on his hammer. "Sure you're not a going to favor only one of us. If Young Pip has a half-holiday, do as much for old Orlick." I suppose he had been about five-and-twenty when he'd become a vampire, but he usually spoke of him-self as an ancient person.

"Why, what'll you do with a half-holiday, if you get it?" said Joe.

"What'll I do with it! What'll he do with it? I'll do as much with it as him," said Orlick.

"As to Pip, he's going uptown," said Joe.

"Well then, as to old Orlick, he's a going uptown," retorted that worthy. "Two can go uptown. Tain't only one wot can go uptown."

"Don't lose your temper," said Joe.

"Shall if I like," growled Orlick. "Some and their uptowning! Now, master! Come. No favouring in this shop. Be a man!"

The master refusing to entertain the subject until the journeyman was in a better temper, Orlick plunged at the furnace, drew out a red-hot bar, made at me with it as if he were going to run it through my body, whisked it round my head, laid it on the anvil, hammered it out, as if it were I, I thought, and the sparks were my spurting blood.

"As in general you stick to your work as well as most men," said Joe, "let it be a half-holiday for all."

My sister had been standing silent in the yard, within hearing— she was a most unscrupulous spy and listener—and she instantly looked in at one of the windows.

"Like you, you fool!" said she to Joe, "giving holidays to great idle hulkers like that. You are a rich man, upon my life, to waste wages in that way. I wish I was his master!"

"You'd be everybody's master, if you durst," retorted Orlick, with an ill-favoured grin.

"Let her alone," said Joe.

"I'd be a match for all noodles and all rogues," returned my sister, beginning to work herself into a mighty rage. "And I couldn't be a match for the rogues, without being a match for you, who are the worst rogue between this and France. Now!"

"You're a foul shrew, Mother Gargery," growled the vampire. "If that makes a judge of rogues, you ought to be a good'un."

"Let her alone, will you?" said Joe.

"What did you say?" cried my sister, beginning to scream. "What did you say? What did that vampire Orlick say to me, Pip? What did he call me, with my husband standing by? Oh! oh! oh!" Each of these exclamations was a shriek.

"Ah-h-h!" growled the vampire journeyman, between his teeth, which were pointed fangs, as true to his nature. "I'd hold you, if you was my wife. I'd hold you under the pump, and choke it out of you."

"I tell you, let her alone," said Joe.

"Oh! To hear him!" cried my sister, with a clap of her hands and a scream together. "That Orlick! In my own house!"

What could the wretched Joe do now, after his disregarded interruptions, but stand up to his journeyman, and ask him what he meant by interfering betwixt himself and Mrs. Joe, and further whether he was man enough to come on? Without so much as pulling off their singed and burnt aprons, they went at one another, like two giants. But, if any man or Scapegrace in that neighbourhood could stand up long against Joe, I never saw him.

Orlick, as if he had been of no more account than the furry young gentleman, was very soon among the coal-dust, and in no hurry to come out of it. Then Joe unlocked the door and picked up my sister, who had dropped insensible at the window (but who had seen the fight first, I think), and who was carried into the house and laid down, and who was recommended to revive.

Then came that singular calm and silence which succeed all uproars, such a lull that I went upstairs to bed. Before dawn, with no more fuss in the night to disturb me, I dressed and went to see if anything new happened in the night. When I came down, I found Joe and Orlick sweeping up, without any other traces of discomposure than a slit in one of Orlick's nostrils, which was neither expressive nor ornamental. They had apparently worked through the night and shared a pot of beer from the Jolly Bargemen in a peaceable manner. The lull had a sedative and philosophical influence on Joe, who followed me out into the road to say, as a parting observation that might do me good, "On the rampage, Pip, and off the rampage, Pip:—such is Life!"

With what absurd emotions I found myself again going to Miss

Havisham's matters little here. Nor, how I passed and re-passed the gate many times before I could make up my mind to ring.

Miss Sarah Pocket came to the gate. No Estella.

"How, then? You here again?" said Miss Pocket, nursing a fresh puncture wound on her neck. "What do you want?"

When I said that I only came to see how Miss Havisham was, Sarah evidently deliberated whether or no she should send me about my business. But unwilling to hazard the responsibility, she let me in.

Everything was unchanged, and Miss Havisham was alone.

"Well?" said she, fixing her eyes upon me. "I hope you want nothing? You'll get nothing."

"No indeed, Miss Havisham. I only wanted you to know that I am doing very well in my apprenticeship, and am always much obliged to you."

"There, there!" with the restless fingers. "Come now and then; come on your birthday—Aye! You are looking round for Estella? Hey?"

I had been looking round—in fact, for Estella—and I stammered that I hoped she was well.

"Abroad," said Miss Havisham. "Educating for a lady; far out of reach; prettier than ever, and twice as deadly. Do you feel that you have lost her?"

There was such a malignant enjoyment in her utterance of the last words, and she broke into such a disagreeable laugh, that I was at a loss what to say. She spared me the trouble of considering by dismissing me. When at last Sarah closed the gate on me, I felt more dissatisfied than ever with my home and with my trade and with my wolfishness and with everything. Estella was going to be a lady, fit for a gentleman, not for a werewolf smithy who had no hope of ever becoming a gentleman.

As I loitered along the High Street, looking in disconsolately at the shop windows, and thinking what I would buy if I were a gentleman, who should come out of the bookshop but Mr. Wopsle. As the night was dark and the way was dreary, and almost any companionship on the road was better than none, I made no great resistance to his suggestion that we walk together. I kept my full wolf at bay, just barely, and only had the light furring and snout that occasionally marked the moon coming full. Beyond town, we found a heavy mist out, and it fell wet and thick. We were noticing this, and saying how the mist rose with a change of wind from a certain quarter of our marshes, when we came upon a man slouching under the lee of the turnpike house.

"Halloa!" we said, stopping. "Orlick there?"

"Ah!" he answered, slouching out. "I was standing by a minute, on the chance of company."

"You are late," I remarked, as he wiped something from the corner of his lip that looked suspiciously like blood.

"I stopped for a meal." Orlick not unnaturally answered, "Well? And you're late."

"We have been indulging in an intellectual evening," Mr. Wopsle said.

Old Orlick growled, as if he had nothing to say about that, and we all went on together. I asked him presently whether he had been spending his half-holiday up and down town?

"Yes," said he, "all of it. I come in behind yourself. I didn't see you, but I must have been pretty close behind you. By the by, the guns is going again."

"At the Hulks?" said I.

"Aye! The guns have been going since dark, about. You'll hear one presently."

In effect, we had not walked many yards further, when the well-remembered boom came towards us, deadened by the mist, and heavily rolled away along the low grounds by the river, as if it were pursuing and threatening the fugitive Scapegraces.

"A good night for cutting off in," said Orlick. "We'd be puzzled how to bring down a jail-bird on the wing, tonight."

The subject was a suggestive one to me, and I thought about it in silence. Now and then, the sound of the signal cannon broke upon us again, and again rolled sulkily along the course of the river.

Thus, we came to the village. The way by which we approached it took us past the Three Jolly Bargemen, which we were surprised to find—it being eleven o'clock—in a state of commotion, with the door wide open, and unwonted lights that had been hastily caught up and put down scattered about. Mr. Wopsle dropped in to ask what was the matter (surmising that a convict had been taken), but came running out in a great hurry.

"There's something wrong," said he, without stopping, "up at your place, Pip. Run all!"

"What is it?" I asked, keeping up with him. So did Orlick, at my side.

"I can't quite understand. The house seems to have been violently entered when Joe Gargery was out. Supposed by Scapegraces. Somebody has been attacked and hurt."

We ran too fast to admit of more being said, and we made no stop until we got into our kitchen. It was full of people; the whole village was there, or in the yard; and there was a surgeon, and there was Joe. The bystanders drew back when they saw me, and so I became aware of my sister, lying without sense or movement on the bare boards where she had been knocked down by a tremendous blow on the back of the head, dealt by some unknown hand when her face was turned towards the fire, destined never to be on the rampage again, or so it seemed, while she was the wife of Joe.

CHAPTER 14

As MY SISTER'S NEAR relation, a Scapegrace popularly known to be under obligations to her, I was a more legitimate object of suspicion than any one else. Fortunately, I could account for my time and had witnesses to my whereabouts for most of the day. In the clear light of next morning, I began to consider the matter of who could have attacked my sister.

Joe had been at the Three Jolly Bargemen, smoking his pipe, from a quarter after eight o'clock to a quarter before ten. While he was there, my sister had been seen standing at the kitchen door, and had exchanged goodnight with a farm-labourer going home. The man could not be more particular as to the time at which he saw her than that it must have been before nine. When Joe went home at five minutes before ten, he found her struck down on the floor, and promptly called in assistance. The fire had not then burnt unusually low, nor was the snuff of the candle very long; the candle, however, had been blown out.

Nothing had been taken away from any part of the house. Neither, beyond the blowing out of the candle, which stood on a table between the door and my sister, and was behind her when she stood facing the fire and was struck, was there any disarrangement of the kitchen, excepting such as she had made, in falling and bleeding. But, there was one remarkable piece of evidence on the spot. She had been struck with something blunt and heavy, on the head and spine. After the blows were dealt, something heavy had been thrown down at her with considerable violence, as she lay on her face. And on the ground beside her, when Joe picked her up, was a convict's leg-silver, which had been filed asunder.

Now, Joe, examining this silver with a smith's eye, declared it to have been filed asunder some time ago. The hue and cry going off to the Hulks, and people coming thence to examine the silver, Joe's opinion was corroborated. They did not undertake to say when it had left the containment ships to which it undoubtedly had once belonged; but they claimed to know for certain that that particular manacle had not been worn by either of the two Scapegraces who had escaped last night. Further, one of those two was already retaken, and had not freed himself of his silver.

Knowing what I knew, I set up an inference of my own here. I believed the silver to be my convict's silver—the silver cuff I had seen and heard him filing at, on the marshes—but my mind did not accuse him of having put it to its latest use. I believed one of two other persons to have become possessed of it, and to have turned it to this cruel account: either Orlick, or the strange man who had shown me the file.

It was horrible to think that I had provided the weapon, however undesignedly, but I could hardly think otherwise. The Constables and the Bow Street men from London were about the house for a week or two. They took up several obviously wrong Scapegraces, and they ran their heads very hard against wrong ideas, and persisted in trying to fit the circumstances to the ideas, instead of trying to extract ideas from the circumstances. The vampire Orlick somehow escaped their notice, though my sister did have a bite mark on her neck. The strange man, of course, was nowhere to be found, and who would believe me if I suggested he could have come back to commit the crime based on the evidence I would rather not discuss, my convict's silver cuff.

Long after these constitutional powers had dispersed, my sister lay very ill in bed. Her sight was disturbed, so that she saw objects multiplied, and grasped at visionary teacups and wineglasses instead of the realities. Her hearing was greatly impaired; her memory also; and her speech was unintelligible. Mr. Pumblechook became a frequent visitor, and was, in fact and unfortunately, with us when she succumbed to her injuries at last.

In his argument to revive her, Mr. Pumblechook made the case that my sister needn't have to be abandoned in her state, that he could help her yet live and find her purpose, that it would be a waste to lose Mrs. Gargery when she could yet be brought back to us. My immediate reaction was to gasp and recoil in horror at the very idea, and to urge Joe not to listen to Pumblechook's ridiculous scheme. I had feared my sister enough in life, but as a Recommissioned? But I was young and Joe was trusting. It made sense to Joe that perhaps it wasn't Mrs. Joe's time to be buried in the churchyard with our parents and brothers, but to be recommissioned into a new state of function- ality and peace. Joe felt it his obligation to allow my sister to live as full a life as she could manage, even in death. He agreed to give Mr. Pumblechook a chance to work his particular skills on the corpse.

After several hours alone with her and his bokor stores of herbs and potions in her room, Pumblechook did reanimate Mrs. Joe to a state of something resembling life. I describe it as more of a state of existence, for anyone who knew my sister would hardly recog- nize a spark of life in her without her usual carrying on. But she was indeed with us, as she used to look but with a blank new sort of ex- pression on her face.

No longer did her eyes shine with malevolence or her brow wrin- kle in consternation or her lips turn up in a sneer when she made conversation. Her colouring, too, had gone a bit pale, or in fact grey to tell the truth of the matter. Her speech never quite returned right. But she could groan and she could attempt to make words, often the wrong words, like baker for bacon, and she could move and ramble about the house. Her temper was greatly improved, and she was patient. She did not seem to recognize what Tickler had been to her in the past, for she put it to use in retrieving items from the upper shelves of the pantry that she could not otherwise reach without losing a hand or some fingers up on a high shelf where they occasioned some difficulty to retrieve for reattachment.

A tremulous uncertainty of the action of all her limbs soon became a part of her regular state, and afterwards, at intervals of two or three months, she would often put her hands to her head and moan. Her housekeeping often needed correcting, as she would stop in the middle of emptying the dustpan and try to knit the contents into a blanket, or to garnish her best dress. She tried to roast and serve her beaver bonnet for dinner on more than one occasion. We were at a loss to find a suitable attendant for her, until a circumstance happened conveniently to relieve us. Mr. Wopsle's greataunt met her end and was already in such a decayed state as to be denied any chance of recommissioning by even the best of bokors, let alone that hack Pumblechook, allowing Biddy to become a part of our establishment.

It may have been about a month after my sister's reappearance in the kitchen when Biddy came to us with a small speckled box containing the whole of her worldly effects, and became a blessing to the household. Above all, she was a blessing to Joe, for the dear old fellow was sadly cut up by the constant contemplation of the wreck of his wife, and had been accustomed, while attending on her of an evening, to turn to me every now and then and say, with his blue eyes moistened, "Such a fine figure of a woman as she once were, Pip!"

Biddy instantly took the cleverest charge of her as though she had studied her from infancy. Joe became able in some sort to appreciate the greater quiet of his life, and to get down to the Jolly Bargemen now and then for a change that did him good.

CHAPTER 15

I FELL INTO A REGULAR routine of apprenticeship life, varied only by the arrival of my birthday and my paying another visit to Miss Havisham. I found Miss Sarah Pocket still on duty, though much

paler and always bleeding from the neck, at the gate. Miss Havisham was just as I had left her, and she spoke of Estella in the very
same way, if not in the very same words. The interview lasted but a
few minutes, and she gave me a guinea when I was going, and told
me to come again on my next birthday, which indeed became our
custom. I tried to decline taking the guinea on the first occasion,
but with no better effect than causing her to ask me very angrily, if
I expected more? There was no convincing her to chase me around
the room to try to get it back. Then, and after that, I simply took it.

So unchanging was the dull old house, the yellow light in the
darkened room, the faded spectre in her chair at the dressing-table,
invisible in the looking glass. I felt as if the stopping of the clocks
had stopped time in that mysterious place. And yet still, I suffered
under the embarrassment of my trade, my secret transformations,
and the house I lived in. How could I ever be more than I was on
a regular basis, less than I was upon a full moon, and be worthy of
Estella in general?

Imperceptibly I became conscious of a change in Biddy. Her
shoes came up at the heel, her hair grew bright and neat, her hands
were always clean. She was not beautiful—she was common, and
could not be like Estella—but she was pleasant and wholesome and
sweet-tempered. She had not been with us more than a year (I
remember her being newly out of mourning at the time it struck
me), when I observed to myself one evening that she had curiously
thoughtful and attentive eyes, very pretty eyes.

It came of my lifting up my own eyes from writing some passages from a book, and seeing Biddy observant of my actions. I laid
down my pen, and Biddy stopped in her needlework without laying
it down.

"Biddy," said I, "how do you manage it? Either I am very stupid,
or you are very clever."

"What is it that I manage? I don't know," returned Biddy,
smiling.

She managed our whole domestic life, and wonderfully, too; but

I did not mean that, though that made what I did mean more surprising.

"How do you manage, Biddy," said I, "to learn everything that I learn, and always to keep up with me?"

I was beginning to be rather vain of my knowledge, for I spent my birthday guineas on it, and set aside the greater part of my pocket-money for similar investment; though I have no doubt, now, that the little I knew was extremely dear at the price.

"I might as well ask you," said Biddy, "how *you* manage? With your changes, I mean. And everything else. It must be painful, how it wracks you. And then, to go on about your business next day?"

"It just happens. I try to control it and not let it get the best of me."

"Which must be why you moan so, when we lock you in. How does it feel?"

"It feels wild, Biddy. Overwhelming. I get a craving that requires all my concentration to master."

"A craving." Her eyes were wide. She leaned a little forward in her chair. "For what? What do you crave?"

I'd never told anyone of the cravings and perhaps I shouldn't have mentioned it to sweet Biddy, but it was too late to change course. "For meat, Biddy. Raw, fresh meat. And not just offered to me, no. I long to chase, to hunt, to . . . yes, Biddy, to kill."

I should have looked away, ashamed. Had I been speaking to Estella, I never would have confessed it in the first place. But I held Biddy's gaze, whether to judge the effect of my words or to seek her approval, I know not.

"But of course." She nodded and placed a hand over mine. "Of course, Pip. You become something wild, a wolf! The bloodlust is a natural effect, do you suppose?"

"I suppose," I agreed. She did not turn her eyes to the floor or look away. She didn't recoil in disgust, as Estella likely would have, or even offer sympathy for my plight. She seemed, in fact, fascinated and very understanding.

"A good thing, then, we see to keeping you locked away at full moon time. For your own safety."

"And you're not afraid to be the one to lock me away, Biddy? I don't frighten you?"

"Oh, not at all." She waved me off and went back to her sewing. "You wouldn't hurt anyone, Pip. Never on purpose."

"But that's the thing, Biddy. When I turn wolf, I don't always have control."

"Nonsense." Biddy waved off the notion, like swatting a fly. "Deep down, you're always Pip and you know right from wrong."

I leaned back in my wooden chair, and looked at Biddy sewing away with her head on one side. Astonishing, as Joe would say, that she would have such faith in me, even at my most wolfish, when even most of society believed werewolves to be inherently bad and ready to perpetrate any given crime, most especially murderous ones. I began to think her rather an extraordinary girl. Beyond that she had no fear of the wolf, she was equally accomplished in the terms of our trade, and the names of our different sorts of work, and our various tools. In short, whatever I knew, Biddy knew. Theoretically, she was already as good a silversmith as I, or better, for I became weak and fainted if I handled too much silver at once. I was better at the blacksmithing.

"You are one of those, Biddy," said I, "who make the most of every chance. You never had a chance before you came here, and see how improved you are!"

Biddy looked at me for an instant, and went on with her sewing. "I was your first teacher though; wasn't I?" said she, as she sewed.

"Biddy!" I exclaimed, in amazement. "Why, you are crying!"

"No I am not," said Biddy, looking up and laughing. "What put that in your head?"

What could have put it in my head but the glistening of a tear as it dropped on her work? I recalled the hopeless circumstances by which she had been surrounded in the miserable little shop. I reflected that even in those untoward times there must have been latent in Biddy what was now developing, for, in my first uneasiness and discontent I had turned to her for help, as a matter of course.

Biddy sat quietly sewing, shedding no more tears, and while I looked at her and thought about it all, it occurred to me that perhaps I had not been sufficiently grateful to Biddy.

"Yes, Biddy," I observed, when I had done turning it over, "you were my first teacher, and that at a time when we little thought of ever being together like this, in this kitchen."

"Ah, poor thing!" replied Biddy. It was like her self-forgetfulness to transfer the remark to my sister, and to get up and be busy about her, making her more comfortable. "That's sadly true!"

"Well!" said I, "we must talk together a little more, as we used to do. And I must consult you a little more, as I used to do. Let us have a quiet walk on the marshes next Sunday, Biddy, and a long chat."

My sister was never left alone now, but Joe more than readily undertook the care of her on that Sunday afternoon. Biddy and I went out together. It was summertime, and lovely weather. When we came to the riverside and sat down on the bank, with the water rippling at our feet, I resolved that it was a good time and place for the admission of Biddy into my inner confidence.

"Biddy," said I, after binding her to secrecy, "I want to be a gentleman."

"Oh, I wouldn't, if I was you!" she returned. "I don't think it would answer. A werewolf in polite company?"

"Biddy," said I, with some severity, "I have particular reasons for wanting to be a gentleman. I have been accepted in some polite company."

"It's not the same though, is it?" Biddy observed. "You've told me that Miss Havisham is a vampire, so it does seem she would be more willing to keep company of other Scapegraces. Does she even know what you are?"

"She suspects, if she does not know outright. I'm certain she must suspect by now, for all the times I've gone hairy when she was giving chase or managed an extraordinary feat like catching a stake hurling through midair between my teeth."

"Exactly, Pip. Things ordinary boys can't do. Suppose you were to give yourself away in a drawing room of regular people, not vampire gentility such as Miss Havisham? They would accuse you of something sinister, no doubt, and give you a shoddy trial and turn you right out to a containment ship."

I shook my head. "They would not turn me out without reason, Biddy. I don't see why I couldn't be a gentleman and a werewolf, had I the means. There are plenty of vampire gentlemen."

"Well, it is acceptable for them, isn't it? Many of them were gentlemen first, vampires later. But a wolf is most often born a wolf, as you know, and there's not many wolves born to gentlefolk. At least, not that stay among gentlefolk."

"And why shouldn't there be?"

Biddy sighed, as if she would rather not have to say but would carry on for the sake of honesty and friendship. "Well, I suppose the ugly transformations, the shedding all over the furniture, and eating the family pets or an occasional sibling or housemaid. Perhaps accidentally swallowing the family jewels, snarling at the neighbours. Who knows what sorts of things proper folks find unacceptable that we live with happily, even develop a fondness for, really? The gentry aren't like us."

"They are, perhaps, more than we think, Biddy. It would be unfair of us to judge."

"Us, judge?" Biddy shook her head, as if to clear her thoughts. "You know best, Pip; but don't you think you are happier as you are? Making a transformation in polite society would be dreadful awkward."

"Biddy," I exclaimed, impatiently, "I am not at all happy as I am. I am disgusted with my calling and with my life. I have never taken to either, since I was bound. Don't be absurd."

"Was I absurd?" said Biddy, quietly raising her eyebrows. "I am sorry for that. I didn't mean to be. I only want you to do well, and to be comfortable."

"Well, then, understand once for all that I never shall or can be comfortable—or anything but miserable—there, Biddy!—unless I can lead a very different sort of life from the life I lead now."

"That's a pity!" said Biddy, shaking her head with a sorrowful air.

Now, I, too, had so often thought it a pity, that, I was half inclined to shed tears of vexation when Biddy gave utterance to her sentiment and my own. I told her she was right, and I knew it was much to be regretted, but still it was not to be helped.

"If I could have settled down," I said to Biddy, plucking up the short grass within reach, much as I had once upon a time pulled my feelings out of my hair and kicked them into the brewery wall. "If I could have settled down and been but half as fond of the forge as I was when I was little, I know it would have been much better for me. You and I and Joe would have wanted nothing then, and Joe and I would perhaps have gone partners when I was out of my time, and I might even have grown up to keep company with you, and we might have sat on this very bank on a fine Sunday, quite different people. I should have been good enough for *you*. Shouldn't I, Biddy?"

Biddy sighed as she looked at the ships sailing on, and returned for answer, "Yes; I am not over-particular. Werewolves are fine by me." It scarcely sounded flattering, but I knew she meant well.

"Instead of that," I said, plucking up more grass and chewing a blade or two, "see how I am going on. Dissatisfied, and uncomfortable, and—what would it signify to me, being hairy and common, if nobody had told me so!"

Biddy turned her face suddenly towards mine, and looked far more attentively at me than she had looked at the sailing ships.

"It was neither a very true nor a very polite thing to say," she remarked, directing her eyes to the ships again. "Who said it?"

I was disconcerted, for I had broken away without quite seeing where I was going. It was not to be shuffled off now, however, and I answered, "The beautiful young lady at Miss Havisham's, and she's more beautiful than anybody ever was, and I admire her dreadfully, and I want to be a gentleman on her account." Having made this lunatic confession, I began to throw my torn-up grass into the river, as if I had some thoughts of following it.

"Do you want to be a gentleman to spite her or to gain her over?" Biddy quietly asked me, after a pause.

"I don't know," I moodily answered.

"Because, if it is to spite her," Biddy pursued, "I should think— but you know best—that might be better and more independently done by caring nothing for her words. And if it is to gain her over, I should think—but you know best—she was not worth gaining over."

Exactly what I myself had thought, many times. Exactly what was perfectly manifest to me at the moment. But how could I, a poor dazed village lad, avoid that wonderful inconsistency into which the best and wisest of men fall every day?

"It may be all quite true," said I to Biddy, "but I admire her dreadfully."

Biddy was the wisest of girls, and she tried to reason no more with me. She put her hand, which was a comfortable hand though roughened by work, upon my hands, one after another, and gently took them out of my hair. Then she softly patted my shoulder in a soothing way, and I felt vaguely convinced that I was very much ill-used by somebody, or by everybody; I can't say which.

"I am glad of one thing," said Biddy, "and that is, that you have felt you could give me your confidence, Pip. And I am glad of another thing, and that is, that of course you know you may depend upon my keeping it and always so far deserving it."

"Biddy." I got up, put my arm round her neck, and gave her a kiss. "I shall always tell you everything."

"Till you're a werewolf gentleman," said Biddy.

"You know I never shall be, so that's always."

"Ah!" said Biddy, quite in a whisper, as she looked away at the ships. "Shall we walk a little further, or go home?"

I said to Biddy we would walk a little further, and we did so, and the summer afternoon toned down into the summer evening, and it was very beautiful. I began to consider whether I was not more naturally and wholesomely situated, after all, in these circumstances than playing moving target by candlelight in the room with the stopped clocks, and being despised by Estella. I thought it would be very good for me if I could get her out of my head, with all the rest of those remembrances and fancies, and could go to work determined to relish what I had to do, and stick to it, and make the best of it. I asked myself that if Estella were beside me at that moment instead of Biddy, would she make me miserable? I was obliged to admit that I did know it for a certainty, and I said to myself, "Pip, what a fool you are!"

"Biddy," said I, when we were walking homeward, "I wish you could put me right."

"I wish I could!" said Biddy.

"If I could only get myself to fall in love with you. You don't mind my speaking so openly to such an old acquaintance?"

"Oh dear, not at all!" said Biddy. "Don't mind me."

"If I could only get myself to do it, that would be the thing for me."

"But you never will, you see," said Biddy.

It did not appear quite so unlikely to me that evening, as it would have done if we had discussed it a few hours before. In my heart I believed her to be right; and yet I took it rather ill, too, that she should be so positive on the point.

When we came near the churchyard, we had to cross an embankment, and get over a stile. There started up, from the gate, or from the rushes, or from the ooze (which was quite in his stagnant way), Old Orlick.

"Halloa!" he growled, "where are you two going?"

"Where should we be going, but home? The sun has set." He was quite late for work, as always.

"Well, then," said he, "I'm jiggered if I don't see you home!"

Biddy was much against his going with us, and said to me in a whisper, "Don't let him come; I don't like him."

As I did not like him either, I took the liberty of saying that we thanked him, but we didn't want seeing home. He received that piece of information with a yell of laughter, and dropped back, but came slouching after us at a little distance. Curious to know whether Biddy suspected him of having had a hand in that murderous attack of which my sister had never been able to give any account, I asked her why she did not like him.

"Oh!" she replied, glancing over her shoulder as he slouched after us, "because I—I am afraid he likes me."

"Did he ever tell you he liked you?" I asked indignantly.

"No," said Biddy, glancing over her shoulder again. "He never told me, but he looks at me as the old cat at the Wopsles used to look at the fresh catch when the fishmonger delivered. As if he would like a taste of me, and I would prefer not to be tasted. By him."

However novel and peculiar this testimony of attachment, I did not doubt the accuracy of the interpretation. I was outraged upon Old Orlick's daring to admire her.

"But it makes no difference to you, you know," said Biddy, calmly.

"No, Biddy, only I don't like it; I don't approve of it."

I kept an eye on Orlick after that night.

And now, because my mind was not confused enough before, I complicated its confusion fifty thousand-fold, by having states and seasons when I was clear that Biddy was immeasurably better than Estella, and that the plain honest working life to which I was born had nothing in it to be ashamed of, but offered me sufficient means of self-respect and happiness. At those times, I would decide that I was growing up in a fair way to be partners with Joe and to keep company with Biddy—when all in a moment some confounding remembrance of the Havisham days would fall upon me like a destructive missile, and scatter my wits again.

If my time had run out, it would have left me still at the height of my perplexities, I dare say. It never did run out, however, but was brought to a premature end, as I proceed to relate.

CHAPTER 16

IT WAS A SATURDAY night four years into my apprenticeship with Joe. I sat with a group assembled round the fire at the Three Jolly Bargemen, attentive to Mr. Wopsle as he read the newspaper aloud about a recent spike in vampire attacks around the countryside.

A strange gentleman, with an air of authority not to be disputed, and with a manner expressive of knowing something secret about every one of us that would effectually do for each individual if he chose to disclose it, left the back of the settle, and came into the space between the two settles, in front of the fire, where he remained standing, his left hand in his pocket, and he biting the forefinger of his right.

"From information I have received," said he, looking round at us as we all quailed before him, "I have reason to believe there is a silversmith among you, by name Joseph—or Joe—Gargery. Which is the man?"

"Here is the man," said Joe.

The strange gentleman beckoned him out of his place, and Joe went.

"You have an apprentice," pursued the stranger, "commonly known as Pip? Is he here?"

"I am here!" I cried.

The stranger did not recognize me, but I recognized him as

the gentleman I had met on the stairs, on the occasion of my second visit to Miss Havisham. I had known him the moment I saw him looking over the settle, and now that I stood confronting him with his hand upon my shoulder, I checked off again in detail his large head, his dark complexion, his deep-set eyes, his bushy black eyebrows, his large watch-chain, his strong black dots of beard and whisker, and even the smell of scented soap on his great hand.

"I wish to have a private conference with you two," said he, when he had surveyed me at his leisure. "It will take a little time. Perhaps we had better go to your place of residence."

Amidst a wondering silence, we three walked out of the Jolly Bargemen, and in a wondering silence walked home. We went in the front door at Joe's choosing. Our conference was held in the state parlour, which was feebly lighted by one candle.

It began with the strange gentleman's sitting down at the table, drawing the candle to him, and looking over some entries in his pocketbook. He then put up the pocketbook and set the candle a little aside, after peering round it into the darkness at Joe and me.

"My name," he said, "is Jaggers, and I am a lawyer in London. I have unusual business to transact with you, that it is not of my originating. If my advice had been asked, I should not have been here. It was not asked, and you see me here. What I have to do as the confidential agent of another, I do. No less, no more."

Finding that he could not see us very well from where he sat, he got up, and threw one leg over the back of a chair and leaned upon it; thus having one foot on the seat of the chair, and one foot on the ground.

"Now, Joseph Gargery, I am the bearer of an offer to relieve you of this young fellow your apprentice. You would not object to cancel his indentures at his request and for his good? You would want nothing for so doing?"

"Lord forbid that I should want anything for not standing in Pip's way," said Joe, staring. "No. I do not want anything."

I thought Mr. Jaggers glanced at Joe, as if he considered him a fool for his disinterestedness. But I was too much bewildered between breathless curiosity and surprise, to be sure of it.

"Very well," said Mr. Jaggers. "Now, I return to this young fellow. And the communication I have got to make is, that he has great expectations."

Joe and I gasped and looked at one another.

"I am instructed to communicate to him," said Mr. Jaggers, throwing his finger at me sideways, "that he will come into a handsome property. Further, that it is the desire of the present possessor of that property, that he be immediately removed from this place, and be brought up as a gentleman—in a word, as a young fellow of great expectations."

My dream was out. My wild fancy was surpassed by sober reality. Miss Havisham was going to make my fortune on a grand scale. A werewolf and a gentleman I would be.

"Now, Mr. Pip," pursued the lawyer, "I address the rest of what I have to say to you. You are to understand, first, that it is the request of the person from whom I take my instructions that you always bear the name of Pip. You will have no objection, I dare say, to your great expectations being encumbered with that easy condition. But if you have any objection, this is the time to mention it."

My heart beat so fast, and there was such a singing in my ears, that I could scarcely stammer I had no objection.

"I should think not! Now you are to understand, secondly, Mr. Pip, that the name of the person who is your liberal benefactor remains a profound secret, until the person chooses to reveal it. I am empowered to mention that it is the intention of the person to reveal it at first hand. When or where that intention may be carried out, I cannot say; no one can say. It may be years hence. Now, you are distinctly to understand that you are most positively prohibited from making any inquiry on this head, or any allusion or reference, however distant, to any individual whomsoever as *the* individual, in all the communications you may have with me. The condition is laid down. Your acceptance of it, and your observance of it as binding, is the only remaining condition that I am charged with, by the person from whom I take my instructions. That person is the person from whom you derive your expectations, and the secret is solely held by that person and by me. Again, not a very difficult condition with which to encumber such a rise in fortune; but if you have any objection to it, this is the time to mention it. Speak out."

Once more, I stammered with difficulty that I had no objection.

"I should think not! Now, Mr. Pip, I have done with stipulations." Though he called me Mr. Pip, and began rather to make up to me, he still could not get rid of a certain air of bullying suspicion. "We come next, to mere details of arrangement. You must know that, although I have used the term 'expectations' more than once, you are not endowed with expectations only. There is already lodged in my hands a sum of money amply sufficient for your suitable education and maintenance. You will please consider me your guardian. It is considered that you must be better educated, in accordance with your altered position, and that you will be alive to the importance and necessity of at once entering on that advantage."

I said I had always longed for it.

"Never mind what you have always longed for, Mr. Pip," he retorted. "Keep to the record. Am I answered that you are ready to be placed at once under some proper tutor? Is that it?"

I stammered yes, that was it.

"Good. There is a certain tutor, of whom I have some knowledge, who I think might suit the purpose," said Mr. Jaggers. "The gentleman I speak of is one Mr. Matthew Pocket."

Ah! I caught at the name directly. Miss Havisham's relation. The Matthew whom Mr. and Mrs. Camilla had spoken of. The Matthew whose place was to be at Miss Havisham's head, when she lay dead, in her bride's dress on the bride's table.

"You know the name?" said Mr. Jaggers, looking shrewdly at me, and then shutting up his eyes while he waited for my answer.

My answer was, that I had heard of the name.

"Oh!" said he. "What do you say of it?"

"I say it sounds fine."

"Good. You should know then that your people have found you. Your benefactor, your tutor, and all your fellow pupils—quite exactly in the same state as you."

"Apprentices?" I said, but I had every certainty that wasn't what he meant at all. I could guess that he meant Scapegraces, but I couldn't be sure and didn't hazard the guess lest the offer be removed at hint of my monthly change. A second look at his black brows, however, that seemed to grow even as we spoke, led me to believe that he was one of us as well, a werewolf. I grew quite excited at the thought that I could not only meet and fraternize with those of my own kind, at last, but that I could be a werewolf and still have great expectations rather than only grave expectations at the thought of being an outcast, a convict, and dying in captivity.

"Scapegraces," he said, quite outright.

Everything I had begun to believe about myself and my kind was being proven false, and all my dreams were suddenly becoming quite real.

"Scapegraces who learn and achieve and are welcome in society?" It seemed too good to be true. "You know I am a werewolf, not a vampire."

He nodded. "There are werewolves who own land or property and become scholars, physicians, merchants, gentlemen, or even lawyers." He waggled his bushy black brows. "It's rare, of course, and we keep our wolf side hidden to avoid attracting suspicion. You can't expect to achieve any of that here. I understand Joe Gargery occasionally works with silver. It weakens us, you are aware? Saps the strength completely. You must be very powerful indeed, to be up and about and not always sick in bed."

"Me? Powerful?" I smiled at the idea, but I did recall the sound thrashing I'd delivered to the furry young gentleman. Perhaps he had a point. Powerful, I repeated in my mind.

"Powerful," Mr. Jaggers repeated to me. "Perhaps an alpha in the making. Think of all that you could be, given this extraordinary opportunity to learn from Mr. Matthew Pocket, or any tutor you wish. Mr. Pocket specializes in teaching ways to control your transformation and be able to do it at will and not just under a full moon, an important skill for gentlemen wolves. It is widely considered impolite to go beasty in the middle of a drawing room, as you might imagine. You had better try Mr. Pocket in his own house. The way shall be prepared for you, and you can see his son first, who is in London. When will you come to London?"

I said (glancing at Joe, who stood looking on, motionless), that I supposed I could come directly.

"First," said Mr. Jaggers, "you should have some new clothes to come in, and they should not be working-clothes. You'll want some money. Shall I leave you twenty guineas?"

He produced a long purse, with the greatest coolness, and counted them out on the table and pushed them over to me.

"Well, Joseph Gargery? You look dumbfoundered?" he said.

"I *am!*" said Joe, in a very decided manner.

"It was understood that you wanted nothing for yourself, remember?"

"It were understood," said Joe. "And it are understood. And it ever will be similar according."

"But what," said Mr. Jaggers, swinging his purse—"what if it was in my instructions to make you a present, as compensation?"

"As compensation what for?" Joe demanded.

"For the loss of his services."

Joe laid his hand upon my shoulder with the touch of a woman. I have often thought him since, like the steam-hammer that can crush a man or pat an eggshell, in his combination of strength with gentleness. "Pip is that hearty welcome to go free with his services, to honor and fortun', as no words can tell him. But if you think as Money can make compensation to me for the loss of the little child—what come to the forge—and ever the best of friends!—"

Oh, dear good Joe, whom I was so ready to leave and so unthankful to, I see you again, with your muscular smithy's arm before your eyes, and your broad chest heaving, and your voice dying away. Oh, dear good faithful tender Joe, I feel the loving tremble of your hand upon my arm, as solemnly this day as if it had been the rustle of an angel's wing!

But I encouraged Joe at the time. I was lost in the mazes of my future fortunes, and could not retrace the bypaths we had trodden together. I begged Joe to be comforted, for (as he said) we had ever been the best of friends, and (as I said) we ever would be so. Joe scooped his eyes with his disengaged wrist, as if he were bent on gouging himself, but said not another word.

"Well, Mr. Pip," Mr. Jaggers said. "I think the sooner you leave here—as you are to be a gentleman—the better. Some days after the next full moon, you shall receive my printed address. You can take a hackney-coach at the stagecoach office in London, and come straight to me. Understand, that I express no opinion, one way or other, on the trust I undertake. I am paid for undertaking it, and I do so."

Something came into my head, which induced me to run after him as he was going down to the Jolly Bargemen, where he had left a hired carriage.

"I beg your pardon, Mr. Jaggers."

"Halloa!" said he, facing round, "what's the matter?"

"I wish to be quite right, Mr. Jaggers, and to keep to your directions; so I thought I had better ask. Would there be any objection to my taking leave of any one I know, about here, before I go away?"

"No," said he, looking as if he hardly understood me.

"I don't mean in the village only, but uptown?"

"No," said he. "No objection."

I thanked him and ran home again, and there I found that Joe had already locked the front door and vacated the state parlour, and was seated by the kitchen fire with a hand on each knee, gazing intently at the burning coals. I, too, sat down before the fire and gazed at the coals, and nothing was said for a long time.

My sister was in her cushioned chair in her corner, and Biddy sat at her needlework before the fire, and Joe sat next Biddy, and I sat next Joe in the corner opposite my sister. The more I looked into the glowing coals, the more incapable I became of looking at Joe; the longer the silence lasted, the more unable I felt to speak.

At length I got out, "Joe, have you told Biddy?"

"No, Pip," returned Joe, still looking at the fire, and holding his knees tight, as if he had private information that they intended to make off somewhere, "which I left it to yourself, Pip."

"I would rather you told, Joe."

"Pip's a gentleman of fortun' then," said Joe, "and God bless him in it!"

Biddy dropped her work, and looked at me. Joe held his knees and looked at me. I looked at both of them. After a pause, they both heartily congratulated me, but there was a certain touch of sadness in their congratulations that I rather resented.

I took it upon myself to impress Biddy (and through Biddy, Joe) with the grave obligation I considered my friends under, to know nothing and say nothing about the maker of my fortune. It would all come out in good time, I observed, and in the meanwhile nothing was to be said, save that I had come into great expectations from a mysterious patron. Biddy nodded her head thoughtfully at the fire as she took up her work again.

I never could have believed it without experience, but as Joe and Biddy became more at their cheerful ease again, I became quite gloomy. Dissatisfied with my fortune, of course I could not be; but it is possible that I may have been, without quite knowing it, dissatisfied with myself.

With my elbow on my knee and my face upon my hand, I looked into the fire, as those two talked about my going away, and about what they should do without me, and all that.

"A week after Saturday night," said I, when we sat at our supper of bread and cheese. "That's full moon. I'll soon go."

"Yes, Pip," observed Joe, whose voice sounded hollow in his beer-mug. "You'll soon go."

"Soon, soon go," said Biddy.

"I have been thinking, Joe, that when I go downtown on Monday, and order my new clothes, I shall tell the tailor that I'll come and put them on there, or that I'll have them sent to Mr. Pumblechook's. It would be very disagreeable to be stared at by all the people here."

"Mr. and Mrs. Hubble might like to see you in your new gen-teel figure, too, Pip," said Joe, industriously cutting his bread, with his cheese on it, in the palm of his left hand, and glancing at my un-tasted supper as if he thought of the time when we used to compare slices. "So might Wopsle. And the Jolly Bargemen might take it as a compliment."

"That's just what I don't want, Joe. They would make such a business of it—such a coarse and common business—that I couldn't bear myself."

"Ah, that indeed, Pip!" said Joe. "If you couldn't abear your-self—"

Biddy asked me here, as she sat holding my sister's plate, "Have you thought about when you'll show yourself to Mr. Gargery, and your sister, and me? You will show yourself to us; won't you?"

"Biddy," I returned with some resentment, "you are so exceed-ingly quick that it's difficult to keep up with you."

"She always were quick," observed Joe.

"If you had waited another moment, Biddy, you would have heard me say that I shall bring my clothes here in a bundle one evening—most likely on the evening before I go away."

Biddy said no more. Handsomely forgiving her, I soon exchanged an affectionate goodnight with her and Joe, and went up to bed. When I got into my little room, I sat down and took a long look at it, as a mean little room that I should soon be parted from and raised above, forever. The sun had been shining brightly all day on the roof of my attic, and the room was warm. As I put the window

open and stood looking out, I saw Joe come slowly forth at the dark
door, below, and take a turn or two in the air; and then I saw Biddy
come, and bring him a pipe and light it for him. He never smoked
so late, and it seemed to hint to me that he wanted comforting, for
some reason or other.

He presently stood at the door immediately beneath me, smoking his pipe, and Biddy stood there, too, quietly talking to him, and
I knew that they talked of me, for I heard my name mentioned in an
endearing tone by both of them more than once. I would not have
listened for more, if I could have heard more; so I drew away from
the window, and sat down in my one chair by the bedside, feeling it
very sorrowful and strange that this first night of my bright fortunes
should be the loneliest I had ever known.

Looking towards the open window, I saw light wreaths from Joe's
pipe floating there, and I fancied it was like a blessing from Joe—
not obtruded on me or paraded before me, but pervading the air we
shared together. I put my light out, and crept into bed; and it was
an uneasy bed now, and I never slept the old sound sleep in it any
more.

CHAPTER 17

WITH MORNING CAME THE realization that it was not all a dream,
but quite real. My life had changed. What lay heaviest on my mind
was the consideration that six days stood in my way of departure. I
feared that something might happen to London in the meanwhile,
and that, when I got there, it would be either greatly deteriorated
or clean gone.

Joe and Biddy were very sympathetic and pleasant when I

spoke of our approaching separation, but they only referred to it when I did. After breakfast, Joe brought out my indentures from the press in the best parlour, and we put them in the fire. I was free. With all the novelty of my emancipation on me, I went to church with Joe.

After our early dinner, I strolled out alone, feeling restless and wild under the nearly full moon. If I had often thought before, with something allied to shame, of my companionship with the fugitive whom I had once seen limping among those graves, what were my thoughts on this Sunday, when the place recalled the wretch, ragged and shivering, with his felon silver! My comfort was that it happened a long time ago, and that he had doubtless been transported a long way off, and that he was dead to me, and might be veritably dead into the bargain.

No more low, wet grounds, no more dikes and sluices, no more of these grazing cattle, who suddenly looked respectfully at me with my great expectations. Well they should, all the nights I spared them of my wolfish cravings. Even now, the thought of rare fresh beef intrigued. I growled in their direction, but I would not give in to the urge to devour. Farewell, monotonous acquaintances of my childhood, henceforth I was for London and greatness! I made my exultant way to the old battery, and, lying down there to consider the question whether Miss Havisham intended me for Estella, fell asleep.

When I awoke, I was much surprised to find Joe sitting beside me, smoking his pipe. He greeted me with a cheerful smile on my opening my eyes, and said, "As being the last time, Pip, I thought I'd foller."

"And, Joe, I am very glad you did so."

"Thankee, Pip."

"You may be sure, dear Joe," I went on, after we had shaken hands, "that I shall never forget you."

"No, no, Pip!" said Joe, in a comfortable tone, "I'm sure of that. Aye, old chap!"

Somehow, I was not best pleased with Joe's being so mightily secure of me.

"I have always wanted to be a gentleman," I informed Joe at last. "I often speculated on what I would do, if I were one."

"Have you though?" said Joe. "Astonishing!"

"It's a pity now, Joe, that you did not get on a little more, when we had our lessons here; isn't it?"

"Well, I don't know," returned Joe. "I'm so awful dull. I'm only master of my own trade. But it's no more of a pity now, than it was—this day twelvemonth—don't you see?"

What I had meant was, that when I came into my property and was able to do something for Joe, it would have been much more agreeable if he had been better qualified for a rise in station. He was so perfectly innocent of my meaning, however, that I thought I would mention it to Biddy in preference.

So, when we had walked home and had had tea, I took Biddy into our little garden by the side of the lane.

"I'll never forget you, Biddy," I said. "I am glad, though, that you will be here to help Joe on, a little."

"How, help him on?" asked Biddy, with a steady sort of glance.

"Well! Joe is a dear good fellow, but he is rather backward in some things. For instance, Biddy, in his learning and his manners."

Although I was looking at Biddy as I spoke, and although she opened her eyes very wide when I had spoken, she did not look at me.

"Oh, his manners! Won't his manners do then?" asked Biddy, plucking a black-currant leaf.

"My dear Biddy, they do very well here—"

"Oh! They *do* very well here?" interrupted Biddy, looking closely at the leaf in her hand.

"Hear me out, but if I were to remove Joe into a higher sphere, as I shall hope to remove him when I fully come into my property, they would hardly do him justice."

"And don't you think he knows that?" asked Biddy.

It was such a very provoking question, that I said, "Biddy, what do you mean?"

"Have you never considered that he may be proud?" Biddy rubbed the leaf to pieces between her hands, and the smell of a black-currant bush has ever since recalled to me that evening in the little garden by the side of the lane.

"Proud?" I repeated, with disdainful emphasis.

"Oh! There are many kinds of pride," said Biddy, looking full at me and shaking her head. "He may be too proud to let any one take him out of a place that he is competent to fill, and fills well and with respect. To tell you the truth, I think he is."

"Now, Biddy, I am very sorry to see this in you. You are envious, and grudging. You are dissatisfied on account of my rise in fortune, and you can't help showing it."

"If you have the heart to think so," returned Biddy, "say so. Say so over and over again, if you have the heart to think so."

"If you have the heart to be so, you mean, Biddy," said I, in a virtuous and superior tone. "Don't put it off upon me. I am very sorry to see it, and it's a—it's a bad side of human nature. I did intend to ask you to use any little opportunities you might have after I was gone, of improving dear Joe. But after this I ask you nothing. I am extremely sorry to see this in you, Biddy."

"Whether you scold me or approve of me, you may equally depend upon my trying to do all that lies in my power, here, at all times. And whatever opinion you take away of me, shall make no difference in my remembrance of you. Yet a gentleman should not be unjust neither," said Biddy, turning away her head.

I again warmly repeated that it was a bad side of human nature, and Biddy went into the house, and I went out at the garden gate and took a dejected stroll until supper-time; again feeling it very sorrowful and strange that this, the second night of my bright fortunes, should be as lonely and unsatisfactory as the first.

The next morning, with my outlook improved, I went into town to arrange for new clothes, boots, and other things I would need for my great transformation—not from boy to wolf, but from common boy to gentleman. When I had ordered everything I wanted, I directed my steps towards Pumblechook's, and, as I approached that man's place of business, I saw him standing at his door.

He waited for me with great impatience. He had been out early with the chaise-cart, and had called at the forge and heard the news. He had prepared a light meal in the parlour, and he ordered his Recommissioned shopman to "come out of the gangway" as my sacred person passed. I cringed at sight of him, as usual.

"My dear friend," said Mr. Pumblechook, taking me by both hands, when he and I were alone, "I give you joy of your good fortune. Well deserved, well deserved!"

This was coming to the point, and I thought it a sensible way of expressing himself.

"To think," said Mr. Pumblechook, after snorting admiration at me for some moments, "that I should have been the humble instrument of leading up to this is a proud reward."

I begged Mr. Pumblechook to remember that nothing was to be ever said or hinted, on that point.

"My dear young friend, you must be hungry, you must be exhausted. Be seated." Mr. Pumblechook gestured to the table and chairs. "Here's one or two little things had round from the Boar, that I hope you may not despise. But do I see afore me, him as I ever sported with in his times of happy infancy? And may I—*may* I—?"

This may I meant might he shake hands? I consented, and he was fervent, and then sat down again.

"Here is wine," said Mr. Pumblechook. "Let us drink, thanks to Fortune, and may she ever pick out her favourites with equal judgment! And—may I—may I—?"

I said he might, and he shook hands with me again, and emptied his glass and turned it upside down. I did the same; and if I had turned myself upside down before drinking, the wine could not have gone more direct to my head.

"And your sister," he resumed, after a little steady eating, "which

had the honour of bringing you up by hand! It's a sad picter, to reflect that she's no longer equal to fully understanding the honour.
But she's with us, at least, thanks to me. May—"

I saw he was about to come at me again, and I stopped him.

"We'll drink to her," I said.

"Let us never be blind," said Mr. Pumblechook, "to her faults of
temper, but it is to be hoped she meant well."

At about this time, I began to observe that he was getting
flushed in the face; as to myself, I felt all face, steeped in wine,
and smarting.

I mentioned to Mr. Pumblechook that I wished to have my new
clothes sent to his house, and he was ecstatic on my so distinguish-
ing him. I mentioned my reason for desiring to avoid observation
in the village, and he lauded it to the skies. There was nobody
but himself, he intimated, worthy of my confidence, and—in short,
might he? Then he asked me tenderly if I remembered our boyish
games at sums, and how we had gone together to have me bound
apprentice, and, in effect, how he had ever been my favourite fancy
and my chosen friend?

By degrees he fell to reposing such great confidence in me, as
to ask my advice in reference to his own affairs. He mentioned
that there was a great increase in demand for Recommissioneds in
household service. What alone was wanting to the realization of
a vast fortune, he believed, was capital. He needed capital to hire
and train more retrievers, a very select few of whom he intended to
make into bokors.

"Retrievers?" I asked.

"Retrievers are designed to ferret out and discover the dead
worthy of recommissioning. It takes a special corpse, Pip; one
that died a quiet death while in good physical condition, no flesh-
wounds. Unfortunately, the Recommissioned themselves are ill-
equipped for such an office as they no longer possess the ability to
distinguish between corpses in their prime and those not worthy of
the office. A well-trained bokor then employs his gifts to recommis-

sion the dead back to a state quite like living, so that they can put their new lives to good purpose."

"Like becoming domestic servants or soldiers?" It hardly sounded like a purpose that suited them as much as it suited those with a need for cheap, subservient labour.

"Indeed." Mr. Pumblechook speared a large chunk of liver, ate it, and continued. "It takes special skills to be a bokor, Pip. Not just anyone can undertake the office. It's a very involved and secret process. With more help, I can meet the increased demand. People die every day, Pip."

"Yes, Mr. Pumblechook." I wanted to say more but I found myself simply staring at him like a fish on the plate, were we having fish.

"Why shouldn't they be put to good use then? To be allowed to find some basic purpose for us after we die, Pip, is there any greater gift?"

I thought over all the sermons I had ever sat through with Joe in his finery, and I thought perhaps Mr. Pumblechook would not win the approval of the church. I was yet unsure that my changing condition from boy to wolf could win the approval of the church, and so I said nothing.

"Capital, Pip! If I had the capital, through a sleeping partner perhaps, sir. The partner having nothing to do but walk in whenever he pleased to examine the books and take his profits—a full fifty per cent! A young gentleman of spirit and property might make the perfect partner. What do you think, eh Pip?"

I wished him luck in his endeavour. I did not know what else to think.

We drank all the wine, and Mr. Pumblechook pledged himself over and over again to keep Joseph up to the mark (I don't know what mark), and to render me efficient and constant service (I don't know what service). He also made known to me for the first time in my life, and certainly after having kept his secret wonderfully well, that he had always said of me, "That boy is no common boy, and mark me, his fortun' will be no common fortun'." He said with a tearful smile that it was a singular thing to think of now.

Finally, I went out into the air, just in time as it turned out. My hands were covered in a shaggy down. I didn't need to paw my nose to know that it had gone to snout, for I could still smell the wine on Mr. Pumblechook's breath though I was clearing some distance of him. My bones began to stretch. I started to run. With the wine in my blood, I remembered little of the wolfish night, besides baying at the moon before I woke next morning unclothed and under a hedge.

I had scant luggage to take with me to London, for little of the little I possessed was adapted to my new station. But I began packing that same afternoon, and wildly packed up things that I knew I should want next morning in a fiction that there was not a moment to be lost.

So, Tuesday, Wednesday, and Thursday passed. On Friday morning, I went to Mr. Pumblechook's to put on my new clothes and pay my visit to Miss Havisham. It being market morning at a neighbouring town some ten miles off, Mr. Pumblechook was not at home. I had not told him exactly when I meant to leave, and was not likely to shake hands with him again before departing. This was all as it should be, and I went out with every hope that I had enough silver tucked in my pockets to stay full boy and not turn into partial wolf along the way to Miss Havisham's.

I went circuitously by all the back ways, just in case, and rang at the bell constrainedly, on account of the stiff long fingers of my gloves. Sarah Pocket came to the gate, and positively reeled back when she saw me so changed.

"You?" said she. "You? Good gracious! What do you want?"

"I am going to London, Miss Pocket. I want to say goodbye to Miss Havisham."

As I was not expected, she went to ask about my admittance. After a very short delay, she returned and took me up, staring at me all the way.

Miss Havisham was taking exercise by chasing mice around the long spread table, spearing them on her crutch stick, and raising them with a triumphant hurrah after each successful skewering. The room was lighted as of yore, and at the sound of our entrance, she stopped and turned. She was then just abreast of the rotted bride-cake.

"Don't go, Sarah," she said. "Well, Pip?"

"I start for London, Miss Havisham, tomorrow," I was exceedingly careful what I said, "and I thought you would kindly not mind my taking leave of you."

"This is a gay figure, Pip," said she, making her crutch stick play round me, mouse tails dangling, as if she, the sinister fairy godmother who had changed me, were bestowing the finishing gift.

"I have come into such good fortune since I saw you last, Miss Havisham," I murmured. "And I am so grateful for it!"

"Aye!" said she, looking at the discomfited and envious Sarah, with delight. "I have seen Mr. Jaggers. I have heard about it, Pip. So you go tomorrow?"

"Yes, Miss Havisham."

"And you are adopted by a rich person? Not named? And Mr. Jaggers is made your guardian?"

"Yes, Miss Havisham."

She quite gloated on these questions and answers, so keen was her enjoyment of Sarah Pocket's jealous dismay.

"Well! You have a promising career before you. Be good—deserve it—and abide by Mr. Jaggers's instructions." She looked at me, and looked at Sarah, and Sarah's countenance wrung out of her watchful face a cruel smile. "Goodbye, Pip!—you will always keep the name of Pip, you know."

"Yes, Miss Havisham."

She stretched out her hand, and I went down on my knee and put it to my lips. I had not considered how I should take leave of her; it came naturally to me at the moment. She looked at Sarah Pocket with triumph in her weird eyes, and so I left my sinister fairy godmother, with both her hands on her mouse-laden crutch stick, standing in the midst of the dimly lighted room beside the rotten bride-cake that was hidden in cobwebs.

Sarah Pocket conducted me down, as if I were a ghost who must be seen out. She could not get over my appearance, and was in the last degree confounded. Or perhaps she was reeling from blood loss and about to faint, for it looked as if Miss Havisham had recently made a meal of her.

Clear of the house, I made my way back to Pumblechook's, took off my new clothes, made them into a bundle, and went back home in my older dress, the clothes I had shed and had gathered back up from where they were strewn across the field earlier in the week.

And now, those six days that were to have run out so slowly had run out fast and were gone. As the evenings had dwindled away, to five, to four, to three, to two, I had become more and more appreciative of the society of Joe and Biddy. On this last evening, I dressed myself out in my new clothes for their delight, and sat in my splendour until bedtime. We had a hot supper on the occasion, graced by the inevitable roast fowl, substituted just in time for the beaver bonnet my sister meant to cook, and we were all very low, and none the higher for pretending to be in spirits.

I was to leave our village in the morning, carrying my little hand-portmanteau, and I had told Joe that I wished to walk away all alone. I am afraid—sore afraid—that this purpose originated in my sense of the contrast there would be between us, if we went to the coach together.

Such dreams I had! There were coaches in my broken sleep, going to wrong places instead of to London, and having in the traces, now wolves, now pigs, now men—never horses. Suddenly, I had a vision of myself all in my wolfish glory eating the horses, and the coach unable to move on from the stretch of road outside the forge. When I had such dreams, I sometimes feared that I would wake up out of doors, covered from head to toe in blood, proving the dream quite real. Fortunately, I woke up in bed.

Biddy was up so early to get my breakfast that I smelt the smoke of the kitchen fire when I started up with a terrible idea that it must be late in the afternoon. I got up from the meal, saying with a sort of briskness, as if it had only just occurred to me, "Well! I suppose I must be off!" and then I kissed my sister who was nodding and dribbling green ooze from her nose, as she had often since her recommissioning, and kissed Biddy, and threw my arms around Joe's neck. Then I took up my little portmanteau and walked out.

The last I saw of them was, when I presently heard a scuffle behind me, and looking back, saw Joe waving his strong right arm above his head, crying huskily, "Hooroar!" and Biddy put her apron to her face.

I walked away at a good pace, thinking it was easier to go than I had supposed it would be. The village was very peaceful and quiet, and the light mists were solemnly rising, as if to show me the world, and I had been so innocent and little there, and all beyond was so unknown and great, that in a moment with a strong heave and sob I broke into tears. It was by the finger-post at the end of the village, and I laid my hand upon it, and said, "Goodbye, oh my dear, dear friend!"

So subdued I was by those tears, and by their breaking out again in the course of the quiet walk, that when I was on the coach, and it was clear of the town, I deliberated with an aching heart whether I would not get down when we changed horses and walk back, and have another evening at home, and a better parting. We changed, and I had not made up my mind. And while I was occupied with these deliberations, I would fancy an exact resemblance to Joe in some man coming along the road towards us, and my heart would beat high—as if he could possibly be there!

We changed again, and yet again, and it was now too late and too far to go back, and I went on. And the mists had all solemnly risen now, and the world lay spread before me. And I looked down to find my hands growing hairy and realized it was yet too close to full moon to be without silver, and I hadn't remembered to pack any let alone fill my pockets.

THIS IS THE END OF THE FIRST STAGE OF PIP'S EXPECTATIONS.

CHAPTER 18

THE RELIEF OF SEEING the four horses, alive and well, pulling the stagecoach, enabled me to enjoy the ride, five hours long as it was, and the sights of the Cross Keys, Wood Street, Cheapside, London. A little intimidated by the immensity of London, I think I might have had some faint doubts whether it was not rather ugly, crooked, narrow, and dirty instead of the lovely, straight, wide, and gleaming I had imagined.

Mr. Jaggers had duly sent me his address in Little Britain, "just out of Smithfield, and close by the coach-office."

I had scarcely had time to enjoy the coach, and the fact that the hair had stopped growing on my hands and I remained perfectly boyish, when I observed the coachman beginning to get down, as if we were going to stop presently. And stop we presently did, in a gloomy street, at certain offices with an open door, whereon was painted MR. JAGGERS.

I went into the front office with my little portmanteau in my hand and asked, Was Mr. Jaggers at home?

"He is not," returned the clerk. "He is in court at present. Am I addressing Mr. Pip?"

"Yes."

"Mr. Jaggers left word, would you wait in his room. He couldn't say how long he might be, having a case on. But it stands to reason, his time being valuable, that he won't be longer than he can help."

With those words, the clerk opened a door, and ushered me into an inner chamber at the back. Mr. Jaggers's room was lit by a sky-light only, and was a most dismal place. There were not so many papers about as I should have expected to see; and there were some odd objects about, that I should not have expected to see—such as an old rusty pistol, a silver sword in a scabbard, several strange-looking boxes and packages, and two dreadful casts on a shelf, of faces peculiarly swollen and unappealing. Mr. Jaggers's own high-backed chair was of deadly black horsehair, with rows of brass nails round it, like a coffin. I fancied I could see how he leaned back in it, and bit his forefinger at the clients.

I sat down in the cliental chair placed over against Mr. Jaggers's chair, and became fascinated by the dismal atmosphere of the place. I wondered whether the two swollen face casts were of Mr. Jaggers's family, and, if he were so unfortunate as to have had a pair of such ill-looking relations, why he stuck them on that dusty perch for the flies to settle on, instead of giving them a place at home.

Of course I had no experience of a London summer day, and my spirits may have been oppressed by the hot exhausted air, and by the dust and grit that lay thick on everything. But I sat wondering and waiting in Mr. Jaggers's close room, until I really could not bear the two casts on the shelf above Mr. Jaggers's chair, and got up and went out.

When I told the clerk that I would take a turn in the air while I waited, he advised me to go round the corner and I should come into Smithfield. Smithfield was not to my liking. I kept walking with all possible speed, and turned into a street where I saw the great black dome of Saint Paul's bulging at me from behind a grim stone building, which a bystander said was Newgate Prison, which I knew housed a containment block for Scapegraces. I shuddered.

Following the wall of the jail, I found the roadway covered with straw to deaden the noise of passing vehicles. From this, and from the quantity of people standing about smelling strongly of spirits and beer, I inferred that the trials were on.

I went back to the office to ask if Mr. Jaggers had come in yet, and I found he had not, and I strolled out again. This time, I made the tour of Little Britain, and turned into Bartholomew Close; and now I became aware that other people were waiting about for Mr. Jaggers, as well as I. There were two men of ghoulish appearance lounging in Bartholomew Close, one of whom said to the other when they first passed me, that "Jaggers would do it if it was to be done." There was a knot of three men and two women standing at a corner, and one of the women was crying on her dirty shawl, and the other comforted her by saying, as she pulled her own shawl over her shoulders, "Jaggers is for him, 'Melia, and what more *could* you have when all spells fail us?" These testimonies to the popularity of my guardian made a deep impression on me, and I admired and wondered more than ever.

At length, as I was looking out at the iron gate of Bartholomew Close into Little Britain, I saw Mr. Jaggers coming across the road towards me. All the others who were waiting saw him at the same time, and there was quite a rush at him. Mr. Jaggers, putting a hand on my shoulder and walking me on at his side without saying anything to me, addressed himself to his followers.

First, he took the two ghoulish men.

"Now, I have nothing to say to *you*," said Mr. Jaggers, throwing his finger at them. "I want to know no more than I know. As to the result, it's a toss-up. I told you from the first it was a toss-up. Have you paid Wemmick?"

"We made the money up this morning, sir," said one of the men, submissively, while the other perused Mr. Jaggers's face.

"Very well; then you may go," said Mr Jaggers, waving his hand at them to put them behind him.

"And now you!" said Mr. Jaggers, suddenly stopping, and turning on the two women with the shawls, from whom the three men had meekly separated, "Amelia, is it?"

"Yes, Mr. Jaggers."

"And do you remember," retorted Mr. Jaggers, "that but for me you wouldn't be here and couldn't be here?"

"Oh yes, sir!" exclaimed both women together. "Goddess bless you, sir, well we knows that!"

"Then why," said Mr. Jaggers, "do you come here?"

"My Bill, sir! My magic, it's not working to set him free," the crying woman pleaded.

"Now, I tell you what!" said Mr. Jaggers. "Once for all. If you don't know that your Bill's in good hands, I know it. And if you come here bothering about your Bill, I'll make an example of both your Bill and you, and let him slip through my fingers. Have you paid Wemmick?"

"Oh yes, sir! Every farden."

"Very well. Then you have done all you have got to do. Say another word—one single word—and Wemmick shall give you your money back."

This terrible threat caused the two women to fall off immediately. No one remained. Without further interruption, we reached the front office, where we found the clerk, and walked on by him.

My guardian then took me into his own room, and while he lunched, standing, from a sandwich-box and a pocket-flask of sherry (he seemed to bully his very sandwich as he ate it), informed me what arrangements he had made for me. I was to go to "Barnard's Inn," to young Mr. Pocket's rooms, where a bed had been sent in for my accommodation. I was to remain with young Mr. Pocket until Monday, when I was to go with him to his father's house on a visit, that I might try how I liked it. Also, I was told what my allowance was to be—it was a very liberal one—and had handed to me, from one of my guardian's drawers, the cards of certain tradesmen with whom I was to deal for all kinds of clothes, and such other things as I could in reason want.

"You will find your credit good, Mr. Pip," said my guardian, whose flask of sherry smelt like a whole caskful, as he hastily refreshed himself. "But I shall by this means be able to check your bills, and to pull you up if I find you outrunning the constable. Of course you'll go wrong somehow, but that's no fault of mine."

After I had pondered a little over this encouraging sentiment, I asked Mr. Jaggers if I could send for a coach? He said I was so near my destination that a coach was not worthwhile. Wemmick should walk round with me, if I pleased.

I then found that Wemmick was the clerk in the next room. Another clerk was rung up to take his place while he was out, and I accompanied him into the street, after shaking hands with my guardian. We found a new set of Scapegraces lingering outside, but Wemmick made a way among them.

"I tell you it's no use." He addressed the crowd. "He won't have a word to say to one of you."

We soon got clear of the crowd, and went on side by side. Casting my eyes on Mr. Wemmick as we went along, to see what he was like in the light of day, I found him to be a dry man, rather short in stature, with a mouth continually gaping like a letter-box awaiting mail and a square wooden face, whose expression seemed to have been imperfectly chipped out with a dull-edged chisel. The chisel had made three or four of these attempts at embellishment over his nose, but had given them up without an effort to smooth them off.

I judged him to be a bachelor from the frayed condition of his linen, and he appeared to have sustained a good many bereavements; for he wore at least four mourning rings, besides a brooch representing a lady and a weeping willow at a tomb with an urn on it. I noticed, too, that several rings and seals hung at his watch chain, as if he were quite laden with remembrances of departed friends. He had glittering eyes—small, keen, and black—and I noticed something in them that made me start. Recognition. He, too, was one of my kind.

"So you were never in London before?" said Mr. Wemmick to me.

"No," I said.

"I was new here once," said Mr. Wemmick. "Now I know the moves of it."

"Is it a very wicked place?" I asked, more for the sake of saying something than for information.

"You may get cheated, robbed, and murdered in London. There are plenty of people anywhere who'll do that for you, but here you'll be the one charged of the crime done to you and sent off to spend your life on a containment ship."

"If there is bad blood between you and them," said I, to soften it off a little.

"Oh! I don't know about bad blood," returned Mr. Wemmick. "There's not much bad blood about. If you're a Scapegrace, you're a victim and a target all in one. It keeps Jaggers in business just defending all the false charges brought against our kind let alone the legitimate complaints."

He almost made me wonder why any of us would stay in London, but I knew the answer. In London, I could be a gentleman. It was worth any risk.

Mr. Wemmick wore his hat on the back of his head, and looked straight before him: walking in a self-contained way as if there were nothing in the streets to claim his attention.

"Do you know where Mr. Matthew Pocket lives?" I asked Mr. Wemmick.

"Yes," said he, nodding in the direction. "At Hammersmith, west of London. About five miles off."

"Do you know him?"

"Why, you're a regular cross-examiner!" said Mr. Wemmick, looking at me with an approving air. "Yes, I know him. And here we are at Barnard's Inn."

My depression was not alleviated by the announcement, for I had supposed that establishment to be a hotel kept by Mr. Barnard, to which the Blue Boar in our town was a mere public-house. Whereas I now found Barnard to be a fiction, and his inn the dingiest collection of shabby buildings ever squeezed together in a rank corner as a club for tomcats.

We entered this haven through a wicket-gate, and came into an introductory passage into a melancholy little square that looked to me like a flat burying-ground with the most dismal trees in it, and the most dismal sparrows, and the most dismal cats, and the most dismal houses (in number half a dozen or so), that I had ever seen. I thought the windows of the sets of chambers into which those houses were divided were in every stage of dilapidated blind and curtain, crippled flower-pot, cracked glass, dusty decay, and miserable makeshift; while TO LET, TO LET, TO LET, glared at me from empty rooms, as if no new wretches ever came there, and the vengeance of the soul of Barnard was being slowly appeased by the gradual suicide of the present occupants and their unholy interment under the gravel, a potential boon for Mr. Pumblechook.

So imperfect was this realization of the first of my great expectations that I looked in dismay at Mr. Wemmick. Grave expectations indeed.

"Ah! The retirement reminds you of the country. So it does me." He had quite mistaken me.

He led me into a corner and conducted me up a flight of stairs, which appeared to me to be slowly collapsing into sawdust, to a set of chambers on the top floor. MR. POCKET, JUN., was painted on the door, and there was a label on the letter-box, "RETURN SHORTLY."

"He hardly thought you'd come so soon," Mr. Wemmick explained. "You don't want me any more?"

"No, thank you," I said.

"As I keep the cash," Mr. Wemmick observed, "we shall most likely meet pretty often. Good day."

"Good day."

When we had shaken hands and he was gone, I opened the staircase window and nearly beheaded myself, for, the lines had rotted away, and it came down like the guillotine. Happily it was so quick that I had not put my head out. After this escape, I was content to take a foggy view of the Inn through the window's encrusting dirt, and to stand dolefully looking out, saying to myself that London was decidedly overrated.

Mr. Pocket's idea of "shortly" was not mine, for I had nearly maddened myself with looking out for half an hour, and had written my name with my finger several times in the dirt of every pane in the window before I heard footsteps on the stairs. My nails were looking sharp, as they did when they were wolfish, and I wished I'd brought a file. A silver file.

Gradually there arose before me the hat, head, neckcloth, waistcoat, trousers, boots of a member of society of about my own standing. He had a paper-bag under each arm and a pottle of strawberries in one hand, and was out of breath.

"Mr. Pip?" said he.

"Mr. Pocket?" said I.

"Dear me!" he exclaimed. "I am extremely sorry, but I knew there was a coach from your part of the country at midday, and I thought you would come by that one. The fact is, I have been out on your account—not that that is any excuse—for I thought, coming from the country, you might like a little meat after dinner, and I went to Covent Garden Market to get it good."

I felt as if my eyes would start out of my head. I acknowledged his attention incoherently, and began to think this was a dream. I smelled an aroma like burnt porridge.

"Dear me!" said Mr. Pocket, Junior. "This door sticks so!"

As he wrestled with the door while the paper-bags were under his arms, I begged him to allow me to hold them. He handed them over with an agreeable smile, and combatted with the door as if it were a wild beast. It yielded so suddenly at last that he staggered back upon me, and I staggered back upon the opposite door, and we both laughed. But still I felt as if my eyes must start out of my head, and as if this must be a dream.

"Pray come in," said Mr. Pocket, Junior. "Allow me to lead the way. I am rather bare here, but I hope you'll be able to make out tolerably well till Monday. My father thought you would get on more agreeably through tomorrow with me than with him, and might like to take a walk about London. I am sure I shall be very happy to show London to you. As to our table, you won't find that bad, I hope, for it will be supplied from our coffee-house here, and at your expense, such being Mr. Jaggers's directions. As to our lodging, it's not by any means splendid. This is our sitting-room—just such chairs and tables and carpet, you see, as they could spare from home. You mustn't give me credit for the tablecloth and spoons and castors, because they come for you from the coffee-house. This is my little bedroom; rather musty, but Barnard's is musty. This is your bedroom; the furniture's hired for the occasion, but I trust it will answer the purpose. If you should want anything, I'll go and fetch it. The chambers are retired, and we shall be alone together, but we shan't fight, I dare say. But dear me, I beg your pardon, you're holding the meat all this time. Pray let me take these bags from you. I am quite ashamed."

As I stood opposite to Mr. Pocket, Junior, delivering him the bags, One, Two, I saw the starting appearance come into his own eyes that I knew to be in mine, and he said, falling back, "Lord bless me, you're the prowling boy!"

"And you," said I, "are the furry young gentleman!"

CHAPTER 19

THE FURRY YOUNG GENTLEMAN and I circled around, contemplating one another in Barnard's Inn, until we both burst out laughing.

"The idea of its being you!" said he.

"The idea of its being *you!*" said I.

We circled again, and laughed again.

"Well!" said the furry young gentleman, reaching out his hand, which was still slightly furry after all. I knew him to be what he was, which is what I was. We were a couple of young werewolves in London. "It's all over now, I hope, and it will be magnanimous in you if you'll forgive me for having knocked you about so."

I supposed he could afford to be magnanimous now that we'd had established at our earlier meeting who was the alpha among us. And yet, of course, I relied on him to teach me my way around London, putting us on more equal terms. We shook hands warmly, as rolling over on our bellies in polite society would never do.

"You hadn't come into your good fortune at that time?" said Herbert Pocket. "I heard it had happened very lately. *I* was rather on the lookout for good fortune then."

"No I hadn't then. Only very lately," I confirmed. "And indeed, you were on the lookout for good fortune?"

"Yes. Miss Havisham had sent for me, to see if she could take a fancy to me. But she couldn't. At all events, she didn't."

I thought it polite to remark that I was surprised to hear that.

"Bad taste," said Herbert, laughing, "but a fact. Yes, she had sent for me on a trial visit, and if I had come out of it successfully, I suppose I should have been provided for; perhaps I should have been what-you-may-called it to Estella."

"What's that?" I asked, with sudden gravity.

He arranged meat on plates while we talked, which divided his attention, and was the cause of his having made this lapse of a word. "Victimized. Sacrificed. Savaged. What's-his-named. Any word of that sort."

"By Estella?"

"Pooh!" said he, "She's a barbarian."

"Miss Havisham?"

"I don't say no to that, but I meant Estella. That girl's hard and haughty and capricious to the last degree, and has been brought up by Miss Havisham to wreak revenge on all Scapegraces."

"Oh, that. All in fun," I said. "What relation is she to Miss Havisham?"

"None," said he. "Only adopted."

"Do you really think she means to wreak revenge on all Scapegraces? I thought perhaps only on vampires, though I could never figure out why. Miss Havisham herself is a vampire."

"Lord, Mr. Pip!" said he. "Don't you know?"

"No," said I.

"Dear me! It's quite a story, and shall be saved till dinnertime. And now let me take the liberty of asking you a question. How did you come there, that day?"

I told him, and he was attentive until I had finished, and then burst out laughing again, and asked me if I was sore afterwards? I didn't ask him if he was, for my conviction on that point was perfectly established.

"Mr. Jaggers is your guardian, I understand?" he went on.

"Yes."

"You know he is Miss Havisham's man of business and solicitor, and has her confidence when nobody else has?"

This was bringing me (I felt) towards dangerous ground. I answered with a constraint I made no attempt to disguise, that I had seen Mr. Jaggers in Miss Havisham's house on the very day of our combat, but never at any other time, and that I believed he had no recollection of having ever seen me there.

"He was so obliging as to suggest my father for your tutor, and he called on my father to propose it. My father is Miss Havisham's cousin, but there is not much familiarity between them."

Herbert Pocket had a frank and easy way with him that was very taking. I had never seen any one then, and I have never seen any one since, who more strongly expressed to me, in every look and tone, a natural incapacity to do anything secret and mean. There was something wonderfully hopeful about his general air, and something that at the same time whispered to me he would never be very successful or rich. I don't know how this was. I became imbued with the notion on that first occasion before we sat down to dinner, but I cannot define by what means.

He was still a furry young gentleman, and had a certain conquered languor about him in the midst of his spirits and briskness that did not seem indicative of natural strength. He had not a handsome face, but it was better than handsome, being extremely amiable and cheerful. His figure was a little ungainly, as if he were always on the brink of turning full wolf, but it looked as if it would always be light and young.

As he was so communicative, I felt that reserve on my part would be a bad return. I therefore told him my small story, and laid stress on my being forbidden to enquire as to who my benefactor was. I further mentioned that I had been brought up a silversmith in a country place, and knew very little of the ways of politeness. I would take it as a great kindness in him if he would give me a hint whenever he saw me at a loss or going wrong.

"With pleasure," said he, "though I venture to prophesy that you'll want very few hints. I dare say we shall be often together, and I should like to banish any needless restraint between us. Will you do me the favour to begin at once to call me by my Christian name, Herbert?"

I thanked him and said I would. I informed him in exchange that my Christian name was Philip.

"I don't take to Philip," he said, with a smile. "It sounds like a moral boy out of the schoolyard, who was so lazy that he fell into a pond, or so fat that he couldn't see out of his eyes, or so avaricious that he locked up his cake till the mice ate it, or so determined to go out on a midnight hunt that he got himself sucked dry by vampires who lived handy in the neighbourhood. I tell you what I should like. We are so harmonious—would you mind it?"

"I shouldn't mind anything that you propose," I answered, "but I don't understand you."

"Would you mind Lowell for a familiar name? It means young wolf."

"I should like it very much."

"Then, my dear Lowell." He turned round to open the door. "Here we have the makings of a full dinner, but I am suddenly thinking we would be better served to catch our fill out of doors."

"You mean—to hunt? But it's not a full moon."

"We do not need a full moon, Lowell. We have London at our paws. One thing my father will teach you is to be able to control your transformations, both to hold them off and to bring them on. You remember our fight? I simply had to provoke you."

"This is true. But would it be ungentlemanly of us, Herbert?"

He shrugged. "Your lessons haven't started yet. I could show you a bit of London."

I was tempted, but how—Herbert forced his head into my stomach. I groaned and felt my bones shift, my hair begin to grow.

"Aha, you see?" Herbert hit me again, a swipe across the jaw. I staggered back. "Hit me now. Come on."

"With pleasure." I delivered a solid punch to his nose, already growing snoutish.

We shed our clothes before stretching and shifting out of them. I ran out after Herbert, my tail growing even as we ran. I followed him down the stairs and out into the yard. He ran fast, entirely lycanthrope now. I felt the last of my joints stretch out of place and into my wolfish state. I caught up with him in a single pounce.

We ran through the streets, past hissing cats and scattering children, street vendors, and shop fronts. We ran all the way to Hyde

Park and bounded through the grass. Herbert darted in through some trees and came out with a rabbit between his teeth. I left him devouring his snack and went off to explore. I played along the banks of the river and frightened a young couple meeting by some trees. I caught scent of something new, something delicious, and went off in pursuit. A fierce craving overtook me, sending me nearly to a frenzy. The last thing I remembered was cornering a fat pheasant at the edge of the park before waking at early dawn with feathers scattered all around me, and some stuck in my teeth. I rose, stretched, and went off in search of Herbert. I found him curled up in tall grass.

"How are we to get home?" I asked, making some effort to cover myself. I'd never woken up from a wolfish episode so far from home without my clothes.

"We'll find something, my dear Lowell." Herbert yawned, stretched, brushed some rabbit fur from his chest before rising. "Follow my lead."

He strutted without any apparent fear of discovery across the open field. I cowered at his side, covering myself with my hands as we walked.

"I don't know what happened," I said. "I don't remember."

"It's the bloodlust." Herbert nodded. "On scent of tempting prey, it takes over and makes us all beast. It only lasts as long as we're wolfish."

A few lanes from the park, we borrowed some clothes drying on a line in an alleyway.

"We'll bring them back after laundering them," Herbert said. "No sense in stealing, my dear Lowell."

Once at home again and properly clothed in our own garments, we sat down to a breakfast of strawberries and cold meat, what would have been our dinner the previous night had we not gone out to dine al fresco.

"I must beg of you to take the top of the table, because the meal is of your providing," Herbert said. This I would not hear of, so he took the top, and I faced him. It was a nice little breakfast, and it acquired additional relish from being eaten under those independent circumstances, with no old people by, and with London all around us.

The table was, as Mr. Pumblechook might have said, the lap of luxury, it being entirely furnished forth from the coffee-house. As we dined, I reminded Herbert of his promise to tell me about Miss Havisham.

"True," he replied. "I'll redeem it at once. Now, concerning Miss Havisham. Miss Havisham, you must know, was a spoilt child. Her mother died when she was a baby, and her father denied her nothing. Her father was a country gentleman down in your part of the world, and was a brewer. It is indisputable, though I'm not sure why, that while you cannot possibly be genteel and bake, you may be as genteel as never was and brew. You see it every day."

"Yet a gentleman may not keep a public-house; may he?" I said. We had passed a few of those in our ramblings of the night.

"Not on any account," returned Herbert. "But a public-house may keep a gentleman. Well! Mr. Havisham was very rich and very proud. So was his daughter."

"Miss Havisham was an only child?" I hazarded.

"Stop a moment, I am coming to that. No, she was not an only child; she had a half-brother. Her father privately married again— his cook, I rather think."

"I thought he was proud."

"My good Lowell, so he was. He married his second wife privately, because he was proud, and in course of time *she* died. When she was dead, I apprehend he first told his daughter what he had done, and then the son became a part of the family, residing in the house you are acquainted with. As the son grew a young man, he turned out riotous, extravagant, undutiful—altogether bad. At last his father disinherited him; but he softened when he was dying, and left him well off, though not nearly so well off as Miss Havisham."

"I see. Go on."

Herbert paused to finish a strawberry, then went on. "Miss Havisham was now an heiress, and you may suppose was looked after as a great match. Her half-brother had now ample means again, but what with debts and what with new madness wasted them most fearfully again. There were stronger differences between brother and sister than there had been between him and his father, and it is suspected that he cherished a deep and mortal grudge against Miss Havisham as having influenced the father's anger. Now, I come to the cruel part of the story.

"Oh dear."

"Quite right. There appeared upon the scene a certain man who made love to Miss Havisham. I never saw him (for this happened five-and-twenty years ago, before you and I were born, Lowell), but I have heard my father mention that he was a showy man, not to be mistaken for a gentleman. Well! This man pursued Miss Havisham closely, and professed to be devoted to her. I believe she had not shown much susceptibility up to that time; but all the susceptibility she possessed certainly came out then, and she passionately loved him. There is no doubt that she perfectly idolized him."

"Even though he was not a gentleman?" I found it hard to believe, so important had it become to me to impress Estella with my gentlemanly ways.

Herbert shook his head. "He preyed on her affection in that systematic way, that he got great sums of money from her. He induced her to buy her brother out of a share in the brewery (which had been weakly left him by his father) at an immense price, on the plea that when he was to be her husband he would manage it all. Your guardian was not at that time in Miss Havisham's counsels, and she was too haughty and too much in love to be advised by any one. Her relations were poor and scheming, with the exception of my father; he was poor enough, but not jealous. The only independent one among them, he warned her that she was doing too much for this man, and was placing herself too unreservedly in his power.

She took the first opportunity of angrily ordering my father out of the house, in his presence, and my father has never seen her since."

I thought of her having said, "Matthew will come and see me at last when I am laid dead upon that table;" and I asked Herbert whether his father was so inveterate against her?

"It's not that," said he, "but she charged him, in the presence of her intended husband, with being disappointed in the hope of fawning upon her for his own advancement, and, if he were to go to her now, it would look true—even to him—and even to her. Back to the man and Miss Havisham. He preyed on her for more than her money. He took her blood."

"Her blood? He was the vampire who turned her?"

"Indeed, Lowell. He was her sire, as they say."

"And, Miss Havisham? She allowed him to make her a vampire?"

Herbert nodded. "He promised they could spend eternity together. The wedding day was fixed, the dresses were bought, the honeymoon was planned out, the guests were invited. He weakened her with daily feedings, just enough to keep her complacent, and made her vampire days before their wedding, as it takes a few days to regain one's strength. The day came, but not the bridegroom. He wrote her a letter—"

"Which she received," I struck in, "when she was dressing for her marriage? At twenty minutes to nine?"

"At the hour and minute," Herbert confirmed. "At which she afterwards stopped all the clocks. What was in it, further than that it most heartlessly broke the marriage off, I can't tell you, because I don't know. When she recovered from the shock, and the blood loss, for he left her so weakened from all the feedings, she laid the whole place waste, as you have seen it, and she has never since looked upon the light of day. She claims that she will live long enough to see that Scapegraces are struck down from this earth, as an act of vengeance upon the vampire who brought her to the brink of death and abandoned her."

"All Scapegraces, you think? Truly?" I asked, after considering it.

"As I know of it; and indeed I only know so much, through piecing it out for myself. My father always avoids the topic, and, even when Miss Havisham invited me to go there, he has told me no more of it than was absolutely requisite for my safety. He thinks her harmless to our kind, for now, and intent on destroying vampires first. But I have forgotten one thing. It has been supposed that the man to whom she gave her misplaced confidence acted throughout in concert with her half-brother; that it was a conspiracy between them; and that they shared the profits."

"I wonder he didn't marry her and get all the property," I said.

"He may have been married already, and her cruel mortification may have been a part of her half-brother's scheme," said Herbert. "Mind! I don't know that."

"What became of the two men?" I asked, after again considering the subject.

"They fell into deeper shame and degradation—if there can be deeper—and ruin."

"Are they alive now?"

"I don't know."

"You said just now that Estella was not related to Miss Havisham, but adopted. When adopted?"

Herbert shrugged his shoulders. "There has always been an Estella, since I have heard of a Miss Havisham. I believe Miss Havisham invites our kind over so that Estella can study Scapegraces and get to know our ways and our weaknesses to bring about our eventual destruction. I know no more. And now, Lowell," said he, finally throwing off the story as it were, "there is a perfectly open understanding between us. All that I know about Miss Havisham, you know."

"And all that I know," I retorted, "you know."

"I fully believe it. So there can be no competition or perplexity between you and me. And as to the condition on which you hold your advancement in life—namely, that you are not to enquire or discuss to whom you owe it—you may be very sure that it will never

be encroached upon, or even approached, by me, or by any one belonging to me."

In truth, he said this with so much delicacy, that I felt the subject done with, even though I should be under his father's roof for
years and years to come. Yet he said it with so much meaning, too,
that I felt he as perfectly understood Miss Havisham to be my bene-
factress, as I understood the fact myself. Why, I had yet to fully understand. I harboured the secret hope that she intended me as a
bridegroom for Estella, but now perhaps it seemed that she meant
me as a murder victim. Impossible! Miss Havisham liked me, I had
thought. And Estella had kissed me the once, when I'd defeated
Herbert. Would she have kissed me if she'd intended to kill me? I
hardly knew.

It seemed to me that if vampires and werewolves were naturally
contentious toward one another, and Miss Havisham was determined to wipe out vampires, perhaps a werewolf union for Estella
would give her strength to meet her purpose. Perhaps Herbert had
it wrong after all and Miss Havisham wasn't bent on the destruction
of all Scapegraces, but only of the vampire kind.

At any rate, after clearing the topic of Miss Havisham out of our
way, we were very gay and sociable, and I asked him, in the course
of conversation, what he did for a living.

"I'm a capitalist," he said. "That is, an insurer of ships in the
city."

I had grand ideas of the wealth and importance of insurers of
ships in the city, and I began to think with awe of having laid a
young insurer on his back, blackened his enterprising eye, and cut
his responsible head open. But again there came upon me, for my
relief, that odd impression that Herbert Pocket would never be very
successful or rich.

"I shall not rest satisfied with merely employing my capital in insuring ships. I want to engage in transport of Scapegraces. Ocean
voyages are particularly trying for our kind as we must spend a good
deal of time locked up away from fellow passengers. I shall buy up

some ships and arrange a network of travel opportunities for were-wolves, and perhaps other Scapegraces. I'm most interested in connecting with others, to create a worldwide network of werewolves for our common good. My father has shown that we can be gentlemen. Why shouldn't we be accepted and treated with the same decency and respect as everyone else? We should not have to hide who we are or risk being sent off to the country or worse, locked away in containment ships."

"You're absolutely right."

"Yes." He shook his head. "I dream of having an Office of Werewolf Welfare and Education in every country, on every shore. Who better to promote our interests and inspire understanding of our kind than ourselves?"

"You will make a convincing representative," I said.

I wavered again, and began to think here were greater expectations than my own.

"I think I shall trade, also," said he, putting his thumbs in his waist-coat pockets, "to the West Indies, for sugar, tobacco, and rum. Also to Ceylon, specially for elephants' tusks. I will need the income to help support my educational endeavours."

"You will want a good many ships," I said.

"A perfect fleet," he responded.

Quite overpowered by the magnificence of these transactions, I asked him where the ships he insured mostly traded to at present?

"I haven't begun insuring yet," he replied. "I am looking about me."

Somehow, that pursuit seemed more in keeping with Barnard's Inn. I said (in a tone of conviction), "Ah-h!"

"Yes. I work in an accounting house, and am looking for ways to step up from it."

"Is an accounting house profitable?" I asked.

"To—do you mean to the young fellow who's in it?" he asked, in reply.

"Yes, to you."

"Why, n-no, not to me." He said this with the air of one carefully reckoning up and striking a balance. "Not directly profitable. That is, it doesn't pay me much of anything, and I have to—keep myself."

This certainly had not a profitable appearance, and I shook my head as if I would imply that it would be difficult to acquire much accumulative capital from such a source of income.

"But the thing is," said Herbert Pocket, "that you look about you. That's the grand thing. You are in an accounting house, you know, and you look about you for new opportunities to arise. When you have once made your capital, you have nothing to do but employ it."

This was very like his way of conducting that encounter in the garden; very like. His manner of bearing his poverty, too, exactly corresponded to his manner of bearing that defeat. It seemed to me that he took all blows and buffets now with just the same air as he had taken mine then. Yet, having already made his fortune in his own mind, he was so unassuming with it that I felt quite grateful to him for not being puffed up. It was a pleasant addition to his naturally pleasant ways, and we got on famously. In the evening we went out for a walk in the streets and went half-price to the theatre. We didn't allow ourselves to turn or go hunting but we both developed a thin coating of fur, bushy brows, and slight snout, which all went unnoticed at the theatre. London was grand!

On the Monday morning at a quarter before nine, Herbert went to the accounting house to report and I bore him company. He was to come away in an hour or two to attend me to Hammersmith, and I was to wait about for him. When Herbert came, we went and had lunch, then went back to Barnard's Inn, got my little portmanteau, and took the coach for Hammersmith.

CHAPTER 20

WE ARRIVED THERE AT two or three o'clock in the afternoon, and had very little way to walk to Mr. Pocket's house. Lifting the latch of a gate, we passed direct into a little garden overlooking the river, where Mr. Pocket's children were playing. Mrs. Pocket was sitting on a garden chair under a tree, reading, with her legs upon another garden chair. Mrs. Pocket's two nursemaids were looking about them while the children played.

"Mamma," said Herbert, "this is young Mr. Pip." Upon which Mrs. Pocket received me with an appearance of amiable dignity.

She looked up from her book, fixed her eyes upon me, and said, "I hope your mamma is quite well?"

This unexpected inquiry put me into such a difficulty that I began saying in the absurdest way that if there had been any such person I had no doubt she would have been quite well and would have been very much obliged.

Mrs. Pocket forgot me, and went on reading.

I found, now I had leisure to count them, that there were no fewer than six little Pockets present, in various stages of tumbling up. I had scarcely arrived at the total when a seventh was heard, as in the region of air, howling dolefully.

"If there ain't Baby!" said Flopson, appearing to think it most surprising. "Make haste up, Millers."

Millers, who was the other nurse, retired into the house, and by degrees the child's wailing was hushed and stopped, as if it were a young ventriloquist with something in its mouth. Mrs. Pocket read all the time, and I was curious to know what the book could be.

We were waiting, I supposed, for Mr. Pocket to come out to us. Millers came down with the baby, which was actually a pup

in wolfish state, handed it to Flopson, which Flopson was handing it to Mrs. Pocket, "Here! Take the baby, mum, and give me
your book."

Mrs. Pocket acted on the advice, and inexpertly danced the
swaddled pup a little in her lap, while the other children played
about it. This had lasted but a very short time, when Mrs. Pocket
issued summary orders that they were all to be taken into the house
for a nap.

Under these circumstances, when Flopson and Millers had got
the children into the house, like a little flock of sheep, and Mr.
Pocket came out of it to make my acquaintance, I was not much
surprised to find that Mr. Pocket was a gentleman with a rather
perplexed expression of face, and with his very gray hair disordered
on his head, as if he didn't quite see his way to putting anything
straight.

Mr. Pocket said he was glad to see me, and he hoped I was not
sorry to see him.

"For, I really am not," he added, with his son's smile, "an alarming personage."

He was a young-looking man, in spite of his thick black brows
and his very gray hair, and his manner seemed quite natural. When
he had talked with me a little, he said to Mrs. Pocket, with a rather
anxious contraction of his abundant eyebrows, "Belinda, I hope you
have welcomed Mr. Pip?"

And she looked up from her book, and said, "Yes."

I found out within a few hours that Mrs. Pocket was the only
daughter of a certain quite accidental deceased knight, who created
his own baronetcy. Be that as it may, he had directed Mrs. Pocket
to be brought up from her cradle as one who in the nature of things
must marry a title, and who was to be guarded from the acquisition
of plebeian domestic knowledge.

So successful a watch and ward had been established over the
young lady by this judicious parent, that she had grown up highly
ornamental, but perfectly helpless and useless. With her charac-

ter thus happily formed, in the first bloom of her youth she had encountered Mr. Pocket, who was also in the first bloom of youth,
and not quite decided whether to roam the wild from full moon to
full moon or become domesticated. Mrs. Pocket tamed him in no
time and they had married quickly without the knowledge of her
judicious parent. The judicious parent, upon finding out his daughter had married a werewolf instead of the titled gentleman he had
in mind for her, threatened to withhold his blessing, as well as his
money, should any of his acquaintance discover his son-in-law's
monthly condition. Mr. Pocket took up the study of controlling his
transformations that he later went on to teach, and the judicious
handsomely settled a dower upon the couple. Mrs. Pocket was in
general the object of a queer sort of respectful pity, because she had
not married a title. If it were widely known outside of the Scapegrace community that she had in fact married a werewolf, she would
have been scorned and ruined.

Mr. Pocket took me into the house and showed me my room,
which was a pleasant one, and so furnished as that I could use it
with comfort for my own private sitting room. He then knocked
at the doors of two other similar rooms, and introduced their occupants, by name Drummle and Startop. Drummle, an old-looking
young man of a heavy sort of body, was whistling. Startop, younger
in years and appearance, was reading and holding his head, as if he
thought himself in danger of exploding it with too strong a charge
of knowledge.

By degrees I learnt, chiefly from Herbert, that Mr. Pocket had
been educated at Harrow and at Cambridge, where he had distinguished himself. It was there that he had studied the account of lycanthropic control and correction, and on such means now made
his living.

It came to my knowledge, through what passed between Mrs.
Pocket and Drummle, that Drummle, whose Christian name was
Bentley, was actually the next heir but one to a baronetcy. It fur-
ther appeared that the book I had seen Mrs. Pocket reading in

the garden was all about titles. Drummle didn't say much, but in his limited way, he spoke as one of the elect, and recognized Mrs. Pocket as a woman and a sister.

After dinner the children were introduced. There were four little girls, and two little boys, besides the baby who was evidently male, and the baby's next successor who was as yet neither. They were brought in by Flopson and Millers, while Mrs. Pocket looked at the children as if she rather didn't quite know what to make of them.

"Here! Give me your fork, mum, and take the baby," said Flopson. "Don't take it that way, or you'll get its head under the table."

Thus advised, Mrs. Pocket took it the other way, and got its head upon the table, which was announced to all present by a prodigious concussion.

"Dear, dear! Give it me back, mum," said Flopson. "Miss Jane, come and dance for the baby, do!"

One of the little girls, a mere mite who seemed to have prematurely taken upon herself some charge of the others, stepped out of her place by me, and danced to and from the baby until it stopped whining and barked. Then, the children laughed, and Mr. Pocket laughed, and we all laughed and were glad.

Flopson, by dint of holding the puppy by the scruff of its neck, then got it safely into Mrs. Pocket's lap, and gave it the meat bones to gnaw, at the same time recommending Mrs. Pocket make sure the bones didn't splinter and choke the "baby." Then, the two nurses left the room.

I was made very uneasy by Mrs. Pocket's falling into a discussion with Drummle respecting two baronetcies, while she ate a sliced orange steeped in sugar and wine, and forgot all about the pup on her lap, who gnawed the bones to stubs. At length little Jane, perceiving its young life to be imperiled, softly left her place, and with many small artifices coaxed the dangerous snacks away. Mrs. Pocket finishing her orange at about the same time, and not approving of this, said to Jane, "You naughty child, how dare you take Baby's bones? Go and sit down this instant!"

"Mamma dear," lisped the little girl, "Baby ood have choked."

"How dare you tell me so?" retorted Mrs. Pocket. "Go and sit down in your chair this moment!"

"Belinda," remonstrated Mr. Pocket, from the other end of the table, "how can you be so unreasonable? Jane only interfered for the protection of Baby."

"I will not allow anybody to interfere," said Mrs. Pocket. "I am surprised, Matthew, that you should expose me to the affront of interference."

"Good God!" cried Mr. Pocket, in an outbreak of desolate desperation. "Are infants to be choked into their tombs, and is nobody to save them? May he survive for his first transformation! We've already lost one boy not having the advantage of being whelped under a full moon."

"I will not be interfered with by Jane," said Mrs. Pocket, with a majestic glance at that innocent little offender. "Jane, indeed!"

"Hear this!" Mr. Pocket helplessly exclaimed to the elements. "Babies are not to be choking on bones before first transformation!"

We all looked awkwardly at the tablecloth while this was going on. A pause succeeded, during which the honest and irrepressible pup made a series of leaps and woofs at little Jane, who appeared to me to be the only member of the family (irrespective of servants) with whom it had any decided acquaintance.

"Mr. Drummle," said Mrs. Pocket, "will you ring for Flopson? Jane, you undutiful little thing, go and lie down. Now, Baby darling, come with Ma!"

The pup was the soul of honor, and protested with all its might. It doubled itself up the wrong way over Mrs. Pocket's arm, wiggled and squirmed, paws up to its furry face, and was carried out in the highest state of mutiny. And it gained its point after all, for I saw it through the window within a few minutes being cradled by little Jane.

In the evening there was rowing on the river. Mr. Pocket felt that rowing was a great sport for engaging one's concentration and putting off transformations. As Drummle and Startop had each a boat, I resolved to set up mine, and to cut them both out. I was pretty good at most exercises in which country boys are adepts, but I was conscious of wanting elegance of style for the Thames, not to say for other waters. I at once engaged to place myself under the tutelage of the rower of a prize-wherry in the neighbourhood, to whom I was introduced by my new allies.

There was a supper-tray after we got home at night. After supper, we took part in some exercises of provoking each other to see if we could hold off our transformations in such an event. Herbert was star pupil, and I thought it had to do more with his natural disposition than with any relation to our instructor. Drummle, of course, made accusations of favoritism and in fact got so distressed by the simplest insult (Startop called him a scurvy lout) that he went running into the woods in full metamorphosis and did not return until morning. Startop and I handled the exercise tolerably well, though my ears grew a bit pointed and my tongue thickened so as to prevent my speech.

Mr. Pocket was in good spirits, though he remarked that he could see he had some work ahead of him.

CHAPTER 21

AFTER TWO OR THREE days, when I had established myself in my room and had gone backwards and forwards to London several times, and had ordered all I wanted of my tradesmen, Mr. Pocket and I had a long talk together. He knew more of my intended career than I knew myself, for he referred to his having been told by Mr. Jaggers that I was not designed for any profession, and that I should be well enough educated for my destiny if I could "hold my own" with the average of young men in prosperous circumstances, and become more gentleman than wolf. I acquiesced, of course, knowing nothing to the contrary.

He advised my attending certain places in London for the acquisition of such skills as I wanted, and my investing him with the functions of explainer and director of all my studies. He hoped that with intelligent assistance I should meet with little to discourage me, and should soon be able to dispense with any aid but his.

When these points were settled, and so far carried out as that I had begun to work in earnest, it occurred to me that if I could retain my bedroom in Barnard's Inn, my life would be agreeably varied, while my manners would be none the worse for Herbert's society. Mr. Pocket did not object to this arrangement. I went off to Little Britain to Mr. Jaggers about my circumstances.

"If I could buy the furniture now hired for me," said I, "and one or two other little things, I should be quite at home there."

"Do it!" said Mr. Jaggers, with a short laugh. "I told you you'd get on. Wemmick! Take Mr. Pip's written order, and pay him twenty pounds."

Wemmick led me into my guardian's room.

"Pray," I said, as the two odious casts with the twitchy leer upon them caught my sight again, "whose likenesses are those?"

"These?" said Wemmick, getting upon a chair, and blowing the dust off the horrible heads before bringing them down. "These are two celebrated ones. Famous clients of ours. This chap murdered his master."

"Is it like him?" I asked, recoiling from the brute.

"Like him? It's himself, you know. The cast was made in Newgate, directly after he was taken down. You had a particular fancy for me, hadn't you, Old Artful?" said Wemmick, as he turned one of his rings as if in tribute. "Portable property, from the man himself," he said, gesturing then to his ring. "That's what you need to see you through life, portable property. Always get it off them when you can."

I looked again at all his rings, portable property. He seemed to be preparing for his future, and not perpetually in mourning after all.

"Did that other creature come to the same end?" I asked. "He has the same look."

"You're right," said Wemmick. "Yes, he came to the same end. Wizard, this one was. Not powerful enough to save himself from his fate, however. Say, if at any odd time when you have nothing better to do, you wouldn't mind coming over to see me at Walworth, I could offer you a bed, and I should consider it an honour."

I said I should be delighted to accept his hospitality.

"Thankee, then we'll consider that it's to come off, when convenient to you. Have you dined with Mr. Jaggers yet?"

"Not yet."

"Well," said Wemmick, "he'll give you wine, and good wine. I'll give you punch, and not bad punch. And now I'll tell you something. When you go to dine with Mr. Jaggers, look at his housekeeper."

"Shall I see something very uncommon?"

"Well," said Wemmick, "you'll see a wild beast tamed. Not so very uncommon, you'll tell me. I reply, that depends on the original wildness of the beast, and the amount of taming. It won't lower your opinion of Mr. Jaggers's powers. Keep your eye on it."

I told him I would do so, with all the interest and curiosity that his preparation awakened.

CHAPTER 22

I HADN'T HAD THE PLEASURE to meet a great number of my kind, but Bentley Drummle most certainly ranked among the most disagreeable of werewolves. Heavy in figure, movement, and comprehension, he had a large, awkward tongue that seemed to always protrude as he panted, even in full human form. He lolled about in his room sure as his tongue lolled about in his mouth. He was idle, proud, stingy, reserved, and suspicious. He came of rich people down in Somersetshire who had nursed this combination of qualities until they made the discovery that the transformations they thought to be an odd novelty of childhood were to continue under full moons for the rest of Bentley Drummle's life. Thus, Bentley had come to Mr. Pocket when he was a head taller than that gentleman, and half a dozen heads thicker than most gentlemen.

Startop had been spoilt by a weak mother and kept at home when he ought to have been at school, but he was devotedly attached to her, and admired her beyond measure. He had a woman's delicacy of feature, and was—"as you may see, though you never saw her," said Herbert to me—"exactly like his mother, except when in wolfish form, and then he looks more Afghan hound than wolf to be sure." It was but natural that I should take to him much more kindly than to Drummle, and that, even in the earliest evenings of our boating, he and I should pull homeward abreast of one another, conversing from boat to boat, while Bentley Drummle came up in our wake alone, under the overhanging banks and among the rushes. He would always creep inshore like some uncomfortable creature, even when the tide would have sent him fast upon his way.

The nights usually ended with Drummle unable to hold off his transformation despite the concentration required for the boating exercise, and one of us would have to board, risking our lives to right his vessel, and knock him into the water to shock the wolf right out of him. Being a fiercely determined sort of creature, even cold water often failed to bring Drummle back to humanity and he would simply paddle ashore and storm off into the woods, determined to hunt down some innocent creatures in the night.

Herbert was my companion and friend. I presented him with a half-share in my boat, which was the occasion of his often coming down to Hammersmith; and my possession of a half-share in his chambers often took me up to London. We used to walk between the two places at all hours, and sometimes to run and hunt, though his father would never have approved. I have affection for the road yet.

These were the surroundings among which I settled down, and applied myself to my education. I soon contracted expensive habits, and began to spend an amount of money that within a few short months I should have thought almost fabulous; but through good and evil I stuck to my studies. Between Mr. Pocket and Herbert I got on fast. I learned methods of meditation and chanting when I felt the wolf coming on, and was eventually able to go a whole full moon without changing. Though, the transformation came in full force but a few days later, and wracked me so strongly that I ended up much to my shame as similar to Bentley Drummle, in the woods chasing after forest creatures, and possibly eating one for I woke covered in blood with small bones all around me.

"A natural occurrence," Mr. Pocket insisted. "Nature will out."

He further explained that holding off an entire transformation at full moon was a necessary skill, occasionally required, but that it would always come back to us for it was not in our constitutions to be entirely human at all times. "For every held-off transformation, there is a stronger and more violent transformation," was Mr. Pocket's favorite law of physics.

In event of danger, I learned to bring the transformation on at will, for we were most certainly stronger as wolves than as men, not to mention with sharper instincts and senses. Once I began to master the skill, it was one I was glad I hadn't had years earlier, for who knows what an untried youth in wolf form might have done to an aggressor, such as my sister. At any rate, I had a much easier time of holding off my changes than of bringing them on. Mr. Pocket explained that it had to do with my natural disposition. People disposed to high tempers and strong reactions tended to go wolfish with much less effort. I thought of Bentley Drummle.

As my studies continued to progress, it occurred to me that I had not seen Mr. Wemmick for some weeks. I thought I would write him a note and propose to go home with him on a certain evening. He replied that it would give him much pleasure, and that he would expect me at the office at six o'clock. Thither I went, and there I found him.

"Did you think of walking down to Walworth?" said he.

"Certainly," said I, "if you approve."

"Very much," was Wemmick's reply, "for I have had my legs under the desk all day, and shall be glad to stretch them. Now, I'll tell you what I have got for supper, Mr. Pip. I have got a stewed steak—which is of home preparation—and a cold roast fowl—which is from the cook's-shop. You don't object to an aged parent, I hope?"

I really thought he was still speaking of a dish for dinner, until he added, "Because I have got an aged parent at my place." I then said what politeness required, relieved that he was not proposing we dine on human flesh.

"So, you haven't dined with Mr. Jaggers yet?" he pursued, as we walked along.

"Not yet."

"He told me so this afternoon when he heard you were coming. I expect you'll have an invitation tomorrow. He's going to ask your pals, too. Three of 'em; ain't there?"

Although I was not in the habit of counting Drummle as one of my intimate associates, I answered, "Yes."

"Well, he's going to ask the whole gang, and whatever he gives you, he'll give you good. Don't look forward to variety, but you'll have excellence."

We talked so that I hardly realized we had already arrived in the district of Walworth.

It appeared to be a collection of back lanes, ditches, and little gardens, and to present the aspect of a rather dull retirement. Wemmick's house was a little wooden cottage in the midst of plots of garden, and the top of it was cut out and painted like a battery mounted with guns.

"My own doing," said Wemmick. "Looks pretty. Don't it?"

I highly commended it. I think it was the smallest house I ever saw, with the queerest Gothic windows and a Gothic door almost too small to use.

"That's a real flagstaff, you see," said Wemmick, "and on Sundays I run up a real flag. Then look here. After I have crossed this bridge, I hoist it up—so—and cut off the communication. Handy during full moon." The bridge was a plank, and it crossed a chasm about four feet wide and two deep. "At nine o'clock every night, Greenwich time," said Wemmick, "the gun fires. There he is, you see! And when you hear him go, I think you'll say he's a Stinger."

"Then, at the back," said Wemmick, "out of sight, so as not to impede the idea of fortification, there's a pig, and there are fowls and rabbits. Never hunt in the wild what you can raise on your own, I like to say. Safer. You know where your meat has been. And I knock together my own little frame, you see, and grow cucumbers. You'll judge at supper what sort of a salad I can raise."

He conducted me to a bower about a dozen yards off, which was approached by such ingenious twists of path that it took quite a long time to reach. In this retreat, our glasses were already set. Our punch was cooling in an ornamental lake.

"I am my own engineer, and my own carpenter, and my own plumber, and my own gardener, and my own Jack of all Trades," said Wemmick, in acknowledging my compliments. "Well, it's a good thing, you know. It gives me something to focus on so as to put off transformations, brushes the Newgate cobwebs away, and pleases the Aged. You wouldn't mind being at once introduced to the Aged, would you? It wouldn't put you out?"

I expressed the readiness I felt, and we went into the castle. There we found, sitting by a fire, a very old man in a flannel coat: clean, cheerful, comfortable, and well cared for, but intensely deaf.

"Well aged parent," said Wemmick, shaking hands with him in a cordial and jocose way, "how am you?"

"All right, John; all right!" replied the old man.

"Here's Mr. Pip, aged parent," said Wemmick, "and I wish you could hear his name. Nod away at him, Mr. Pip; that's what he likes. Nod away at him, if you please, like winking!"

We left the Aged bestirring himself to feed the fowls, and we sat down to our punch in the arbor. Wemmick told me, as he smoked a pipe, that it had taken him a good many years to bring the property up to its present pitch of perfection.

"I hope Mr. Jaggers admires it?" I said.

"Never seen it," said Wemmick. "Never heard of it. Never seen the Aged. Never heard of him. No, the office is one thing, and private life is another. When I go into the office, I leave the Castle behind me, and when I come into the Castle, I leave the office behind me. If it's not in any way disagreeable to you, you'll oblige me by doing the same. I don't wish it professionally spoken about."

The supper was excellent, and though the Castle was rather subject to dry-rot insomuch that it tasted like a bad nut, and though the pig might have been further off, I was heartily pleased with my whole entertainment. Nor was there any drawback on my little turret bedroom, beyond there being such a very thin ceiling between me and the flagstaff, that when I lay down on my back in bed, it seemed as if I had to balance that pole on my forehead all night.

Wemmick was up early in the morning, and I am afraid I heard him cleaning my boots. After that, he fell to gardening, and I saw him from my Gothic window pretending to employ the Aged, and nodding at him in a most devoted manner. Our breakfast was as good as the supper, and at half-past eight precisely we started for Little Britain. By degrees, Wemmick got dryer and harder as we went along, and his mouth tightened.

CHAPTER 23

Not long after, as Wemmick had told me it would happen, I accepted an invitation to dine with Jaggers.

"No ceremony," Jaggers stipulated, "and no dinner dress, and say tomorrow. Come here, and I'll take you home with me."

When I and my friends repaired to him at six o'clock next day, he conducted us to Gerrard Street, Soho, to a house on the south side of that street. Rather a stately house of its kind, but dolefully in want of painting, and with dirty windows. He took out his key and opened the door, and we all went into a stone hall, bare, gloomy, and little used. So, up a dark brown staircase into a series of three dark brown rooms on the first floor.

Dinner was laid in the best of these rooms; the second was his dressing-room; the third, his bedroom. The table was comfortably laid and at the side of his chair was a capacious dumb-waiter, with a variety of bottles and decanters on it, and four dishes of fruit for dessert. I noticed throughout, that he kept everything under his own hand, and distributed everything himself.

There was a bookcase in the room filled with books on evidence, Scapegrace laws, Scapegrace criminal biography, trials, acts of Parliament against Scapegraces, and such things. The furniture was all very solid and good. It had an official look, however, and there was nothing merely ornamental to be seen.

As he had scarcely seen my three companions until now—for he and I had walked together—he stood on the hearth-rug, after ringing the bell, and took a searching look at them. To my surprise, he seemed at once to be principally if not solely interested in Drummle.

"Pip," he said, putting his large hand on my shoulder and moving me to the window, "I don't know one from the other. Who's the Spider?"

"The spider?" said I.

"The blotchy, sprawly, sulky fellow."

"That's Bentley Drummle. The other, with the delicate face, is Startop."

Not making the least account of "the one with the delicate face," he returned, "Bentley Drummle is his name, is it? I like the look of that fellow."

He immediately began to talk to Drummle: not at all deterred by his replying in his heavy reticent way, but apparently led on by it to screw discourse out of him. I was looking at the two, when there came between us the housekeeper, with the first dish for the table.

She was a woman of about forty, I supposed—but I may have thought her younger than she was. Rather tall, of a lithe nimble figure, extremely pale, with large faded eyes, and a quantity of streaming hair. I cannot say whether any diseased affection of the heart caused her lips to be parted as if she were panting, and her face to bear a curious expression of suddenness and flutter. She was a Scapegrace, undoubtedly, to be in with Jaggers, but to look at her I couldn't tell if she were werewolf, vampire, witch, or goblin. She reminded of the witches from Macbeth, that I had seen on stage, but yet there was something mysteriously indefinable about her.

She set the dish on, touched my guardian quietly on the arm with a finger to notify that dinner was ready, and vanished—not literally, I saw her quit the room. We took our seats at the round table, and my guardian kept Drummle on one side of him, while Startop sat on the other. It was a noble dish of fish that the housekeeper had put on table, and we had a joint of equally choice mutton afterwards, and then an equally choice bird.

Induced to take particular notice of the housekeeper, both by her own striking appearance and by Wemmick's preparation, I observed that whenever she was in the room she kept her eyes attentively on my guardian, and that she would remove her hands from any dish she put before him, hesitatingly, as if she dreaded his calling her back.

Dinner went off gaily, and although my guardian seemed to follow rather than originate subjects, I knew that he wrenched the weakest part of our dispositions out of us. For myself, I found that I was expressing my tendency to lavish expenditure, and to patronize Herbert, and to boast of my great prospects, before I quite knew that I had opened my lips. It was so with all of us, but with no one more than Drummle. His grudging and suspicious nature was screwed out of him before the fish was taken off.

It was not then, but when we had got to the cheese, that our conversation turned upon our rowing feats, and that Drummle was rallied for coming up behind of a night in that slow beastly way of his. Drummle, upon this, informed our host that he much preferred our room to our company, and that as to skill he was more than our master, and that as to strength he could scatter us like chaff. By some invisible agency, my guardian wound him up to a pitch little short of ferocity about this trifle; and he fell to baring his teeth and his arms to show how fierce and muscular he was, and we all fell to baring teeth and arms in a ridiculous manner, almost enough to make us all turn into our wolfish selves. Being near Drummle was often enough to make me wolfish, no matter what the cycle of the moon.

The housekeeper was at that time clearing the table; my guardian, taking no heed of her, but with the side of his face turned from her, was leaning back in his chair biting the side of his forefinger and showing an interest in Drummle, that, to me, was quite inexplicable. Suddenly, he clapped his large hand on the housekeeper's, like a trap, as she stretched it across the table. So suddenly and smartly did he do this, that we all stopped in our foolish contention.

"If you talk of strength," said Mr. Jaggers, "I'll show you a wrist. Molly, let them see your wrist."

Her entrapped hand was on the table, but she had already put her other hand behind her waist.

"Master," she said, in a low voice, with her eyes attentively and entreatingly fixed upon him. "Don't."

"I'll show you a wrist," repeated Mr. Jaggers, with an immovable determination to show it. "Molly, let them see your wrist."

"Master," she again murmured. "Please!"

"Molly," said Mr. Jaggers, not looking at her, but obstinately looking at the opposite side of the room, "let them see both your wrists. Show them. Come!"

He took his hand from hers, and turned that wrist up on the table. She brought her other hand from behind her, and held the two out side by side. The last wrist was much disfigured—deeply scarred and scarred across and across. When she held her hands out she took her eyes from Mr. Jaggers, and turned them watchfully on every one of the rest of us in succession.

"There's power here," said Mr. Jaggers, coolly tracing out the sinews with his forefinger. "Very few men have the power of wrist that this woman has. It's remarkable what mere force of grip there is in these hands. I have had occasion to notice many hands; but I never saw stronger in that respect, man's or woman's, than these."

While he said these words in a leisurely, critical style, she continued to look at every one of us in regular succession as we sat. The moment he ceased, she looked at him again. "That'll do, Molly," said Mr. Jaggers, giving her a slight nod. "You have been admired, and can go."

She withdrew her hands and went out of the room, and Mr. Jaggers, putting the decanters on from his dumb-waiter, filled his glass and passed round the wine.

"At half-past nine, gentlemen," said he, "we must break up. Pray make the best use of your time. I am glad to see you all. Mr. Drummle, I drink to you."

If his object in singling out Drummle were to bring him out still more, it perfectly succeeded. In a sulky triumph, Drummle showed his morose depreciation of the rest of us, in a more and more offensive degree, until he became downright intolerable. Through all his stages, Mr. Jaggers followed him with the same strange interest. He actually seemed to serve as a zest to Mr. Jaggers's wine.

In our boyish want of discretion I dare say we took too much to drink, and I know we talked too much. We became particularly hot upon some boorish sneer of Drummle's, to the effect that we were too free with our hunting. It led to my remarking, with more zeal than discretion, that it came with a bad grace from him. He hunted regularly, and not just at full moon.

"Well," retorted Drummle, "there are too many deer in the forest. They would starve to death if not for me cutting their numbers down."

"I dare say," I went on, meaning to be very severe, "that you might one day encounter a weredeer that wants to eat you for a change."

We all laughed, except Drummle.

"A weredeer, the idea," said Drummle. "It wouldn't stand a chance against me if it existed at all."

"Come, Mr. Drummle, since we are on the subject, I'll wager you couldn't handle a wereotter if one came across you in the water, where you spend a good deal of your time with your boating skills." If ever there was an exercise in preventing a turn toward wolfishness, the evening had turned out to be one.

Drummle added in a low growl, that we might all go to the devil and shake ourselves. He began to laugh outright, in fact, and sat laughing in our faces with his hands in his pockets, likely to hide the growth of hair, and his hackles raised; plainly signifying that it was quite true, and that he despised us as asses all. Before our eyes, his nose began to take snout and his ears grew straight up to points.

Hereupon Startop took him in hand, though with a much better grace than I had shown, and exhorted him to mind his manners and be a little more agreeable. Startop being a lively, bright young fellow, and Drummle being the exact opposite, the latter was always disposed to resent him as a direct personal affront. He now exposed wolfish fangs and growled in a coarse warning, and Startop tried to turn the discussion aside with some small pleasantry that made us all laugh. Resenting this little success more than anything,

Drummle, without any threat or warning, pulled his furred paws out of his pockets, dropped down to all fours, barked ferociously, and would have pounced on Startop but for our entertainer's housekeeper making an appearance with her mighty hands wrapping right around Drummle's wolfish neck! She had come out of the kitchen so fast that she might have been a whirlwind. And her strength as she pinned Drummle to the floor, as if he were no more than a mewling kitten? Simply astonishing. As fast as she had subdued him, she let him go and ran back to the kitchen.

"Gentlemen," said Mr. Jaggers, deliberately putting down the glass, and hauling out his watch by its massive chain. "I am exceedingly sorry to announce that it's half-past nine."

On this hint we all rose to depart. Drummle gradually came back to himself, scared back to himself, I think it was. Before we got to the street door, Startop was cheerily calling Drummle "old boy," as if nothing had happened. But the old boy was so far from responding, that he would not even walk to Hammersmith on the same side of the way; so Herbert and I, who remained in town, saw them going down the street on opposite sides; Startop leading, and Drummle lagging behind in the shadow of the houses, much as he was wont to follow in his boat.

As the door was not yet shut, I thought I would leave Herbert there for a moment, and run up stairs again to say a word to my guardian. I found him in his dressing-room.

I told him I had come up again to say how sorry I was that anything disagreeable should have occurred, and that I hoped he would not blame me much.

"Pooh!" said he, sluicing his face, and speaking through the water-drops; "it's nothing, Pip. I like that Spider though."

He had turned towards me now, and was shaking his head, and blowing, and toweling himself.

"I am glad you like him, sir," said I—"but I don't."

"No, no," my guardian assented; "don't have too much to do

with him. Keep as clear of him as you can. But I like the fellow, Pip; he is one of the true sort. Why, if I was a fortune-teller—"

Looking out of the towel, he caught my eye.

"But I am not a fortune-teller," he said, letting his head drop into a festoon of towel, and toweling away at his two ears. "You know what I am, don't you? Goodnight, Pip."

"Goodnight, sir."

In about a month after that, the Spider's time with Mr. Pocket was up for good, and, to the great relief of all the house but Mrs. Pocket, he went home to the family hole.

CHAPTER 24

My dear Mr. Pip:—

I write this by request of Mr. Gargery, for to let you know that he is going to London in company with Mr. Wopsle and would be glad if agreeable to be allowed to see you. He would call at Barnard's Hotel Tuesday morning at nine o'clock, when if not agreeable please leave word. Your poor sister is much the same as when you left, perhaps displacing her limbs with more frequency and ever determined to roast or stew her best bonnet. We talk of you in the kitchen every night, and wonder what you are saying and doing. If now considered in the light of a liberty, excuse it for the love of poor old days. No more, dear Mr. Pip, from your ever obliged, and affectionate servant,

Biddy

P.S. He wishes me most particular to write *what larks*. He says you will understand. I hope and do not doubt it will be agreeable to see him, even though a gentleman, for you had ever a good heart, and he is a worthy, worthy man. I have read him all, excepting only the last little sentence, and he wishes me most particular to write again *what larks*.

I received this letter by the post on Monday morning, and therefore its appointment was for next day. Let me confess exactly with what feelings I looked forward to Joe's coming.

With considerable disturbance, some mortification, and a keen sense of incongruity, I met the prospect of a visit from Joe. My greatest reassurance was that he was coming to Barnard's Inn, not to Hammersmith, and consequently would not fall in Bentley Drummle's way. I had little objection to his being seen by Herbert or his father, for both of whom I had a respect; but I had the sharpest sensitiveness as to his being seen by Drummle, whom I held in contempt. So, throughout life, our worst weaknesses and meannesses are usually committed for the sake of the people whom we most despise.

I had begun to be always decorating the chambers in some quite unnecessary and inappropriate way or other. By this time, the rooms were vastly different from what I had found them. I had got on so fast of late, that I had even started a boy to act as footman, a Recommissioned, to my dread, as he did save on expenses for wages, food, and board. I got him from a bokor in town, a competitor of Pumblechook's, which did give me some satisfaction. I was astonished to find a Recommissioned of so young an age for sale, and I took pity on him, having no idea what might become of him on the streets. Even the Recommissioned must have some sort of awareness of their surroundings, I reasoned, after all.

I came into town on the Monday night to be ready for Joe, and I got up early in the morning, and caused the sitting room and breakfast table to assume their most splendid appearance. As the time approached I should have liked to run away, but presently I heard Joe on the staircase. I knew it was Joe by his clumsy manner of coming upstairs, and by the time it took him to read the names on the other floors in the course of his ascent. When at last he stopped outside our door, I could hear his finger tracing over the painted letters of my name, and I afterwards distinctly heard him breathing in at the keyhole. Finally he gave a faint single rap, and Pepper—such was the name of the footman—announced "Mr. Gargery" in his usual monotone.

I thought he never would have done wiping his feet, and that I must have gone out to lift him off the mat, but at last he came in.

"Joe, how are you, Joe?"

"Pip, how AIR you, Pip?"

With his good honest face all glowing and shining, and his hat put down on the floor between us, he caught both my hands and worked them straight up and down, as if I had been the last-patented pump.

"I am glad to see you, Joe. You look well. Give me your hat."

But Joe, taking it up carefully with both hands, like a bird's-nest with eggs in it, wouldn't hear of parting with that piece of property.

"Thank God," said Joe, "I'm well. And your sister, she's no worse than she were. And Biddy, she's ever right and ready. And all friends is no backerder, if not no forarder. 'Ceptin Wopsle; he's had a drop. He's left the Church and went into the playacting. Which the play-acting have likeways brought him to London along with me."

I took what Joe gave me, and found it to be the crumpled play-bill of a small metropolitan theatre, announcing the first appear-ance, in that very week, of "the celebrated Provincial Amateur of Roscian renown, whose unique performance in the highest tragic walk of our National Bard has lately occasioned so great a sensation in local dramatic circles."

"Were you at his performance, Joe?" I inquired.

"I were," said Joe, with emphasis and solemnity.

"Was there a great sensation?"

"Why," said Joe, "yes, there certainly were, partickler when he see the ghost."

Herbert entered the room, as I guessed from Joe's eyes widening as if he'd seen a ghost, and I presented Joe to Herbert, who held out his hand; but Joe backed from it, and held on to his hat.

"Your servant, sir," said Joe, "which I hope as you and Pip get your elths in this close spot? For the present may be a werry good inn, according to London opinions, and I believe its character do stand, but I wouldn't keep a pig in it myself—not in the case that I wished him to fatten wholesome and to eat with a meller flavor on him."

Having borne this flattering testimony to the merits of our dwelling-place, and having incidentally shown this tendency to call me "sir," Joe, being invited to sit down to table, looked all round the room for a suitable spot on which to deposit his hat, as if it were only on some very few rare substances in nature that it could find a resting place. Ultimately, he left it on an extreme corner of the chimney-piece, from which it ever afterwards fell off at intervals.

"Do you take tea, or coffee, Mr. Gargery?" asked Herbert, who always presided of a morning.

"Thankee, sir," said Joe, stiff from head to foot, "I'll take whichever is most agreeable to yourself."

"Say tea then," said Herbert, pouring it out. "When did you come to town, Mr. Gargery?"

"Were it yesterday afternoon?" said Joe, after coughing behind his hand, as if he had had time to catch the whooping-cough since he came. "No it were not. Yes it were. Yes. It were yesterday afternoon."

"Have you seen anything of London yet?"

"Why, yes, sir," said Joe, "me and Wopsle went off straight to look at the Blacking Ware'us. But we didn't find that it come up to its likeness in the red bills at the shop doors; which I meantersay," added Joe, in an explanatory manner, "as it is there drawd too architectooralooral."

I really believe Joe would have prolonged this word into a per-

fect chorus, but for his attention being providentially attracted by
his hat, which was toppling. Then he fell into such unaccountable
fits of meditation, with his fork midway between his plate and his
mouth. I was heartily glad when Herbert left us for the city.

I had neither the good sense nor the good feeling to know that
this was all my fault, and that if I had been easier with Joe, Joe
would have been easier with me. I felt impatient of him and out of
temper with him.

"Us two being now alone, sir,"—began Joe.

"Joe," I interrupted, pettishly, "how can you call me sir?"

Joe looked at me for a single instant with something faintly like
reproach. Utterly preposterous as his cravat was, and as his collars
were, I was conscious of a sort of dignity in the look.

"Us two being now alone," resumed Joe, "and me having the intentions and abilities to stay not many minutes more, I will now
conclude—leastways begin—to mention what have led to my
having had the present honor. I were at the Bargemen t'other night,
Pip;"—whenever he subsided into affection, he called me Pip,
and whenever he relapsed into politeness he called me sir; "when
there come up in his shay-cart, Pumblechook. And his word were,
'Joseph, Miss Havisham she wish to speak to you.'"

"Miss Havisham, Joe?"

"'She wish,' were Pumblechook's word, 'to speak to you.'" Joe sat
and rolled his eyes at the ceiling.

"Yes, Joe? Go on, please."

"Next day, sir," said Joe, looking at me as if I were a long way off,
"having cleaned myself, I go and I see Miss A."

"Miss A., Joe? Miss Havisham?"

"Which I say, sir," replied Joe, with an air of legal formality, as
if he were making his will, "Miss A., or otherways Havisham. Her
expression air then as follering: 'Mr. Gargery. You air in correspondence with Mr. Pip?' Having had a letter from you, I were able to
say 'I am.' (When I married your sister, sir, I said 'I will'; and when I
answered your friend, Pip, I said 'I am.') 'Would you tell him, then,'

said she, 'that which Estella has come home and would be glad to see him.'"

I felt my face fire up as I looked at Joe. I hope one remote cause of its firing may have been my consciousness that if I had known his errand, I should have given him more encouragement.

"Biddy," pursued Joe, "when I got home and asked her fur to write the message to you, a little hung back. Biddy says, 'I know he will be very glad to have it by word of mouth, it is holiday time, you want to see him, go!' I have now concluded, sir," said Joe, rising from his chair, "and, Pip, I wish you ever well and ever prospering to a greater and a greater height."

"But you are not going now, Joe?"

"Yes I am," said Joe.

"But you are coming back to dinner, Joe?"

"No I am not," said Joe.

Our eyes met, and he gave me his hand.

"Pip, dear old chap, life is made of ever so many partings welded together, as I may say. If there's been any fault at all today, it's mine. You and me is not two figures to be together in London; nor yet anywheres else but what is private, and beknown, and understood among friends. It ain't that I am proud, but that I want to be right, as you shall never see me no more in these clothes. I'm wrong in these clothes. I'm wrong out of the forge, the kitchen, or off th' meshes. You won't find half so much fault in me if you think of me in my forge dress, with my hammer in my hand, or even my pipe. You won't find half so much fault in me if, supposing as you should ever wish to see me, you come and put your head in at the forge window and see Joe the blacksmith, there, at the old anvil, in the old burnt apron, sticking to the old work. I'm awful dull, but I hope I've beat out something nigh the rights of this at last. And so GOD bless you, dear old Pip, old chap, GOD bless you!"

I had not been mistaken in my fancy that there was a simple dignity in him. The fashion of his dress could no more come in its way when he spoke these words than it could come in its way in

Heaven. He touched me gently on the forehead, and went out. As soon as I could recover myself sufficiently, I hurried out after him and looked for him in the neighbouring streets; but he was gone.

CHAPTER 25

I<small>T WAS CLEAR THAT</small> I must return to our town next day, and equally clear that I must stay at Joe's. But, when I had secured my box-place by tomorrow's coach, and had been down to Mr. Pocket's and back, I was not convinced on the last point, and began to invent reasons for putting up at the Blue Boar. I should be an inconvenience at Joe's. I was not expected, and my bed would not be ready. I should be too far from Miss Havisham's, and she was exacting and mightn't like it.

All other swindlers upon earth are nothing to the self-swindlers, and with such pretenses did I cheat myself. Having settled that I must go to the Blue Boar, I took my place at the afternoon coach.

At that time, it was customary to carry Scapegrace convicts down to the containment ship docks by stage-coach. As I had often heard of them in the capacity of outside passengers, and had more than once seen them on the high road dangling their silvered legs over the coach roof, I had no cause to be surprised when Herbert, meeting me in the yard, came up and told me there were two Scapegrace convicts going down with me.

They had a gaoler and a Recommissioned with them. The two convicts were handcuffed together, and had silver bands on their legs of a pattern that I knew well. They were werewolf, not vampire, or so I assumed from the look of them and the fact that they'd been out at midday.

They wore the dress that I likewise knew well. Their keeper had a brace of pistols, and the Recommissioned carried a thick-knobbed bludgeon under his arm. One was a taller and stouter man than the other, and appeared, as a matter of course, to have had allotted to him the smaller suit of clothes, but I knew his half-closed eye at one glance. There stood the man whom I had seen on the settle at the Three Jolly Bargemen on a Saturday night, and who had brought me down with his invisible gun!

It was easy to make sure that as yet he knew me no more than if he had never seen me in his life. He looked across at me, and his eye appraised my watch-chain, and then he incidentally spat and said something to the other convict, and they laughed with a clink of their coupling manacle, and looked at something else. The convicts hauled themselves up as well as they could, and the convict I had recognized sat behind me with his breath on the hair of my head, which was still preferable to me than sharing a seat with a Recommissioned dribbling green goo. The Recommissioned ended up in front with the driver.

"Goodbye, Lowell!" Herbert called out as we started. I thought what a blessed fortune it was that he had found another name for me than Pip.

It is impossible to express with what acuteness I felt the convict's breathing, not only on the back of my head, but all along my spine. He seemed to have more breathing business to do than another Scapegrace, and to make more noise in doing it.

The weather was miserably raw, and the two cursed the cold. It made us all lethargic before we had gone far, and when we had left the Halfway House behind, we habitually dozed and shivered and were silent. I dozed off, myself, in considering the question whether I ought to restore a couple of pounds sterling to this creature before losing sight of him, and how it could best be done.

I woke to wonder if I must have slept longer than I had thought, since, although I could recognize nothing in the darkness and the fitful lights and shadows of our lamps, I traced marsh country in the cold damp wind that blew at us. The very first words I heard the convicts interchange were the words of my own thought, "Two one pound notes."

"How did he get 'em?" said the convict I had never seen.

"How should I know?" returned the other. "He had 'em stowed away somehows. Give him by friends, I expect."

"I wish," said the other, with a bitter curse upon the cold, "that I had 'em here."

"Two one pound notes, or friends?"

"Two one pound notes. I'd eat all the friends I ever had. Well? So he says—?"

"So he says," resumed the convict I had recognized— "it was all said and done in half a minute, behind a pile of timber in the dock-yard—'You're a going to be discharged?' Yes, I was. Would I find out that boy that had fed him and kept his secret, and give him them two one pound notes? Yes, I would. And I did."

"More fool you," growled the other. "I'd have spent 'em on drink to wash down my prey. He must have been a green one. Mean to say he knowed nothing of you?"

"Not a ha'porth. Different gangs and different containment ships. He was tried again for breaking containment, and got made a Lifer."

"And was that—Honour!—the only time you worked out, in this part of the country?"

"The only time."

"What might have been your opinion of the place?"

"A most beastly place. Mudbank, mist, swamp, and work; work, swamp, mist, and mudbank. Good cattle for hunting, though. The swamp must make the meat more tender."

They both execrated the place in very strong language, and grad-ually growled themselves out, and had nothing left to say. After overhearing this dialogue, I should assuredly have got down and been left in the solitude and darkness of the highway, but for feel-ing certain that the man had no suspicion of my identity. Indeed, I was not only so changed in the course of nature, but so differently dressed and so differently circumstanced, that it was not at all likely he could have known me without accidental help. Still, the coincidence of our being together on the coach was sufficiently strange to fill me with a dread that some other coincidence might at any moment connect me, in his hearing, with my name.

For this reason, I resolved to alight as soon as we touched the town, and put myself out of his hearing. This device I executed successfully. My little portmanteau was in the boot under my feet; I had but to turn a hinge to get it out; I threw it down before me, got down after it, and was left at the first lamp on the first stones of the town pavement. As to the convicts, they went their way with the coach, and I knew at what point they would be spirited off to the river. In my fancy, I saw the boat with its Scapegrace crew waiting for them at the slime-washed stairs—again heard the gruff "Give way, you!" like an order to dogs—again saw the wicked Noah's Ark lying out on the black water.

I could not have said what I was afraid of, for my fear was altogether undefined and vague, but there was great fear upon me. As I walked on to the hotel, I felt that a dread, much exceeding the mere apprehension of a painful or disagreeable recognition, made me tremble. I am confident that it took no distinctness of shape, and that it was the revival for a few minutes of the terror of childhood.

The coffee-room at the Blue Boar was empty, and I had not only ordered my dinner there, but had sat down to it, before the waiter knew me. As soon as he had apologized for the remissness of his memory, he asked me if he should send Boots for Mr. Pumblechook?

"No," said I, "certainly not."

The waiter appeared surprised, and took the earliest opportunity of putting a dirty old copy of a local newspaper so directly in my way that I took it up and read this paragraph:

Our readers will learn, in reference to the recent romantic rise in fortune of a young artificer in silver of this neighbourhood, that the youth's earliest patron, companion, and friend was a highly respected individual not entirely unconnected with the recommissioned trade. It is not wholly irrespective of our personal feelings that we record HIM as the Mentor of our young Telemachus, for it is good to know that our town produced the founder of the latter's fortunes.

I entertain a conviction, based upon large experience, that if in the days of my prosperity I had gone to the North Pole, I should have met somebody there who would have told me that Pumblechook was my earliest patron and the founder of my fortunes.

CHAPTER 26

THOUGH UP AND DRESSED early, it was too early yet to go to Miss Havisham's. I passed some time walking around Miss Havisham's side of town, which was not Joe's side. I could go to Joe's tomorrow, thinking about my patroness, and painting brilliant pictures of her plans for me.

She had adopted Estella, and she had as good as adopted me. It could not fail to be her intention to bring us together. I chose not to embrace Herbert's theory that Miss Havisham was looking for a victim for Estella. If Miss Havisham was intent on destruction of vampires, she could choose no better match for Estella than a werewolf, albeit a reluctant one. Together, Estella and I could be a formidable force. Or, preferable to my way of thinking, we could settle down to a gentle life with my love overcoming Miss Havisham's influence of bitterness and suspicion.

Indeed, it followed that Miss Havisham reserved it for me to re-store the desolate house, admit the sunshine into the dark rooms, set the clocks a-going and the cold hearths a-blazing, tear down the cobwebs, destroy the vermin—in short, do all the shining deeds of the young knight of romance, and marry the princess. I had stopped to look at the house as I passed. Its seared red brick walls, blocked windows, and strong green ivy clasping even the stacks of chimneys with its twigs and tendons, as if with sinewy old arms, had made up a rich attractive mystery, of which I was the hero.

Estella was the inspiration of it, and the heart of it, of course. But, though she had taken such strong possession of me, though my fancy and my hope were so set upon her, though her influence on my boyish life and character had been all-powerful, I did not, even that romantic morning, invest her with any attributes save those she possessed.

I so shaped out my walk as to arrive at the gate at my old time. I rang the bell with an unsteady hand and turned my back upon the gate while I tried to get my breath and keep my beating heart mod-erately quiet. I heard the side-door open, and a voice beckoning me to enter, but no one came out through the courtyard to greet me. I followed the voice and went inside the dark corridor, but didn't see anyone at first.

Being at last touched on the shoulder, I started and turned. A candle appeared. I started much more naturally then, to find myself confronted by a man in a sober grey dress. The last man I should have expected to see in that place of porter at Miss Havisham's door.

"Orlick!"

"Ah, young master, it's opposed to my orders to hold the gate open. Do come with me."

I followed. "How did you end up here?"

"On my legs," he said, glancing back. The light of the candle added an increased malevolence to his sharp features. "I had my box brought alongside me in a barrow."

"Are you here for good?"

"I ain't here for harm, young master, I suppose?"

I was not so sure of that. I had leisure to entertain the retort in my mind, while he slowly lifted his heavy glance from the floor, up my legs and arms, to my face.

"Then you have left the forge?" I said.

"Do this look like a forge?" replied Orlick, sending his glance all round him with an air of injury. "Now, do it look like it?"

I asked him how long he had left Gargery's forge.

"One day is so like another here," he replied, "that I don't know without casting it up. However, I come here some time since you left."

"I could have told you that, Orlick."

"Ah!" said he, dryly. "But then you've got to be a scholar."

By this time we had come to the main part of the house, where I found his room to be one just within the side-door, with a little window that probably looked over the courtyard but was blocked in such a way as to keep out any light. A lamp added some illumination and I could see his whole space. In its small proportions, it was not unlike the kind of place usually assigned to a gate-porter. Certain keys were hanging on the wall, to which he now added the gate key; and his patchwork-covered bed was in a little inner division or recess. The whole had a slovenly, confined, and sleepy look, like a cage for a human dormouse. He loomed dark and heavy in the shadow of a corner and looked like the human dormouse, or the rat that he was.

"I never saw this room before," I said. "But there used to be no porter here."

"No," he said. "Not till it got about that there was no protection on the premises, and it come to be considered dangerous, with convicts and Tag and Rag and Bobtail going up and down. And then I was recommended to the place as a man who could give another man as good as he brought, and I took it. It's easier than bellowsing and hammering."

My eye had been caught by a gun with a silver-bound stock over the chimney-piece, and his eye had followed mine.

"Well," said I, not desirous of more conversation, "shall I go up to Miss Havisham?"

"Burn me, if I know!" He stretched himself and shook. "My orders ends here, young master. I give this here bell a rap with this here hammer, and you go on along the passage till you meet somebody."

"I am expected, I believe?"

"Burn me twice over if I can say!"

Upon that, I turned down the long passage and he made his bell sound. At the end of the passage, while the bell was still reverberating, I found Sarah Pocket.

"Oh!" she said. "You, is it, Mr. Pip?"

"It is, Miss Pocket. I am glad to tell you that Mr. Pocket and family are all well."

"Are they any wiser?" said Sarah, with a dismal shake of the head. "They had better be wiser than well. Ah, Matthew, Matthew! You know your way, sir?"

'I do." Her head had always reminded me of a walnut, and I understood why Miss Havisham fed on her. Sarah remained plump, though a little pale, and she gave off a smell of toasted nuts to match the shape of her head. I became hungry standing next to her and wondered, if circumstances were different, if I might eat her, too. Perhaps I should have filled my pockets with silver instead of simply relying on my watch chain to help keep me from becoming wolfish.

I ascended the staircase now and tapped in my old way at the door of Miss Havisham's room.

"Pip's rap," I heard her say, immediately. "Come in, Pip."

She was in her chair near the old table, in the old dress, with her two hands crossed on her stick, her chin resting on them, and her eyes on the fire. Sitting near her, with the white shoe, that had never been worn, in her hand, and her head bent as she looked at it, was an elegant lady whom I had never seen.

"Come in, Pip," Miss Havisham continued to mutter, without looking round or up. "Come in, Pip. How do you do, Pip?"

"I heard, Miss Havisham," I said, rather at a loss, "that you were so kind as to wish me to come and see you, and I came directly."

"Well?" she repeated.

The lady whom I had never seen before lifted her eyes and looked archly at me, and then I picked up a scent that was Estella's scent, and I saw that the eyes were Estella's eyes. She was so much changed, was so much more beautiful, so much more womanly, in all things winning admiration. In comparison, I felt as if I hadn't changed at all, same hairy hands and common stare.

She gave me her hand. I stammered something about the pleasure I felt in seeing her again, and about my having looked forward to it, for a long, long time.

"Do you find her much changed, Pip?" asked Miss Havisham, with her greedy look, and striking her stick upon a chair that stood between them, as a sign to me to sit.

"When I came in, Miss Havisham, I thought there was nothing of Estella in the face or figure; but now it all settles down so curiously into the old—"

"What? You are not going to say into the old Estella?" Miss Havisham interrupted. "She was proud and insulting, and you wanted to go away from her. Don't you remember?"

I couldn't possibly forget. "That was long ago," I said, with confusion as to how to proceed. "I didn't know better."

Estella smiled with perfect composure, and said she had no doubt of my having been quite right, and of her having been very disagreeable.

"Is *he* changed?" Miss Havisham asked her.

"Very much," said Estella, looking at me.

"Less hairy and common?" said Miss Havisham, playing with Estella's hair.

Estella laughed, and looked at the shoe in her hand, and laughed again, and looked at me, and put the shoe down. She treated me as a boy still, but she lured me on. I was not actually hairy, of that I was certain, though I'd been feeling very wolfish all of the sudden. As for presenting myself as a gentleman, I could only hope that my lessons had benefitted me.

We sat in the dreamy room among the old strange things, and I learnt that she had but just come home from China, where she learned quite a bit about weaponry, and that she had greatly improved her aim, as she proved with a round of target practice by way of demonstration. I just barely managed to dodge her knives, catching one or two, and had to duck behind the target board when she started tossing her Chinese throwing stars. Then she showed Miss Havisham and me some techniques she learned for meditating to get in touch with her Scapegrace-detecting senses. It seemed to me that she was simply sitting cross-legged on the carpet, but apparently, she was picking up on something called chi.

Next, she was going to London to study with a master of combat. It was settled that I should stay there all the rest of the day, and return to the hotel at night, and to London tomorrow. When we had conversed for a while, Miss Havisham sent us two out to walk in the neglected garden.

Estella and I went out by the gate through which I had strayed to my encounter with the furry young gentleman, now Herbert. I trembled in spirit and worshipped the very hem of her dress. She remained quite composed and most decidedly did not worship any bit of me.

"I must have been a singular little creature to hide and see the fight that day," she said at last, as we came upon the scene of my former altercation. "But I did, and I enjoyed it very much."

"You rewarded me very much."

"Did I?" she replied, in an incidental and forgetful way. "I remember I entertained a great objection to your adversary, because he had no real fight in him. Not like you. Still, it was exciting to see you both, all fur and fangs."

"He and I are great friends now." I thought she scorned were-

wolves, but I began to wonder if she preferred us as wolves to gentlemen the way her eyes shone with the memory.

"Are you? I think I recollect though that you studied with his
father?"

"Yes."

I made the admission with reluctance, for it seemed to have a
boyish look, and she already treated me more than enough like
a boy.

"Since your change of fortune and prospects, you have changed
your companions," said Estella.

"Naturally," said I.

"And necessarily," she added, in a haughty tone; "what was fit
company for you once, would be quite unfit company for you now."

In my conscience, I doubt very much whether I had any lingering intention left of going to see Joe; but if I had, this observation
put it to flight.

"You had no idea of your impending good fortune, in those
times?" said Estella, with a slight wave of her hand, signifying in
the fighting times.

"Not the least."

The air of completeness and superiority with which she walked
at my side, and the air of youthfulness and submission with which
I walked at hers, made a contrast that I strongly felt. It would have
rankled in me more than it did, if I had not regarded myself as elic-
iting it by being so set apart for her and assigned to her.

The garden was too overgrown and rank for walking in with
ease, and after we had made the round of it twice or thrice, we came
out again into the brewery yard. I showed her where I had seen her
walking on the casks, that first old day, and she said, with a cold and
careless look in that direction, "Did I?"

I reminded her where she had come out of the house and given
me my meat and drink, and she said, "I don't remember."

"Not remember that you made me cry?" said I.

"No," said she, and shook her head and looked about her. I

verily believe that her not remembering and not minding in the least, made me cry again, inwardly—and that is the sharpest crying of all.

"You must know," said Estella, condescending to me as a brilliant and beautiful woman might, "that I have no heart—if that has anything to do with my memory."

I got through some jargon to the effect that I took the liberty of doubting that. That I knew better. That there could be no such beauty without it.

"Oh! I have a heart to be stabbed in or shot in, I have no doubt," said Estella, "and of course if it ceased to beat I should cease to be. But you know what I mean. I have no softness there, no—sympathy—sentiment—nonsense. I've killed, you know, Pip."

"Vampires, you mean? You've killed vampires?" I knew Miss Havisham meant for Estella to destroy her kind, but I hoped she hadn't started on werewolves yet. It might change things between us.

"Only vampires, yes, so far. A stake to the heart, and poof. They practically vanish into air. It's what I'm meant to do. There's no place for emotion or sentimentality."

"But you must have a care, Estella. There's danger."

"I'm prepared to face the risks."

"I know. I've seen you fight. But what about—could you be in any trouble with the law? For murder?"

"Over Scapegraces?" She laughed slightly, then grew serious. "Vampires carry more threat, I grant you, than—"

"Than werewolves. I understand." No one took any notice or care of werewolves who might be hurt or killed. "But there are some powerful vampires."

"With important titles, I'm aware. Part of my training involves stealth and subterfuge, slipping away before arousing suspicion. They're awful, unnatural creatures. They must be stopped. I can stop them. Someone has to, and I can. I've been raised to it all these years. It is my sole focus, my only mission. That's what fills my heart, if anything does."

What was it that was borne in upon my mind when she stood still and looked attentively at me? Anything that I had seen in Miss Havisham? No. I looked again, and though she was still looking at me, the suggestion was gone.

What *was* it?

"I am serious," said Estella, not so much with a frown (for her brow was smooth) as with a darkening of her face. "If we are to be thrown much together, you had better believe it at once. No! I have not bestowed my tenderness anywhere. I have never had any such thing. Though, of course, I don't mind fighting with you for practise. We've had some good combat between us, have we not?"

"We have," I agreed, though I was ready for a different sort of closeness with Estella than a wrestling match. I hoped it was not her intention for our combat to go from practise to reality.

In another moment we were in the brewery, so long disused, and she pointed to the high gallery where I had seen her going out on that same first day, and told me she remembered to have been up there, and to have seen me standing scared below. As my eyes followed her white hand, again the same dim suggestion that I could not possibly grasp crossed me. My involuntary start occasioned her to lay her hand upon my arm. Instantly the ghost passed once more and was gone.

What *was* it?

"What is the matter?" asked Estella. "Are you scared again?"

"I should be, if I believed what you said just now," I replied, to turn it off.

"Then you don't? Very well. It is said, at any rate. Let us make one more round of the garden, and then go in. Come! We shall not practise our combat now. You shall be my page, and give me your shoulder."

Her handsome dress trailed upon the ground. She held it in one hand, and with the other lightly touched my shoulder as we walked. We walked round the ruined garden twice or thrice more, and it was all in bloom for me. If the green and yellow growth of weed in the chinks of the old wall had been the most precious flowers that ever blew, it could not have been more cherished in my remembrance.

There was no discrepancy of years between us to remove her far from me. We were of nearly the same age, though of course the age told for more in her case than in mine. Her beauty and her manner gave her an air of inaccessibility that tormented me in the midst of my delight, but I clung to the belief that our patroness meant for us to be together.

CHAPTER 27

UPON MY RETURN AT Barnard's Inn, I found Herbert dining on cold meat and delighted to welcome me back. Having dispatched the footman to the coffee-house for an addition to the dinner, I felt that I must open my breast that very evening to my friend.

Dinner done and we sitting with our feet upon the fender, I said to Herbert, "I have something very particular to tell you. It concerns myself and one other person."

Herbert crossed his feet, looked at the fire with his head on one side, and having looked at it in vain for some time, looked at me because I didn't go on.

"Herbert," said I, "I love—I adore—Estella."

Instead of being transfixed, Herbert replied in an easy matter-of-course way, "Exactly. Well. I know that. What next?"

"How do you know it? I never told you."

"Told me! You have never told me when you have got your hair cut, but I have had senses to perceive it. You have always adored her, ever since I have known you. You brought your adoration and your portmanteau here together."

"Very well, then," said I, to whom this was a new and not unwelcome light, "I have never left off adoring her. She has come back, a most beautiful and most elegant creature. I saw her yesterday. And if I adored her before, I now doubly adore her. You should see the way she handles her weapons."

"Lucky for you then, Lowell," said Herbert, "that you are still alive. Keep in mind her purpose and that those weapons could well be turned on you. Have you any idea yet, of Estella's views on the adoration question?"

I shook my head gloomily. "Oh! She is thousands of miles away from me."

"Caution, my dear Lowell. I have been thinking that Estella surely cannot be a condition of your inheritance if she was never referred to by your guardian. Am I right in so understanding what you have told me, as that he never referred to her, directly or indirectly, in any way? Never even hinted that your patron might have views as to your marriage ultimately?"

"Never."

"Yes; but my dear Lowell, think of her bringing-up, and think of Miss Havisham. Think of what she is herself. This may lead to miserable things. To your death!"

"I keep it under consideration." She was only getting more skilled, but so was I getting stronger. If she had meant to kill me, I thought she might have attempted it by now. Hope remained alive for our eventual union. Fortunately, Herbert saw fit to change the subject.

"May I ask you if you have ever had an opportunity of remarking, down in your part of the country, that the children of not exactly suitable marriages are always most particularly anxious to be married?"

This was such a singular question, that I asked him in return, "Is it so?"

"I don't know," said Herbert, "that's what I want to know. Because it is decidedly the case with us. My poor sister Charlotte, who was next me and died before she was fourteen, was a striking example. Little Jane is the same. In her desire to be matrimonially established, you might suppose her to have passed her short existence in the perpetual contemplation of domestic bliss. Little Alick in a frock has already made arrangements for his union with a suitable young person at Kew. And indeed, I think we are all engaged, except the baby."

"Then you are?" I'd had no idea.

"I am," said Herbert. "But it's a secret."

I assured him of my keeping the secret, and begged to be favoured with further particulars. "May I ask the name?"

"Name of Clara," said Herbert.

"Live in London?"

"Yes, perhaps I ought to mention," said Herbert, who had become curiously crestfallen and meek, since we entered on the interesting theme, "that she is rather below my mother's nonsensical family notions. Her father had to do with the victualling of passenger-ships. I think he was a species of purser. And, of course, a werewolf."

"What is he now?" said I.

"He's an invalid now," replied Herbert. "And still and more often a werewolf."

"Living on—?"

"On the first floor, quite well secured, for the drink sends him in and out of wolfishness," said Herbert. Which was not at all what I meant, for I had intended my question to apply to his means. "I have never seen him, for he has always kept his room since I have known Clara. But I have heard him constantly. He makes tremendous rows—roars, and scratches at the floor." In looking at me and then laughing heartily, Herbert for the time recovered his usual lively manner.

"Don't you expect to see him?" said I.

"Oh yes, I constantly expect to see him," returned Herbert, "because I never hear him, without expecting him to come tumbling through the ceiling. But I don't know how long the rafters may hold."

When he had once more laughed heartily, he became meek again, and told me that the moment he began to realize capital, it was his intention to marry this young lady. He added as a self-evident proposition, engendering low spirits, "But you can't marry, you know, while you're not in the right circumstances."

As we contemplated the fire, and as I thought what a difficult place Herbert was in, I put my hands in my pockets. A folded piece of paper in one of them attracting my attention, I opened it and found it to be the playbill I had received from Joe, relative to the celebrated provincial amateur of Roscian renown. "And bless my heart," I involuntarily added aloud, "it's tonight!"

This changed the subject in an instant, and made us hurriedly resolve to go to the play. So, when I had pledged myself to comfort and abet Herbert in the affair of his heart by all practicable and impracticable means, and when Herbert had told me that his affianced already knew me by reputation and that I should be presented to her, and when we had warmly shaken hands upon our mutual confidence, we blew out our candles, made up our fire, locked our door, and issued forth in quest of Mr. Wopsle and Denmark.

The play provided enough diversion to forget our troubles of an evening. Mr. Wopsle's appearance was often greeted by laughter when perhaps he should have been treated as a character of some gravity and contemplation. We had made some pale efforts in the beginning to applaud Mr. Wopsle, but they were too hopeless to be persisted in. Therefore we had sat, feeling keenly for him, but laughing, nevertheless, from ear to ear.

CHAPTER 28

ONE DAY WHEN I was busy with my books and Mr. Pocket, I received a note that sent me into quite a flutter. It read:

> I am to come to London the day after tomorrow by the midday coach. I believe it was settled you should meet me? At all events, Miss Havisham has that impression, and I write in obedience to it. She sends you her regard.
>
> Yours, ESTELLA

If there had been time, I should probably have ordered several suits of clothes for the occasion. My appetite doubled instantly, the craving to hunt fresh meat springing to the fore. I knew no peace or rest until the day arrived.

When the day arrived, I was worse than ever. I began haunting the coach-office in Wood Street, Cheapside, before the coach had even left the Blue Boar in our town. For all that I knew this perfectly well, I felt it unsafe to let the coach-office out of my sight longer than five minutes at a time. While prowling my watch, I ran into Wemmick.

"Halloa, Mr. Pip," he said. "How do you do? I should hardly have thought this was *your* beat."

I explained that I was waiting to meet somebody who was coming up by coach, and I enquired after the Castle and the Aged.

"Both flourishing thankye," said Wemmick. "However, this is not London talk. Where do you think I am going to?"

"To the office?" said I, for he was tending in that direction.

"Next thing to it," returned Wemmick. "I am going to Newgate. We are in a case just at present, and I have been down the road taking a squint at the scene of action, and thereupon must have a word or two with our client."

"Did your client commit the crime?" I asked.

"Bless your soul and body, no," answered Wemmick, very drily. "But he is accused of it. So might you or I be. Missing goats, blood at the scene. Either of us might be accused of it, you know."

"Only neither of us is," I remarked.

"Yah!" said Wemmick, touching me on the breast with his forefinger. "You're a deep one, Mr. Pip! Would you like to have a look at Newgate? Have you time to spare?"

I had so much time to spare that the proposal came as a relief, even if it did take me from the coach office. We were at Newgate in a few minutes, and we passed through the lodge where some silver fetters were hanging up on the bare walls among the prison rules, into the interior of the containment wing of the jail. It was visiting time when Wemmick took me in, and a potman was going his rounds with beer. The prisoners, behind bars, were buying beer, and talking to friends, and an ugly, disorderly, depressing scene it was.

It struck me that Wemmick walked among the Scapegrace prisoners much as a gardener might walk among his plants. "What, Captain Tom? Are you there? Ah, indeed!" he said. "Is that Black Bill? Why I didn't look for you these two months. How do you find yourself?"

The vampire convicts, few as they numbered, were resting in shadows to escape any light of day coming in through the few barred windows. It was the werewolves, some of them almost fully wolfish, who came to gnash teeth or put paws through the bars, though they were silver bars and chafed the skin. All of them were friendly toward Wemmick. He looked at them while in conference, as if he were taking particular notice of the advance they had made, since last observed, towards coming out in full blow at their trial.

He was highly popular, and I found that he took the familiar department of Mr. Jaggers's business; though something of the state of Mr. Jaggers hung about him, too, forbidding approach beyond certain limits. His personal recognition of each successive client was comprised in a nod, and in his settling his hat a little easier on his head with both hands, and putting his hands in his pockets.

Thus, we walked through Wemmick's greenhouse, until he turned to me and said, "Notice the man I shall shake hands with."

Almost as soon as he had spoken, a portly upright man in a well-worn olive-colored frock-coat, with a peculiar pallor, and eyes that went wandering about when he tried to fix them, came up to a corner of the bars, and put his hand to his hat, which had a greasy and fatty look. He raised his hairy hand in salute.

"How are you, Colonel?" Wemmick asked. Wemmick always maintained complete control over his wolfish instinct in such circumstances. I suppose he learned it from Jaggers. I felt a little wildness rising up in me with the beastliness of the surroundings, but I hummed a little to distract myself as Mr. Pocket had instructed me.

"All right, Mr. Wemmick," he responded.

"Everything was done that could be done, but the evidence was too strong for us, Colonel."

"Yes, it was too strong, sir, but I don't care."

"No, no," said Wemmick, coolly, "you don't care." Then, turning to me, "Served His Majesty, this man. Was a soldier in the line and bought his discharge."

I said, "Indeed? I didn't know a werewolf could serve as soldier."

The man's eyes looked at me, and then looked over my head, and then looked all round me, and then he drew his hand across his lips and laughed. I felt my hackles rise and hummed a little louder.

"I think I shall be out of this on Monday, sir," he said to Wemmick.

"Perhaps," returned my friend, "but there's no knowing."

"I am glad to have the chance of bidding you goodbye, Mr. Wemmick," said the man, stretching out his hand between two bars.

"Thankye," said Wemmick, shaking hands with him. "Same to you, Colonel." They shook hands again, and as we walked away Wemmick said to me, "A very good workman. The Recorder's report is made today, and he is sure to be executed on Monday."

Mr. Wemmick and I parted at the office in Little Britain, where suppliants for Mr. Jaggers's notice were lingering about as usual, and I returned to my watch in the street of the coach-office, with some three hours on hand. I consumed the whole time in thinking how strange it was that I should be encompassed by all this taint of containment prison; that, in my childhood out on our lonely marshes on a winter evening, I should have first encountered it; that, it should have reappeared on two occasions, starting out like a stain that was faded but not gone; that, it should in this new way pervade my fortune and advancement.

While my mind was thus engaged, I thought of the beautiful slayer Estella, proud and refined, coming towards me, and I thought with absolute abhorrence of the contrast between the contained Scapegraces and her. I wished that Wemmick had not met me, or that I had not yielded to him and gone with him, so that, of all days in the year on this day, I might not have had Newgate in my breath and on my clothes. So contaminated did I feel, remembering who was coming, that the coach came quickly after all, and I was not yet free from the soiling consciousness of Mr. Wemmick's conservatory, when I saw her face at the coach window and her hand waving to me.

What was the nameless shadow, which again in that one instant had passed?

CHAPTER 29

IN HER FURRED TRAVELLING dress, Estella seemed more delicately beautiful than she had ever seemed yet, even in my eyes. We stood in the inn yard while she pointed out her luggage to me, and when it was all collected I remembered—having forgotten everything but herself in the meanwhile—that I knew nothing of her destination.

"I am going to Richmond," she told me. "Our lesson is, that there are two Richmonds, one in Surrey and one in Yorkshire, and that mine is the Surrey Richmond. The distance is ten miles. I am to have a carriage, and you are to take me. This is my purse, and you are to pay my charges out of it. Oh, you must take the purse! We have no choice, you and I, but to obey our instructions. We are not free to follow our own devices, you and I."

As she looked at me in giving me the purse, I hoped there was an inner meaning in her words. She said them slightingly, but not with displeasure.

"A carriage will have to be sent for, Estella. Will you rest here a little?"

"Yes, I am to rest here a little, and I am to drink some tea, and you are to take care of me the while."

She drew her arm through mine, as if it must be done, and I requested a waiter who had been staring at the coach like a man who had never seen such a thing in his life, to show us a private sitting room. Upon that, he pulled out a napkin, and led us to the black hole of the establishment, fitted up with a diminishing mirror (quite a superfluous article, considering the hole's proportions), an anchovy sauce-cruet, and somebody's pattens. On my objecting to this retreat, he took us into another room with a dinner table for thirty.

"Some tea for the lady," I said and sent him out of the room.

I was, and I am, sensible that the air of this chamber, in its strong combination of stable with soup-stock, might have led one to infer that the coaching department was not doing well, and that the enterprising proprietor was boiling down the horses for the refreshment department. Yet the room was all in all to me, Estella being in it. I thought that with her I could have been happy there for life. (I was not at all happy there at the time, observe, and I knew it well.)

"Where are you going to, at Richmond?" I asked Estella.

"I am going to live," said she, "at a great expense, with a lady there who has the power to enhance my abilities."

"I suppose you will be glad of learning more?"

"Yes, I suppose so. How do you thrive with Mr. Pocket?"

"I live quite pleasantly there. At least—" It appeared to me that I was losing a chance.

"At least?" repeated Estella.

"As pleasantly as I could anywhere, away from you."

"You silly boy," said Estella, quite composedly, "how can you talk such nonsense? Your friend Mr. Matthew, I believe, is superior to the rest of his family?"

"Very superior indeed. He is nobody's enemy—"

"Don't add but his own," interposed Estella, "for I hate that class of man. But he really is disinterested, and above small jealousy and spite, I have heard?"

"I am sure I have every reason to say so."

"You have not every reason to say so of the rest of his people," said Estella, nodding at me with an expression of face that was at once grave and rallying, "for they beset Miss Havisham with reports and insinuations to your disadvantage. They watch you, misrepresent you, write letters about you (anonymous sometimes), and you are the torment and the occupation of their lives. You can scarcely realize to yourself the hatred those people feel for you."

"They do me no harm, I hope?"

"How could they think to change Miss Havisham's mind on anything? They thought they had only one wolf to contend with in Matthew, and him safely out of the way. That Miss Havisham could take a shine to another, and one not even of blood relation? They're determined to prove that a werewolf can't be a gentleman, and couldn't possibly earn favor at Satis House. But Miss Havisham has her reasons for everything, and has never set any store in their opinions. Only in their blood."

Estella burst out laughing. This was very singular to me, and I looked at her in considerable perplexity.

"I hope I may suppose that you would not be amused if they did me any harm," I said, in my diffident way with her.

"No, no you may be sure of that," said Estella. "You may be certain that I laugh because they fail. Oh, those people with Miss Havisham, and the tortures they undergo! They look for a meal ticket and instead have become the meal."

She laughed again, and even now when she had told me why, her laughter was very singular to me, for I could not doubt it being genuine, and yet it seemed too much for the occasion. I thought there must really be something more here than I knew. She saw the thought in my mind, and answered it.

"It is not easy for even you," said Estella, "to know what satisfaction it gives me to see those people thwarted, or what an enjoyable sense of the ridiculous I have when they are made ridiculous. For you were not brought up in that strange house from a mere baby. I was. You had not your little wits sharpened by their intriguing against you, suppressed and defenceless, under the mask of sympathy and pity and what not that is soft and soothing. I had. You did not gradually open your round childish eyes wider and wider to the discovery of that impostor of a woman who calculates her stores of peace of mind for when she wakes up in the night. I did."

It was no laughing matter with Estella now, nor was she summoning these remembrances from any shallow place. I would not have been the cause of that look of hers for all my expectations in a heap.

"Two things I can tell you," said Estella. "First, you may set your mind at rest that these people never will—never would, in a hundred years—impair your ground with Miss Havisham, in any particular, great or small. Second, I am beholden to you as the cause of their being so busy and so mean in vain, and there is my hand upon it."

As she gave it to me playfully, for her darker mood had been fleeting, I held it and put it to my lips.

"You ridiculous boy," said Estella, "will you never take warning? Or do you kiss my hand in the same spirit in which I once let you kiss my cheek?"

"What spirit was that?" said I.

"I must think a moment. A spirit of contempt for the fawners and plotters."

"If I say yes, may I kiss the cheek again?"

"You should have asked before you touched the hand. But, yes, if you like."

I leaned down, and her calm face was like a statue's.

"Now," said Estella, gliding away the instant I touched her cheek, "you are to take care that I have some tea, and you are to take me to Richmond."

Her reverting to this tone as if our association were forced upon us, and we were mere puppets, gave me pain; but everything in our intercourse did give me pain. Whatever her tone with me happened to be, I could put no trust in it, and build no hope on it; and yet I went on against trust and against hope. Why repeat it a thousand times? So it always was.

The bill paid, and the waiter remembered, and the ostler not forgotten, and the chambermaid taken into consideration, we got into our post-coach and drove away. Turning into Cheapside and rattling up Newgate Street, we were soon under the walls of which I was so ashamed.

"What place is that?" Estella asked me.

I made a foolish pretence of not at first recognizing it, and then told her. As she looked at it, and drew in her head again, murmuring, "Wretches!" I would not have confessed to my visit for any consideration.

"Mr. Jaggers," said I, by way of putting it neatly on somebody else, "has the reputation of being more in the secrets of that dismal place than any man in London."

"He is more in the secrets of every place, I think," said Estella, in a low voice. "You have been accustomed to see him often, I suppose?"

"I have been accustomed to see him at uncertain intervals, ever since I can remember. But I know him no better now, than I did before I could speak plainly. What is your own experience of him? Do you advance with him?"

"Once habituated to his distrustful manner," said I, "I have done very well."

"Are you intimate?" she asked.

"I have dined with him at his private house."

"I fancy," said Estella, shrinking, "that must be a curious place."

"It is a curious place."

We fell into other talk, and it was principally about the way by which we were travelling, and about what parts of London lay on this side of it, and what on that. The great city was almost new to her, she told me, for she had never left Miss Havisham's neighbourhood until she had gone to China, and she had merely passed through London then in going and returning. I asked her if my guardian had any charge of her while she remained here? To that she emphatically said, "God forbid!" and no more.

When we passed through Hammersmith, I showed her where Mr. Matthew Pocket lived, and said it was no great way from Richmond, and that I hoped I should see her sometimes.

"Oh yes, you are to see me. You are to come when you think

proper. You are to be mentioned to the family; indeed you are already mentioned."

I enquired was it a large household she was going to be a member of?

"No. There are only two, mother and daughter. The mother is a lady of some station, though not averse to increasing her income."

"I wonder Miss Havisham could part with you again so soon."

"It is a part of Miss Havisham's plans for me, Pip," said Estella, with a sigh, as if she were tired. "I am to write to her constantly and see her regularly and report how I go on."

We came to Richmond all too soon, and our destination there was a house by the green, a staid old house, where hoops and powder and patches, embroidered coats, rolled stockings, ruffles and swords had had their court days many a time.

A bell sounded gravely in the moonlight, and two maids came lumbering out to receive Estella. It soon became apparent that they were not regular maids, but Recommissioned. And, to my surprise, I learned what happened when you fed a Recommissioned, as Pumblechook had always warned against, for they surged straight for the driver and began to bite him, tearing him limb from limb as they devoured him. Blood spurted everywhere. I felt myself growing wolfish at the sight.

Estella confirmed my fears as she paused to remove her gloves. "Stand back, Pip. They've fed them. Meat would be my guess, for meat makes the Recommissioned most ravenous for human flesh. It's a test of my abilities, no doubt."

She raised up in a delicate position on her toes, one leg in the air, reminding me of a ballerina until she shrieked an ear-splitting sound, leapt, and kicked one of the Recommissioned away from the driver's body. The other maid, still down on all fours with her face in the driver's stomach, looked up, entrails dangling from between her teeth.

The kicked Recommissioned, evidently angered by Estella's actions, got to her feet again slowly, and began a charge at Estella. As the Recommissioned apparently move very sluggishly even while enraged, the charge took some time and Estella was able to attack the second Recommissioned, ripping her head straight from her body to send green goo and entrails all across the lawn, before re-engaging with the first.

I felt perhaps I should do something, but Estella did not need my help and I did not want to interfere with a test of her abilities. I soothed my wolfish instincts down and watched with growing fascination as Estella crouched, preparing to spring on her prey. She waited for several minutes for the Recommissioned to lurch closer. I might have taken out my watch and timed the approach, but I was too entranced in studying Estella in fighting form. Aside from her hair falling from her chignon, a flush on her cheeks, and a small splatter of green goo streaked across the bodice of her gown, she looked relatively unruffled and as lovely as ever.

Finally, she spun around in a pirouette and flew at her opponent, leg outstretched. She knocked the Recommissioned maid into a tree, raised her hand, and lopped off her head with one swift chopping motion.

"Well done," I said, nearly breathless.

She stepped back, brushed her hands, tucked a strand of hair behind her ear, and sighed. "Vampires are much cleaner to kill."

"How did you know what to do?" I mimicked her fatal chopping motion. "With your hands? To decapitate?"

"Oh, a little something I learned in China. Removing their heads, that's the way to end a Recommissioned."

I would not tell her that I was slightly more in awe of her after witnessing her physical display of power and finesse against actual opponents.

A well-dressed, ruddy-faced man that I took to be the butler, and he introduced himself as such, came out to help with Estella's bags.

"We've been eager for you to arrive," he said. "I can't tell you what a chore it was to keep the Recommissioneds occupied once we fed them raw liver. They devoured two of our best footmen and the kitchen cat."

"Oh dear," Estella said. "A shame about the driver, too. How will you get home, Pip?"

"I shall manage," I said. I had a wild side, and I had hunted innocent creatures, this is true. But I would never have a taste for human flesh, I knew beyond all doubt just looking at the poor driver sprawled out across the yard.

The doorway soon absorbed Estella's boxes, and she gave me her hand and a smile, and said goodnight, and was absorbed likewise. And still I stood looking at the house, thinking how happy I should be if I lived there with her, and knowing that I never was happy with her, but always miserable.

With a heavy heart, I began the long walk back to Hammersmith. My heartache only increased along the way. By the time I got to our own door, I thought I might die of aching need, but it turned out the moon was full and perhaps it was the pain of transformation adding to the pain in my heart, and I might bear it as usual after all.

Even if I had wanted to go to Mr. Pocket for advice, the house was all aflutter with Baby's first transformation coming on. Born wolf, Baby had stayed wolfish until the moon. Come morning, he would finally change to boy and resume his normal course of transformations, staying in his human infant form much of the time and changing back to wolf only under the full moon.

I didn't stay at home to be locked in that night, not that anyone remembered to check. I escaped into the wilderness. I ran. I hunted. I must have eaten something small and tasty for I woke with fresh blood on my chin in the morning and some bit of furred flesh, probably rabbit, lodged under my nails. My belly was full, but my heart ached more than ever. Fortunately, I had awoken close to our door, for my clothes had been abandoned I knew not where.

CHAPTER 30

As I HAD GROWN accustomed to my expectations, I disguised their influence on my character as much as possible; but I knew very well that it was not all good. I lived in a state of chronic uneasiness respecting my behavior to Joe. My conscience was not by any means comfortable about Biddy. When I woke up in the night, I used to think, with a weariness on my spirits, that I should have been happier and better if I had never seen Miss Havisham's face, and had risen to manhood content to be partners with Joe in the honest old forge. Many a time of an evening, when I sat alone looking at the fire, I thought, after all, there was no fire like the forge fire and the kitchen fire at home. But if the cost of having Biddy, Joe, and domestic happiness was never having known Estella, it was too great a sacrifice to bear.

Concerning my influence on Herbert, I feared I did him a great disservice and slowed down his progress toward achieving his capital. My lavish habits led his easy nature into expenses that he could not afford, corrupted the simplicity of his life, and disturbed his peace with anxieties and regrets. It often caused me a twinge to think that I had done him evil service in crowding his sparely furnished chambers with incongruous upholstery work, and placing the footman at his disposal.

Eventually, Herbert and I both began to contract a quantity of debt. At Startop's suggestion, we put ourselves down for election into a club called the Savages of the Timberland: the object of which institution I have never divined, if it were not that the members should dine expensively once a full moon (to sate the appetite and prevent hunting of wild creatures); to spar among themselves under the stars; and to cause six footmen to gather them up, with their shed clothing, the next morning. I know that these gratifying social ends were so invariably accomplished that Herbert and I understood nothing else to be referred to in the first standing toast of the society: which ran "Gentlemen, may the present promotion of good feeling ever reign predominant among the Savages of the Timberland."

The Savages spent their money foolishly (the hotel we dined at was in Covent Garden), and the first Savage I saw when I had the honour of joining the Timberland was Bentley Drummle. But here I anticipate a little, for I was not a Savage, and could not be, according to the sacred laws of the society, until I came of age.

In my confidence in my own resources, I would willingly have taken Herbert's expenses on myself; but Herbert was proud, and I could make no such proposal to him. He got into difficulties in every direction.

I was usually at Hammersmith about half the week, and when I was at Hammersmith I haunted Richmond, whereof separately by and by. Herbert would often come to Hammersmith when I was there. As I am now generalizing a period of my life with the object of clearing my way before me, I can scarcely do so better than by at once completing the description of our usual manners and customs at Barnard's Inn.

We spent as much money as we could, and got as little for it as people could make up their minds to give us. We were always more or less miserable, and most of our acquaintances were in the same condition. There was a jolly fiction among us that we were constantly enjoying ourselves, and a skeleton truth that we never did. To the best of my belief, our case was in the last aspect a rather common one.

If we had been less attached to one another, I think we must have hated one another regularly every morning. I detested the chambers beyond expression at that period of repentance, and could not endure the sight of the footman's livery.

One evening, we heard a letter dropped through the slit in the door, and fall on the ground.

"It's for you, Lowell," said Herbert, going out and coming back with it, "and I hope there is nothing the matter." This was in allusion to its heavy black seal and border.

The letter was signed TRABB & CO., and its contents were simply, that I was an honored sir, and that they begged to inform me that Mrs. J. Gargery had lost her head and finally departed us on Monday last at twenty minutes past six in the evening, and that my attendance was requested at the interment on Monday next at three o'clock in the afternoon.

CHAPTER 31

MRS. JOE WAS FINALLY gone. It could only have been a beheading, or so I knew now from experience, and I wondered how that had been managed. Had she put her own head in the oven along with the beaver bonnet and lopped it off with closing the door? I could only imagine until returning home for details.

I had never felt right about the recommissioning. The figure of my sister in her chair by the kitchen fire haunted me night and day. Still, I could not imagine that the place could possibly exist without her. I had now the strangest ideas that she was coming towards me in the street, groaning and dribbling green goo. Or that she would presently knock at the door. In my rooms, too, with which she had never been at all associated, there was at once the blankness of death and a perpetual suggestion of the sound of her voice or the turn of her face or figure, as if she were still alive and had been often there.

Whatever my fortunes might have been, I could scarcely have

recalled my sister with much tenderness. But I suppose there is a shock of regret that may exist without much tenderness. Under its influence (and perhaps to make up for the want of the softer feeling) I was seized with a violent indignation against the assailant from whom she had suffered so much. I felt that on sufficient proof I could have revengefully pursued Orlick, or any one else, to the last extremity.

Having written to Joe, to offer him consolation, and to assure him that I would come to the funeral, I passed the intermediate days in a curious state of mind. I went down early in the morning, and alighted at the Blue Boar in good time to walk over to the forge.

It was fine summer weather again, and, as I walked along, the times when I was a little helpless creature, and my sister did not spare me, vividly returned. But they returned with a gentle tone upon them that softened even the edge of Tickler. At last I came within sight of the house, and saw that Trabb & Co. had put in a funereal execution and taken possession. Two dismally absurd persons, each ostentatiously exhibiting a crutch done up in a black bandage, as if that instrument could possibly communicate any comfort to anybody, were posted at the front door. One of them showed me into the best parlour.

Poor dear Joe, entangled in a little black cloak tied in a large bow under his chin, was seated apart at the upper end of the room; where, as chief mourner, he had evidently been stationed by Trabb. When I bent down and said to him, "Dear Joe, how are you?" he said, "Pip, old chap, you knowed her when she were a fine figure of a—" and clasped my hand and said no more.

Biddy, looking very neat and modest in her black dress, went quietly here and there, and was very helpful. When I had spoken briefly to Biddy, as I thought it not a time for talking, I went and sat down near Joe, and there began to wonder in what part of the house it—she—my sister—was. The air of the parlour being faint with the smell of sweet-cake, I looked about for the table of refreshments.

It was scarcely visible until one had got accustomed to the gloom, but there was a cut-up plum cake upon it, and there were cut-up oranges, and sandwiches, and biscuits, and two decanters that I knew very well as ornaments, but had never seen used in all my life; one full of port, and one of sherry.

Standing at this table, I became conscious of the servile Pumblechook in a black cloak and several yards of hatband, who was alternately stuffing himself, and making obsequious movements to catch my attention. The moment he succeeded, he came over to me (breathing sherry and crumbs), and said in a subdued voice, "May I, dear sir?" and did. Mr. and Mrs. Hubble joined us next. We were all going to "follow," and were all in course of being tied up separately (by Trabb) into ridiculous bundles.

"Pocket-handkerchiefs out, all!" cried Mr. Trabb at this point, in a depressed business-like voice. "Pocket-handkerchiefs out! We are ready!"

So we all put our pocket-handkerchiefs to our faces, as if our noses were bleeding, and filed out two and two; Joe and I; Biddy and Pumblechook; Mr. and Mrs. Hubble. The remains of my poor sister had been brought round by the kitchen door, and, it being a point of undertaking ceremony that the six bearers must be stifled and blinded under a horrible black velvet housing with a white border, the whole looked like a blind monster with twelve human legs, shuffling and blundering along.

The neighbourhood, however, highly approved of these arrangements, and we were much admired as we went through the village. And now the range of marshes lay clear before us, with the sails of the ships on the river growing out of it; and we went into the churchyard, close to the graves of my unknown parents, Philip Pirrip, late of this parish, and Also Georgiana, Wife of the Above. And there my sister was laid quietly in the earth, while the larks sang high above it, and the light wind strewed it with beautiful shadows of clouds and trees. It was, at last, as it should be for my sister in death.

When our fellow mourners were all gone, and when Trabb and his men had crammed their mummery into bags, and were gone, too, the house felt wholesomer. Soon afterwards, Biddy, Joe, and I had a cold dinner together in the best parlour, not in the old kitchen, and there was great restraint upon us. But after dinner, when I made Joe take his pipe, and when I had loitered with him about the forge, and when we sat down together on the great block of stone outside it, we got on better. I noticed that after the funeral Joe changed his clothes so far as to make a compromise between his Sunday dress and working dress; in which the dear fellow looked natural, and like the man he was.

He was very much pleased by my asking if I might sleep in my own little room, and I was pleased, too; for I felt that I had done rather a great thing in making the request. When the shadows of evening were closing in, I took an opportunity of getting into the garden with Biddy for a little talk.

"Biddy," said I, "I think you might have written to me about these sad matters."

"Do you, Mr. Pip?" said Biddy. "I should have written if I had thought that."

"Don't suppose that I mean to be unkind, Biddy, when I say I consider that you ought to have thought that."

"Do you, Mr. Pip?"

She was so quiet, and had such an orderly, good, and pretty way with her, that I did not like the thought of making her cry again. After looking a little at her downcast eyes as she walked beside me, I gave up that point.

"I suppose it will be difficult for you to remain here now, Biddy dear?"

"Oh! I can't do so, Mr. Pip," said Biddy, in a tone of regret but still of quiet conviction. "I have been speaking to Mrs. Hubble, and I am going to her tomorrow. I hope we shall be able to take some care of Mr. Gargery, together, until he settles down."

"How are you going to live, Biddy? If you want any mo—"

"How am I going to live?" repeated Biddy, striking in, with a momentary flush upon her face. "I'll tell you, Mr. Pip. I am going to try to get the place of mistress in the new school nearly finished here. I can be well recommended by all the neighbours, and I hope I can be industrious and patient, and teach myself while I teach others. You know, Mr. Pip," pursued Biddy, with a smile, as she raised her eyes to my face, "the new schools are not like the old, but I learnt a good deal from you after that time, and have had time since then to improve."

"I think you would always improve, Biddy, under any circumstances."

"Ah! Except in my bad side of human nature," murmured Biddy.

It was not so much a reproach as an irresistible thinking aloud. Well! I thought I would give up that point, too. So, I walked a little further with Biddy, looking silently at her downcast eyes.

"I have not heard the particulars of my sister's end, Biddy."

"I had a hand in it, I hate to confess. I left her alone in the kitchen for some minutes to tend something for Mr. Gargery in the forge. When I came back, she had eaten most of the kidney for the pie, and she seemed in a foul temper indeed. I almost thought that none of the sad events of her recent past had happened and she was as blustery on a rampage as she had ever been. She came after me with a pointed stick—"

"Tickler," I interrupted, nodding.

"Tickler," Biddy agreed. "I tried to take it from her, but she was so strong. She got hold of my hand and I thought she was going to bite my fingers like sausages. I managed to pull away—my hands were slippery, still covered in butter from rolling out the paste—and run to the safety of the chimney. I screamed until Mr. Gargery came running, but she proved too strong for even Mr. Gargery, I fear. He did manage to wrest Tickler from her hands and toss it away across the floor, but she wrestled him to the ground and began to bite his neck. He said he wasn't going to fight her, as he was never one to fight her, you know."

"All too well, Biddy." Dear gentle Joe! I thought of the poor carriage driver at the mercy of the two Recommissioned maids.

"She broke the skin, close to his ear. I thought she was going to eat him! I really thought she was, or I never would have—" she choked off in a sob.

"I don't blame you, Biddy." I had seen what the Recommissioned could do in a hunger for human flesh. "Go on."

"While she chewed on Mr. Gargery, she did not notice me climbing out of my hiding space and retrieving Tickler. I picked it up and whacked her, Mr. Pip! I whacked her good and hard, and when once was not enough, I whacked her twice, three times. I whacked her head clean off. That vile green goo flew everywhere. Pardon, Mr. Pip, but it was such a sight. And Mr. Gargery was bleeding. I had no time to fetch her head and see if it would reattach because I had to tend to Mr. Gargery's wounds. I stitched his ear back on myself. Not the least bit crooked, did you notice? It's healing nicely." She beamed with pride.

I lied and said that I had noticed it was on quite straight, when I hadn't really noticed anything about Joe's ear at all.

"Afterwards, I could not get Mrs. Gargery's head back on, though I tried. I did. It was simply too late, I fear. She was gone from us for good."

Biddy cried; the darkening garden, and the lane, and the stars that were coming out, were blurred in my own sight.

"You did the right thing, Biddy," I assured her. "She would have eaten you both. You were very brave. You saved Joe's life, your own as well, and who knows how many others."

"Do you think so, Mr. Pip?" She brightened a little, wiping the tears away with the corner of her apron.

"I know so. Nothing was ever discovered, Biddy, about the attack?"

"Nothing."

"Do you know what is become of Orlick?" I had asked Jaggers to remove him from Miss Havisham's employ, but had feared he would return to the barge.

"I should think from the color of his clothes that he is working in the quarries."

"Of course you have seen him then? Why are you looking at that dark tree in the lane?"

"I saw him there, on the fatal night."

"That was not the last time either, Biddy?"

"No; I have seen him there, since we have been walking here. It is of no use," said Biddy, laying her hand upon my arm, as I was for running out, "you know I would not deceive you. He was not there a minute, and then he was gone."

It revived my utmost indignation, and my fiercest animal instincts, to find that she was still pursued by this fellow. I told her so, and told her that I would spend any money or take any pains to drive him out of that country. She turned our talk to Joe and how he never complained of anything. I knew that she meant to say, of me.

"Indeed, it would be hard to say too much for him," I said. "And, Biddy, we must often speak of these things, for of course I shall be often down here now. I am not going to leave poor Joe alone. Not to mention your calling me Mr. Pip—which appears to me to be in bad taste, Biddy—what do you mean?"

"What do I mean?" asked Biddy, timidly.

"Now, don't echo," I retorted. "You used not to echo, Biddy."

"Used not!" said Biddy. "Oh, Mr. Pip! Used!"

Well! I rather thought I would give up that point, too. After another silent turn in the garden, I fell back on the main position.

"Biddy, I made a remark respecting my coming down here often, to see Joe, which you received with a marked silence. Have the goodness, Biddy, to tell me why."

"Are you quite sure, then, that you WILL come to see him

often?" asked Biddy, stopping in the narrow garden walk, and look-ing at me under the stars with a clear and honest eye.

"Oh dear me!" said I, as if I found myself compelled to give up Biddy in despair. "This really is a very bad side of human nature! Don't say any more, if you please, Biddy. This shocks me very much."

I kept Biddy at a distance during supper, and when I went up to my own old little room, took as stately a leave of her as I could. As often as I was restless in the night, and that was every quarter of an hour, I reflected what an unkindness, what an injury, what an injus-tice, Biddy had done me.

Early in the morning I was to go. Early in the morning I was out, and looking in, unseen, at one of the wooden windows of the forge. There I stood, for minutes, looking at Joe, already at work with a glow of health and strength upon his face that made it show as if the bright sun of the life in store for him were shin-ing on it.

"Goodbye, dear Joe!—No, don't wipe it off—for God's sake, give me your blackened hand!—I shall be down soon and often."

"Never too soon, sir," said Joe, "and never too often, Pip!"

Biddy was waiting for me at the kitchen door with a mug of new milk and a crust of bread.

"Biddy," I said. "I am not angry, but I am hurt."

"No, don't be hurt," she pleaded quite pathetically; "let only me be hurt, if I have been ungenerous."

Once more, the mists were rising as I walked away. If they dis-closed to me, as I suspect they did, that I should not come back, and that Biddy was quite right, all I can say is—they were quite right, too.

CHAPTER 32

As THE MONTHS PASSED, Herbert and I went on from bad to worse in the way of increasing our debts. I came of age before I knew where I was, true to Herbert's earlier prediction.

Herbert himself had come of age eight months before me but as he had no expectations, we hadn't much of a celebration at Barnard's Inn. Instead, we had looked forward to my one-and-twentieth birthday with much speculation, for we had both considered that my guardian could hardly help saying something definite on that occasion.

I took adequate liberties to make the date of my birth widely known. On the day before it, I received an official note from Wemmick informing me that Mr. Jaggers would be glad if I would call upon him at five in the afternoon of the auspicious day. This convinced us that something great was to happen, and threw me into an unusual flutter when I repaired to my guardian's office, a model of punctuality.

In the outer office, Wemmick offered me his congratulations and motioned me with a nod into my guardian's room. It was November, and my guardian was standing before his fire leaning his back against the chimneypiece with his hands under his coattails.

"Well, Pip," he said, "I must call you Mr. Pip today. Congratulations, Mr. Pip. Take a chair, Mr. Pip."

We shook hands and I thanked him. As I sat down, I felt at a disadvantage, which reminded me of that old time when I had been rolled over, tender belly exposed, in the chuchyard.

"Now my young friend," my guardian began, as if I were a witness in the box, "I am going to have a word or two with you."

"If you please, sir."

Mr. Jaggers bent forward to look at the ground, and then threw his head back to look at the ceiling. "Have you anything to ask me?"

"Of course it would be a great relief to me to ask you several questions, sir; but I remember your prohibition. Is my benefactor to be made known to me today?"

"No. Ask another."

I looked about me, but there appeared to be now no possible escape from the inquiry. "Have—I—anything to receive, sir?"

"I thought we should come to it!" Mr. Jaggers crowed triumphantly and called to Wemmick to give him a certain piece of paper. Wemmick appeared, handed it in, and disappeared. "Now, Mr. Pip. Attend, if you please. You have been drawing pretty freely here. Your name occurs pretty often in Wemmick's cash-book; but you are in debt, of course?"

"Yes, sir."

"Now, take this piece of paper in your hand. You have got it? Very good. Now, unfold it and tell me what it is."

"This is a bank-note," I said, looking. "For five hundred pounds."

"And a very handsome sum of money, too, I think. You consider it so?" Mr. Jaggers nodded.

"Undoubtedly."

"Now, that handsome sum of money, Pip, is your own. It is a present to you on this day, in earnest of your expectations. And at the rate of that handsome sum of money per annum, and at no higher rate, you are to live until the donor of the whole appears. That is to say, you will now take your money affairs entirely into your own hands, and you will draw from Wemmick one hundred and twenty-five pounds per quarter, until you are in communication with the benefactor, and no longer with the mere agent. I execute my instructions, and I am paid for doing so. I think them injudicious, but I am not paid for giving any opinion on their merits."

I was beginning to express my gratitude to my benefactor for the great liberality with which I was treated, when Mr. Jaggers stopped me. "I am not paid, Pip, to carry your words to any one."

"There was a question just now, Mr. Jaggers, which you desired me to waive for a moment. I hope I am doing nothing wrong in asking it again?"

"What is it?" said he.

"Is it likely," I said, after hesitating, "that my patron, the benefactor you have spoken of, Mr. Jaggers, will soon come to London," said I, after casting about for a precise form of words, "or summon me anywhere else?"

"Now, here," replied Mr. Jaggers, fixing me for the first time with his dark deep-set eyes, "we must revert to the evening when we first encountered one another in your village. What did I tell you then, Pip?"

"You told me, Mr. Jaggers, that it might be years hence when that person appeared."

"Just so," said Mr. Jaggers, "that's my answer."

As we looked full at one another, I felt my breath come quicker in my strong desire to get something out of him.

"Do you suppose it will still be years hence, Mr. Jaggers?"

"Come!" Mr. Jaggers shook his head. "I'll be plain with you, my friend Pip. That's a question I must not be asked. When that person discloses, you and that person will settle your own affairs. When that person discloses, my part in this business will cease and determine. When that person discloses, it will not be necessary for me to know anything about it. And that's all I have got to say."

We looked at one another until I withdrew my eyes, and looked thoughtfully at the floor. From this last speech I derived the notion that Miss Havisham, for some reason or no reason, had not taken him into her confidence as to her designing me for Estella.

"If that is all you have to say, sir," I remarked, "there can be nothing left for me to say."

I thought to ask Wemmick if he could help me with something I had in mind to assist Herbert with his own prospects, but I deemed it best to see him outside the office, at his home in Walworth, and saved my enquiry for another day.

CHAPTER 33

———

I DEVOTED THE ENSUING SUNDAY afternoon to a pilgrimage to Mr. Wemmick's Castle. On arriving before the battlements, I found the Union Jack flying and the drawbridge up. Undeterred by this show of defiance and resistance, I rang at the gate, and was admitted by the Aged.

"My son, sir, rather had it in his mind that you might happen to drop in, and he left word that he would soon be home from his afternoon's walk. He is very regular in his walks, is my son," the old man said, after securing the drawbridge.

I nodded at the old gentleman as Wemmick himself might have nodded, and we went in and sat down by the fireside.

"You made acquaintance with my son, sir," the old man said, in his chirping way, while he warmed his hands at the blaze, "at his office, I expect?"

I nodded.

I was startled by a sudden click in the wall on one side of the chimney, and the ghostly tumbling open of a little wooden flap with JOHN upon it. The old man, following my eyes, cried with great triumph, "My son's come home!" and we both went out to the drawbridge.

It was worth any money to see Wemmick waving a salute to me from the other side of the moat, when we might have shaken hands across it with the greatest ease. The Aged was so delighted to work the drawbridge that I made no offer to assist him, but stood quiet until Wemmick had come across, and had presented me to Miss Skiffins; a lady by whom he was accompanied. He made the introductions with the lady still on the other side of the moat, however, for she did not cross the drawbridge with him.

"Is Miss Skiffins not to come in?" I asked, as we turned to enter, only to find her opening the door to greet us. "But how—are there two Miss Skiffins?" I looked back across the moat, but she was gone.

"Isn't she bewitching?" Wemmick winked. Miss Skiffins smiled.

"I—oh. Yes. Yes indeed." I had heard of witches, but to my knowledge had never made the acquaintance of one.

Miss Skiffins did not look as I expected a witch to look from the common lore. She had a pleasant appearance, if a little stiff, with auburn hair, a straight nose, and a smooth complexion, no carbuncles or warts to be seen. She might have been some two or three years younger than Wemmick. The cut of her dress from the waist upward, both before and behind, made her figure very like a boy's kite, and was a little too decidedly orange, and her gloves a little too intensely green. But she seemed to be a good sort, and showed a high regard for the Aged.

I was not long in discovering that she was a frequent visitor at the Castle; for, on our going in, and my complimenting Wemmick on his ingenious contrivance for announcing himself to the Aged, he begged me to give my attention for a moment to the other side of the chimney, and disappeared along with Miss Skiffins—poof into thin air.

Presently another click came, and another little door tumbled open with MISS SKIFFINS on it; and she popped back into the room. Then Miss Skiffins shut and she was gone and John tumbled open; then John popped back into the room. Miss Skiffins and John both tumbled open together, and finally shut together, and they both popped back into the room.

I expressed the great admiration with which I regarded them, and he said, "Well, you know, they're both pleasant and useful to the Aged. And by George, sir, it's a thing worth mentioning, that of all the people who come to this gate, the secret of those pulls is only known to the Aged, Miss Skiffins, and me!"

"And Mr. Wemmick made them," added Miss Skiffins, with apparent admiration, "with his own hands out of his own head, no magic necessary."

"With the exception of poofing us in and out of the room," Wemmick added, "which was all the darling Miss Skiffins's doing."

"It helps the demonstration run more smoothly," she acknowledged, with a wink and a nod that took her bonnet off her head and sent it floating across the room to a peg on the wall as if by magic. Quite certainly by magic. She retained her green gloves during the evening as an outward and visible sign that there was company.

Wemmick invited me to take a walk with him round the property, and see how the island looked in wintertime. Thinking that he did this to give me an opportunity of asking him his opinion on a matter, I seized the opportunity as soon as we were out of the Castle.

Having thought of the matter with care, I approached my subject. I informed Wemmick that I was anxious on behalf of Herbert Pocket, and I told him how we had first met, and how we had fought. I glanced at Herbert's home, and at his character, and at his having no means but such as he was dependent on his father for; those, uncertain and unpunctual. I alluded to the advantages I had derived in my first rawness and ignorance from his society, and I confessed that I feared I had but ill repaid them, and that he might have done better without me and my expectations.

For all these reasons (I told Wemmick), and because he was my young companion and friend, and I had a great affection for him, I wished my own good fortune to reflect some rays upon him, and therefore I sought advice from Wemmick's experience and knowledge of men and affairs, how I could best try with my resources to help Herbert to some present income—say of a hundred a year, to keep him in good hope and heart—and gradually to buy him on to some small partnership. I begged Wemmick, in conclusion, to understand that my help must always be rendered without Herbert's knowledge or suspicion, and that there was no one else in the world with whom I could advise.

Wemmick was silent for a little while, and then said with a kind of start, "Well you know, Mr. Pip, I must tell you one thing. This is devilish good of you."

"Say you'll help me to be good then," said I.

"That's not my trade." Wemmick shook his head.

"Nor is this your trading-place," I said.

"You are right," he returned. "You hit the nail on the head. Mr. Pip, I'll put on my considering-cap, and I think all you want to do may be done by degrees. Skiffins (that's her brother) is an accomplished wizard. I'll see if he can conjure something up and go to work for you."

"I thank you ten thousand times."

"On the contrary," said he, "I thank you, for though we are strictly in our private and personal capacity, still it may be mentioned that there *are* Newgate cobwebs about, and it brushes them away."

After a little further conversation to the same effect, we returned into the Castle where we found Miss Skiffins preparing tea the more conventional way, without magic.

"It tastes better," she explained, "when you put in the physical effort."

The responsible duty of making the toast was delegated to the Aged, and that excellent old gentleman was so intent upon it that he seemed to me in some danger of melting his eyes. Miss Skiffins brewed such a jorum of tea that the pig in the back premises became strongly excited, and repeatedly expressed his desire to participate in the entertainment.

We ate the whole of the toast, and drank tea in proportion. After a short pause of repose, Miss Skiffins washed up the tea things by simply waving her hands around and commanding the dishes to meet water, soap, water again for a rinse, and the towel to dry. Once cleaned and dried, the dishes flew like little birds through the air to nest back in the proper place. Then, Miss Skiffins put on her gloves again, and we drew round the fire, and Wemmick said, "Now, Aged Parent, tip us the paper."

Wemmick explained to me while the Aged got his spectacles out, that this was according to custom, and that it gave the old gentleman infinite satisfaction to read the news aloud. At last, the Aged read himself into a light slumber. Of course I knew better than to offer to see Miss Skiffins home, as she had the ability to magically transport, and under the circumstances I thought I had best go first; which I did, taking a cordial leave of the Aged, and having passed a pleasant evening.

Before a week was out, I received a note from Wemmick, dated Walworth, stating that he hoped he had made some advance in that matter appertaining to our private and personal capacities, and that he would be glad if I could come and see him again upon it. So, I went out to Walworth again, and yet again, and yet again, and I saw him by appointment in the City several times.

The upshot was that we found a worthy young wizard who wanted intelligent help, wanted capital, and in due course of time and receipt would want a partner in establishing an office of representation for wizards and witches in other parts of the world, where they were still considered suspect and often burned at the stake. He was not averse to adding werewolves to his course, as they were also widely misunderstood. It was exactly what Herbert wanted, and I wondered what amount of witchcraft had been involved to bring this perfect opportunity into my sphere.

Between the wizard and me, secret articles were signed of which Herbert was the subject, and I paid him half of my five hundred pounds down, and engaged for sundry other payments: some, to fall due at certain dates out of my income: some, contingent on my coming into my property. Miss Skiffins's brother conducted the negotiation. Wemmick pervaded it throughout, but never appeared in it.

The whole business was so cleverly, or magically, managed that Herbert had not the least suspicion of my hand being in it. I never shall forget the radiant face with which he came home one afternoon, and told me, as a mighty piece of news, of his having fallen in with one Clavenger (the young wizard's name), and of Clavenger having shown an extraordinary inclination towards him, and of his belief that the opening had come at last. At length, the thing being done, and he having that day entered Clavenger's House, and he having talked to me for a whole evening in a flush of pleasure and success, I did really cry in good earnest when I went to bed, to think that my expectations had done some good to somebody.

A great event in my life, the turning point of my life, now opens on my view. But, before I proceed to narrate it, and before I pass on to all the changes it involved, I must give one chapter to Estella. It is not much to give to the theme that so long filled my heart.

CHAPTER 34

I HAUNTED THE GROUNDS OF the old house near the green at Richmond enough that one might think me a ghost. Sometimes, under a full moon, I prowled there and woke next morning to find myself naked behind a row of shrubbery. After some difficulty with finding clothes to get home on the first occasion, I'd learned to stash a suit nearby so as to spare myself any potential for future embarrassment.

More than embarrassment, I risked my life to be there, for they were in the habit of practicing combat in the yard with the intent of training to kill Scapegraces. I had witnessed Estella tangling with a vampire first hand. It must have been another of her lessons, for he was brought in a box and let loose, very perturbed by the relocation, in front of her. He put up a decent fight and tried to bite her several times, but she wrestled him to the ground, as she had occasionally managed with me in our pretend combat, and staked him through the heart, dead center. He disappeared in an ashy poof. I nearly cried out in my surprise. Had they known that I lurked but a short distance away, watching, Estella might have had another victim and quite the lesson learned.

The lady with whom Estella was placed, Mrs. Brandley by name, was a widow and a student, now a teacher, of the martial arts. She had one daughter several years older than Estella who had more interest in books than training. The mother looked young, and the daughter looked old. The mother's complexion was pink and lively, especially after turning cartwheels whilst brandishing silver swords in the courtyard. The daughter's complexion had a yellow and withered cast. The mother clearly enjoyed her work, laughing merrily after Estella performed a particularly pretty pirouette, with a dagger in her teeth, which she would then throw straight to the target in a nearby tree. Sometimes I shuddered to see her accuracy. The daughter never laughed, but often offered philosophical statements on why one must not kill fellow creatures for sport.

"We're not out for sport," her mother would answer. "We're out to rid the world of vermin."

Upon hearing, my blood would run cold. Vermin? For certain, she did not mean werewolves, then, for we were *predators* of vermin.

Despite the seemingly unladylike activity of making combat in the yard, they were in what is called a good position, and visited, and were visited by, numbers of people. Little, if any, community of feeling subsisted between them and Estella, but the understanding was established that they were necessary to her, and that she was necessary to them.

I didn't merely watch from the yard, of course. On proper occasions, when the moon was in a waning phase, I would call upon Estella as a welcome visitor. If she one day planned to aim a deadly dagger at me, quite on purpose, I had no suspicion of it. Still, both in Mrs. Brandley's house and out of Mrs. Brandley's house, I suffered every kind and degree of torture that Estella could cause me. The nature of my relations with her, which placed me on terms of familiarity without placing me on terms of favour, conduced to my distraction.

She made use of me to tease, perhaps lure, other Scapegrace admirers, and she turned the very familiarity between herself and me to the account of putting a constant slight on my devotion to her. If I had been her secretary, steward, half-brother, poor relation, I could not have seemed to myself further from my hopes when I was nearest to her. The privilege of calling her by her name and hearing her call me by mine became, under the circumstances, an aggravation of my trials; and while I think it likely that it almost maddened her other lovers, I know, too certainly, that it almost maddened me.

She had admirers in droves. No doubt my jealousy made an admirer of every one who went near her; but there were more than enough of them without that. What a struggle it was, as the full moon neared, to maintain my composure and not go wild and wolfish.

I saw her often at Richmond, I heard of her often in town, and I used often to take her and the Brandleys on the water. There were picnics, fête days, plays, operas, concerts, parties, all sorts of pleasures, through which I pursued her. They were all miseries to me. I never had one hour's happiness in her society, and yet my mind all round the four-and-twenty hours was harping on the happiness of having her with me unto death.

Throughout this part of our intercourse—and it lasted, as will presently be seen, for what I then thought a long time—she habitually reverted to that tone which expressed that our association was forced upon us. There were other times when she would come to a sudden check in this tone and in all her many tones, and would seem to pity me.

"Pip, Pip," she said one evening, coming to such a check, when we sat apart at a darkening window of the house in Richmond; "will you never take warning?"

"Of what?"

"Of me."

"Warning not to be attracted by you, do you mean, Estella, or something more sinister? Have you been training with pistols?"

"And silver bullets?" She arched a thin brow. "If you don't know what I mean, you are blind."

"At any rate," said I, giving up the opportunity to observe that love is blind, for it was apparently deaf and insensitive as well, though not mute. "I have no warning given me just now, for you wrote to me to come to you, this time."

"That's true," said Estella, with a cold careless smile that always chilled me. It was so like the cold smile she flashed after hitting a target dead center. "The time has come round when Miss Havisham wishes to have me for a day at Satis. You are to take me there, and bring me back, if you will. She would rather I did not travel alone, and objects to receiving my maid, for she has a sensitive horror of the Recommissioned. Can you take me?"

"Can I take you, Estella?" I did not dare question why Miss Havisham would have a care for Estella traveling alone, with Estella's level of skills and strength leaving her quite able to handle herself among both mortal ruffians and Scapegrace villains alike. It was enough that she wanted me to perform the service of escort.

"You can then? The day after tomorrow, if you please. You are to pay all charges out of my purse. You hear the condition of your going?"

"And must obey," said I.

This was all the preparation I received for that visit, or for others like it. Miss Havisham never wrote to me, nor had I ever so much as seen her handwriting. We went down on the next day but one, and we found her in the room where I had first beheld her, and it is needless to add that there was no change in Satis House.

She was even more dreadfully fond of Estella than she had been when I last saw them together. There was something positively dreadful in the energy of her looks and embraces. She hung upon Estella's beauty, hung upon her words, hung upon her demonstrated prowess with a pair of daggers, and sat mumbling her own trembling fingers while she looked at her, as though she were devouring the beautiful creature she had reared. Perhaps she wanted to have a taste. I did not see Sarah Pocket on premises, and speculated that Miss Havisham had finally drained the odious woman dry.

From Estella she looked at me, with a searching glance that seemed to pry into my heart and probe its wounds.

"How does she use you, Pip; how does she use you?" she asked me again, with her soul-sucking eagerness, even in Estella's hearing. When we sat by her flickering fire at night, she extorted from Estella, by dint of referring back to what Estella had told her in her regular letters, the names and conditions of the men whom she had fascinated, lured in, and killed, all apparently vampires save a very few. As Miss Havisham dwelt upon this roll, with the intensity of a mind mortally hurt and diseased, she sat with her other hand on her crutch stick, and her chin on that, and her wan bright eyes glaring at me, a very spectre.

I saw in this that Estella was set to wreak Miss Havisham's revenge on Scapegraces, and that she was not to be given to me until she had gratified it for a term. I saw in this a reason for her being beforehand assigned to me. Sending her out to attract and torment and murder, Miss Havisham sent her with the malicious assurance that she was to captivate and kill all admirers, and that all who staked upon that cast were secured to lose. How I could know all I knew and still count myself safe and intended for Estella, I can't explain. Another wolf might have suspected that she meant for me to die at Estella's hands eventually, perhaps sooner than later the way her eyes twinkled to look at me. I saw in this the reason for my being staved off so long and the reason for my late guardian's declining to commit to the formal knowledge of such a scheme.

In a word, I saw in this Miss Havisham as I had her then and there before my eyes, and always had had her before my eyes; and I saw in this, the distinct shadow of the darkened and unhealthy house in which her life was hidden from the sun. I saw what I wanted to believe, that I was the chosen hero to restore the light and laughter to Satis House.

It happened on the occasion of this visit that some sharp words arose between Estella and Miss Havisham. It was the first time I had ever seen them opposed.

We were seated by the fire, as just now described, and Miss Havisham had ordered Estella to perform some of the martial arts routines from her training sessions. She went through the stances with fluidity and grace, and it was like watching a dance, a deadly dance, for every pose represented yet another way to prepare for a kill. After a very involved series of pirouettes, leaps, and kicks, Estella paused to catch her breath.

"What!" said Miss Havisham, flashing her eyes upon her, "are you tired of performing for me?"

"Only a little tired of performing," replied Estella, moving to lean on the great chimneypiece, where she stood looking down at the fire.

"Speak the truth, ingrate!" Miss Havisham passionately struck her stick upon the floor. "You are tired of showing me what you can do. And how are you supposed to survive a vampire attack if you tire so easily?"

Estella looked at her with perfect composure, and again looked down at the fire. Her graceful figure and her beautiful face expressed a self-possessed indifference to the wild heat of the other that was almost cruel.

"You have grown soft away from my influence!" exclaimed Miss Havisham.

"What?" said Estella, preserving her attitude of indifference as she leaned against the great chimneypiece and only moving her eyes. "Do you accuse me of letting emotions slow me down?"

"Do you not?" was the fierce retort.

"You should know," said Estella. "I am what you have made me. Take all the praise, take all the blame; take all the success, take all the failure; in short, take me. I have never formed any emotional attachments. I am as hard and cold as you have made me."

"Oh, look at her, look at her!" cried Miss Havisham, bitterly. "Look at her so thankless and soft, on the hearth where she was reared! Where I took her into this wretched breast when it was first bleeding from its stabs, and where I have lavished years of training upon her!"

"At least I was no party to the compact," said Estella, "for if I could walk and speak, when it was made, it was as much as I could do. But what would you have? You have been provided for me, and I owe everything to you. What would you have?"

"Success," replied the other.

"You have it. I have reduced the numbers of vampires in the region and I continue in my pursuits."

"I would expect a reduction of half, or more," said Miss Havisham. "Perhaps you're getting too attached to your prey, falling in love with them. Love slows you down."

"Mother by adoption," retorted Estella, never departing from the easy grace of her attitude, never raising her voice as the other did, never yielding either to anger or tenderness. "Love is softness. Love is emotion. I've never learned to feel it, and I have never been slowed down. I increase my abilities daily, but I am only one woman."

"One woman with superior skills, thanks to my training!" cried Miss Havisham, turning wildly to me. "Did I never give her a burning purpose? Let her call me mad, let her call me mad!"

"Why should I call you mad," returned Estella. "I, of all people? Does any one live, who knows what set purposes you have, half as well as I do? Does any one live, who knows what a steady memory you have, half as well as I do? I who have sat on this same hearth on the little stool that is even now beside you there, learning your lessons and looking up into your face, when your face was strange and frightened me!"

"Ah, then, you still fear me?" moaned Miss Havisham. "Fear will hold you back from your goals."

"Fear you? No, not now. Not for many years. Remember your teachings. You wanted me to learn to kill vampires as if forgetting what you yourself are. When have you found me false to your teaching? When have you found me unmindful of your lessons? Perhaps only when I return here and spare you? Is that why you're angry with me? That I have obeyed all your teaching, learned to kill Scapegraces of all kinds, and have not yet made an attempt to stake you? Perhaps I really have gone soft, then?" Estella touched her bosom with her hand. "Would you prefer I acted on all my teachings? To kill without pity or remorse? To take the life of any Scapegrace that crosses my path?"

I avoided Estella's gaze, for I dreaded she might be looking at me as well as at Miss Havisham.

"Soft!" moaned Miss Havisham, pushing away her straggly hair with both her hands. "And thankless. After all that I've done for you, Estella. You might as well stake me and have done!"

Estella looked at her for a moment with a kind of calm wonder, but was not otherwise disturbed; when the moment was past, she looked down at the fire again. I wondered if Miss Havisham weren't really wishing to be staked by Estella one day in raising her to such an art.

"I cannot think," said Estella, raising her eyes after a silence "why you should be so unreasonable when I come to see you after a separation. I have never forgotten your wrongs and their causes. I have never been unfaithful to you or your schooling. I have never shown any weakness that I can charge myself with."

"Would it be weakness to show some gratitude?" exclaimed Miss Havisham. "But yes, yes, she would call it so!"

"I begin to think," said Estella, in a musing way, after another moment of calm wonder, "that I almost understand how this comes about. If you had brought up your adopted daughter wholly in the dark confinement of these rooms, and had never let her know that there was such a thing as the daylight by which she had never once seen your face—if you had done that, and then, for a purpose had wanted her to understand the daylight and know all about it, you would have been disappointed and angry?"

Miss Havisham, with her head in her hands, sat making a low moaning, and swaying herself on her chair, but gave no answer.

"Or," said Estella—"which is a nearer case—if you had taught her, from the dawn of her intelligence, with your utmost energy and might, that there was such a thing as daylight, but that it was made to be her enemy and destroyer, and she must always turn against it, for it had blighted you and would else blight her—if you had done this, and then, for a purpose, had wanted her to take naturally to the daylight and she could not do it, you would have been disappointed and angry?"

Miss Havisham sat listening (or it seemed so, for I could not see her face), but still made no answer.

"So," said Estella, "I must be taken as I have been made. The success is not mine, the failure is not mine, but the two together make me."

Miss Havisham had settled down, I hardly knew how, upon the floor, among the faded bridal relics with which it was strewn. I took advantage of the moment—I had sought one from the first—to leave the room, after beseeching Estella's attention to her, with a movement of my hand. When I left, Estella was yet standing by the great chimneypiece, just as she had stood throughout. Miss Havisham's dull hair was all adrift upon the ground, among the other bridal wrecks, and was a miserable sight to see.

It was with a depressed heart that I walked in the starlight for an hour and more, about the courtyard, and about the brewery, and about the ruined garden. When I at last took courage to return to the room, I found Estella sharpening stakes at Miss Havisham's knee. Afterwards, Estella and I played at staking targets and so the evening wore away, and I went to bed.

Before we left next day, there was no revival of the difference between her and Estella, nor was it ever revived on any similar occasion; and there were four similar occasions, to the best of my remembrance. Nor did Miss Havisham's manner towards Estella in anywise change, except that I believed it to have something like fear infused among its former characteristics.

It is impossible to turn this leaf of my life, without putting Bentley Drummle's name upon it; or I would, very gladly.

On a certain occasion when the Savages were assembled in force, and when good feeling was being promoted in the usual manner by nobody's agreeing with anybody else, the presiding Savage called the Timberland to order, forasmuch as Mr. Drummle had not yet toasted a lady; which, according to the solemn constitution of the society, it was the brute's turn to do that day. I thought I saw him leer in an ugly way at me while the decanters were going round, but as there was no love lost between us, that might easily be. What was my indignant surprise when he called upon the company to pledge him to "Estella!"

"Estella who?" said I.

"Never you mind," retorted Drummle.

"Estella of where?" said I. "You are bound to say of where." Which he was, as a Savage.

"Of Richmond, gentlemen," said Drummle, putting me out of the question, "and a peerless beauty."

Much he knew about peerless beauties, a mean, miserable idiot! I whispered to Herbert.

"I know that lady," said Herbert, across the table, when the toast had been honored.

"*Do* you?" said Drummle.

"And so do I," I added, with a scarlet face.

"*Do* you?" said Drummle. "Oh, Lord!"

This was the only retort that the heavy creature was capable of making. I became as highly incensed by it as if it had been barbed with wit, and I immediately rose in my place and said that I could not but regard it as being like the honourable Savage's impudence to propose a lady of whom he knew nothing. Mr. Drummle, upon this, starting up, demanded what I meant by that?

I felt my hackles rising and could see Drummle growing wolfish on the spot. Reminders to use the techniques we had learned at Pocket's to slow or put off our transformations were in vain, for Drummle was ever the beast and I was determined to hold my own. I stripped quickly to avoid ruining my clothes, but Drummle did not give a care to his, popping seams and wrenching free of them. He gave a mighty growl as he turned, sinking to his haunches, and I probably cried out as well, a keening howl that I might have made under a full moon. The pain of flesh and bone shifting and stretching was nothing to the rage that simmered beneath the surface at Bentley Drummle fancying himself a prospect for Estella.

He drew first blood, pawing me across the chest before my hair had fully grown in. I gnashed my teeth and lunged at him, knocking him into a table. He pounced to his feet and charged at me, sending me onto my back. I struggled under him, but he managed to tear a strip of flesh from my shoulder before I found my bearings and kicked him off me again. He ran, and I gave chase, catching him at the door, where I had managed to turn him over and might have had my chance at him if not for Herbert and the other Savages dousing us with ice-cold water, bringing us to our senses, and out of our wolfish haze.

As we came back to ourselves, proposals ensued of how Mr. Drummle and I might solve our Savage differences without resorting to lycanthropic violence. However, it was decided at last (the Timberland being a Court of Honour) that if Mr. Drummle would bring proof of having the lady's acquaintance, that Mr. Pip must express his regret, as a gentleman and a Savage, for having questioned Mr. Drummle's honour. Next day was appointed for the production (lest our honour should take cold from delay), and next day Drummle appeared with a polite little avowal in Estella's hand that she had had the honour of dancing with him several times.

This left me no course but to regret that I had been doubtful of "Drummle's honour." Drummle and I then sat snorting at one another for an hour, while the Timberland engaged in indiscriminate contradiction, and finally the promotion of good feeling was declared to have gone ahead at an amazing rate.

I tell this lightly, but it was no light thing to me. For, I cannot adequately express what pain it gave me to think that Estella should show any favour to a contemptible, clumsy, sulky whelp, so very far below the average, even if I was well aware of her habit of luring Scapegraces to kill them. To the present moment, I could not endure the thought of her stooping to that hound, if even as a temporary flirtation. No doubt I should have been miserable whomsoever she had favoured; but a worthier object would have caused me a different kind and degree of distress.

It was easy for me to find out, and I did soon find out, that Drummle had begun to follow her closely, and that she allowed him to do it. A little while, and he was always in pursuit of her, and he and I crossed one another every day. He held on, in a dull persistent way, and Estella held him on; now with encouragement, now with discouragement, now almost flattering him, now openly despising him, now knowing him very well, now scarcely remembering who he was.

The Spider, as Mr. Jaggers had called him, was used to lying in wait, however, and had the patience of his tribe. Added to that, he had a blockhead confidence in his money and in his family greatness, which sometimes did him good service—almost taking the place of concentration and determined purpose. So, the Spider, doggedly watching Estella, outwatched many brighter insects, and would often uncoil himself and drop at the right nick of time.

At a certain Assembly Ball at Richmond (there used to be Assembly Balls at most places then), where Estella had outshone all other beauties, this blundering Drummle so hung about her, and with so much toleration on her part, that I resolved to speak to her concerning him.

I had no chance at the ball, unfortunately. I fell prey not to Estella, but to the most ungentlemanly of urges: to turn wolf. As all of my attempts to control my transformation failed, I darted from the ballroom just in time, with a tail threatening to burst through my trousers at any moment. If Bentley Drummle had followed, we would certainly have come to blows, perhaps exciting Estella no end. For all she scorned my kind, she seemed to have a strange admiration for watching us fight. I might have convinced myself that her bloodthirsty yearnings were the reason behind her allowing Drummle's attentions, had she not explained when I cornered her on the subject at next opportunity.

When she was waiting for Mrs. Brandley to take her home, and was sitting apart among some flowers, ready to go, I had finally gotten hold of myself and restored to human form. I was with her, for I almost always accompanied them to and from such places.

"Are you tired, Estella?"

"Rather, Pip."

"You should be."

"Say rather, I should not be; for I have my letter to Satis House to write before I go to sleep."

"Recounting tonight's triumph?" said I. "Surely a very poor one, Estella."

"What do you mean? I didn't know there had been any."

"Estella," said I. "Do look at that fellow in the corner yonder, who is looking over here at us."

"Why should I look at him?" returned Estella, with her eyes on me instead. "What is there in that fellow in the corner yonder—to use your words—that I need look at?"

"Indeed, that is the very question I want to ask you," said I. "For he has been hovering about you all night."

"Moths, and all sorts of ugly creatures," replied Estella, with a glance towards him, "hover about a lighted candle. Can the candle help it?"

"No," I returned. "But cannot the Estella help it?"

"Well!" said she, laughing, after a moment, "perhaps. Yes. Anything you like."

"But, Estella, do hear me speak. It makes me wretched that you should encourage a man so generally despised as Drummle. You know he is despised."

"Well?" said she.

"You know he is as ungainly within as without. A deficient, ill-tempered, lowering, stupid fellow."

"Well?" said she. "The better to end him, then. You should not mind so much if he is no friend of yours."

"He isn't. But—" I paused. "You haven't killed a werewolf yet, have you?"

"No. Do you worry that I won't be able to do it? Or do you think I will come for you next? For I have given you warning about what I am, and you have seen me perform."

"I have seen you," I allowed. "And I'm not worried for myself. I wonder, though, if you really intend to lure and dispose of Drummle like the others. He's stronger than you think. Have a care."

"Perhaps he isn't like the others."

"Your intentions are more serious? With Drummle? You know he has nothing to recommend him but money and a ridiculous roll of addle-headed predecessors; now, don't you?"

"Well?" said she again; and each time she said it, she opened her lovely eyes the wider.

To overcome the difficulty of getting past that monosyllable, I took it from her, and said, repeating it with emphasis, "Well! Then that is why it makes me wretched."

I felt the wolf rearing up in me again, but I would not let Drummle triumph. I hummed Old Clem under my breath.

"Pip," said Estella, casting her glance over the room, "don't be foolish about its effect on you. It may have its effect on others, and may be meant to have. It's not worth discussing."

"Yes it is," said I, "because I cannot bear that people should say, 'She throws away her graces and attractions on a mere boor, the lowest in the crowd.'"

If the elegant ladies and gentlemen of the ball had seen me wolfish, I most certainly would have stolen the honour from Drummle as the lowest in the crowd. I thanked Mr. Pocket's good training for allowing me to make my escape and gather my wits in time.

"I can bear it," said Estella.

"Oh! Don't be so proud, Estella, and so inflexible."

"Calls me proud and inflexible in this breath!" said Estella, opening her hands. "And in his last breath reproached me for stooping to a boor!"

"There is no doubt you do," said I, something hurriedly, "for I have seen you give him looks and smiles this very night, such as you never give to—me."

"Do you want me then," said Estella, turning suddenly with a fixed and serious, if not angry, look, "to deceive and entrap you?"

"Do you deceive and entrap him, Estella?"

"Yes, and many others—all of them but you. Here is Mrs. Brandley. I'll say no more."

And now that I have given the one chapter to the theme that so filled my heart, and so often made it ache and ache again, I pass on unhindered, to the event that had impended over me longer yet; the event that had begun to be prepared for, before I knew that the world held Estella, and in the days when her baby intelligence was receiving its first distortions from Miss Havisham's hands.

CHAPTER 35

I WAS THREE-AND-TWENTY YEARS OF age. In the passing years, I hadn't heard another word to enlighten me on the subject of my expectations. We had left Barnard's Inn more than a year, and lived in the Temple. Our chambers were in Garden-court, down by the river.

Mr. Matthew Pocket had deemed me worthy of my gentlemanly stature, that is, I'd learned to control the stages of my transformation when in public, and to presumably seek shelter out of the public eye while the moon was at its fullest. We continued on the best terms as friends, no longer as student and teacher. I had a restless nature, which persisted despite my attempts to rein it in, and continued to wreak havoc with my ability to settle things. Reading, I'd found, was one thing that would soothe me and allow me to keep my composure, so I read for several hours a day. That matter of Herbert's was still progressing, and everything with me was as I have brought it down to the close of the last preceding chapter.

Business had taken Herbert on a journey to Marseilles. I was alone and it was drawing closer to the night of a full moon. Fortunately, it was wretched weather, stormy and wet, and I had no desire to venture out. Violent blasts of rain had accompanied rages of wind, and as another day of it came to a close, I sat down to read.

We lived at the top of the last house, and the wind rushing up the river shook the house that night, like discharges of cannon, or breakings of a sea. I read with my watch upon the table, purposing to close my book at eleven o'clock. As I shut it, Saint Paul's, and all the many church-clocks in the City—some leading, some accompanying, some following—struck that hour. The sound was curiously flawed by the wind; and I was listening, and thinking how the wind assailed and tore it, when I heard a footstep on the stair.

"There is some one down there, is there not?" I called out, looking down.

"Yes," said a voice from the darkness beneath.

"What floor do you want?"

"The top. Mr. Pip."

"That is my name.—There is nothing the matter?"

"Nothing the matter," returned the voice. And the man came on.

I stood with my lamp held out over the stair rail, and he came slowly within its light. In the instant, I had seen a face that was strange to me, yet familiar at once.

Moving the lamp as the man moved, I made out that he was substantially dressed, but roughly, like a voyager by sea. That he had long silver-grey hair. That his age was about sixty. That he was a muscular man, strong on his legs, and that he was browned and hardened by exposure to weather. As he ascended the last stair or two, and the light of my lamp included us both, I saw, with a stupid kind of amazement, that he was holding out both his hands to me.

"Pray what is your business?" I asked him. How could I know him?

"My business?" he repeated, pausing. "Ah! Yes. I will explain my business, by your leave."

"Do you wish to come in?"

"Yes," he replied. "I wish to come in, master."

I took him into the room I'd just left and set the lamp down near my book. He looked about him with the strangest air—an air of wondering pleasure, as if he had some part in the things he admired—and he pulled off a rough outer coat, and his hat. Then, I saw that his head was furrowed, and that the long silver-grey hair receded slightly at the temples. But, I saw nothing that in the least explained him. On the contrary, I saw him next moment, once more holding out both his hands to me.

"What do you mean?" said I, half suspecting him to be mad.

He stopped looking at me, and slowly rubbed his right hand over his head. I noticed that the top of his hand was sporting a some-what thick covering of silver-grey hair. A fellow wolf? I sniffed. Yes. I smelled it on him now, his essence. What I didn't smell was fear. He was a bold one.

"It's disapinting to a wolfman," he said, in a coarse broken voice, "arter having looked for'ard so distant, and come so fur; but you're not to blame for that—neither on us is to blame for that. I'll speak in half a minute. Give me half a minute, please."

He sat down on a chair that stood before the fire, and covered his forehead with his large furred hands. I looked at him atten-tively then, and looked at my own hands, also covered with a tawny down, and recoiled a little from him. I did not know him.

"There's no one nigh," said he, looking over his shoulder; "is there?"

"Why do you, a stranger coming into my rooms at this time of the night, ask that question?" I shifted my stance, legs spread. I felt the wildness rising up in me. Having had some experience with sparring, I was prepared to hold my ground, as man or wolf.

"You're a game one," he returned, shaking his head at me with a deliberate affection, at once most unintelligible and most exasper-ating. "I'm glad you've grow'd up, a game one! But don't catch hold of me. You'd be sorry arterwards to have done it."

I knew him! Even yet I could not recall a single feature, but I knew him! If the wind and the rain had driven away the interven-ing years, had swept us to the churchyard where we first stood face to face on such different levels, I could not have known my convict more distinctly than I knew him now as he sat in the chair before the fire. A moment before, I had not been conscious of remotely suspecting his identity.

He came back to where I stood, and again held out both his hands. Not knowing what to do—for, in my astonishment I had lost my self-possession—I reluctantly gave him my hairy hands. He grasped them heartily, raised them to his nose, sniffed them, and still held them.

"You acted noble, my boy," said he. "Noble, Pip! And I have never forgot it!"

At a change in his manner as if he were even going to embrace me, I laid a hand upon his breast and put him away.

"Stay!" said I. "Keep off! If you have come here to thank me for what I did when I was a mere pup, it was not necessary. Still, however you have found me out, there must be something good in the feeling that has brought you here, and I will not repulse you; but surely you must understand that—I—"

My attention was so attracted by the singularity of his fixed look at me that the words died away on my tongue.

"We're the same, you and I. We can look out for one another, Pip. It's the way of the pack. We share a bond as werewolves."

True, that wolves were pack animals, as we had learned at Mr. Pocket's, but I had all the pack I could handle with Herbert, the other Pockets, and the Savages. I did not feel I needed to add this lone wolf to my pack.

"You was a saying," he observed, when we had confronted one another in silence, "that surely I must understand. What, surely must I understand?"

"That I cannot wish to renew that chance intercourse with you of long ago, under these different circumstances. I am glad to believe you have recovered yourself. I am glad to tell you so. I am glad that, thinking I deserve to be thanked, you have come to thank me. But our ways are different ways. You are wet, and you look weary. Will you drink something before you go?"

He had replaced his neckerchief loosely, and had stood, keenly observant of me, biting a long end of it. "I think," he answered, still with the end at his mouth and still observant of me, "that I *will* drink (I thank you) afore I go."

There was a tray ready on a side-table. I brought it to the table near the fire, and asked him what he would have? He touched one of the bottles without looking at it or speaking, and I made him some hot rum and water. I tried to keep my hand steady while I did so, but his look at me as he leaned back in his chair with the long draggled end of his neckerchief between his teeth—evidently forgotten—made my hand, growing more paw-like in my ability to focus on holding off the change, very difficult to master. When at last I put the glass to him, I saw with amazement that his eyes were full of tears.

Up to this time I had remained standing, not to disguise that I wished him gone. But I was softened by the softened aspect of the man, and felt a touch of reproach.

"I hope," said I, hurriedly putting something into a glass for myself, and drawing a chair to the table, "that you will not think I spoke harshly to you just now. I had no intention of doing it, and I am sorry for it if I did. I wish you well and happy!"

As I put my glass to my lips, he glanced with surprise at the end of his neckerchief, dropping from his mouth when he opened it, and stretched out his hand. I gave him mine, and then he drank, and drew his sleeve across his eyes and forehead.

"How are you living?" I asked him.

"I've been a sheep-farmer, stock-breeder, other trades besides, away in the new world," said he; "many a thousand mile of stormy water off from this."

"I hope you have done well?" It seemed unusual, that a werewolf might be put in charge of breeding stock or keeping sheep.

"I've done wonderfully well. There's others went out alonger me as has done well, too, but no man has done nigh as well as me. I'm famous for it. It seems wolfish types have a way of making livestock do one's bidding."

"I am glad to hear it."

"I hope to hear you say so, my dear boy."

Without stopping to try to understand those words or the tone in which they were spoken, I turned off to a point that had just come into my mind.

"Have you ever seen a messenger you once sent to me," I enquired, "since he undertook that trust?"

"Never set eyes upon him. I warn't likely to it."

"He came faithfully, and he brought me the two one pound notes. I was a poor boy then, as you know, and to a poor boy they were a little fortune. But, like you, I have done well since, and you must let me pay them back. You can put them to some other poor boy's use." I took out my purse.

He watched me as I laid my purse upon the table and opened it, and he watched me as I separated two one pound notes from its contents. They were clean and new, and I spread them out and handed them over to him. Still watching me, he laid them one upon the other, folded them long-wise, gave them a twist, set fire to them at the lamp, and dropped the ashes into the tray.

"May I make so bold," he said then, with a smile that was like a frown, and with a frown that was like a smile, "as ask you *how* you have done, since you and me was out on them lone shivering marshes?"

"How I have done?"

"Ah." He emptied his glass, got up, and stood at the side of the fire, with his hairy hand on the mantel. He put a foot up to the bars, to dry and warm it. The wet boot began to steam, but he neither looked at it, nor at the fire, but steadily looked at me with silver-grey eyes. At last, I began to tremble.

When I mastered myself so that my tongue was no longer so thick in my mouth that I was about to begin panting, I told him I had been chosen to succeed to some property.

"Might a mere warmint ask what property?" said he.

I faltered, "I don't know."

"Could I make a guess, I wonder," said the Convict, "at your income since you come of age! As to the first figure now. Five?"

With my heart beating like a heavy hammer of disordered action, I rose out of my chair, and stood with my hand upon the back of it, looking wildly at him.

"Concerning a guardian," he went on. "There ought to have been some guardian, or such-like, whiles you was a minor. Some lawyer, maybe. As to the first letter of that lawyer's name now. Would it be J?"

All the truth of my position came flashing on me. The disappointments, dangers, disgraces, consequences of all kinds, rushed in in such a multitude that I was borne down by them and had to struggle for every breath I drew. My bones begin to stretch. I had to calm my pulse from the shock or I would turn wolf before the moon was even full.

"Jaggers," he confirmed, as I closed my eyes and hummed softly to myself, a trick to soothe the nerves. "However, did I find you out? Why, I wrote from Portsmouth to a person in London, for particulars of your address. That person's name? Why, Wemmick."

I could not have spoken one word, though it had been to save my life. I concentrated on the humming until the bones stopped groaning under my skin. My hair, I trusted, had grown some, and I couldn't stop it entirely. My nose had lengthened, but was not yet a snout. I would not turn beast. Not now! I swayed on my feet. He caught me, drew me to the sofa, put me up against the cushions, and bent on one knee before me, bringing the face that I now well remembered, and that I shuddered at, very near to mine.

"Yes, Pip, dear boy, I've made a gentleman on you! It's me wot has done it! I swore that time, sure as ever I earned a guinea, that guinea should go to you. I swore arterwards, sure as ever I spec'lated and got rich, you should get rich. I lived rough, that you should live smooth; I worked hard, that you should be above work. What odds, dear boy? Do I tell it, fur you to feel a obligation? Not a bit. I tell it, fur you to know as that there hunted dunghill dog that you saved got his head so high that he could make a gentleman—and, Pip, you're him!"

The abhorrence in which I held the man, the dread I had of him, the repugnance with which I shrank from him, could not have been exceeded if he had been turned full wolf and crouched on the attack.

"Look'ee here, Pip. I'm your second father. You're my son—more to me nor any son. We're bonded like pup and sire, ever since that night on the moors. I've put away money, only for you to spend. When I was on my own, roaming the wild till I half forgot wot men's and women's faces wos like, I see yourn. I see you there a many times, as plain as ever I see you on them misty marshes. 'Lord strike me dead!' I says each time—and I goes out in the air to say it under the open heavens—'but wot, if I gets liberty and money, I'll make that boy a gentleman!' A werewolf gentleman, aye. And I done it. Why, look at you, dear boy! Look at these here lodgings o'yourn, fit for a lord! A lord? Ah! You shall show money with lords for wagers, and beat 'em!"

In his heat and triumph, and in his knowledge that I had been nearly fainting, which felt for all the world like being a pup on my back again, he did not remark on my reception of all this. It was the one grain of relief I had.

"Look'ee here!" He went on, taking my watch out of my pocket, and turning towards him a ring on my finger, which I never wore on full moon but had deemed safe enough earlier in the day. I recoiled from his touch as if he had been a snake. "A gold 'un and a beauty: that's a gentleman's, I hope! A diamond all set round with rubies; that's a gentleman's, I hope! Look at your linen; fine and beautiful! Look at your clothes; better ain't to be got! And your books, too," turning his eyes round the room, "mounting up, on their shelves, by hundreds! And you read 'em; don't you? I see you'd been a reading of 'em when I come in. Ha, ha, ha! You shall read 'em to me, dear boy! And if they're in foreign languages wot I don't understand, I shall be just as proud as if I did."

Again he took both my hands and put them to his lips, while my blood pounded fierce within me.

"Don't you mind talking, Pip," said he, after again drawing his

sleeve over his eyes and forehead, as the click came in his throat
which I well remembered—and he was all the more horrible to
me that he was so much in earnest. "You can't do better nor keep
quiet, dear boy. You ain't looked slowly forward to this as I have;
you wosn't prepared for this as I wos. But didn't you never think it
might be me?"

"Oh no, no," I returned, "Never, never!"

"Well, you see it wos me, and single-handed. Never a soul in it
but my own self and Mr. Jaggers."

"Was there no one else?" I asked.

"No," said he, with a glance of surprise. "Who else should there
be? And, dear boy, how good looking you have growed! There's
bright eyes somewheres—eh? Isn't there bright eyes somewheres,
wot you love the thoughts on?"

Oh Estella, Estella!

"They shall be yourn, dear boy, if money can buy 'em. Not that
a gentleman like you, so well set up as you, can't win 'em off of his
own game; but money shall back you! Let me finish wot I was a
telling you, dear boy. From that there hut and that there hiring-
out, I got money left me by my master (which died, and had been
the same as me), and got my liberty and went for myself. In every
single thing I went for, I went for you. 'Lord strike a blight upon it,'
I says, wotever it was I went for, 'if it ain't for him!' It all prospered
wonderful. As I giv' you to understand just now, I'm famous for it.
It was the money left me, and the gains of the first few year wot I
sent home to Mr. Jaggers—all for you—when he first come arter
you, agreeable to my letter."

Oh that he had never come! That he had left me at the forge—
far from contented, yet, by comparison happy!

"And then, dear boy, it was a recompense to me, look'ee here,
to know in secret that I was making a werewolf gentleman. Serves
'em all right. The blood horses of them colonists might fling up the
dust over me as I was walking; what do I say? I says to myself, 'I'm
making a better gentleman nor ever you'll be!' When one of 'em

says to another, 'He was a convict, a few year ago, and is a ignorant common fellow now, for all he's lucky,' what do I say? I says to
myself, 'If I ain't a gentleman, nor yet ain't got no learning, I'm the
owner of such. All on you owns stock and land; which on you owns
a brought-up London gentleman?' This way I kep myself a going.
And this way I held steady afore my mind that I would for certain
come one day and see my boy, and make myself known to him, on
his own ground."

He laid his hand on my shoulder. I shuddered at the thought that
for anything I knew, his hand might be stained with blood, and not
just blood of simple forest creatures. I knew what it was to be out in
the wild, to feel the heady charge of freedom and power that came
with being a wolf in the night.

"It warn't easy, Pip, for me to leave them parts, nor yet it warn't
safe. But I held to it, and the harder it was, the stronger I held, for I
was determined, and my mind firm made up. At last I done it. Dear
boy, I done it!"

I tried to collect my thoughts, but I was stunned and it was hard
to pay attention with fighting my way through the self-protective
urge to change forms.

"Where will you put me?" he asked, presently. "I must be put
somewheres, dear boy."

"To sleep?"

"Yes. And to sleep long and sound," he answered; "for I've been
sea-tossed and sea-washed, months and months."

"My friend and companion is absent." I rose from the sofa. "You
must have his room."

"He won't come back tomorrow; will he?"

"No." I answered almost mechanically, in spite of my utmost efforts. "Not tomorrow."

"Because, look'ee here, dear boy," he said, dropping his voice,
and laying a long finger on my breast in an impressive manner,
"caution is necessary."

"How do you mean? Caution?" I arched a heavy brow.

"It's Death!"

"What's death?"

"I was sent for life. It's death to come back. There's been over-much coming back of late years. I'm a convict yet, eh? I should certainly be hanged in a silver noose if took."

Nothing was needed but this; the wretched man, after loading wretched me with his gold and silver chains for years, had risked his life to come to me, and I held it there in my keeping! If I had loved him instead of abhorring him; if I had been attracted to him by the strongest admiration and affection, instead of shrinking from him with the strongest repugnance; it could have been no worse. On the contrary, it would have been better, for his preservation would then have naturally and tenderly addressed my heart.

My first care was to close the shutters, so that no light might be seen from without, and then to close and make fast the doors. While I did so, he stood at the table drinking rum and gnawing on a biscuit. When I saw him thus engaged, I saw my convict on the marshes at his meal again. It almost seemed to me as if he must stoop down presently, to file at his leg.

When I had gone into Herbert's room, and had shut off any other communication between it and the staircase than through the room in which our conversation had been held, I asked him if he would go to bed? He said yes, but asked me for some of my "gentleman's linen" to put on in the morning. I brought it out, and laid it ready for him, and my blood again pounded when he again took me by both hands to give me goodnight.

I got away from him, without knowing how I did it, and mended the fire in the room where we had been together, and sat down by it, afraid to go to bed. For an hour or more, I remained too stunned to think; and it was not until I began to think, that I began fully to know how wrecked I was, and how the ship in which I had sailed was gone to pieces.

Miss Havisham's intentions towards me were all a mere dream.

Estella was not designed for me. I only suffered in Satis House as a convenience, a sting for the greedy relations, a model with a mechanical heart to practise on when no other practise was at hand; perhaps a live victim for Estella when the time came, as Herbert had long ago suspected. But, sharpest and deepest pain of all, that it was for the convict, a convict guilty of I knew not what crimes and liable to be taken out of those rooms where I sat thinking and hanged at the Old Bailey door, that I had deserted Joe.

I would not have gone back to Joe now. I would not have gone back to Biddy now, for any consideration. My sense of my own worthless conduct to them was suddenly apparent to me and greater than every consideration. No wisdom on earth could have given me the comfort that I should have derived from their simplicity and fidelity. I could never, never, undo what I had done.

In every rage of wind and rush of rain, I heard pursuers. With these fears upon me, I began to imagine that I'd had mysterious warnings of this man's approach. That, for weeks gone by, I had passed faces in the streets that I had thought like his. That these likenesses had grown more numerous, as he, coming over the sea, had drawn nearer. That his wicked spirit had somehow sent these messengers to mine, and that now on this stormy night he was as good as his word, and with me.

Crowding up with these reflections came the remembrance that I had seen him with my childish eyes to be a desperately violent man; that I had seen him down in the ditch tearing and fighting like a wild beast; that his vampire convict cohort had declared him to be a murderer. Out of such remembrances I brought into the light of the fire a half-formed terror that it might not be safe to be shut up there with him in the dead of the wild solitary night. This impelled me to take a candle and go in and look at my dreadful burden.

He had rolled a handkerchief round his head, and his face was set in sleep. But he was asleep, and quietly, too, though he had a pistol lying on the pillow. Assured of this, I softly removed the key to the outside of his door, and turned it on him before I again sat down by the fire. Gradually I slipped from the chair and lay on the floor. When I awoke without having parted in my sleep with the perception of my grave expectations, the clocks of the eastward churches were striking five, the candles were wasted out, the fire was dead, and the wind and rain intensified the thick black darkness.

THIS IS THE END OF THE SECOND STAGE OF PIP'S EXPECTATIONS.

CHAPTER 36

UPON WAKING, THE NEED for precautions to ensure the safety of my dreaded visitor superseded my muddled worries for my future endeavours.

Keeping him safely concealed in the chambers without arousing suspicion seemed impossible. True, I no longer had a footman. Shortly after my sister attacked Biddy and Joe for the last time, I had severed Pepper's head and put an end to him out of pity and dread for what he might one day become. I had never hired a manservant, but I did have an inflammatory old housekeeper, assisted by an animated rag-bag whom she called her niece. At first, I'd thought that the niece was a Recommissioned, but it turned out that she was simply slow to respond and entirely uninterested in anything, especially in working. To keep a room secret from the pair of them would be to invite curiosity and exaggeration. They both had weak eyes, which I had long attributed to their chronically looking in at keyholes, and they were always at hand when not wanted; indeed that was their only reliable quality besides larceny. Not to get up a mystery with these people, I resolved to announce in the morning that my uncle had unexpectedly come from the country.

While deciding on this course, the hair on the back of my neck rose in warning. I hadn't much neck hair at the time, being perfectly human, but my wolf senses were aroused nonetheless. It was dark on the stairs, the lights having been blown out in the storm, but I didn't need to wait on the watchman's lantern. Nostrils flaring with the scent of danger, or at least of an unannounced presence, I prowled cautiously down the steps and followed my nose to a man crouching in a corner.

The man made no answer when I asked him what he was doing on premises and he ran off at questioning. It troubled me that there should have been a lurker on the stairs, on that night of all nights in the year, and I asked the watchman whether he had admitted at his gate any gentleman who had perceptibly been dining out?

"The night being so bad, sir," said the watchman, "uncommon few have come in at my gate. Besides them three gentlemen that I have named, I don't call to mind another since about eleven o'clock, when a stranger asked for you."

"My uncle," I muttered. "Yes. You saw him, sir?"

"Yes. Oh yes. Likewise the person with him."

"Person with him!" I repeated.

"I judged the person to be with him," returned the watchman. "The person stopped, when he stopped to make enquiry of me, and the person took this way when he took this way."

"What sort of person?"

The watchman had not particularly noticed. He said a working person; to the best of his belief, he had a dust-coloured kind of clothes on, under a dark coat. The watchman made more light of the matter than I did, and naturally, not having my reason for attaching weight to it.

When I returned to my rooms, which I thought it well to do without prolonging explanations, my mind was much troubled by these two circumstances taken together. Some diner out or diner at home, who had not gone near this watchman's gate, might have strayed to my staircase and dropped asleep there. Or, my nameless visitor might have brought some one with him to show him the way. Still, joined, they had an ugly look to one as prone to distrust and fear as the changes of a few hours had made me.

I lit my fire, which burnt with a raw pale flare at that time of the morning, and fell into a doze before it. I seemed to have been dozing a whole night when the clock struck six. All this time, I had not been able to consider my own situation, nor could I do so yet. I had not the power to attend to it. As to forming any plan for the future, I could as soon have formed an elephant. When I opened the shutters and looked out at the wet wild morning, I thought how miserable I was, but hardly knew why, or how long I had been so, or on what day of the week I made the reflection, or even who I was that made it.

At last, the old woman and the niece came in—the latter with a head not easily distinguishable from her dusty broom—and testified surprise at sight of me and the fire. I imparted how my uncle had come in the night and was then asleep, and how the breakfast preparations were to be modified accordingly. Then I washed and dressed while they knocked the furniture about and made a dust; and so, in a sort of dream or sleep-waking, I found myself sitting by the fire again, waiting for my convict to come to breakfast.

By and by, his door opened and he came out. I could not bring myself to bear the sight of him, and I thought he had a worse look by daylight.

"I do not even know," said I, speaking low as he took his seat at the table, "by what name to call you. I have given out that you are my uncle."

"That's it, dear boy! Call me uncle."

"You assumed some name, I suppose, on board ship?"

"Yes, dear boy. I took the name of Provis and I mean to keep it."

"What is your real name?" I asked him in a whisper.

"Magwitch," he answered, in the same tone; "chrisen'd Abel."

"What were you brought up to be?"

"A werewolf, dear boy."

He answered quite seriously, and used the word as if it denoted some profession.

"When you came in at the gate last night and asked the watchman the way here, had you any one with you?"

"With me? No, dear boy."

"But there was some one there?"

"I didn't take particular notice," he said, dubiously, "not knowing the ways of the place. But I think there *was* a person, too, come in alonger me."

"Are you known in London?"

"I hope not!" he said.

"Were you known in London, once?"

"Not over and above, dear boy. I was in the provinces mostly."

"Were you tried—in London?"

"Which time?" said he, with a sharp look.

"The last time."

He nodded. "First knowed Mr. Jaggers that way. Jaggers was for me."

It was on my lips to ask him what he was tried for, but he took up a knife, gave it a flourish, and with the words, "And what I done is worked out and paid for!" fell to at his breakfast.

He ate in a ravenous way that was very disagreeable, and all his actions were uncouth, noisy, and greedy. Some of his teeth had failed him since I saw him eat on the marshes, and as he turned his food in his mouth, and turned his head sideways to bring his strongest fangs to bear upon it, he looked terribly like the hungry old dog I remembered. If I had begun with any appetite, he would have taken it away, and I should have sat much as I did—repelled from him by an insurmountable aversion, and gloomily looking at the cloth.

"I'm a heavy grubber, dear boy," he said, as a polite kind of apology when he made an end of his meal, "but I always was. If it had been in my constitution to be a lighter grubber, I might ha' got into lighter trouble. Similarly, I must have my smoke."

As he said so, he got up from table, and putting his hand into the breast of the pea-coat he wore, brought out a short black pipe, and a handful of loose tobacco. Having filled his pipe, he put the surplus tobacco back again, as if his pocket were a drawer. Then, he took a live coal from the fire with the tongs, and lit his pipe at it, and then turned round on the hearth-rug with his back to the fire, and went through his favourite action of holding out both his hands for mine.

"And this," said he, dandling my hands up and down in his, as he puffed at his pipe—"and this is the gentleman what I made! The real genuine one! It does me good fur to look at you, Pip. All I stip'late, is, to stand by and look at you, dear boy!"

I released my hands as soon as I could, and found that I was beginning slowly to settle down to the contemplation of my condition. What I was chained to, and how heavily, became intelligible to me, as I heard his hoarse voice, and sat looking up at his furrowed head with its silver grey hair at the sides.

"I mustn't see my gentleman a footing it in the mire of the streets. My gentleman must have horses, Pip! Horses to ride, and horses to drive, and horses for his servant to ride and drive as well."

He took out of his pocket a great thick pocketbook, bursting with papers, and tossed it on the table.

"There's something worth spending in that there book, dear boy. It's yourn. All I've got ain't mine; it's yourn. Don't you be afeerd on it. There's more where that come from. I've come to the old country fur to see my gentleman spend his money like a gentleman. That'll be my pleasure. And blast you all!" he wound up, looking round the room and snapping his fingers once with a loud snap, "blast you every one, from the judge in his wig, to the colonist a stirring up the dust, I'll show a better gentleman than the whole kit on you put together!"

"Stop!" said I, almost in a frenzy of fear and dislike, "I want to speak to you. I want to know what is to be done. I want to know how you are to be kept out of danger, how long you are going to stay, what projects you have."

"Look'ee here, Pip," said he, laying his hand on my arm in a suddenly altered and subdued manner. "First of all, look'ee here. I forgot myself half a minute ago. What I said was low, more like a mangy old dog than a proud wolf; that's what it was; doggish. Look'ee here, Pip. I ain't a going to be a dog."

"First," I resumed, half groaning, "what precautions can be taken against your being recognised and seized?"

"Well, dear boy, the danger ain't so great. Without I was informed agen, the danger ain't so much to signify. There's Jaggers, and there's Wemmick, and there's you. Who else is there to inform?"

"Is there no chance person who might identify you in the street?" said I.

"Well," he returned, "there ain't many. Nor yet I don't intend to advertise myself in the newspapers by the name of A.M. come back from Botany Bay; and years have rolled away, and who's to gain by it? Still, look'ee here, Pip. If the danger had been fifty times as great, I should ha' come to see you, mind you, just the same."

"And how long do you remain?"

"How long?" said he, taking his black pipe from his mouth, and dropping his jaw as he stared at me. "I'm not a going back. I've come for good."

"Where are you to live?" said I. "Where will you be safe?"

"Dear boy," he returned, "there's disguising wigs can be bought for money, and there's hair powder, and spectacles, and black clothes— shorts and what not. Others has done it safe afore, and what others has done afore, others can do agen. As to the where and how of living, dear boy, give me your own opinions on it."

"You take it smoothly now," said I, "but you were very serious last night, when you swore it was Death. Wigs and disguises will only work as you remain completely human. Someone could know you as wolf."

"It would be Death," said he, putting his pipe back in his mouth, "and Death by the silver rope, in the open street not fur from this, and it's serious that you should fully understand it to be so. What then, when that's once done? Here I am. To go back now 'ud be as bad as to stand ground—worse. Besides, Pip, I'm here, because I've meant it by you, years and years. As to what I dare, I'm a old wolf now, as has dared all manner of traps since first he was fledged, and I'm not afeerd to pounce on more. And now let me have a look at my gentleman agen."

Once more, he took me by both hands and surveyed me with an air of admiring proprietorship: smoking with great complacency all the while.

It appeared to me that I could do no better than secure him some quiet lodging hard by, of which he might take possession when Herbert returned in two or three days. That the secret must be confided to Herbert as a matter of unavoidable necessity was plain to me. But it was by no means so plain to Mr. Provis (I resolved to call him by that name), who reserved his consent to Herbert's participation until he should have seen him and formed a favourable judgment of his physiognomy. "And even then, dear boy," said he, pulling a greasy little clasped black Testament out of his pocket, "we'll have him on his oath."

To state that my terrible patron carried this little black book about the world solely to swear people on in cases of emergency, would be to state what I never quite established; but this I can say, that I never knew him put it to any other use. The book itself had the appearance of having been stolen from some court of justice, and perhaps his knowledge of its antecedents, combined with his own experience in that wise, gave him a reliance on its powers as a sort of binding spell or witchlike charm. On this first occasion of his producing it, I recalled how he had made me swear fidelity in the churchyard long ago, and how he had described himself last night as always swearing to his resolutions in his solitude.

As he was at present dressed in a seafaring slop suit, in which he

looked as if he had some parrots and cigars to dispose of, I next discussed with him what dress he should wear. He had in his own mind
sketched a dress for himself that would have made him something
between a dean and a dentist. It was with considerable difficulty
that I won him over to the assumption of a dress more like a prosperous farmer's; and we arranged that he should cut his hair close,
and wear a little powder. Lastly, as he had not yet been seen by the
laundress or her niece, he was to keep himself out of their view until
his change of dress was made.

The greatest risk would be for him to be seen in his full wolf
form, running wild, where anyone who knew him might see him
and identify him. Disguises would be useless to him in his wolfish
state. It was of the utmost importance to find a place to keep him
safely locked away from prying eyes, especially during full moon.

It would seem a simple matter to decide on these precautions;
but in my dazed, not to say distracted, state, it took so long, that I
did not get out to further them until two or three in the afternoon.
He was to remain shut up in the chambers while I was gone, and
was on no account to open the door.

There being to my knowledge a respectable lodging-house in
Essex Street, almost within hail of my windows, I first of all repaired
to that house, and was so fortunate as to secure the second floor for
my uncle, Mr. Provis. I then went from shop to shop, making such
purchases as were necessary to the change in his appearance.

Next day the clothes I had ordered all came home, and he put
them on. Whatever he put on, became him less (it dismally seemed
to me) than what he had worn before. The more I dressed him
and the better I dressed him, the more he looked like the slouching Scapegrace on the marshes. This effect on my anxious fancy
was partly referrable, no doubt, to his old face and manner growing
more familiar to me; but I believe, too, that he dragged one of his
legs as if there were still a weight of silver on it, and that from head
to foot there was werewolf in the very grain of the man.

The influences of his solitary hut-life and wildness in his veins lent a savage air that no dress could tame. He'd tried a touch of powder. He'd cut his grizzled hair, which did have some slight effect toward improving his appearance, though it would have to be trimmed again after every full moon. No end of agonies the thought of the impending full moon caused me, but I locked us in tight with plenty of meat in our separate rooms—a bowl of rum added to the water dish in his—and I daresay we passed the night comfortably enough indoors without ever crossing paths, though Herbert's room needed some small repairs the next day.

This is written of, I am sensible, as if it had lasted a year. It lasted about five days. Expecting Herbert all the time, I dared not go out, except when I took Provis for an airing after dark. At length, one evening when dinner was over and I had dropped into a slumber quite worn out, I was roused by the welcome footstep on the staircase. Provis, who had been asleep, too, staggered up at the noise I made, and in an instant I saw his jackknife shining in his hand.

"Quiet! It's Herbert!" I said, and Herbert came bursting in.

"Lowell, my dear fellow, how are you? I seem to have been gone a twelvemonth! Why, so I must have been, for you have grown quite thin and pale! Lowell, my—Halloa! I beg your pardon."

He was stopped in his running on and in his shaking hands with me by seeing Provis. Provis, regarding him with a fixed attention, was slowly putting up his jackknife, and groping in another pocket for something else.

"Herbert, my dear friend," I said, shutting the double doors, while Herbert stood staring and wondering. "Something very strange has happened. This is—a visitor of mine."

"It's all right, dear boy!" said Provis coming forward, with his little clasped black book, and then addressing himself to Herbert. "Take it in your right hand. Lord strike you dead on the spot, if ever you split in any way sumever! Kiss it!"

"Do so, as he wishes it," I said to Herbert. So, Herbert, looking at me with a friendly uneasiness and amazement, complied, and

Provis immediately shaking hands with him, said, "Now you're on your oath, you know. And never believe me on mine, if Pip shan't make a gentleman on you!"

CHAPTER 37

I CAN'T BEGIN TO DESCRIBE the astonishment and disquiet of Herbert, when he and I and Provis sat down before the fire, and I recounted the whole of the secret. From Herbert's expression, I could see a reflection of my own feelings, and what I saw did not flatter me. I couldn't well hide my repugnance towards the man who had done so much for me from my friend who knew me so well.

For his part, Provis had no idea of the possibility that I could find any fault with my good fortune. His boast that he had made me a gentleman, and that he had come to see me live like one, was made for me as much as for himself. And that it was a highly agreeable boast to both of us, and that we must both be very proud of it, was a conclusion quite established in his own mind.

"Though, look'ee here, Pip's comrade," he said to Herbert, after having discoursed for some time. "I know very well that once since I come back—for half a minute—I've been a mangy cur. I said to Pip, I knowed as I had been a low dog. But don't you fret yourself on that score. I ain't made Pip a gentleman, and Pip ain't a going to make you a gentleman, not fur me not to know what's due to ye both. Dear boy, and Pip's comrade, you two may count upon me always having a gen-teel muzzle on. Muzzled I have been since that half a minute when I was betrayed into lowness, muzzled I am at the present time, muzzled I ever will be."

"Certainly," Herbert said, but he looked as if there were no specific consolation in this, and remained perplexed and dismayed.

We were anxious for the time when Provis would go to his lodging and leave us together, but he was evidently jealous of leaving us together, and sat late. It was midnight before I took him round to Essex Street, saw him safely in at his own dark door, and locked him in with the caution to keep away from windows, especially in the event of growing wolfish. When the key turned to lock him in for the night, I experienced the first moment of relief I had known since the night of his arrival.

I always looked about me in taking my guest out after dark, and in bringing him back, and I looked about me now. Difficult as it is in a large city to avoid the suspicion of being watched, when the mind is conscious of danger in that regard, I could not persuade myself that any of the people within sight cared about my movements. The few who were passing passed on their several ways, and the street was empty when I turned back into the Temple. Nobody had come out at the gate with us. Nobody went in at the gate with me. As I crossed by the fountain, I saw his lighted back windows looking bright and quiet, and, when I stood for a few moments in the doorway of the building where I lived, before going up the stairs, Garden Court was as still and lifeless as the staircase was when I ascended it.

Herbert spoke some sound words of sympathy and encouragement. I realized how fortunate I was to have a friend as we sat down to consider what was to be done.

The chair that Provis had occupied still remaining where it had stood, Herbert unconsciously took it, but next moment started out of it, pushed it away, and took another. He had no occasion to say after that that he had conceived an aversion for my patron, neither had I occasion to confess my own. We interchanged that confidence without shaping a syllable.

"What is to be done?" I said, once Herbert settled in a new chair.

"My poor dear Lowell," he replied, holding his head, "I am too stunned to think."

"So was I, Herbert, when the blow first fell. Still, something must be done. He is intent upon various new expenses—horses, and carriages, and lavish appearances of all kinds. He must be stopped somehow."

"You mean that you can't accept—"

"How can I?" I interposed, as Herbert paused. "Think of him! Look at him!"

An involuntary shudder passed over both of us.

"Yet I am afraid the dreadful truth is, Herbert, that he is attached to me, strongly attached to me. Was there ever such a fate?"

"My poor dear Lowell," Herbert repeated.

"Then, after all, stopping short here, never taking another penny from him, think what I owe him already." I sighed. "Then again, I am heavily in debt—very heavily for me, who have now no expectations, or very grave expectations at that. How did I ever believe I could be a gentleman? A werewolf from the low country, a gentleman? I have been bred to no calling, and I am fit for nothing."

"Well, well, well!" Herbert remonstrated. "Don't say fit for nothing."

"What am I fit for? I know only one thing that I am fit for, and that is, to go for a soldier. And I might have gone, my dear Herbert, but for the prospect of taking counsel with your friendship." And, I didn't mention, for the idea of working closely with Recommissioneds.

Of course I broke down there. Herbert, beyond seizing a warm grip of my hand, pretended not to know it.

"Anyhow, my dear Lowell, soldiering won't do. If you were to renounce this patronage and these favors, I suppose you would do so with some faint hope of one day repaying what you have already had. Not very strong, that hope, if you went soldiering! Besides, it's absurd. You would be infinitely better in Clavenger's House, small as it is. I am working up towards a partnership, you know."

Poor fellow! He little suspected with whose money.

"But there is another question," said Herbert. "This is an ignorant, determined man, who has long had one fixed idea. More than that, he seems to me (I may misjudge him) to be a man of a desperate and fierce character."

"I know he is," I returned. "Let me tell you what evidence I have seen of it." And I told him what I had not mentioned in my narrative, of that encounter with the vampire convict.

"See, then," said Herbert. "Think of this! He comes here at the peril of his life, for the realisation of his fixed idea. In the moment of realisation, after all his toil and waiting, you cut the ground from under his feet, destroy his idea, and make his gains worthless to him. Do you see nothing that he might do, under the disappointment?"

"I have seen it, Herbert, and dreamed of it, ever since the fatal night of his arrival. Nothing has been in my thoughts so distinctly as his putting himself in the way of being taken."

"Then you may rely upon it," said Herbert, "that there would be great danger of his doing it. That is his power over you as long as he remains in England, and that would be his reckless course if you forsook him."

I was so struck by the horror of this idea, which had weighed upon me from the first, and that to go through with it would surely make me a murderer that I could not rest in my chair, but began pacing to and fro. I said to Herbert, meanwhile, that even if Provis were recognized and taken by his own fault, I should be wretched as the cause, however innocently. Even though I was so wretched in having him at large and near me, and even though I would far rather have worked at the forge all the days of my life than I would ever have come to this!

But there was no staving off the question, what was to be done?

"The first and the main thing to be done," said Herbert, "is to get him out of England. You will have to go with him, and then he may be induced to go."

"But get him where I will, could I prevent his coming back?"

"My good Lowell, with Newgate in the next street, there must

be far greater hazard in your making him reckless here than else-
where. If a pretext to get him away could be made out of that vampire convict, or out of anything else in his life, it would benefit us."

"There, again!" said I, stopping before Herbert, with my open
hands held out, as if they contained the desperation of the case. "I
know nothing of his life. It has almost made me mad to sit here of
a night and see him before me, so bound up with my fortunes and
misfortunes, and yet so unknown to me, except as the miserable
wretch who terrified me two days in my childhood!"

Herbert got up, and linked his arm in mine, and we slowly walked
to and fro together, studying the carpet.

"Lowell." Herbert stopped. "Do you feel convinced that you can
take no further benefits from him?"

"Fully. Surely you would, too, if you were in my place?"

"And you feel convinced that you must break with him? And
you have, and are bound to have, that tenderness for the life he has
risked on your account, that you must save him, if possible, from
throwing it away. Then you must get him out of England before you
stir a finger to extricate yourself. That done, extricate yourself, in
Heaven's name, and we'll see it out together."

It was a comfort to shake hands upon it, and walk up and down
again, with only that done.

"I think the only way I can get a knowledge of his history is that
I must ask him point blank," I reasoned aloud.

"Yes. Ask him," said Herbert, "when we sit at breakfast in the
morning."

With this project formed, we went to bed. I had the wildest
dreams concerning him, and woke fearful of his being found out as
a returned transport. Waking, I never lost that fear.

He came round at the appointed time, took out his jackknife,
and sat down to his meal. He was full of plans "for his gentleman's
coming out strong, and like a gentleman," and urged me to begin
speedily spending from the pocketbook that he had left in my possession. He considered the chambers and his own lodging as tempo-

rary residences, and advised me to look out at once for a "fashionable crib" near Hyde Park, in which he could have "a shake-down."

"After you were gone last night, I told my friend of the struggle that the soldiers found you engaged in on the marshes, when we came up. You remember?" I addressed him without a word of preface as soon as he had made an end of his breakfast, and was wiping his knife on his leg.

"Remember!" said he. "I think so!"

"We want to know something about that man—and about you. It is strange to know no more about either, and particularly you, than I was able to tell last night. Is not this as good a time as another for our knowing more?"

"Well!" he said, after consideration. "You're on your oath, you know, Pip's comrade?"

"Assuredly," replied Herbert.

"As to anything I say, you know," he insisted. "The oath applies to all."

"I understand it to do so."

"And look'ee here! Wotever I done is worked out and paid for," he insisted again.

"So be it," Herbert and I agreed.

He took out his black pipe and was going to fill it when, looking at the tangle of tobacco in his hand, he seemed to think it might perplex the thread of his narrative. He put it back again, stuck his pipe in a button-hole of his coat, spread a hand on each knee, and after turning an angry eye on the fire for a few silent moments, looked round at us and said what follows.

CHAPTER 38

"Dear boy and Pip's comrade." He looked at us both with a white hot flame glowing in his silver-grey eyes. "I am not going to recount my life like a song, or a storybook. I'll sum it up short and handy: in containment and out of containment, in containment and out of containment, in containment and out of containment. There, you've got it.

"I've been done everything to, pretty well—except hanged. I've been locked up as much as a silver tea-kittle. I've been carted here and carted there, and put out of this town, and put out of that town, and stuck in the stocks, and whipped and worried and drove. I've no more notion where I was born than you have—if so much. I first become aware of myself down in Essex, a thieving turnips for my living. Summun had run away from me—a man—a tinker—and he'd took the fire with him, and left me wery cold.

"I know'd my name to be Magwitch, chrisen'd Abel. How did I know it? Much as I know'd the birds' names in the hedges to be chaffinch, sparrer, thrush. I might have thought it was all lies together, only as the birds' names come out true, I supposed mine did. So fur as I could find, there warn't a soul that see young Abel Magwitch but wot caught fright at him, and either drove him off, or took him up. I was took up, took up, to that extent that I reg'larly grow'd up took up.

"This is the way it was, that when I was a ragged little creetur as much to be pitied as ever I see (not that I looked in the glass, for there warn't many insides of furnished houses known to me), I got the name of being barbarian. "This is a terrible barbarian," they says to prison wisitors, picking out me. "May be said to live in containments, this boy." They always went on about the Devil when I come back from a night under the moon covered in blood. But what the

Devil was I to do? I must put something into my stomach, mustn't I? It's a natural urge for us to hunt, in't it? Howsomever, I'm a getting low, and I know what's due. Dear boy and Pip's comrade, don't you be afeerd of me being low.

"Tramping, begging, thieving, hunting, working sometimes when I could—though that warn't as often as you may think. Would you ha' been over-ready to give me work yourselves—a bit of a poacher, a bit of a labourer, a bit of a wagoner, a bit of a haymaker, a bit of a hawker, a bit of most things that don't pay and lead to trouble, and then turning wolfish every so often. A deserting soldier learnt me to read and write. I warn't locked up as often now as formerly, but I wore out my good share of key-metal still.

"You don't ha' to be guilty of any crime to be locked up as a Scapegrace. Just turning wolf is crime enough but they always nabbed me on missing livestock, cows, sheep, and the like. Any fool excepting wampires knows wild deer and rabbit taste better'n the man-raised meat any day of the week. But lock us up they will, and they did. In containment, they wrap you in silver chains until you have no strength to go wolfish. After a while, they seem to forget you ever were wolfish in the first place, or think you cured and let you go, until which time they pick you up again. A hard life, it is, for a wolf on the streets, without name or coin.

"At Epsom races, a matter of over twenty years ago, I got acquainted wi' a man whose skull I'd crack wi' this poker to see him now. His right name was Compeyson; and that's the wampire, dear boy, what you see me a pounding in the ditch, according to what you truly told your comrade arter I was gone last night.

"He set up fur a gentleman, this Compeyson, as wampires often manage to do. He'd been to a public boarding-school and had learning. He was a smooth one to talk, and was a dab at the ways of gentlefolks. He was good-looking, too. It was the night afore the great race, when I found him on the heath. Him and some more was a sitting among the tables when I went in, and the landlord (which had a knowledge of me, and was a sporting one) called him out, and said to Compeyson, 'I think this is a man that might suit you, with special skills of his own.'

"Compeyson, he looks at me very noticing, and I look at him. He has a watch and a chain and a ring and a breast-pin and a handsome suit of clothes.

"'To judge from appearances, you're out of luck,' says Compeyson to me.

"'Yes, master, and I've never been in it much.' (I had come out of Kingston Containment last on a vagrancy committal. I was rangy and unkempt, night after a full moon and my prey had escaped me.)

"'Luck changes,' says Compeyson; 'perhaps yours is going to change.'

"I says, 'I hope it may be so. There's room.'

"'What can you do?' says Compeyson.

"'Eat and drink,' I says; 'hunt.'

"Compeyson laughed, looked at me again very noticing, give me five shillings, and appointed me for next night. Same place.

"I went to Compeyson next night, same place, and Compeyson took me on to be his man and pardner. A werewolf suited his need, he said. A werewolf ha' the muscle and determination to serve him quite well. Wampires don't like to work much, as you know, if they have someone can do for them, wi' the added fact that a werewolf can move around during the day when a wampire must lie low, out of the sun. And what was Compeyson's business in which we was to go pardners? Compeyson's business was the swindling, handwriting forging, stolen bank-note passing, and such-like. All sorts of traps as Compeyson could set with his head, and keep his own legs out of and get the profits from and let another man in for, was Compeyson's business. He'd no more heart than a silver file, he was as cold as death, and he had the head of the Devil afore mentioned.

"There was another in with Compeyson, as was called Arthur— not as being so chrisen'd, but as a surname. He was a shadow to look at. Him and Compeyson had been in a bad thing with a rich lady some years afore, and they'd made a pot of money by it, which wampires especially need as they live so long. They sank low, they did, feasting on tavern wretches and labouring folk for all hours of the night, sleeping all the day. Compeyson betted and gamed, and he'd have run through the king's taxes. Compeyson had a wife who he kicked mostly, and snacked on sometimes, though he wouldn't make her a wampire no matter how she begged. Arthur didn't take to the way of life and he began to get weak and sick.

"I became a poor tool in Compeyson's hands. Arthur lived at the top of Compeyson's house (over nigh Brentford it was), and Compeyson kept a careful account against him for board and lodging, in case he should ever get better to work it out. But Arthur soon settled the account. The second or third time as ever I see him, he come a tearing down into Compeyson's parlour late at night, in only a flannel gown, with his hair all in a sweat, and he says to Compeyson's wife, 'Sally, she really is upstairs alonger me, now, and I can't get rid of her. She's all in white,' he says, 'wi' white flowers in her hair, and she's awful mad, and she's got a shroud hanging over her arm, and she says she'll put it on me at five in the morning.'

"Says Compeyson: 'Why, you fool, don't you know she's got a living body? I turned her, not killed her. And how should she be up there, without coming through the door, or in at the window, and up the stairs?'

"'I don't know how she's there,' says Arthur, shivering dreadful with the horrors, 'but she's standing in the corner at the foot of the bed, awful mad. And over where her heart's broke—you broke it!— there's drops of blood.'

"Compeyson spoke hardy, but he was always a coward. 'Go up alonger this drivelling sick man,' he says to his wife, 'and, Magwitch, lend her a hand, will you?' But he never come nigh himself.

"Compeyson's wife and me took him up to bed again, and he raved most dreadful. 'Why look at her!' he cries out. 'She's a shaking the shroud at me! Don't you see her? Look at her eyes! Ain't it awful to see her so mad?' Next he cries, 'She'll put it on me, and then I'm done for! Take it away from her, take it away!' And then he catched hold of us, and kep on a talking to her, and answering of her, till I half believed I see her myself.

"Compeyson's wife, being used to him, giv him some liquor to get the horrors off, and by and by he quieted. 'Oh, she's gone. You're a good creetur,' he says to Compeyson's wife, 'don't leave me, whatever you do, and thank you!'

"He rested pretty quiet till it might want a few minutes of five, and then he starts up with a scream, and screams out, 'Here she is! She's got the shroud again. She's unfolding it. She's coming out of the corner. She's coming to the bed. Hold me, both on you—one of each side—don't let her touch me with it. Hah! She missed me that time. Don't let her throw it over my shoulders. Don't let her lift me up to get it round me. She's lifting me up. Keep me down!' Then he lifted himself up hard, and slammed himself down on the bedpost. It splintered right through his heart and he was dead, poof, turned to dust. Gone.

"Compeyson took it easy as a good riddance for both sides. Him and me was soon busy, and first he swore me (being ever artful) on my own book—this here little black book, dear boy, what I swore your comrade on.

"Not to go into the things that Compeyson planned, and I done—which 'ud take a week—I'll simply say to you, dear boy, and Pip's comrade, that that man got me into such nets as made me his slave. I was always in debt to him, always under his thumb, always a working, always a getting into danger. He was younger than me, but he'd got craft, and he'd got learning, and he overmatched me five hundred times told and no mercy. My Missis as I had the hard time wi'—Stop though! I ain't brought *her* in—"

He looked about him in a confused way, as if he had lost his place in the book of his remembrance; and he turned his face to the fire, and spread his hands broader on his knees, and lifted them off and put them on again.

"There ain't no need to go into it," he said, looking round once more. "The time wi' Compeyson was a'most as hard a time as ever

I had. Did I tell you as I was tried, alone, for misdemeanour, while with Compeyson?"

I answered, "No."

"Well!" he said, "I *was*, and got convicted. I was took up on suspicion, that was twice or three times in the four or five year that it lasted, but evidence was wanting. At last, me and Compeyson was both committed for felony—on a charge of putting stolen notes in circulation—and there was other charges behind. Compeyson says to me, 'Separate defences, no communication,' and that was all. And I was so miserable poor, that I sold all the clothes I had, except what hung on my back, afore I could get Jaggers.

"When we was put in the dock, I noticed first of all what a gentleman Compeyson looked, wi' his curly hair and his black clothes and his white pocket-handkercher, and what a common sort of a wretch I looked, with my ragged clothes and shaggy hair, and general ranginess as it was getting close to full moon. When the prosecution opened and the evidence was put short, aforehand, I noticed how heavy it all bore on me, and how light on him. When the evidence was giv in the box, I noticed how it was always me that had come for'ard, and could be swore to, how it was always me that the money had been paid to, how it was always me that had seemed to work the thing and get the profit.

"But when the defence come on, then I see the plan plainer; for, says the counsellor for Compeyson, 'My lord and gentlemen, here you has afore you, side by side, two persons as your eyes can separate wide; one, the younger, well brought up, who will be spoke to as such; one, the elder, ill brought up, and a Scapegrace besides who will be spoke to as such; one, the younger, seldom if ever seen in these here transactions, and only suspected; t'other, the elder, always seen in 'em and always wi' his guilt brought home. Can you doubt, if there is but one in it, which is the one, and, if there is two in it, which is much the worst one?' And such-like. And when it come to character, warn't it Compeyson as had been to the school, and warn't it his schoolfellows as was in this position and in that, and warn't it him as had been know'd by witnesses in such clubs and societies, and nowt to his disadvantage? And isn't it always the wampires getting away with passing as full human as long as they could find a way to come out in sunlight and not burn to a crisp? A covered coach, in his case, and covering almost every inch of skin with clothes and veils.

"And warn't it me as had been tried afore, and as had been know'd up hill and down dale in Bridewells and Containments! And known to turn werewolf under a full moon, and two days from a moon with court going late so I might turn right in front of them and look like a terror indeed. And when it come to speech-making, warn't it Compeyson as could speak to 'em wi' his face dropping every now and then into his white pocket-handkercher—ah! and wi' verses in his speech, too—and warn't it me as could only say, 'Gentlemen, this man at my side is a wampire and a most precious rascal'? And when the verdict come, warn't it Compeyson as was recommended to mercy on account of good character and bad company, and not his fault for being wampire. And warn't it me as got never a word but Guilty and the scorn of being born a wolf when how could I help how I was born? And when I says to Compeyson, 'Once out of this court, I'll smash that face of yourn!' ain't it Compeyson as prays the Judge to be protected, and gets two turnkeys stood betwixt us? And when we're sentenced, ain't it him as gets seven year, and me fourteen, and ain't it him as the Judge is sorry for, because he might a done so well, and ain't it me as the Judge perceives to be a old offender of wiolent passion, likely to come to worse?"

Provis had worked himself into a state of great excitement, but he checked it, took two or three short breaths, swallowed as often, and stretching out his hand towards me said, in a reassuring manner, "I ain't a going to be low, dear boy!"

He had so heated himself that he took out his handkerchief and wiped his face and head and neck and hands, before he could go on.

"I had said to Compeyson that I'd smash that face of his, and I swore Lord smash mine to do it. We was in the same containment ship, but I couldn't get at him for long, though I tried. At last I come behind him and hit him on the cheek to turn him round and get a smashing one at him, when I was seen and seized. The black-hole of that ship warn't a strong one, to a judge of black-holes that could swim and dive. I escaped to the shore, and I was a hiding among the graves there, envying them as was in 'em and all over, when I first see my boy!"

He regarded me with a look of affection that made him almost abhorrent to me again, though I had felt great pity for him.

"By my boy, I was giv to understand as Compeyson was out on them marshes, too. Upon my soul, I half believe he escaped in his terror, to get quit of me, not knowing it was me as had got ashore. I hunted him down. I smashed his face. 'And now,' says I 'as the worst thing I can do, caring nothing for myself, I'll drag you back.' I could have ended him there, dragged him into the sun or stabbed him through the heart, but he deserved more than an easy end. He deserved to live his immortal life locked in a cage wi' only the rats to drink dry of blood. I'd have swum off, towing him by the hair, if it had come to that, and I'd a got him aboard without the soldiers.

"Of course he'd much the best of it to the last—his character was so good. He had escaped when he was made half wild by me and my murderous intentions; and his punishment was light. I was put in heavy silver chains, heavier than the silver leg clamp, brought to trial again, and sent for life. I didn't stop for life, dear boy and Pip's comrade, being here."

He wiped himself again, as he had done before, and then slowly took his tangle of tobacco from his pocket, and plucked his pipe from his button-hole, and slowly filled it, and began to smoke.

"Is he dead?" I asked, after a silence.

"Is who dead, dear boy?"

"Compeyson."

"He hopes I am, if he's alive, you may be sure," with a fierce look. "I never heerd no more of him."

Herbert had been writing with his pencil in the cover of a book. He softly pushed the book over to me, as Provis stood smoking with his eyes on the fire, and I read in it:—

"Young Havisham's name was Arthur. Compeyson is the man who professed to be Miss Havisham's lover."

I shut the book and nodded slightly to Herbert, and put the book by; but we neither of us said anything, and both looked at Provis as he stood smoking by the fire.

CHAPTER 39

WHY SHOULD I PAUSE to ask how my relations with Provis might affect my pursuit of Estella? Or how my love for Estella affected my shrinking from Provis? Why should I compare the state of mind in which I had tried to rid myself of the stain of the containment prison before meeting her at the coach-office, with the state of mind in which I now reflected on the abyss between Estella in her pride and beauty, and Provis, the returned transport? The road would be none the smoother for it. The end would be none the better for it.

A new fear had sprung up in my mind by his narrative; or rather, his narrative had given shape to the fear that was already there. If Compeyson were alive and should discover his return, I could hardly doubt the consequence. That Compeyson stood in mortal fear of him made it certain that he would turn Provis in at any opportunity.

Never had I breathed, and never would I breathe—or so I resolved—a word of Estella to Provis. But, I said to Herbert that before I could go abroad, I must see both Estella and Miss Havisham. This was when we were left alone on the night of the day when Provis told us his story. I resolved to go out to Richmond next day, and I went.

On my presenting myself at Mrs. Brandley's, Estella's maid was called to tell that Estella had gone into the country. Where? To Satis House, as usual. Not as usual, I said, for she had never yet gone there without me. When was she coming back? There was an air of reservation in the answer which increased my perplexity, and the answer was, that her maid believed she was only coming back at all for a little while. I could make nothing of this, except that it was meant that I should make nothing of it, and I went home again in complete discomfiture.

Another night consultation with Herbert after Provis was gone home (I always took him home, locked him in, and always looked well about me) led us to the conclusion that nothing should be said about going abroad until I came back from Miss Havisham's.

Next day, I feigned that I was under a binding promise to go down to Joe. Provis was to be strictly careful while I was gone, and Herbert was to take the charge of him that I had taken. Having thus cleared the way for my expedition to Miss Havisham's, I set off by the early morning coach before it was yet light. When we drove up to the Blue Boar after a drizzly ride, I saw Bentley Drummle coming out under the gateway, toothpick in hand, to look at the coach.

As he pretended not to see me, I pretended not to see him. It was a very lame pretense on both sides; the lamer, because we both went into the coffee-room, where he had just finished his breakfast, and where I ordered mine. It was poisonous to me to see him in the town, for I very well knew why he had come there.

Pretending to read a smeary newspaper, I sat at my table while he stood before the fire. By degrees it became an enormous injury to me that he stood before the fire. And I got up, determined to have my share of it. I had to put my hand behind his legs for the poker when I went up to the fireplace to stir the fire, but still pretended not to know him.

"Is this a cut?" said Mr. Drummle.

"Oh!" said I, poker in hand. "It's you, is it? How do you do?"

With that, I poked tremendously, and having done so, planted myself side by side with Mr. Drummle, my shoulders squared and my back to the fire.

"You have just come down?" said Mr. Drummle, edging me a little away with his shoulder.

"Yes," said I, edging him a little away with my shoulder.

"Beastly place," said Drummle. "Your part of the country, I think?"

"Yes," I assented. "I am told it's very like your Shropshire."

"Not in the least like it," said Drummle.

I felt here, through a tingling in my blood, that Mr. Drummle and I were about to come to blows again, and this time there were no Savages to tear us apart. The hair on my neck stood up and I barely suppressed a low sinister growl.

"Large tract of marshes about here, I believe?" said Drummle. I could smell his fear in the air, sharper than the fire, and I realised he kept up conversation in an attempt to maintain his composure. He had learned something from Mr. Pocket after all.

"Yes. What of that?" said I, inching closer, for I was not afraid of him and suddenly my lessons were the furthest thing from my mind. I let my lip curl up in a sneer.

"I am going out for a ride in the saddle," he said, hiding his furring hands behind his back. "I mean to explore those marshes for amusement. Out-of-the-way villages there, they tell me. Curious little public-houses—and smithies—and that. Waiter! Is that horse of mine ready?"

"Brought round to the door, sir."

"I say. Look here, you sir. The lady won't ride today. The weather won't do. And I don't dine, because I'm going to dine at the lady's."

"Very good, sir."

Then, Drummle glanced at me, with an insolent triumph on his great-jowled face that cut me to the heart, dull as he was, and so exasperated me, that I felt inclined to take him in my arms and seat him on the fire. It was his way perhaps of assuring me there was no need to fight, for he had already won. Estella was his. No amount of my pummeling, tearing him limb from limb, or even killing him would do if she would be the one to look after his wounds, or mourn him. I had no idea if she had a mind to kill him herself or if she took him for other reasons. His money? His power? To clear her way to abandon Miss Havisham and take Drummle as her partner as I had dreamed to be?

"Mr. Drummle, I did not seek this conversation," I said. "And I don't think it an agreeable one. And therefore, with your leave, I will suggest that we hold no kind of communication in future."

"Quite my opinion," said Drummle. "And what I should have suggested myself, or done—more likely—without suggesting. But don't lose your temper. Haven't you lost enough without that?"

I looked stonily at the opposite wall, as if there were no one present, and forced myself to silence. I saw him through the window, seizing his horse's mane, and mounting in his blundering brutal manner, and sidling and backing away. The slouching shoulders and ragged hair of this man who attended him reminded me of Orlick.

Too heavily out of sorts to care much at the time whether it were he or no, or after all to touch the breakfast, I washed the weather and the journey from my face and hands, and went out to the memorable old house that it would have been so much the better for me never to have entered, never to have seen.

CHAPTER 40

AT SATIS HOUSE, I chose not to ring the bell and wait to be let in. My wolf's instincts aroused, I made my own way through the house for what I hoped was a visit but knew might turn out to be some sort of confrontation. In the room where the dressing-table stood, and where the wax-candles burnt on the wall, I found Miss Havisham and Estella. Miss Havisham was seated on a settee near the fire, looking over Estella's shoulder as Estella, on a cushion at her feet, sharpened stakes. They both raised their eyes as I went in, and both clearly saw an alteration in me from the look they interchanged.

"And what wind," said Miss Havisham, "blows you here, Pip?"

Though she looked steadily at me, I saw that she was rather confused. Estella paused a moment in her whittling with her eyes upon me. I fancied that I read in the action of her fingers that she perceived I had discovered my real benefactor.

"Miss Havisham," I said. "I went to Richmond yesterday, to speak to Estella; and finding that some wind had blown *her* here, I followed."

Miss Havisham motioning to me for the third or fourth time to sit down, I took the chair by the dressing-table, which I had often seen her occupy. With all that ruin at my feet and about me, it seemed a natural place for me, that day.

"What I had to say to Estella, Miss Havisham, I will say before you, presently—in a few moments."

Miss Havisham continued to look steadily at me. I could see in the action of Estella's fingers as they worked that she attended to what I said. She would not meet my gaze.

"I have found out who my patron is. It is not a fortunate discovery, and is not likely ever to enrich me in reputation, station, fortune, anything. There are reasons why I must say no more of that. It is not my secret, but another's."

As I was silent for a while, looking at Estella and considering how to go on, Miss Havisham repeated, "It is not your secret, but another's. Well?"

"When you first caused me to be brought here, Miss Havisham, when I belonged to the village over yonder, that I wish I had never left, I suppose I did really come here, as any other chance boy might have come—as a kind of servant, to gratify a want or a whim, and to be paid for it?"

"Aye, Pip." Miss Havisham steadily nodded her head. "You did."

"And that Mr. Jaggers—"

"Mr. Jaggers," said Miss Havisham, taking me up in a firm tone, "had nothing to do with it, and knew nothing of it. His being my lawyer, and his being the lawyer of your patron is a coincidence. He holds the same relation towards numbers of Scapegraces, and it might easily arise. Be that as it may, it did arise, and was not brought about by any one."

Any one might have seen in her haggard face that there was no suppression or evasion so far.

"But when I fell into the mistake I have so long remained in, at least you led me on?" I said.

"Yes," she returned, again nodding steadily, "I let you go on."

"Was that kind?"

"For God's sake, who am I that I should be kind?" cried Miss Havisham, striking her stick upon the floor and flashing into wrath so suddenly that Estella glanced up at her in surprise.

It was a weak complaint to have made, and I had not meant to make it. I told her so as she sat brooding after this outburst.

"Well, well, well!" she said. "What else?"

"I was liberally paid for my old attendance here," I said, to soothe her, "in being apprenticed, and I have asked these questions only for my own information. What follows has another (and I hope more disinterested) purpose. In humouring my mistake, Miss Havisham, you punished—practised on—perhaps you will supply whatever term expresses your intention, without offence—your self-seeking relations?"

"I did. Why, they would have it so! So would you. What has been my history, that I should be at the pains of entreating either them or you not to have it so! You made your own snares. I never made them."

Waiting until she was quiet again—for this, too, flashed out of her in a wild and sudden way—I went on.

"I have been thrown among one family of your relations, Miss Havisham, and have been constantly among them since I went to London. I know them to have been as honestly under my delusion as I myself. And I should be false and base if I did not tell you, whether it is acceptable to you or no, and whether you are inclined to give credence to it or no, that you deeply wrong both Mr. Matthew Pocket and his son Herbert, if you suppose them to be otherwise than generous, upright, open, and incapable of anything designing or mean."

"They are your friends," said Miss Havisham.

"They made themselves my friends," said I, "when they supposed me to have superseded them; and when Sarah Pocket, Miss Georgiana, and Mistress Camilla were not my friends, I think. The Scapegraces showed more humanity than the humans."

This contrasting of them with the rest seemed, I was glad to see, to do them good with her. She looked at me keenly for a little while. "What do you want for them?"

"Only," said I, "that you would not confound them with the others. They may be of the same blood, but, believe me, they are not of the same nature, and I don't mean to refer to the werewolf-human physical differences but also of who they are inside."

"I see what you mean to say. The monsters are the humans, eh?" She cackled. "What do you want for them?"

"I am not so cunning, you see," I said in answer, conscious that I reddened a little, "as that I could hide from you, even if I desired, that I do want something. Miss Havisham, if you would spare the money to do my friend Herbert a lasting service in life, but which from the nature of the case must be done without his knowledge, I could show you how."

"Why must it be done without his knowledge?" she asked, settling her hands upon her stick, that she might regard me the more attentively.

"Because," said I, "I began the service myself, more than two years ago, without his knowledge, and I don't want to be betrayed. Why I fail in my ability to finish it, I cannot explain. It is a part of the secret which is another person's and not mine."

She gradually withdrew her eyes from me, and turned them on the fire. All this time Estella whittled on. When Miss Havisham had fixed her attention on me, she said, speaking as if there had been no lapse in our dialogue, she said, "What else?"

"Estella," said I, turning to her now, and trying to command my trembling voice, "you know I love you. You know that I have loved you long and dearly."

She raised her eyes to my face, on being thus addressed, and her fingers plied their work, and she looked at me with an unmoved countenance. I saw that Miss Havisham glanced from me to her, and from her to me.

"I should have said this sooner, but for my long mistake. It induced me to hope that Miss Havisham meant us for one another. While I thought you could not help yourself, as it were, I refrained from saying it. But I must say it now."

Preserving her unmoved countenance, and with her fingers still going, Estella shook her head.

"I have no hope that I shall ever call you mine, Estella. I am ignorant what may become of me very soon, how poor I may be, or where I may go. Still, I love you. I have loved you ever since I first saw you in this house."

Looking at me perfectly unmoved and with her fingers busy, she shook her head again.

"It would have been cruel in Miss Havisham, horribly cruel, to practise on the susceptibility of a poor boy, and to torture me through all these years with a vain hope and an idle pursuit, if she had understood that werewolves, unlike vampires, are still human most of the time, with human emotions and attachments. But I think she did not. I think that, in the pursuit of her revenge, she forgot I might develop feelings, Estella. Feelings of love."

I saw Miss Havisham put her hand to her heart and hold it there, as she sat looking by turns at Estella and at me.

"It seems," said Estella, very calmly, "that there are sentiments, fancies—I don't know how to call them—which I am not able to comprehend. When you say you love me, I know what you mean, as a form of words, but nothing more. You address nothing in my breast. You touch nothing there. I don't care for what you say at all. I have tried to warn you of this, now, have I not?"

I said in a miserable manner, "Yes."

"Yes. But you would not be warned, for you thought I did not mean it. Now, did you not think so?"

"I thought and hoped you could not mean it. You, so young, untried, and beautiful, Estella! Surely it is not in nature."

"It is in my nature," she returned. And then she added, with a stress upon the words, "It is in the nature formed within me, as being wolf is in yours. I can do no more."

"If I can learn to control my wolfishness, you can learn to love," I said. "Is it not true that Bentley Drummle is in town here, and pursuing you? We would make a better team, you and I. We've fought together here, for show. We could do it together, for a purpose."

"Not your purpose, Pip. Not your fight. Learn to love? I have learned to kill. You wish to kill, Pip? At my side? To prey on fellow Scapegraces?" She raised a brow. I couldn't help but flinch at the sound of it, when spoken out loud. "I am a slayer, Pip. And you are a werewolf."

"And so is Drummle!"

"Ah, but he has no heart or mind. You are human as well as wolf, Pip, with a heart, but not for killing, truly. It is quite true regarding Mr. Drummle pursuing me, and my accepting."

"You encourage him, and ride out with him, and he dines with you this very day? You cannot love him, Estella!"

Her fingers stopped for the first time, as she retorted rather angrily, "What have I told you? Do you still think, in spite of it, that I do not mean what I say?"

"You would never marry him, Estella?"

She looked towards Miss Havisham, and considered for a moment with her work in her hands. Then she said, "Why not tell you? I am going to be married to him."

"Marry him?" I dropped my face into my hands, but was able to control myself better than I could have expected, considering what agony it gave me to hear her say those words. When I raised my face again, there was such a ghastly look upon Miss Havisham's, that it impressed me, even in my passionate hurry and grief. "Could you not affect your revenge more potently by simply killing him? Or do you mean to practise your arts for some time? Play with him? He should be an easy mark. Estella, dearest Estella." I reached to take her hand. She pulled back. "Do not let Miss Havisham lead you into this fatal step. Put me aside for ever—you have done so, I well know—but bestow yourself on some worthier person than Drummle."

"What does his worthiness matter? He is a means to an end."

"You mean, to end him?" I asked.

"I am going," she said again, in a gentler voice, "to be married to him. The preparations for my marriage are making, and I shall be married soon. It has nothing to do with my mother by adoption. It is my own act."

"Your own act, Estella, to fling yourself away upon a brute?"

"On whom should I fling myself away?" she retorted, with a smile. "Should I fling myself away upon the man who would the soonest feel that I have endangered him and brought him nothing? That I cost him the joy that he might feel with another, more suited? There! It is done. I shall do well enough, and so will my husband. As to leading me into what you call this fatal step, Miss Havisham would have had me not marry; but I am tired of following her instincts. It is time I followed my own. It is no longer just about achieving her revenge, but about eradicating vampires for the good of all. Drummle is a tool, nothing more. A means to an end."

"Such a mean brute, such a stupid brute!" I urged, in despair.

"Don't be afraid of my being a blessing to him," said Estella. "I shall not be that. Come! Here is my hand. Do we part on this, you visionary pup—or man?"

"Oh, Estella!" I answered, as my bitter tears fell fast on her hand, do what I would to restrain them. "Even if I remained in England and could hold my head up with the rest, how could I see you Drummle's wife?"

"You won't need to see it." She smiled impassively. "Simply stay out of my way for a time. This will pass."

"Never, Estella!"

"You will get me out of your thoughts in a week."

"Out of my thoughts! You are part of my existence, part of myself. You have been in every line I have ever read since I first came here, the hairy common boy whose poor heart you wounded even then. You have been in every prospect I have ever seen since—on the river, on the sails of the ships, on the marshes, in the clouds. Estella, to the last hour of my life, you cannot choose but remain part of my character, part of the little good in me, part of the evil. But, in this separation, I associate you only with the good; and I will faithfully hold you to that always, for you must have done me far more good than harm, let me feel now what sharp distress I may. Oh God bless you, God forgive you!"

In what ecstasy of unhappiness I got these broken words out of myself, I don't know. The rhapsody welled up within me, like blood from an inward wound, and gushed out. I held her hand to my lips some lingering moments, and so I left her. But ever afterwards, I remembered—and soon afterwards with stronger reason—that while Estella looked at me merely with incredulous wonder, the spectral figure of Miss Havisham, her hand still covering her heart, seemed all resolved into a ghastly stare of pity and remorse.

All done, all gone! So much was done and gone, that when I

went out at the gate, the light of the day seemed of a darker colour than when I went in. I hadn't meant to stay so late. Under the light of the moon, I began my transformation. For the sake of safety, I stripped and concealed my clothes where I knew I could find them again upon my eventual return, should I ever return.

For a while, I hid myself among some lanes and bypaths, and reeled from the pain of the change as it took over. Once sufficiently covered by my own wild growth of hair, and unrecognisable as human though still very much human in my mind, I struck off to run all the way to London. I could not go back to the inn and risk seeing Drummle there. The danger was too great that we would engage and I did not doubt that I would tear him to shreds despite his physical advantage. To murder him would leave me no better than the convict I was so desperate to remove from my life.

On the way to London, I ran wildly, down streets, keeping to the shadows. In fear of being seen under the street lamps and at risk of being accused of some crime, I ran down a dark alley and encountered a vampire just sinking his teeth into the tender flesh of a victim's neck.

"Help!" She flailed uselessly in his much-stronger arms. "Someone! No, don't eat me!"

I stopped behind them, reared up on hind legs, and howled. I was quite a sight, I realised, when stretched up at full height, all bulky fur, and fangs, and teeth. I dreaded to invoke greater terror in the vampire's prey, but she needed saving and I knew no other way. One look at me over the vampire's shoulder and she fainted and fell limp in his arms, poor dear. But she might thank me later.

I inched closer and growled, as threatening as I could manage.

The vampire dropped his victim, turned, and gave me a nod, blood dripping from his extended fangs. "Eh, what do you want?"

He didn't seem to think me a threat? I sprung, slamming him to the cobblestones and tearing a chunk out of his neck much as he had attempted to devour his prey. I leaned over him, breathing hot into his face as he shrieked in pain, and bared my fangs. Now I could smell the fear.

"Leave me alone!" He was strong in his struggling, but he was no match for me.

I revelled in his weakness. Even a dead, cold thing like a vampire could be intimidated given the right circumstances. Without a stake to the heart or direct sunlight, I could not kill him. But I could torture him with pain. I could tear him to shreds. Perhaps I could wrench his head off, and that might indeed kill him as sure as it would end a Recommissioned.

"No," he started to beg. "Please. I'll leave town. I'll eat animals! No more humans for me. I promise. Just let—let me go!"

His victim revived enough to whimper at the sight of us and run off to safety.

I snarled at his cowering form, but I was not unaffected by his fearful pleas. Estella was right. I knew he was a beast, and he was cruel. Given the chance, he would terrorize innocents without a hint of remorse. And yet, I could not kill him. I did not have the hunger for human, or vampire, flesh. I had no desire to willingly end the life of something that so closely resembled a human. I backed away, leaving him in the alley, and I ran.

My inner beast took over and guided me away from the city lights and into the dense brush alongside the road, and further to the forest. I woke naked and hungry, huddled in the moss near the split trunk of an old ash tree. Apparently, I hadn't killed last night, not for sport or food. No poor forest creature had died to sate my savage appetite.

It was some time after dawn that I crossed London Bridge, having begged a robe off a monk driving a cart along a quiet lane on the outskirts. Pursuing the narrow intricacies of the streets, my readiest access to the Temple was close by the riverside, through Whitefriars. I was not expected till much later in the day, but I had my keys on a chain worn round my neck, and, if Herbert were still locked up in his chamber, sleeping off the change, I could get in without disturbing him.

As it seldom happened that I came in at that Whitefriars gate after the Temple was closed, and as I was very muddy and weary, I did not take it ill that the night-porter, still on duty, examined me with much attention as he held the gate a little way open for me to pass in. To help his memory I mentioned my name.

"I was not quite sure, sir, but I thought so. Here's a note, sir. The messenger that brought it, said would you be so good as to read it?"

Much surprised by the request, I took the note. It was directed to Philip Pip, Esquire, and on the top of the superscription were the words, "PLEASE READ THIS, HERE." I opened it and read inside, in Wemmick's writing—"DON'T GO HOME."

CHAPTER 41

As soon as I had read the warning, I made my way to Fleet Street, and there got a late hackney chariot and drove to Wemmick's, DON'T GO HOME running through my head along the way. Why I was not to go home, and what had happened at home, and whether Provis was safe at home, were questions occupying my mind so busily that one might have supposed there could be no more room for any other theme. Even when I thought of Estella, and how we had parted forever, and when I recalled all the circumstances of our parting, and all her looks and tones, and the action of her fingers while she sharpened stakes—even then I was pursuing, here and there and everywhere, the caution, Don't go home.

It was a relief to arrive.

"Halloa, Mr. Pip!" said Wemmick. "You did come home, then?"

"Yes," I returned. "But I didn't go home."

"That's all right." He rubbed his hands.

I thanked him for his friendship and caution, and our discourse proceeded in a low tone.

"Now, Mr. Pip," said Wemmick, "I accidentally heard, yesterday morning, being in a certain place where I once took you—even between you and me, it's as well not to mention names when avoidable—"

"Much better not. I understand you." He meant Newgate.

"I heard there by chance, yesterday morning, that you at your chambers in Garden Court, Temple, had been watched, and might be watched again."

"By whom?" said I.

"I wouldn't go into that," said Wemmick, evasively, "it might clash with official responsibilities. I heard it, as I have in my time heard other curious things in the same place. I don't tell it you on information received. I heard it."

He arranged the Aged's breakfast neatly on a little tray, and excused himself to deliver it.

"This watching of me at my chambers (which I have once had reason to suspect)," I said to Wemmick when he came back, "is connected to a person we both know?"

Wemmick looked very serious. "I couldn't undertake to say that, of my own knowledge. I mean, I couldn't undertake to say it was at first. But it either is, or it will be, or it's in great danger of being."

"You have heard of a man of bad character, whose true name is Compeyson?" I asked.

He answered with one other nod.

"Is he living? Is he in London?"

He gave me one other nod, then gave me one last nod, and went on with his breakfast.

"Now," said Wemmick, "questioning being over," which he emphasised and repeated for my guidance, "I come to what I did, after hearing what I heard. I went to Garden Court to find you; not finding you, I went to Clavenger's to find Mr. Herbert."

"And him you found?" said I, with great anxiety.

"And him I found. Without mentioning any names or going into any details, I gave him to understand that if he was aware of anybody—Tom, Jack, or Richard—being about the chambers, or about the immediate neighbourhood, he had better get Tom, Jack, or Richard out of the way while you were out of the way."

"He would be greatly puzzled what to do?"

"He *was* puzzled what to do; not the less, because I gave him my opinion that it was not safe to try to get Tom, Jack, or Richard too far out of the way at present. Mr. Pip, I'll tell you something. Under existing circumstances, there is no place like a great city when you are once in it. Don't break cover too soon. Lie close. Wait till things slacken, before you try the open, even for foreign air."

I thanked him for his valuable advice, and asked him what Herbert had done?

"Mr. Herbert," said Wemmick, "after being all of a heap for half an hour, struck out a plan. He mentioned to me as a secret, that he is courting a young lady who has, as no doubt you are aware, a bedridden Pa. Which Pa, having been in the Purser line of life, lies a-bed in a bow-window where he can see the ships sail up and down the river. You are acquainted with the young lady, most probably?"

"Not personally," said I.

Clara had objected to me as an expensive companion who did Herbert no good, but she was changing her opinion as Herbert's prospects increased.

"The house with the bow-window," said Wemmick, "being by the riverside and being kept, it seems, by a very respectable widow who has a furnished upper floor to let, Mr. Herbert put it to me, what did I think of that as a temporary tenement for Tom, Jack, or Richard? Now, I thought very well of it, for three reasons I'll give you. That is to say: Firstly, it's altogether out of all your beats, and is well away from the usual heap of streets great and small. Secondly, without going near it yourself, you could always hear of the safety of Tom, Jack, or Richard, through Mr. Herbert. Thirdly, after a while and when it might be prudent, if you should want to slip Tom, Jack, or Richard on board a foreign packet-boat, there he is—ready."

Much comforted by these considerations, I thanked Wemmick again and again, and begged him to proceed.

"Well, sir! Mr. Herbert threw himself into the business with a will, and by nine o'clock last night he housed Tom, Jack, or Richard—whichever it may be—you and I don't want to know—quite successfully. Another great advantage of all this is that it was done without you, and when, if any one was concerning himself about your movements, you must be known to be ever so many miles off and quite otherwise engaged. It brings in more confusion, and you want confusion."

Wemmick, having finished his breakfast, here looked at his watch, and began to get his coat on.

"And now, Mr. Pip," he said, slipping his hands through the sleeves, "I have probably done the most I can do. Here's the address. There can be no harm in your going here tonight, and seeing for yourself that all is well with Tom, Jack, or Richard, before you go home—which is another reason for your not going home last night. But, after you have gone home, don't go back there. You are very welcome, I am sure, Mr. Pip, and let me finally impress one important point upon you." He laid his hands upon my shoulders, and added in a solemn whisper, "Avail yourself of this evening to lay hold of his portable property. You don't know what may happen to him. Don't let anything happen to the portable property."

"I'll take it under advisement."

"Time's up," said Wemmick. "I must be off. If you had nothing more pressing to do than to keep here till dark, that's what I should advise. Dress yourself in something of mine or of the Aged's. Good day."

I soon fell asleep before Wemmick's fire. When it was quite dark, I slipped away again.

CHAPTER 42

The SPOT TO WHICH Wemmick had directed me, Mill Pond Bank, was not easy to find, and eight o'clock had struck before I got there. All that water-side region was unknown ground to me. It was a fresh kind of place, all circumstances considered, where the wind from the river had room to turn itself round.

Selecting from the few houses upon Mill Pond Bank a house with a wooden front and three stories of bow-window, I looked at the plate upon the door, and read there MRS. WHIMPLE. That being the name I wanted, I knocked, and an elderly woman of a pleasant and thriving appearance responded. Herbert followed right behind her, much to my relief. It was an odd sensation to see his very familiar face established quite at home in that very unfamiliar room and I found myself looking at him, much as I looked at the corner-cupboard with the glass and china, the shells upon the chimney-piece, and the colored engravings on the wall.

"All is well, Lowell," said Herbert. "He is quite satisfied, though eager to see you. My dear girl is with her father. If you'll wait till she comes down, I'll make you known to her, and then we'll go up stairs. *That's* her father."

I had become aware of an alarming growling overhead, and had probably expressed the fact in my countenance.

"I am afraid he is a sad old rascal," said Herbert, smiling. "I have never seen him. Don't you smell rum? He is always at it."

"At rum?" said I.

"Yes," returned Herbert, "and you may suppose how mild it makes his gout."

While he thus spoke, the growling noise became a prolonged roar, and then died away.

He seemed to have hurt himself very much, for he gave another furious roar.

"To have Provis for an upper lodger is quite a godsend to Mrs. Whimple," said Herbert, "for of course people in general won't stand that noise. A curious place, Lowell. Isn't it?"

"It is a curious place, but remarkably well kept and clean."

"Mrs. Whimple is the best of housewives," Herbert said. "I really do not know what my Clara would do without her motherly help. For, Clara has no mother of her own, Lowell, and no relation in the world but old Gruffandgrim."

"Surely that's not his name, Herbert?"

"No, no," said Herbert, "that's my name for him. His name is Mr. Barley."

Herbert had told me on former occasions, and now reminded me, that he first knew Miss Clara Barley when she was completing her education at an establishment at Hammersmith, and that on her being recalled home to nurse her father, he and she had confided their affection to the motherly Mrs. Whimple, by whom it had been fostered and regulated with equal kindness and discretion, ever since.

As we were thus conversing in a low tone while Old Barley's sustained growl vibrated in the beam that crossed the ceiling, the room door opened, and a very pretty, slight, dark-eyed girl of twenty or so came in with a basket in her hand: whom Herbert tenderly relieved of the basket, and presented, blushing, as "Clara." She really was a most charming girl, and might have passed for a captive fairy, whom that truculent Ogre, Old Barley, had pressed into his service.

I looked at Clara with pleasure and admiration, when suddenly the growl swelled into a roar again, and a frightful bumping noise was heard above. Upon this Clara said to Herbert, "Papa wants me, darling!" and ran away.

Clara returned soon afterwards, and Herbert accompanied me upstairs to see our charge. As we passed Mr. Barley's door, he was heard hoarsely muttering within, and then singing in a loud voice, which Herbert explained he could keep up half the night.

In his two cabin rooms at the top of the house, which were fresh and airy, and in which Mr. Barley was less audible than below, I found Provis comfortably settled. He expressed no alarm, and seemed to feel none that was worth mentioning, but it struck me that he was softened. I could not have said how, but so it was.

The opportunity that the day's rest had given me for reflection had resulted in my fully determining to say nothing to him respecting Compeyson. For anything I knew, his animosity towards the man might otherwise lead to his seeking him out and rushing on his own destruction. Therefore, when Herbert and I sat down with him by his fire, I asked him first of all whether he relied on Wemmick's judgment and sources of information?

"Aye, aye, dear boy!" he answered, with a grave nod. "Jaggers knows."

"Then, I have talked with Wemmick," said I, "and have come to tell you what caution he gave me and what advice."

I told him how Wemmick had heard, in Newgate Containment (whether from officers or prisoners I could not say), that he was under some suspicion, and that my chambers had been watched. I said it was safest for us to go abroad. As to altering my way of living by enlarging my expenses, I put it to him that in our present unsettled and difficult circumstances, it would be simply ridiculous to raise any suspicion by changing my habits.

He could not deny this, and indeed was very reasonable throughout. His coming back was a venture, he said, and he had always known it to be a venture. He would do nothing to make it a desperate venture, and he had very little fear of his safety with such good help.

"We are both good watermen, Lowell, and could take him down the river ourselves when the right time comes," Herbert suggested. "No boat would then be hired for the purpose, and no boatmen, saving at least a chance of suspicion, and any chance is worth saving. We have the advantage, as most werewolves dread the water and no one would suspect the water route. Father's unusual techniques will benefit us as we can use our training to control our transformations as needed, even wet and cold. We can keep a boat at the Temple stairs and practise our route after dark."

I liked this scheme, and Provis was quite elated by it. We agreed that it should be carried into execution, and that Provis should never recognize us if we came below Bridge, and rowed past Mill Pond Bank. But we further agreed that he should pull down the blind in that part of his window, which gave upon the east, whenever he saw us and all was right.

Our conference being now ended, and everything arranged, I rose to go, remarking to Herbert that he and I had better not go home together, and that I would take half an hour's start of him.

"I don't like to leave you here," I said to Provis, "though I cannot doubt your being safer here than near me. Goodbye!"

"Dear boy," he answered, clasping my hands, "I don't know when we may meet again, and I don't like goodbye. Say goodnight!"

"Goodnight! Herbert will go regularly between us, and when the time comes you may be certain I shall be ready. Goodnight, goodnight!"

We thought it best that he should stay in his own rooms. We left him on the landing outside his door, holding a light over the stair rail to light us downstairs. Looking back at him, I thought of the first night of his return, when our positions were reversed, and when I little supposed my heart could ever be as heavy and anxious at parting from him as it was now.

When we got to the foot of the stairs, I asked Herbert whether he had preserved the name of Provis. He replied, certainly not, and that the lodger was Mr. Campbell. He also explained to the widow that he was in care of Mr. Campbell, and felt a strong personal interest in his being well cared for, and living a secluded life. So, when we went into the parlour where Mrs. Whimple and Clara were seated at work, I said nothing of my own interest in Mr. Campbell, but kept it to myself.

When I had taken leave of the gentle, dark-eyed Clara, I felt as if the house in Mill Pond Bank had grown quite a different place, full of redeeming hope and trust and love. And then I thought of Estella, and of our parting, and went home very sadly.

Next day I set myself to get the boat. It was soon done, and the boat was brought round to the Temple stairs, and rested where I could reach her within a minute or two. Then, I began to go out as for training and practise, sometimes alone, sometimes with Herbert. I was often out in cold, rain, and sleet, but always looking about me to see that I was not followed.

CHAPTER 43

SOME WEEKS PASSED WITHOUT bringing any change. We waited for Wemmick, and he made no sign. If I had never known him out of Little Britain, and had never enjoyed the privilege of being on a familiar footing at the Castle, I might have doubted him.

My worldly affairs began to wear a gloomy appearance. More than one creditor pressed me for money, but I had quite determined that it would be a heartless fraud to take more money from my patron in the existing state of my uncertain thoughts and plans. Therefore, I had Herbert bring Provis his unopened pocketbook to hold in his own keeping.

As the time wore on, an impression settled heavily upon me that Estella was married. Fearful of having it confirmed, though it was all but a conviction, I avoided the newspapers, and begged Herbert never to speak of her to me.

One raw evening, I thought I would comfort myself with dinner and a visit to the theatre. I watched Mr. Wopsle's play and I could tell the exact moment when he, a character on the stage, had taken note of my presence in the audience. And I observed, as the play progressed, that he devoted much of it to staring in my direction as if he were lost in amazement.

There was something so remarkable in the increasing glare of Mr. Wopsle's eye, and he seemed to be turning so many things over in his mind and to grow so confused, that I could not make it out. I was still thinking of it when I came out of the theatre and found him waiting for me near the door.

"How do you do?" I shook hands with him as we turned down the street together. "I saw that you saw me."

"Saw you, Mr. Pip!" he returned. "Yes, of course I saw you. But who else was there?"

"Who else?"

"It is the strangest thing." Mr. Wopsle drifted into his lost look again. "And yet I could swear to him."

Becoming alarmed, I entreated Mr. Wopsle to explain his meaning.

"Whether I should have noticed him at first but for your being there," Mr. Wopsle said, going on in the same lost way, "I can't be positive. Yet I think I should."

Involuntarily I looked round me, for these mysterious words gave me a chill.

"Oh! He can't be in sight," Mr. Wopsle said. "He went out before I went off. I saw him go. I had a ridiculous fancy that he must be with you, Mr. Pip, till I saw that you were quite unconscious of him, sitting behind you there like a ghost."

"Indeed?" I encouraged him.

"Mr. Pip, you remember in old times a certain Christmas Day, when you were quite a child, and I dined at Gargery's, and some soldiers came to the door to get a pair of handcuffs mended?"

"I remember it very well."

"And you remember that there was a chase after two convicts, and that we joined in it, and that Gargery took you on his back, and that I took the lead, and you kept up with me as well as you could?"

"I remember it all very well." Better than he thought, except the last clause.

"Then, Mr. Pip, one of those two prisoners sat behind you to-night. I saw him over your shoulder."

"Steady!" I thought. I asked him then, "Which of the two do you suppose you saw?"

"The one who had been mauled," he answered readily, "and I'll swear I saw him! The more I think of him, the more certain I am of him. That face is too hard to mistake, with the forehead so prominent and gaze red as blood." He shuddered.

"This is very curious!" I gave the best show I could put on of its being nothing more to me. "Very curious indeed!"

I cannot exaggerate the enhanced disquiet into which this conversation threw me, or the special and peculiar terror I felt at Compeyson's having been behind me "like a ghost." If he had ever been out of my thoughts for a few moments together since the hiding had begun, it was in those very moments when he was closest to me. I could not doubt, either, that he was there, because I was there, and that, however slight an appearance of danger there might be about us, danger was always near and active.

I put such questions to Mr. Wopsle as, when did the man come in? He could not tell me. He saw me, and over my shoulder he saw the man. How was he dressed? Prosperously, and all in black, but not noticeably otherwise. When Mr. Wopsle had imparted to me all that he could recall or I extract, and when I had treated him to a little appropriate refreshment, after the fatigues of the evening, we parted. It was between twelve and one o'clock when I reached the Temple, and the gates were shut. No one was near me when I went in and went home.

Herbert had come in, and we held a very serious council by the fire. But there was nothing to be done, saving to communicate to

Wemmick what I had that night found out, and to remind him that we waited for his hint. As I thought that I might compromise him if I went too often to the Castle, I made this communication by letter. I wrote it before I went to bed, and went out and posted it. Again, no one was near me.

Herbert and I agreed that we could do nothing else but be very cautious. And we were very cautious indeed—more cautious than before, if that were possible—and I for my part never went near Mill Pond Bank, except when I rowed by, and then I only looked at the area as I looked at anything else.

CHAPTER 44

THE NEXT DAY, I was invited to dinner with Jaggers and felt that I could not turn him down, especially when he mentioned that Wemmick would be there.

"Did you send that note of Miss Havisham's to Mr. Pip, Wemmick?" Mr. Jaggers asked, soon after we began dinner.

"No, sir," returned Wemmick. "It was going by post, when you brought Mr. Pip into the office. Here it is." He handed it to his principal instead of to me.

"It's a note of two lines, Pip," said Mr. Jaggers, handing it on. "She sent up to me by Miss Havisham on account of her not being sure of your address. She tells me that she wants to see you on a little matter of business you mentioned to her. You'll go down?"

"Yes," said I, casting my eyes over the note, which was exactly in those terms. "At once, I think."

"If Mr. Pip has the intention of going at once," said Wemmick to Mr. Jaggers, "he needn't write an answer, you know."

Receiving this as an intimation that it was best not to delay, I settled that I would go tomorrow, and said so. Wemmick drank a glass of wine, and looked with a grimly satisfied air at Mr. Jaggers, but not at me.

"So, Pip! Our friend the Spider," said Mr. Jaggers, "has played his cards. He has won the pool."

It was as much as I could do to assent.

"Hah! He is a promising fellow—in his way—but he may not have it all his own way. The stronger will win in the end, but the stronger has to be found out first. If he should turn to, and beat her—"

"Surely," I interrupted, with a burning face and heart, "you do not seriously think that he is scoundrel enough for that, Mr. Jaggers?"

"I didn't say so, Pip. I am putting a case. If he should turn to and beat her, he may possibly get the strength on his side. If it should be a question of intellect, he certainly will not. It would be chance work to give an opinion how a fellow of that sort will turn out in such circumstances, because it's a toss-up between two results."

"May I ask what they are?"

"A fellow like our friend the Spider," answered Mr. Jaggers, "either beats or cringes. He may cringe and growl, or cringe and not growl; but he either beats or cringes. Ask Wemmick *his* opinion."

"Either beats or cringes," said Wemmick, not at all addressing himself to me.

Well, surely he would cringe, and not beat. As much as I could not bear to think of Estella being beaten, I could not imagine the man, or wolf, capable of it. She was well trained, impeccably skilled, simply magnificent.

"So here's to Mrs. Bentley Drummle," said Mr. Jaggers, taking a decanter of choicer wine from his dumb-waiter, and filling for each of us and for himself, "and may the question of supremacy be settled to the lady's satisfaction! To the satisfaction of the lady *and* the gentleman, it never will be. Now, Molly, Molly, Molly, Molly, how slow you are today!"

She was at his elbow when he addressed her, putting a dish upon the table. As she withdrew her hands from it, she fell back a step or two, nervously muttering some excuse. And a certain action of her fingers, as she spoke, arrested my attention.

"What's the matter?" said Mr. Jaggers.

"Nothing. Only the subject we were speaking of," I said, "was rather painful to me."

The action of her fingers was like the action of whittling stakes. She stood looking at her master, not understanding whether she was free to go, or whether he had more to say to her and would call her back if she did go. Her look was very intent. Surely, I had seen exactly such eyes and such hands on a memorable occasion very lately!

He dismissed her, and she glided out of the room. But she remained before me as plainly as if she were still there. Those hands, those eyes, that flowing hair that I compared with other hands, other eyes, other hair, and with what those might be after twenty years of a brutal husband and a stormy life.

I looked again at those hands and eyes of the housekeeper, and thought of the inexplicable feeling that had come over me when I last walked—not alone—in the ruined garden, and through the deserted brewery. I thought how the same feeling had come back when I saw a face looking at me, and a hand waving to me from a stagecoach window. How it had come back again and had flashed about me like lightning, when I had passed in a carriage—not alone—through a sudden glare of light in a dark street. I thought of Estella, to the fingers with their whittling action, and the attentive eyes. And I felt absolutely certain that this woman was Estella's mother.

Mr. Jaggers had seen me with Estella, and was not likely to have missed the sentiments I had been at no pains to conceal. He nodded when I said the subject was painful to me, clapped me on the back, put round the wine again, and went on with his dinner.

Only twice more did the housekeeper reappear, and then her stay in the room was very short, and Mr. Jaggers was sharp with her. But her hands were Estella's hands, and her eyes were Estella's eyes, and if she had reappeared a hundred times I could have been neither more sure nor less sure that my conviction was the truth.

It was a dull evening, for Wemmick drew his wine, when it came round, quite as a matter of business, and with his eyes on his chief, sat in a state of perpetual readiness for cross-examination.

We took our leave early, and left together.

"Well!" said Wemmick, "that's over! He's a wonderful man, without his living likeness, but I feel that I have to screw myself up when I dine with him, and I dine more comfortably un-screwed."

I felt that this was a good statement of the case, and told him so.

"Wouldn't say it to anybody but yourself," he answered. "I know that what is said between you and me goes no further."

I asked him if he had ever seen Miss Havisham's adopted daughter, Mrs. Bentley Drummle. He said no. To avoid being too abrupt, I then spoke of the Aged and of Miss Skiffins. He looked rather sly when I mentioned Miss Skiffins, and stopped in the street to blow his nose, with a roll of the head, and a flourish not quite free from latent boastfulness.

"Wemmick, do you remember telling me, before I first went to Mr. Jaggers's private house, to notice that housekeeper?"

"Did I?" he replied. "Ah, I dare say I did. Deuce take me. I know I did. I find I am not quite unscrewed yet."

"A wild beast tamed, you called her."

"And what do you call her?"

"The same. How did Mr. Jaggers tame her, Wemmick?"

"That's his secret. She has been with him many a long year."

"I wish you would tell me her story. I feel a particular interest in being acquainted with it. You know that what is said between you and me goes no further."

"Well!" Wemmick began. "I don't know her story—that is, I

don't know all of it. But what I do know I'll tell you. We are in our private and personal capacities, of course."

"Of course."

"A score or so of years ago, that woman was tried at the Old Bailey for murder, and was acquitted. She was a very handsome young woman, and I believe had some gypsy blood in her. Anyhow, it was hot enough when it was up, as you may suppose."

"But she was acquitted."

"Mr. Jaggers was for her," pursued Wemmick, with a look full of meaning. "He worked the case in a way quite astonishing. It was a desperate case, and it was comparatively early days with him then, and he worked it to general admiration. In fact, it may almost be said to have made him. He worked it himself at the police office, day after day for many days. The murdered person was a woman—a woman a good ten years older, very much larger, and very much stronger. Jaggers took Molly's word that the woman was a vampire. Officially, it was a case of jealousy. They both led tramping lives, and this woman Molly in Gerrard Street here had been married very young to a tramping man who took a fancy to the other woman. No body was found, in keeping with the woman being a vampire. When staked, poof, you know they turn to dust?"

I nodded. I had seen Estella in action. "But Molly's not a Scapegrace? And Jaggers took her case?"

"On account of her victim being a vampire, and Molly's husband at the time a werewolf. Being married to a werewolf is as good as being one yourself, in that you're one of the pack by association. The eyewitness said he saw Molly stab the woman dead in a barn near Hounslow Heath. There had been a violent struggle, perhaps a fight. Molly was bruised and scratched and torn, and had been held by the throat, at last, choked, and bitten. Now, there was no reasonable evidence to implicate any person but Molly. On the improbabilities of her having been able to do it, Mr. Jaggers principally rested his case. You may be sure," said Wemmick, touching me on the sleeve, "that he never dwelt upon the strength of her hands then, though he sometimes does now."

I had told Wemmick of his showing us her wrists, that day of the dinner party.

"Well, sir!" Wemmick went on. "It happened—happened, don't you see?—that Molly was so very artfully dressed from the time of her apprehension that she looked much slighter than she really was. In particular, her sleeves had been so skillfully contrived that her arms had quite a delicate look. She had only a bruise or two about her—nothing for a wolf's mate—but the backs of her hands were lacerated, and the question was, was it with fingernails or teeth? Now, Mr. Jaggers showed that she had struggled through a great lot of brambles which were not as high as her face, but which she could not have got through and kept her hands free of harm. Bits of those brambles were actually found in her skin and put in evidence. The brambles in question were found on examination to have torn little shreds of her dress, which had little spots of blood upon it here and there."

"Her own blood?" I questioned.

Wemmick shrugged and went on. "But what follows is the boldest point Jaggers made to knock down the prosecution's claim. They were setting up their case to show that in proof of her jealousy for the time he spent with the vampire woman, Molly was under strong suspicion of having, at about the time of the murder, frantically destroyed her child by this werewolf tramping man—some three years old—to revenge herself upon him.

"Mr. Jaggers argued that the marks on her were bramble marks, not fingernails or bites. 'Marks of brambles,' he said, 'and we show you the brambles. You say they are marks of fingernails,' he said, 'and you set up the hypothesis that she destroyed her child. You must accept all consequences of that hypothesis. For anything we know, she may have destroyed her child, and the child in clinging to her may have scratched her hands. What then? You are not trying her for the murder of her child; why don't you? As to this case, if you will have scratches, we say that, for anything we know, you may have accounted for them, assuming for the sake of argument that you have not invented them? You have no body. You have a drunk eyewitness. Molly had no reason to go after the woman.' To sum up, sir," said Wemmick, "Mr. Jaggers put on a show altogether too much for the jury, and they gave in."

"Has she been in his service ever since?"

"Yes, but not only that," said Wemmick. "She went into his service immediately after her acquittal, tamed as she is now. She has since been taught one thing and another in the way of her duties, but she was tamed from the beginning."

"Do you remember the sex of the child?"

"Said to have been a girl."

"You have nothing more to say to me tonight?" I asked.

"Nothing. I got your letter and destroyed it. Nothing."

We exchanged a cordial goodnight, and I went home, with new matter for my thoughts, though with no relief from the old.

CHAPTER 45

WITH MISS HAVISHAM'S NOTE in my pocket to serve as my credentials for so soon reappearing at Satis House, in case her waywardness should lead her to express any surprise at seeing me, I went down again by the coach next day. Eager to get into town unnoticed, I alighted at the Halfway House, and breakfasted there, and walked the rest of the distance.

An elderly woman, whom I had seen before as one of the servants who lived in the supplementary house across the back courtyard, opened the gate. The lit candle stood in the dark passage within, as of old, and I took it up and ascended the staircase alone. Miss Havisham was not in her own room, but was in the larger room across the landing. Looking in at the door, after knocking in vain, I saw her sitting on the hearth in a ragged chair, close before, and lost in the contemplation of, the ashy fire.

Doing as I had often done, I went in, and stood touching the old chimney-piece, where she could see me when she raised her eyes. As I stood thinking how, in the progress of time, I, too, had come to be a part of the wrecked fortunes of that house, her eyes rested on me. She stared, and said in a low voice, "Is it real?"

"It is I, Pip. Mr. Jaggers gave me your note yesterday, and I have lost no time."

"Thank you. Thank you."

As I brought another of the ragged chairs to the hearth and sat down, I remarked a new expression on her face, as if she were afraid of me.

"I want," she said, "to pursue that subject you mentioned to me when you were last here, and to show you that I am not all stone. But perhaps you can never believe, now, that there is anything human in my heart?"

When I said some reassuring words, she stretched out her tremulous right hand, as though she would touch me, but she recalled it again before I understood the action, or knew how to receive it.

"You said, speaking for your friend, that you could tell me how to do something useful and good. Something that you would like done?"

"Something that I would like done very much."

"What is it?"

I began explaining to her that secret history of the partnership. I had not got far into it, when I judged from her looks that she was not thinking of what I said.

"Do you break off," she asked then, with her former air of being afraid of me, "because you hate me too much to bear to speak to me?"

"No, no," I answered, "how can you think so, Miss Havisham! I stopped because I thought you were not following what I said."

"Perhaps I was not," she answered, putting a hand to her head. "Begin again, and let me look at something else. Stay! Now tell me."

She set her hand upon her stick in the resolute way that sometimes was habitual to her, and looked at the fire with a strong expression of forcing herself to attend. I went on with my explanation, and told her how I had hoped to complete the transaction out of my means, but how in this I was disappointed. That part of the subject (I reminded her) involved matters which could form no part of my explanation, for they were the weighty secrets of another.

"So!" said she, assenting with her head, but not looking at me. "And how much money is wanting to complete the purchase?"

I was rather afraid of stating it, for it sounded a large sum. "Nine hundred pounds."

"If I give you the money for this purpose, will you keep my secret as you have kept your own?"

"Quite as faithfully."

"And your mind will be more at rest?"

"Much more at rest."

"Are you very unhappy now?" She asked this question, still without looking at me, but in an unwonted tone of sympathy. I could not reply at the moment, for my voice failed me. She put her left arm across the head of her stick, and softly laid her forehead on it.

"I am far from happy, Miss Havisham; but I have other causes of disquiet than any you know of. They are the secrets I have mentioned."

After a little while, she raised her head, and looked at the fire. "It is noble in you to tell me that you have other causes of unhappiness. Is it true?"

"Too true."

"Can I only serve you, Pip, by serving your friend? Regarding that as done, is there nothing I can do for you yourself?"

"Nothing. I thank you for the question. I thank you even more for the tone of the question. But there is nothing."

She presently rose from her seat, and looked about the blighted room for the means of writing. There were none there, and she took from her pocket a yellow set of ivory tablets, mounted in tarnished gold, and wrote upon them with a pencil in a case of tarnished gold that hung from her neck.

"You are still on friendly terms with Mr. Jaggers?"

"Quite. I dined with him yesterday."

"This is an authority to him to pay you that money, to lay out at your irresponsible discretion for your friend. I keep no money here; but if you would rather Mr. Jaggers knew nothing of the matter, I will send it to you."

"Thank you, Miss Havisham. I have not the least objection to receiving it from him."

She read me what she had written. It was direct and clear, and evidently intended to absolve me from any suspicion of profiting by the receipt of the money. I took the tablets from her hand, and it trembled again, and it trembled more as she took off the chain to which the pencil was attached, and put it in mine. All this she did without looking at me.

"My name is on the first leaf. If you can ever write under my name, 'I forgive her,' though ever so long after my broken heart is dust, pray do it!"

"Oh, Miss Havisham, I can do it now. There have been sore mistakes, and my life has been a blind and thankless one. I want forgiveness and direction far too much to be bitter with you."

She turned her face to me for the first time since she had averted it, and, to my amazement, I may even add to my terror, dropped on her knees at my feet, with her folded hands raised to me.

To see her with her worn face kneeling at my feet gave me a shock through my whole frame. I entreated her to rise, and got my arms about her to help her up, but she only pressed that hand of mine which was nearest to her grasp, and hung her head over it and wept. I had never seen her shed a tear before, and, in the hope that the relief might do her good, I bent over her without speaking. She was not kneeling now, but was down upon the ground.

"Oh!" she cried, despairingly. "What have I done! What have I done!"

"If you mean, Miss Havisham, what have you done to injure me, let me answer. Very little. I should have loved her under any circumstances, and she has never tried to kill me, whatever your directions were to that effect. Is she married?"

"Yes."

It was a needless question, for a new desolation in the desolate house had told me so.

"What have I done! What have I done!" She wrung her hands, and crushed her white hair, and returned to this cry over and over again. "What have I done!"

I knew not how to answer, or how to comfort her. That she had done a grievous thing in taking an impressionable child to mould into the form that her wild resentment, spurned affection, and wounded pride found vengeance in, I knew full well. But that, in shutting out the light of day, she had shut out infinitely more. In secluding herself, she had shielded herself from a thousand natural and healing influences. Her mind, brooding solitary, had grown diseased, as all minds do and must and will that reverse the appointed order of their Maker. She chose this life, such sorrow, and she inflicted it on innocents in her midst.

Could I look upon her without compassion, seeing her punishment in the ruin she was, in her profound unfitness for this earth on which she was placed, in the vanity of sorrow which had become a master mania, like the vanity of penitence, the vanity of remorse, the vanity of unworthiness, and other monstrous vanities that have been curses in this world?

"Until you spoke to her the other day, and until I saw in you a looking glass that showed me what I once felt myself—for I can't see my reflection any other way, you know—I did not know what

I had done. How I loathe what I am, what I have become! How I loathe them all, Scapegraces!"

"We are Scapegraces, Miss Havisham. You and I both," I observed. "It doesn't have to be a hateful condition."

"So you showed me, Pip, for you are more human than most. I had almost lost that part of me that remembered what it was to be human, but you brought it back to me. What have I done! What have I done!"

"Miss Havisham," I said, when her cry had died away, "you may dismiss me from your mind and conscience. But Estella is a different case, and if you can ever undo any scrap of what you have done amiss in keeping a part of her right nature away from her, it will be better to do that than to bemoan the past through a hundred years."

"Yes, yes, I know it. But, Pip—my dear!" There was an earnest womanly compassion for me in her new affection. "My dear! Believe this: when she first came to me, I meant to save her from misery like my own. By training her to kill my kind, I meant to assure that she would never fall prey to a Scapegrace's scheming ways, to suffer as I have."

"Well, well! I hope so."

"But as she grew, and showed such promise, my expectations grew along with her. I began to think that she alone could wipe out the entire Scapegrace population. As my expectations grew, hers grew all the greater. I made her hard and cold, a killer."

"She is very skilled." I did not wish to comment on Estella's coldness or Miss Havisham's part in it, as she showed such remorse.

"Aye, skilled," Miss Havisham agreed. "She has left me. She married to achieve her independence, to pursue her goals without my over-reaching interference, and to have what I did not. So cold, so hard. What have I done?" Miss Havisham said again after sitting some moments in quiet contemplation. "If you knew all my story, you would have some compassion and a better understanding of me."

"Miss Havisham," I answered, as delicately as I could, "I believe

I may say that I do know your story, and have known it ever since I first left this neighbourhood. Does what has passed between us give me any excuse for asking you a question relative to Estella? Not as she is, but as she was when she first came here?"

She remained on the ground, with her arms on the ragged chair, and her head leaning on them. "Go on."

"Whose child was Estella?"

She shook her head.

"You don't know? But Mr. Jaggers brought her here, or sent her here? Will you tell me how that came about?"

"I had been shut up in these rooms a long time," she said in a cautious whisper. "I don't know how long; you know what time the clocks keep here, when I told him that I wanted a little girl to rear and train, and save from my fate. I had first seen him when I sent for him to lay this place waste for me, having read of him in the news-papers, before I parted from the world and my humanity. He told me that he would look about him for such an orphan child. One night he brought her here asleep, and I called her Estella."

"Might I ask her age then?"

"Two or three. She herself knows nothing, but that she was left an orphan and I adopted her."

So convinced I was of that woman's being her mother that I wanted no evidence to establish the fact in my own mind. But, to any mind, I thought, the connection here was clear and straight.

What more could I hope to do by prolonging the interview? I had succeeded on behalf of Herbert. Miss Havisham had told me all she knew of Estella. I had said and done what I could to ease her mind. No matter with what other words we parted; we parted.

I blinked against the fading sunlight when I went downstairs into the natural air. I called to the woman who had opened the gate when I entered, that I would not trouble her just yet, but would walk round the place before leaving. I had a presentiment that I should never be there again, and I felt that the dying light was suited to my last view of it.

By the wilderness of casks that I had walked on long ago, and on which the rain of years had fallen since, rotting them in many places, and leaving miniature swamps and pools of water upon those that stood on end, I made my way to the ruined garden. I went all round it, by the corner where Herbert and I had fought our battle, round by the paths where Estella and I had walked. So cold, so lonely, so dreary all!

Taking the brewery on my way back, I raised the rusty latch of a little door at the garden end of it, and walked through. I was going out at the opposite door—not easy to open now, for the damp wood had started and swelled, and the hinges were yielding, and the threshold was encumbered with a growth of fungus—when I turned my head to look back. A childish association revived with wonderful force in the moment of the slight action, and I fancied that I saw Miss Havisham's silhouette in the window again, about to bite a new victim. So strong was the impression that I stood shuddering from head to foot before I knew it was a fancy.

The mournfulness of the place and time, and the great terror of this illusion, though it was but momentary, caused me to feel an indescribable awe as I came out between the open wooden gates where I had once wrung my hair after Estella had wrung my heart. Passing on into the front courtyard, I hesitated whether to call the woman to let me out at the locked gate of which she had the key, or first to go up stairs and assure myself that Miss Havisham was as safe and well as I had left her. I took the latter course and went up.

I looked into the room where I had left her, and I saw her nearing the window, pulling back the curtain as if to let in the light. For a moment, it seemed a healing step that she should, at last, seek the sun, even a setting one. Then I remembered what sunlight did to vampires. The light came through parted curtains, and I called out a warning just as I saw a great flaming light spring up and realised it was Miss Havisham. She ran at me, shrieking, with a whirl of fire blazing all about her, and soaring at least as many feet above her head as she was high.

I had a double-caped great-coat on, and over my arm another thick coat. Somehow, I got them off, wrapped her, threw her down, and got them over her. I dragged the great cloth from the table for the same purpose, and with it dragged down the heap of rotten-ness in the midst, and all the ugly things that sheltered there. We were on the ground struggling like desperate enemies. The closer I covered her, the more wildly she shrieked and tried to free her-self. I knew nothing until I knew that we were on the floor by the great table, and that patches of tinder yet alight were floating in the smoky air, which, a moment ago, had been her faded bridal dress.

Then, I looked round and saw the disturbed beetles and spiders running away over the floor, and a servant coming in with breath-less cries at the door.

"Wolf!" the servant screamed. "Wolf!"

I hadn't even realised I had transformed to a great extent, the process of saving Miss Havisham distracting me from any self-awareness. I had lost all restraint, and the high stress of the situa-tion must have sent my body into chaos, forcing the wolf in me out for my own protection. But I hadn't changed enough to be unrec-ognizable as human. My body stayed the same, perhaps sporting a thick coat of hair, and my ears had gone sharp along with my snout lengthening.

I gnashed my teeth in the woman's direction, forcing her to flee from the room in search of further assistance. I still held Miss Hav-isham down with all my strength, like a prisoner who might escape. I thought she might try. She was insensible, and I was afraid to have her moved, or even touched. I fancied (I think I did) that, if I let her go, the fire would break out again and consume her. I breathed slowly, meditating as Matthew Pocket had instructed, allowing me to change back to man while the servants came running, no doubt with pitchforks. They seemed startled to find no wolf at all, just Pip, and their very injured mistress. If they realised my true nature, there was no chance to address it with Miss Havisham in urgent need of care. When I got up, on the surgeon's coming to her with other aid,

I was astonished to see that both my hands were burnt, for I had no knowledge of it through the sense of feeling.

On examination it was pronounced that she had received serious hurts, but that they of themselves were far from hopeless. Nervous shock, the surgeon suggested, but I knew her true condition and wondered if she would heal. Vampires were rumoured to have astounding healing powers, but she might have harmed herself on purpose in her self-loathing. I had no idea. By the surgeon's directions, her bed was laid upon the great table, which happened to be well suited to the dressing of her injuries. When I saw her again, an hour afterwards, she lay, indeed, where I had seen her strike her stick, and had heard her say that she would lie one day.

Though every vestige of her dress was burnt, as they told me, she still had something of her old ghastly bridal appearance; for, they had covered her to the throat with white cotton-wool. As she lay with a white sheet loosely overlying that, the phantom air of something that had been and was changed was still upon her.

I found, on questioning the servants, that Estella was in Paris, and I got a promise from the surgeon that he would write to her by the next post. Miss Havisham's family I took upon myself, intending to communicate with Mr. Matthew Pocket only, and leave him to do as he liked about informing the rest. This I did next day, through Herbert, as soon as I returned to town.

There was a stage, that evening, when she spoke collectedly of what had happened, though with a certain terrible vivacity. Her burns seemed to have healed, but the emotional scars ran deep. Towards midnight she began to wander in her speech, and after that it gradually set in that she said innumerable times in a low solemn voice, "What have I done!" And then, "When she first came, I meant to save her from misery like mine." And then, "Take the pencil and write under my name, 'I forgive her!'" She never changed the order of these three sentences, but she sometimes left out a word in one or other of them; never putting in another word, but always leaving a blank and going on to the next word.

As I could do no service there, and as I had, nearer home, that pressing reason for anxiety and fear which even her wanderings could not drive out of my mind, I decided, in the course of the night, that I would return by the early morning coach, walking on a mile or so, and being taken up clear of the town. At about six o'clock of the morning, therefore, I leaned over her and touched her lips with mine, just as they said, not stopping for being touched, "Take the pencil and write under my name, 'I forgive her.'"

CHAPTER 46

Two or three times in the night, and again in the morning, my hands had been dressed. My left arm was a good deal burned to the elbow, and, less severely, as high as the shoulder. My wolfish thick hair might have served as some protection to my skin, but I had not the healing power of a vampire. Painful as it was, I felt thankful it was no worse. My right hand was not so badly burnt but that I could move the fingers. It was bandaged, of course, but much less inconveniently than my left hand and arm, those requiring a sling. I could only wear my coat like a cloak, loose over my shoulders and fastened at the neck. My hair had been caught by the fire, but not my head or face.

When Herbert had been down to Hammersmith and seen his father, he came back to me at our chambers, and devoted the day to attending on me. He was the kindest of nurses, and at stated times took off the bandages, and steeped them in the cooling liquid that was kept ready, and put them on again, with a patient tenderness.

At first, as I lay quiet on the sofa, I found it painfully difficult, I might say impossible, to get rid of the impression of the glare of the flames, their hurry and noise, and the fierce burning smell. If I dozed for a minute, I was awakened by the memory of Miss Havisham's cries, and by her running at me with all that height of fire above her head.

Neither of us spoke of the boat, but we both thought of it. That was made apparent by our avoidance of the subject, and by our agreeing—without agreement—to make my recovery of the use of my hands a question of so many hours, not of so many weeks.

My first question when I saw Herbert had been, of course, whether all was well down the river? As he replied in the affirmative, with perfect confidence and cheerfulness, we did not resume the subject until the day was wearing away. But then, as Herbert changed the bandages, more by the light of the fire than by the outer light, he went back to it spontaneously.

"I sat with Provis last night, Lowell, two good hours."

"Where was Clara?"

"Dear little thing!" said Herbert. "She was up and down with Gruffandgrim all the evening. I don't think he will last much longer."

"And then you will be married, Herbert?"

"How can I take care of the dear child otherwise? I was speaking of Provis. Do you know, Lowell, he improves. He was very communicative last night, and told me more of his life. You remember his breaking off here about some woman that he had had great trouble with?"

"I had forgotten that, Herbert, but I remember it now you speak of it."

"Well! He went into that part of his life, and a dark wild part it is. Shall I tell you? Or would it worry you just now?"

"Tell me by all means. Every word."

Herbert bent forward to look at me more nearly, as if my reply had been rather more hurried or more eager than he could quite account for.

"It seems," said Herbert, "that the woman was a young woman, and a jealous woman, and a revengeful woman; revengeful, Lowell, to the last degree."

"To what last degree?"

"Murder."

"How did she murder? Whom did she murder?"

"Why, the deed may not have merited quite so terrible a name," said Herbert, "but, she was tried for it, and Mr. Jaggers defended her, and the reputation of that defence first made his name known to Provis. It was another and a stronger woman who was the victim, a suspected vampire. There had been a struggle—in a barn. Who began it, or how fair it was, or how unfair, may be doubtful. How it ended, also doubtful, for there was no body, only dust. An eyewitness placed Provis's woman at the scene with a bloody stake."

"Was the woman brought in guilty?" I winced. I thought of Jaggers's Molly, Estella's mother.

"No. She was acquitted.—My poor Lowell, I hurt you!"

"It is impossible to be gentler, Herbert. Yes? What else?"

"This acquitted young woman and Provis had a little child, of whom Provis was exceedingly fond. On the evening of the very night when the object of her jealousy was staked, as I tell you, the young woman presented herself before Provis and swore that she would destroy the child (which was in her possession), and he should never see it again. Then, she vanished—There's the worst arm comfortably in the sling once more, and now there remains but the right hand, which is a far easier job.—You don't think your breathing is affected, my dear boy? You seem to breathe quickly."

"Perhaps I do, Herbert. Did the woman keep her oath?"

"There comes the darkest part of Provis's life. She did."

"That is, he says she did."

"Why, of course, my dear boy," returned Herbert, in a tone of surprise, and again bending forward to get a nearer look at me. "He says it all. I have no other information."

"No, to be sure."

"Now, whether," pursued Herbert, "he had used the child's

mother ill, or whether he had used the child's mother well, Provis doesn't say. She had shared some four or five years of the wretched life he described to us at this fireside, and he seems to have felt pity for her, and forbearance towards her. Therefore, fearing he should be called upon to depose about this destroyed child, and so be the cause of her death, he hid himself (much as he grieved for the child), kept himself dark, as he says, out of the way and out of the trial, and was only vaguely talked of as a certain man called Abel, out of whom the jealousy arose. After the acquittal, she disappeared, and thus he lost the child and the child's mother."

"I want to ask—"

"A moment, my dear boy, and I have done. That evil genius, Compeyson, the worst of scoundrels among many scoundrels, knowing of his keeping out of the way at that time and of his reasons for doing so, of course afterwards held the knowledge over his head as a means of keeping him poorer and working him harder. It was clear last night that this barbed the point of Provis's animosity."

"I want to know," said I, "and particularly, Herbert, whether he told you when this happened?"

"Particularly? Let me remember, then, what he said as to that. His expression was, 'a round score o' year ago, and a'most directly after I took up wi' Compeyson.' How old were you when you came upon him in the little churchyard?"

"I think in my seventh year."

"Aye. It had happened some three or four years then, he said, and you brought into his mind the little girl so tragically lost, who would have been about your age."

"Herbert," I said, after a short silence, in a hurried way. "Look at me. You are not afraid that I am in any fever, or that my head is much disordered by the accident of last night?"

"N-no, my dear boy," said Herbert, after taking time to examine me. "You are rather excited, but you are quite yourself."

"I know I am quite myself. I simply want to make sure you believe I am in complete control of my faculties when I tell you what

I have put together. The man we have in hiding down the river, is Estella's Father. Estella is of wolfish blood. She's one of us."

CHAPTER 47

WHAT DIFFERENCE IT MADE that Estella had werewolf in her blood, or why I was hot on tracing out and proving Estella's parentage, I cannot say. But I was seized with a feverish conviction that I ought to hunt the matter down and that I ought to see Mr. Jaggers, and come at the bare truth. I really do not know whether I felt that I did this for Estella's sake, or whether I wanted to give some hope to Magwitch, something to cling to besides his devotion to me. Perhaps the latter possibility may be the nearer to the truth.

At any rate, I became consumed with the idea that I had to go to Gerrard Street that night, straightaway. Herbert's concern that, if I did, I should probably be laid up and stricken useless when our fugitive's safety would depend upon me most, restrained my impatience. On the understanding that, come what would, I was to go to Mr. Jaggers tomorrow, I submitted to stay peacefully at home and let Herbert nurse my wounds. Early next morning we went out together, and at the corner of Giltspur Street by Smithfield, I left Herbert to go his way into the City, and took my way to Little Britain.

There were periodic occasions when Mr. Jaggers and Wemmick went over the office accounts, and checked off the vouchers, and put all things straight. Fortunately, today was one of those occasions. I was not sorry to have Mr. Jaggers and Wemmick together, as Wemmick would then hear for himself that I said nothing to compromise him.

My appearance, with my arm bandaged and my coat loose over my shoulders, favoured my object. Although I had sent Mr. Jaggers a brief account of the accident as soon as I had arrived in town, I had to give him all the details now. While I described the disaster, Mr. Jaggers stood, according to his wont, before the fire. Wemmick leaned back in his chair, staring at me, with his hands in the pockets of his trousers, and his pen in his mouth.

My narrative finished, and their questions exhausted, I then produced Miss Havisham's authority to receive the nine hundred pounds for Herbert. Mr. Jaggers looked a bit surprised, but he presently handed the demand over to Wemmick, with instructions to draw the check for his signature. While that was in course of being done, I looked on at Wemmick as he wrote, and Mr. Jaggers looked on at me.

"I am sorry, Pip," he said, as I put the check in my pocket, when he had signed it, "that we do nothing for you."

"Miss Havisham was good enough to ask me whether she could do nothing for me, and I told her no."

"I should not have told her no, if I had been you," said Mr Jaggers. "But every man ought to know his own business best."

"Every man's business," said Wemmick, rather reproachfully towards me, "is portable property."

As I thought the time was now come for pursuing the theme I had at heart, I turned to Mr. Jaggers. "I did ask something of Miss Havisham, however, sir. I asked her to give me some information relative to her adopted daughter, and she gave me all she possessed."

"Did she?" said Mr. Jaggers, bending forward to look at his boots and then straightening himself. "Hah! I don't think I should have done so, if I had been Miss Havisham. But she ought to know her own business best."

"I know more of the history of Miss Havisham's adopted child than Miss Havisham herself does, sir. I know her mother."

Mr. Jaggers looked at me enquiringly, and repeated "Mother?"

"I have seen her mother within these three days. And so have you, sir. And you have seen her still more recently."

"Yes?" said Mr. Jaggers.

"Perhaps I know more of Estella's history than even you do," said I. "I know her father, too."

A certain stop that Mr. Jaggers came to in his manner assured me that he did not know who her father was. This I had strongly suspected from Provis's account (as Herbert had repeated it) of his having kept himself dark, which led me to conclude that he himself had not been Mr. Jaggers's client until some four years later, when he could have no reason for claiming his identity. I could not be sure of this unconsciousness on Mr. Jaggers's part before, though I was quite sure of it now.

"So! You know the young lady's father, Pip?" said Mr. Jaggers.

"Yes," I replied, "and his name is Provis—from New South Wales."

Even Mr. Jaggers started when I said those words. "And on what evidence, Pip, does Provis make this claim?"

"He does not make it," said I, "and has never made it, and has no knowledge or belief that his daughter is in existence."

Then I told him all I knew, and how I knew it, with the exception that I left him to infer that I knew from Miss Havisham what I in fact knew from Wemmick. I did not look towards Wemmick until I had finished all I had to tell, and had been for some time silently meeting Mr. Jaggers's look. When I did at last turn my eyes in Wemmick's direction, I found that he was intent upon the table before him.

"Hah!" said Mr. Jaggers at last, as he moved towards the papers on the table. "What item was it you were at, Wemmick, when Mr. Pip came in?"

But I could not submit to be thrown off in that way, and I made a passionate, almost an indignant appeal, to him to be more frank and manly with me. I represented myself as being surely worthy of some little confidence from him, in return for the confidence I had just now imparted.

"I don't blame you," I said. "Or suspect him, or mistrust you. I simply want assurance of the truth."

"Why would you want it?" he asked, as if I were a child asking for a sweet that would only spoil my dinner.

"As little as you care for such poor dreams"—I was ready with a response—"I have loved Estella dearly and long, and that although I have lost her, and must live a bereaved life, whatever concerns her is nearer and dearer to me than anything else in the world."

Mr. Jaggers stood quite still and silent under this appeal.

I turned to Wemmick. "Wemmick, I know you to be a man with a gentle heart. I have seen your pleasant home, and your old father, and the innocent, cheerful ways with which you refresh your business life. And I entreat you to say a word for me to Mr. Jaggers, and to represent to him that, all circumstances considered, he ought to be more open with me!"

I have never seen two men look more oddly at one another than Mr. Jaggers and Wemmick did after this apostrophe. At first, a misgiving crossed me that Wemmick would be instantly dismissed from his employment, but it melted as I saw Mr. Jaggers relax into something like a smile, and Wemmick become bolder.

"What's all this?" said Mr. Jaggers. "You with an old father, and you with pleasant and playful ways?"

"Well!" returned Wemmick. "If I don't bring 'em here, what does it matter?"

"Pip," said Mr. Jaggers, laying his hand upon my arm, and smiling openly, "this man must be the most cunning impostor in all London."

"Not a bit of it," returned Wemmick, growing bolder and bolder. "I think you're another."

Again they exchanged their former odd looks, each apparently still distrustful that the other was taking him in.

"You with a pleasant home?" said Mr. Jaggers.

"Since it don't interfere with business," returned Wemmick, "let it be so. Now, I look at you, sir, I shouldn't wonder if you might be planning and contriving to have a pleasant home of your own one of these days, when you're tired of all this work."

Mr. Jaggers nodded his head retrospectively two or three times, and actually drew a sigh. "Pip, we won't talk about 'poor dreams'; you know more about such things than I, having much fresher experience of that kind. But now about this other matter. I'll put a case to you. Mind! I admit nothing."

He waited for me to declare that I quite understood that he expressly said that he admitted nothing.

"Now, Pip," said Mr. Jaggers, "put this case. Put the case that a woman, under such circumstances as you have mentioned, held her child concealed, and was obliged to communicate the fact to her legal adviser, on his representing to her that he must know, with an eye to his defence, how the fact stood about that child. Put the case that, at the same time he held a trust to find a child for an eccentric rich lady to adopt and bring up."

"I follow you, sir." I didn't mention that Miss Havisham was more than eccentric. I was certain he was well aware she was a vampire and not speaking it out loud for reasons of his own.

"Put the case that he lived in an atmosphere of evil, and that all he saw of children was their being generated in great numbers for certain destruction. Put the case that pretty nigh all the Scapegrace children he saw in his daily business life he had reason to look upon as so much spawn, to develop into the fish that were to come to his net—to be prosecuted, defended, forsworn, made orphans, bedevilled somehow."

"I follow you, sir."

"Put the case, Pip, that here was one pretty little child out of the heap who could be saved. The father believed her dead, and dared make no stir about it. Over the mother, the legal adviser had this power: 'I know what you did, and how you did it. You came so and so, you did such and such things to divert suspicion. I have tracked you through it all, and I tell it you all. Part with the child, unless it should be necessary to produce it to clear you, and then it shall be produced. Give the child into my hands, and I will do my best to bring you off. If you are saved, your child is saved, too; if you are lost, your child is still saved.' Put the case that this was done, and that the woman was cleared."

"I understand you perfectly."

"But that I make no admissions. Put the case, Pip, that passion and the terror of death had a little shaken the woman's intellects, and that when she was set at liberty, she was scared out of the ways of the world, and went to him to be sheltered. Put the case that he took her in, and that he kept down the old, wild, violent nature whenever he saw an inkling of its breaking out, by asserting his power over her in the old way. Do you comprehend the imaginary case?"

"Quite."

"Put the case that the child grew up, and was married for money. That the mother was still living. That the father was still living. That the mother and father, unknown to one another, were dwelling within so many miles, furlongs, yards if you like, of one another. That the secret was still a secret, except that you had got wind of it. Put that last case to yourself very carefully."

"I do."

"I ask Wemmick to put it to *himself* very carefully."

And Wemmick said, "I do."

"For whose sake would you reveal the secret? For the father's? I think he would not be much the better for the mother. For the mother's? I think if she had done such a deed she would be safer where she was. For the daughter's? I think it would hardly serve her to establish her parentage for the information of her husband, and to drag her back to disgrace, after an escape of twenty years, pretty secure to last for life."

I looked at Wemmick, whose face was very grave. He gravely touched his lips with his forefinger. I did the same. Mr. Jaggers did the same. "Now, Wemmick," said the latter then, resuming his usual manner, "what item was it you were at when Mr. Pip came in?"

CHAPTER 48

WITH THE CHECK IN my pocket, I went to Miss Skiffins's brother, the wizard, and I had the great satisfaction of concluding my arrangement for the advancement of Herbert's prospects. It was the only good thing I had done, and the only completed thing I had done, since I was first apprised of my great expectations.

Herbert would become a full partner of Clavenger's and take charge of opening an Office of Werewolf Affairs in the East. Happy as I was to set Herbert up for success, I found that I must prepare for a separation from my friend, as if the last anchor were loosening its hold, and I should soon be driving with the winds and waves. Still unaware of my part in his changing fortunes, Herbert would come home of a night and tell me of these changes, and would sketch airy pictures of himself conducting Clara Barley to the land of the Arabian Nights, and of me going out to join them (with a caravan of camels, I believe), and of our all going up the Nile and seeing wonders.

We had now got into the month of March. My left arm, though it presented no bad symptoms, took so long to heal that I was still unable to get a coat on. My right arm was tolerably restored. On a Monday morning, when Herbert and I were at breakfast, I received the following letter from Wemmick by the post.

"Walworth. Burn this as soon as read. Early in the week, or say Wednesday, you might do what you know of, if you felt disposed to try it. Now burn."

When I had shown this to Herbert and had put it in the fire—but not before we had both got it by heart—we considered what to do. For, of course my being disabled could now be no longer kept out of view.

"I have thought it over again and again," said Herbert, "and I think I know a better course than taking a Thames waterman. Take Startop. A good fellow, a skilled hand, fond of us, and enthusiastic and honourable."

I had thought of him more than once.

"But how much would you tell him, Herbert?"

"It is necessary to tell him very little. Let him suppose it a mere freak, but a secret one, until the morning comes. Then, let him know that there is urgent reason for your getting Provis aboard and away. You go with him?"

"No doubt."

"Where?"

It had seemed to me, in the many anxious considerations I had given the point, almost indifferent what port we made for—Hamburg, Rotterdam, Antwerp. The place signified little, so long as he was out of England. I had always proposed to myself to get him well down the river in the boat, certainly well beyond Gravesend, which was a critical place for search or enquiry if suspicion were afoot. As foreign steamers would leave London at about the time of high-water, our plan would be to get down the river by a previous ebb-tide, and lie by in some quiet spot until we could pull off to one. The time when one would be due where we lay, wherever that might be, could be calculated pretty nearly, if we made enquiries beforehand.

Herbert assented to all this, and we went out immediately after breakfast to pursue our investigations. We found that a steamer for Hamburg was likely to suit our purpose best, and we directed our thoughts chiefly to that vessel, but we noted down what other foreign steamers would leave London with the same tide. We then separated for a few hours: I, to get at once such passports as were necessary; Herbert, to see Startop at his lodgings. We both did what we had to do without any hindrance, and when we met again at one o'clock reported it done. I, for my part, was prepared with passports; Herbert had seen Startop, and he was more than ready to join.

Those two should pull a pair of oars, we settled, and I would steer. Our charge would be sitter, and keep quiet. As speed was not our object, we should make way enough. We arranged that Herbert should not come home to dinner before going to Mill Pond Bank that evening, and that he should not go there at all tomorrow evening. Tuesday, he should prepare Provis to come down to some stairs hard by the house. After Tuesday, until we took him on board, Provis would have no further communication with us in any way.

These precautions well understood by both of us, I went home.

On opening the outer door of our chambers with my key, I found a letter in the box, directed to me. It had been delivered by hand, and its contents were these:—

> If you are not afraid to come to the old marshes tonight or tomorrow night at nine, and to come to the little sluice-house by the limekiln, you had better come. If you want information regarding your uncle Provis, you had much better come and tell no one, and lose no time. You must come alone. Bring this with you.

I had had load enough upon my mind before the receipt of this strange letter. What to do now, I could not tell. And the worst was that I must decide quickly, or I should miss the afternoon coach, which would take me down in time for tonight. Tomorrow night I could not think of going, for it would be too close upon the time of the flight. And again, for anything I knew, the proffered information might have some important bearing on the flight itself.

If I had had ample time for consideration, I believe I should still have gone. Having hardly any time for consideration—my watch showing me that the coach started within half an hour—I resolved to go. I should certainly not have gone, but for the reference to my uncle Provis. That, coming on Wemmick's letter and the morning's busy preparation, turned the scale.

Yielding to the letter, upon re-read, in the same mechanical kind of way, I left a note in pencil for Herbert, telling him that as I should be so soon going away, I knew not for how long, I had decided to hurry down and back, to ascertain for myself how Miss Havisham was faring. I had then barely time to get my great-coat, lock up the chambers, and make for the coach-office by the short byways. If I had taken a hackney-chariot and gone by the streets, I should have missed my aim. Going as I did, I caught the coach just as it came out of the yard. I was the only inside passenger, jolting away knee-deep in straw, when I finally had a chance to gather my wits.

I really had not been myself since the receipt of the letter. It had so bewildered me. Now I began to wonder at myself for being in the coach, and to doubt whether I had sufficient reason for being there, and to consider whether I should get out presently and go back. Still, the reference to Provis by name mastered everything. I reasoned as I had reasoned already without knowing it, in case any harm should befall him through my not going, how could I ever forgive myself!

It was dark, and the journey seemed long and dreary to me. Avoiding the Blue Boar, I put up at an inn of minor reputation down the town, and ordered some dinner. While it was preparing, I went to Satis House and enquired for Miss Havisham. She was healed from her burns, but still not up and around.

As I was not able to cut my dinner, with my arms still not to rights, the old landlord with a shining bald head did it for me. This bringing us into conversation, he was so good as to entertain me with my own story—of course with the popular feature that Pumblechook was my earliest benefactor and the founder of my fortunes.

"Do you know the young man?" said I. "Does he ever come back to this neighbourhood?"

"Know him!" repeated the landlord. "Ever since he was—no height at all. Aye, he comes back now and again, and gives the cold shoulder to the man that made him."

"What man is that?"

"Him that I speak of," said the landlord. "Mr. Pumblechook. It would turn a man's blood to white wine winegar to hear him tell of it, sir."

I thought, "Yet Joe, dear Joe, you never tell of it. Long-suffering and loving Joe, you never complain. Nor you, sweet-tempered Biddy!"

"Your appetite's been touched like by your accident," said the landlord, glancing at the bandaged arm under my coat. "Try a tenderer bit."

"No, thank you," I replied, turning from the table to brood over the fire. "I can eat no more. Please take it away."

I had never been struck at so keenly, for my thanklessness to Joe, as through the brazen impostor Pumblechook. The falser he, the truer Joe; the meaner he, the nobler Joe.

My heart was deeply and most deservedly humbled as I mused over the fire for an hour or more. The striking of the clock aroused me, and I got up, got my coat, and went out. I had previously sought in my pockets for the letter, that I might refer to it again; but I could not find it, and was uneasy to think that it must have been dropped in the straw of the coach. I knew very well, however, that the appointed place was the little sluice-house by the limekiln on the marshes, and the hour nine. Towards the marshes I now went straight, having no time to spare.

CHAPTER 49

THE SKY GREW DARK, the moon full. With the excitement of the past few days, I had forgotten to consider the phases of the moon. I struggled against the feelings I'd ignored in my distraction. I had no time to spare, no luxury to lose my head, or my way, to wild abandon. Humming Joe's favourite forge song, Old Clem, I left the enclosed lands, and walked out upon the marshes. The song was simple and meaningless, except that it reminded me of Joe, but it kept me focused and strong to help ward off the change. I stroked my silver watch chain, hoping for a further weakening effect as I walked.

The direction that I took was not that in which my old home lay, nor that in which we had pursued the convicts. My back was turned towards the distant hulks as I walked on, and, though I could see the old lights away on the spits of sand, I saw them over my shoulder. I knew the limekiln as well as I knew the old battery, but they were miles apart.

It was another half-hour before I drew near to the kiln. The lime burned with a sluggish stifling smell, but the fires were made up and left, and no workmen were visible. Hard by was a small stone-quarry. It lay directly in my way, and had been worked that day, as I saw by the tools and barrows that were lying about.

Coming up again to the marsh level out of this excavation—for the rude path lay through it—I saw a light in the old sluice-house. I quickened my pace, and knocked at the door. Waiting for a reply, I looked about me, noticing how the sluice was abandoned and broken, and how the house—of wood with a tiled roof—would not be proof against the weather much longer, if it were so even now, and how the mud and ooze were coated with lime, and how the choking vapor of the kiln crept in a ghostly way towards me. Still there was no answer, and I knocked again. No answer still, and I tried the latch.

It rose under my hand, and the door yielded. Looking in, I saw a lit candle on a table, a bench, and a mattress on a truckle bedstead. As there was a loft above, I called, "Is there any one here?" but no voice answered. Then I looked at my watch, and, finding that it was past nine, called again, "Is there any one here?" There being still no answer, I went out at the door, irresolute what to do.

It was beginning to rain fast. I turned back into the house, and stood just within the shelter of the doorway, looking out into the night. While I considered that someone must have been there lately and must soon be coming back, or the candle would not be burning, it came into my head to look if the wick were long. I turned round to do so, and had taken up the candle in my hand, when it was extinguished by some violent shock. The next thing I comprehended was that I had been caught in a strong noose, thrown over my head from behind.

"Now, I've got you!" A sinister voice broke the silence.

It took barely a second for me to realise, from the weakening of my limbs, that the noose was made of silver chain, and that such a large quantity of silver was around me that I could barely remain on my feet.

"What is this?" I struggled. "Who is it? Why?"

Not only were my arms pulled close to my sides, wrapped around with more chain, but the pressure on my bad arm caused me exquisite pain. Sometimes, a strong man's hand, sometimes a strong man's chest, was set against my mouth to deaden my cries, and with a hot breath always close to me, I struggled ineffectually in the dark, while I was fastened tight to the wall.

"And now," said the suppressed voice, "call out again, and I'll make short work of you!"

Faint from weakness and sick with the pain of my injured arm, bewildered by the surprise, and yet conscious how easily this threat could be put in execution, I desisted, and tried to ease my arm were it ever so little. But, it was bound too tight for that. I felt as if, having been burnt before, it were now being boiled. Earlier, I had struggled not to turn wolf, now I wished more than ever that I could. If only I could summon the strength!

The sudden exclusion of the night, and the substitution of black darkness in its place, warned me that the man had closed a shutter. After groping about for a little, he found the flint and steel he wanted, and began to strike a light. I strained my sight upon the sparks that fell among the tinder, and upon which he breathed and breathed, match in hand, but I could only see his lips, and the blue point of the match; even those but fitfully. The tinder was damp—no wonder there—and one after another the sparks died out.

The man was in no hurry, and struck again with the flint and steel. As the sparks fell thick and bright about him, I could see his hands, and touches of his face, and could make out that he was seated and bending over the table; but nothing more. Presently I saw his blue lips again, breathing on the tinder, and then a flare of light flashed up, and showed me the vampire, Orlick.

He lit the candle from the flaring match with great deliberation, and dropped the match, and trod it out. Then he put the candle away from him on the table, so that he could see me, and sat with his arms folded on the table and looked at me. I made out that I was fastened to a stout perpendicular ladder a few inches from the wall—a fixture there—the means of ascent to the loft above.

"Now," said he, when we had surveyed one another for some time, "I've got you."

"Unbind me. Let me go!"

"Ah!" he returned, "I'll let you go. I'll let you go to the moon. I'll let you go to the stars. All in good time."

"Why have you lured me here?"

"Don't you know?" said he, with a deadly look.

"Why have you set upon me in the dark?"

"Because I mean to do it all myself. One keeps a secret better than two. Oh, you enemy, you enemy!"

His enjoyment of the spectacle I furnished, as he sat with his arms folded on the table, shaking his head at me and hugging himself, had a malignity in it that made me tremble. As I watched him in silence, he put his hand into the corner at his side, and took up a gun with a silver-bound stock.

"Do you know this?" said he, making as if he would take aim at me. "Do you know where you saw it afore? Speak, wolf!"

"Yes," I answered.

"You cost me that place. You did. Speak!"

"What else could I do?" I had, in fact, asked Jaggers to remove Orlick from his post at Miss Havisham's, as I did not think his presence a positive influence there.

"You did that, and that would be enough, without more. How dared you to come betwixt me and a young woman I liked? It was you as always give Old Orlick a bad name to her."

Was this all about Biddy? "You gave it to yourself. You gained it for yourself. I could have done you no harm, if you had done yourself none. At any rate, you couldn't expect her to take up with a vampire."

"You're a liar. And you'll take any pains, and spend any money, to drive me out of this country, will you?" said he, repeating my words to Biddy in the last interview I had with her. "Now, I'll tell you a piece of information. It was never so well worth your while to get me out of this country as it is tonight. Ah! If it was all your money twenty times told, to the last brass farden!" As he shook his heavy hand at me, with his fangs extended from his snarling lips, I felt that it was true.

"What are your plans for me?"

"I'm a going," he said, bringing his fist down upon the table with a heavy blow, and rising as the blow fell to give it greater force. "I'm a going to have your life!"

He leaned forward staring at me, slowly unclenched his hand, and drew it across his mouth as if his mouth watered for me, and sat down again.

"You was always in Old Orlick's way since ever you was a child. You goes out of his way this present night. He'll have no more on you. You're dead."

I felt that I had come to the brink of my grave. For a moment I looked wildly round my trap for any chance of escape. There was too much silver, and I was too weak to beat it from having fought so long to hold off the change.

"More than that," he said, folding his arms on the table again, "I won't have a rag of you, I won't have a bone of you, left on earth. I'll put your body in the kiln—I'd carry two such to it, on my shoulders—and, let people suppose what they may of you, they shall never know nothing."

My mind, with inconceivable rapidity, followed out all the consequences of such a death. Estella's father would believe I had deserted him, would be taken, would die accusing me. Even Herbert would doubt me, when he compared the letter I had left for him with the fact that I had called at Miss Havisham's gate for only a moment. Joe and Biddy would never know how sorry I had been that night, none would ever know what I had suffered, how true I had meant to be, what an agony I had passed through. The death close before me was terrible, but far more terrible than death was the dread of being misremembered after death. And so quick were my thoughts, that I saw myself despised by unborn generations—Estella's children, and their children—while the wretch's words were yet on his lips.

"Now, wolf," said he, "afore I kill you like any other beast—which is wot I mean to do and wot I have tied you up for—I'll have a good look at you and a good goad at you. Oh, you enemy!"

It had passed through my thoughts to cry out for help; though few could know better than I the solitary nature of the spot, and the hopelessness of aid. But as he sat gloating over me, I was supported by a scornful detestation of him that sealed my lips. Above all things, I resolved that I would not entreat him, and that I would die making some last poor resistance to him.

He had been drinking, and his eyes were red and bloodshot. Around his neck was slung a tin bottle, as I had often seen his drink slung about him in other days. He brought the bottle to his lips, and took a fiery drink from it. I smelt the stench of rum and blood upon him. I wondered what poor animal or man had died to provide it.

"Wolf!" said he, folding his arms again, "Old Orlick's a going to tell you somethink. It was you as did for your shrew sister."

"It was you, villain."

"I tell you it was your doing. I tell you it was done through you," he retorted, catching up the gun, and making a blow with the stock at the vacant air between us. "I come upon her from behind, as I come upon you tonight. I giv' it her! I was going to drink her dry, make her vampire so's she could torture you right. But the taste! Most bitter blood I ever had. I couldn't take it, so I beat her instead, solid whacks to her head with the hammer. I left her for dead, and if there had been a limekiln as nigh her as there is now nigh you, she shouldn't have come to life again. But it warn't Old Orlick as did it; it was you. You was favoured, and Orlick was bullied and beat. Ol' human Joe Gargery thinking he could take a vampire? And he did, too. Whoever heard of a human strong enough to beat down a vamp?"

I smiled despite my weakness and pain. "Joe's goodness is his strength. No wicked thing could hurt Joe. You can count on it."

"Now you pays for it." He ignored me. "You done it. Now you pays for it."

He drank again, and became more ferocious. I saw by his tilting of the bottle that there was no great quantity left in it. I distinctly understood that he was working himself up with its contents to make an end of me. I knew that every drop it held was a drop of my life.

When he had drunk this second time, he rose from the bench on which he sat, and pushed the table aside. Then, he took up the candle, and, shading it with his murderous hand so as to throw its light on me, stood before me, looking at me and enjoying the sight.

"Wolf, I'll tell you something more. It was Old Orlick as you tumbled over on your stairs that night."

I saw the staircase with its extinguished lamps. I saw the shadows of the heavy stair rails, thrown by the watchman's lantern on the wall. I saw the rooms that I was never to see again. Here, a door half open. There, a door closed.

"And why was Old Orlick there? I'll tell you something more, wolf. You and her *have* pretty well hunted me out of this country, so far as getting a easy living in it goes, and I've took up with new companions, and new masters."

Her? I wondered did he mean my sister? Miss Havisham?

"I've had a firm mind and a firm will to have your life, since you was down here at your sister's burying. I han't seen a way to get you safe, and I've looked arter you to know your ins and outs. For, says Old Orlick to himself, 'Somehow or another I'll have him!' What! When I looks for you, I finds your uncle Provis, eh?"

Vampires had a general reputation for being clever and resourceful. Orlick had the resourceful, but the clever was not to be found. I could find a way to beat him. I had to find a way.

"You with a uncle, too! Why, I know'd you at Gargery's when you was so small a wolf that I could have chucked you away dead (as I'd thoughts o' doing, odd times, when I see you loitering amongst the pollards on a Sunday), and you hadn't found no uncles then. No, not you! But when Old Orlick come for to hear that your uncle Provis had most like wore the leg-silver wot Old Orlick had picked up, filed asunder, on these meshes ever so many year ago, and wot he kep by him till he dropped your sister with it, like a bullock, as he means to drop you—hey?—when he come for to hear that—hey?"

In his savage taunting, he flared the candle so close at me that I turned my face aside to save it from the flame.

"Ah!" he cried, laughing, after doing it again, "the burnt child dreads the fire! Old Orlick knowed you was burnt. Old Orlick knowed you was smuggling your uncle Provis away. Old Orlick's a match for you and know'd you'd come tonight! Now I'll tell you something more, wolf, and this ends it. There's them that's as good a match for your uncle Provis as Old Orlick has been for you. Let him 'ware them, when he's lost his nevvy! Let him 'ware them, when no man can't find a rag of his dear relation's clothes, nor yet a bone of his body. There's them that can't and that won't have Magwitch—yes, I know the name!—alive in the same land with them, and that's had such sure information of him when he was alive in another land, as that he couldn't and shouldn't leave it unbeknown and put them in danger. 'Ware Compeyson, Magwitch, and the gallows!"

Earlier, he'd referred to serving a new master. Even in my weakened state, I realized his new master was Compeyson.

He flared the candle at me again, smoking my face and hair, and for an instant blinding me, and turned his powerful back as he replaced the light on the table. I had thought a prayer, and had been with Joe and Biddy and Herbert, before he turned towards me again.

"Have a care, Orlick," I warned him. "You burn me, and the whole place could catch and burn with you in it. Do you have the confidence to get out in time?"

"I've no fear of fire, wolf. I'd get out. I'm not the one wrapped up in chains."

There was a clear space of a few feet between the table and the opposite wall. Within this space, he now slouched backwards and forwards. His great strength seemed to sit stronger upon him than ever before, as he did this with his hands hanging loose and heavy at his sides, and with his eyes scowling at me. I had no grain of hope left. Wild as my inward hurry was, and wonderful the force of the pictures that rushed by me instead of thoughts, I could yet clearly understand that, unless he had resolved that I was within a few moments of surely perishing out of all knowledge, he would never have told me what he had told.

Of a sudden, he stopped, took the cork out of his bottle, and tossed it away. Light as it was, I heard it fall like a plummet. He swallowed slowly, tilting up the bottle by little and little, and now he looked at me no more. The last few drops of blood he poured into the palm of his hand, and licked up. Then, with a sudden hurry of violence and swearing horribly, he threw the bottle from him, and stooped; and I saw in his hand a hammer with a long heavy handle. I guessed the hammer was silver.

The resolution I had made did not desert me, for, without uttering one vain word of appeal to him, I struggled with all my might. It was only my head and my legs that I could move, but to that extent I struggled with all the force, until then unknown, that was within me. Despite the silver, I felt myself beginning to transform. In the same instant, I heard a shout, saw a figure and a gleam of light, and heard an enormous crack and tumult.

Orlick struggled with someone, or something. I could only see him between flashes as he moved in front of the candle, now and then, darting to and fro as he fought off—something. At last, he leaned back over the candle. A hand held a stake, hovering over him, into him, and poof! Orlick turned to dust. Candlelight illuminated his aggressor.

"My training has paid off, you see," she said, brushing the dust from her familiar white hands. *Estella*. "Do not think I do it for you, Pip. I've been following this one since he worked for Miss Havisham. Great is my surprise to find that he torments you here. It is my sole purpose in life to end vampires, my only reason for existing. I used to think it my purpose to also end werewolves but you have shown me the humanity of your kind and now, I'm not so certain."

She approached and leaned over me.

"Of our kind," I repeated, feeling my pain increase as the silver chains chafed my skin, feeling weaker by the minute. "Our kind."

And as I thought perhaps she was going to ask what I meant, loosen my chains, or even kiss me—I lost consciousness entirely.

When I woke, it was to the sound of voices and activity, a crack of light coming in through the door. Daytime, at last? I was lying unbound, on the floor, in the same place, with my head on some one's knee. Estella?

My eyes were fixed on the ladder against the wall, when I came to myself—had opened on it before my mind saw it—and thus as I recovered consciousness, I knew that I was in the place where I had lost it. I was lying looking at the ladder, when there came between me and it a face. The face of a local boy who worked for Pumblechook's competitor as a bokor's apprentice.

"I think he's all right!" the boy said. "But ain't he just pale as a Recommissioned, though!"

At these words, the face of him who supported me looked over into mine, and I saw my supporter to be—"Herbert! Great Heaven!"

"Softly," said Herbert. "Gently, Lowell. Don't be too eager."

"And our old comrade Startop!" I cried, as he, too, bent over me.

"Remember what he is going to assist us in," said Herbert, "and be calm."

The allusion made me spring up, though I dropped again from the pain in my arm.

"The time has not gone by, Herbert, has it? What night is tonight? How long have I been here?" For, I had a strange and strong misgiving that I had been lying there a long time—a day and a night—two days and nights—more.

"The time has not gone by. It is Monday."

"Thank God! Estella, where is she?"

"Estella?" Herbert looked at me. "She has not been here."

"Indeed. She saved me. She put a stake in Old Orlick. Right there!" I pointed to the pile of dust and clothes that had once been Orlick, but no stake remained. No trace of Estella lingered to prove she had been there. But she had. I knew. She had saved me.

"You have all tomorrow, Tuesday, to rest in," said Herbert, tossing my suggestion of Estella's presence off as a mental lapse or deciding to deal with it later, I couldn't tell. "But you can't help groaning, my dear Lowell. What hurt have you got? Can you stand?"

"Yes, yes, I can walk. I have no hurt but in this throbbing arm."

They laid the arm bare, and did what they could. It was violently swollen and inflamed, and I could scarcely endure to have it touched. But, they tore up their handkerchiefs to make fresh bandages, and carefully replaced it in the sling, until we could get to the town and obtain some cooling lotion to put upon it. In a little while we had shut the door of the dark and empty sluice-house, and

were passing through the quarry on our way back. The bokor's boy
went before us to lead.

Entreating Herbert to tell me how he had come to my rescue—
which at first he had flatly refused to do, but had insisted on my remaining quiet—I learnt that I had in my hurry dropped the letter,
open, in our chambers, where he, coming home to bring with him
Startop whom he had met in the street on his way to me, found it,
very soon after I was gone. Its tone made him uneasy, and the more
so because of the inconsistency between it and the hasty letter I
had left for him.

His uneasiness increasing instead of subsiding, after a quarter
of an hour's consideration, he set off for the coach-office with
Startop, who volunteered his company, to make enquiry when
the next coach went down. Finding that the afternoon coach was
gone, and finding that his uneasiness grew into positive alarm, he
resolved to follow in a post-chaise. So he and Startop arrived at
the Blue Boar, fully expecting there to find me, or tidings of me;
but, finding neither, went on to Miss Havisham's, where they lost
me. Hereupon they went back to the hotel (doubtless at about
the time when I was hearing the popular local version of my own
story) to refresh themselves and to get some one to guide them
out upon the marshes. Among the loungers under the Boar's arch-
way happened to be the bokor's boy, and he had seen me passing
from Miss Havisham's in the direction of my dining-place. Thus
the bokor's boy became their guide, and with him they went out to
the sluice-house, though by the town way to the marshes, which
I had avoided.

When I told Herbert what had passed within the house, he
seemed to be a little more convinced that Estella had been there,
put an end to Orlick, and loosened my chains. For the present,
under the circumstances, we deemed it prudent to make rather light
of the matter to the bokor's boy. When we parted, I presented him
with two guineas.

Wednesday being so close upon us, we determined to go back

to London that night, three in the post-chaise. It was still daylight when we reached the Temple, and I went at once to bed, and lay in bed all day.

My terror, as I lay there, of falling ill, and being unfit for tomorrow, was so besetting, that I wonder it did not disable me of itself. So anxiously awaited, charged with such consequences, its results so impenetrably hidden, though so near.

No precaution could have been more obvious than our refraining from communication with him that day, though it increased my restlessness. As the day closed in and darkness fell, my overshadowing dread of being disabled by illness before tomorrow morning altogether mastered me. My burning arm throbbed, and my burning head throbbed, and I fancied I was beginning to wander. I counted up to high numbers, to make sure of myself, and repeated passages that I knew in prose and verse.

They kept me very quiet all day, and kept my arm constantly dressed, and gave me cooling drinks. Whenever I fell asleep, I awoke with the notion I had had in the sluice-house, that a long time had elapsed and the opportunity to save him was gone. About midnight I got out of bed and went to Herbert, with the conviction that I had been asleep for four-and-twenty hours, and that Wednesday was past. It was the last self-exhausting effort of my fretfulness, for after that I slept soundly.

Wednesday morning was dawning when I looked out the window. The winking lights upon the bridges were already pale, the coming sun was like a marsh of fire on the horizon. As I looked along the clustered roofs, with church-towers and spires shooting into the unusually clear air, the sun rose up, and a veil seemed to be drawn from the river. From me, too, a veil seemed to be drawn, and I felt strong and well.

Herbert lay asleep in his bed, and our old fellow-student lay asleep on the sofa. I could not dress myself without help, but I made up the fire, which was still burning, and got some coffee ready for them. In good time they, too, started up strong and well, and we admitted the sharp morning air at the windows, and looked at the tide that was still flowing towards us.

"When it turns at nine o'clock," said Herbert, cheerfully, "look out for us, and stand ready, you over there at Mill Pond Bank!"

CHAPTER 50

It WAS MARCH. ONE of those days when the sun shines hot and the wind blows cold. We had our pea-coats with us, and I took a bag. Of all my worldly possessions, I took no more than the few necessaries. Where I might go, what I might do, or when I might return, were questions utterly unknown to me. I didn't vex my mind with them, for it was wholly set on Provis's safety.

We headed down to the Temple stairs. Of course, I had taken care that the boat should be ready and everything in order. We went on board and cast off, Herbert in the bow, I steering. It was then about high-water—half-past eight.

The tide, beginning to run down at nine, and being with us until three, we intended still to creep on after it had turned, and row against it until dark. We should then be well in those long reaches below Gravesend, between Kent and Essex, where the river is broad and solitary and where lone public houses are scattered here and there, of which we could choose one for a resting place. There, we meant to lie by all night. The steamer for Hamburg and the steamer for Rotterdam would start from London at about nine on Thursday morning.

The crisp air, the sunlight, the movement on the river, and the moving river itself, freshened me with new hope. I felt mortified to be of so little use in the boat, but there were few better oarsmen than my two friends. They rowed with a steady stroke that was to last all day.

Old London Bridge was soon passed, and the White Tower and Traitor's Gate, and we were in among the tiers of shipping. Here, at her moorings, was tomorrow's steamer for Rotterdam, of which we took good notice. Here, tomorrow's for Hamburg, under whose bowsprit we crossed. And now I, sitting in the stern, could see, with a faster beating heart, Mill Pond Bank and Mill Pond stairs.

"Is he there?" said Herbert.

"Not yet."

"Right! He was not to come down till he saw us. Can you see his signal?"

"Not well from here; but I think I see it.—Now I see him! Pull both. Easy, Herbert. Oars!"

We touched the stairs lightly for a single moment, and he was on board, and we were off again. Looking as like a river-pilot as my heart could have wished, he had a boat-cloak with him, and a black canvas bag.

"Dear boy!" he said, putting his arm on my shoulder as he took his seat. "Faithful dear boy, well done. Thankye, thankye!"

I silently thanked Estella for saving me, for saving her father. Neither of them would ever know.

At the stairs where we had taken him aboard, and ever since, I had looked warily for any token of our being suspected. I had seen none. We certainly had not been, and at that time as certainly we were not either attended or followed by any boat.

He had his boat-cloak on him, and looked, as I have said, a natural part of the scene. It was remarkable (but perhaps the wretched life he had led accounted for it) that he was the least anxious of any of us. He was not indifferent, for he told me that he hoped to live to see his gentleman one of the best of gentlemen in a foreign country.

"If you knowed, dear boy," he said to me, "what it is to sit here alonger my dear boy and have my smoke, arter having been day

by day betwixt four walls, you'd envy me. But you don't know
what it is."

"I think I know the delights of freedom," I answered, thinking
again of Estella's magnificence as she plunged that dagger straight
through the heart of Old Orlick.

"Ah," said he, shaking his head gravely. "But you don't know it
equal to me. You must have been under lock and key, dear boy, to
know it equal to me—but I ain't a going to be low."

"If all goes well," I said, "you will be perfectly free and safe again
within a few hours."

"Well," he returned, drawing a long breath. "I hope so."

"And think so?"

"Aye, I s'pose I think so, dear boy." He dipped his hand in the
water over the boat's gunwale, and smiled with that softened air
upon him which was not new to me.

The air felt cold upon the river, but it was a bright day, and the
sunshine was very cheering. The tide ran strong, and our steady
stroke carried us on thoroughly well. Our oarsmen were so fresh, by
dint of having occasionally let her drive with the tide for a minute
or two, that a quarter of an hour's rest proved full as much as they
wanted.

We got ashore among some slippery stones while we ate and
drank what we had with us, and looked about. It was like my own
marsh country, flat and monotonous, and with a dim horizon. The
winding river turned and turned, and the great floating buoys upon
it turned and turned, and everything else seemed stranded and still.
For now the last of the fleet of ships was round the last low point
we had headed.

We pushed off again, and made what way we could. It was
much harder work now, but Herbert and Startop persevered and
rowed until the sun went down. By that time the river had lifted
us a little, so that we could see above the bank. As the night was
fast falling, and as the moon, being past the full (thank goodness
for us all), would not rise early, we held a little council; a short

one, for clearly our course was to lie by at the first lonely tavern we could find. They plied their oars once more, and I looked out for anything like a house. Thus we held on, speaking little, for four or five dull miles.

At this dismal time we were evidently all possessed by the idea that we were followed. As the tide made, it flapped heavily at irregular intervals against the shore. Whenever such a sound came, one or other of us was sure to start, and look in that direction. Sometimes, "What was that ripple?" one of us would say in a low voice. Or another, "Is that a boat yonder?" And afterwards we would fall into a dead silence, and I would sit impatiently thinking with what an unusual amount of noise the oars worked in the thowels.

At length we descried a light and a roof, and presently afterwards ran alongside a little causeway made of stones that had been picked up hard by. Leaving the rest in the boat, I stepped ashore, and found the light to be in a window of a public-house. It was a dirty place enough, and I dare say not unknown to smuggling adventurers. There was a good fire in the kitchen, and there were eggs and bacon to eat, and various liquors to drink. Also, there were two double-bedded rooms—"such as they were," the landlord said. No other company was in the house than the landlord, his wife, and a grizzled male creature, the "Jack" of the little causeway, who was as slimy and smeary as if he had been low-water mark, too.

With this assistant, I went down to the boat again, and we all came ashore, and brought out the oars, and rudder and boat-hook, and all else, and hauled her up for the night. We made a very good meal by the kitchen fire, and then apportioned the bedrooms: Herbert and Startop were to occupy one; I and our charge the other.

While we were comforting ourselves by the fire after our meal, the Jack asked me if we had seen a four-oared galley going up with the tide? When I told him no, he said she must have gone down then, and yet she "took up too," when she left there.

"They must ha' thought better on't for some reason or another," said the Jack, "and gone down."

"A four-oared galley, did you say?" said I.

"A four," said the Jack, "and two sitters."

"Did they come ashore here?"

"They put in with a stone two-gallon jar for some beer. I'd ha' been glad to pison the beer myself," said the Jack, "or put some rattling physic in it."

"Why?"

"*I* know why," said the Jack. He spoke in a slushy voice, as if much mud had washed into his throat.

"He thinks," said the landlord, a weakly meditative man with a pale eye, who seemed to rely greatly on his Jack,—"he thinks they was, what they wasn't."

"*I* knows what I thinks," observed the Jack.

"*You* thinks Custom House, Jack?" said the landlord.

"I do," said the Jack.

This dialogue made us all uneasy, and me very uneasy. The dismal wind was muttering round the house, the tide was flapping at the shore, and I had a feeling that we were caged and threatened. When I had induced Provis to go up to bed, I went outside with my two companions (Startop by this time knew the state of the case), and held another council. Whether we should remain at the house until near the steamer's time, which would be about one in the afternoon, or whether we should put off early in the morning, was the question we discussed. On the whole we deemed it the better course to lie where we were, until within an hour or so of the steamer's time, and then to get out in her track, and drift easily with the tide. Having settled to do this, we returned into the house and went to bed.

I lay down with the greater part of my clothes on, and slept well for a few hours. When I awoke, the wind had risen, and the sign of the house (the Ship) was creaking and banging about, with noises that startled me. Rising softly, for my charge lay soundly sleeping, I looked out of the window. It commanded the cause-way where we had hauled up our boat, and, as my eyes adapted themselves to the light of the clouded moon, I saw two men looking into her. They passed by under the window, looking at nothing else, and they did not go down to the landing-place which I could discern to be empty, but struck across the marsh in the direction of the Nore.

My first impulse was to call up Herbert, but reflecting that he and Startop had had a harder day than I, and were fatigued, I forbore. Going back to my window, I could see the two men moving over the marsh. In that light, however, I soon lost them, and, feeling very cold, lay down to think of the matter, and fell asleep again.

We were up early. As we walked to and fro, all four together, before breakfast, I deemed it right to recount what I had seen. Again our charge was the least anxious of the party. It was very likely that the men belonged to the Custom House, he said quietly, and that they had no thought of us. Still wary, I proposed that he and I should walk away together to a distant point we could see, and that the boat should take us aboard there, or as near there as might prove feasible, at about noon. Soon after breakfast he and I set forth, without saying anything at the tavern.

He smoked his pipe as we went along, and sometimes stopped to clap me on the shoulder. As we approached the point, I begged him to remain in a sheltered place while I went on to reconnoiter. He complied, and I went on alone. There was no boat off the point, nor any boat drawn up anywhere near it, nor were there any signs of the men having embarked there. But, to be sure, the tide was high, and there might have been some footprints under water.

When he looked out from his shelter in the distance, and saw that I waved my hat to him to come up, he rejoined me, and there we waited until we saw our boat coming. We got aboard easily, and rowed out into the track of the steamer. By that time it wanted but ten minutes of one o'clock, and we began to look out for her smoke.

But, it was half-past one before we saw any sign of her, and soon afterwards we saw behind it the smoke of another steamer. As they were coming on at full speed, we got the two bags ready, and took that opportunity of saying goodbye to Herbert and Startop. We had all shaken hands cordially, and neither Herbert's eyes nor mine were quite dry, when I saw a four-oared galley shoot out from under the bank but a little way ahead of us, and row out into the same track.

Meantime the galley, which was very skillfully handled, had crossed us, let us come up with her, and fallen alongside. Of the two sitters one held the rudder-lines, and looked at us attentively—as did all the rowers. The other sitter was wrapped up, much as Provis was, and seemed to shrink, and whisper some instruction to the steerer as he looked at us. Not a word was spoken in either boat.

Startop could make out, after a few minutes, which steamer was first, and gave me the word "Hamburg," in a low voice as we sat face to face. She was nearing us very fast, and the beating of her paddles grew louder and louder. I felt as if her shadow were absolutely upon us, when the galley hailed us. I answered.

"You have a returned Transport there," said the man who held the lines. "That's the man, wrapped in the cloak. His name is Abel Magwitch, otherwise Provis. I apprehend that man, and call upon him to surrender, and you to assist."

At the same moment, without giving any audible direction to his crew, he ran the galley abroad of us. They had pulled one sudden stroke ahead, had got their oars in, had run athwart us, and were holding on to our gunwale, before we knew what they were doing. This caused great confusion on board the steamer, and I heard them calling to us, and heard the order given to stop the paddles, and heard them stop, but felt her driving down upon us irresistibly. In the same moment, I saw the steersman of the galley reach over and lay his hand on Magwitch's shoulder, and saw that both boats were swinging round with the force of the tide, and saw that all hands on board the steamer were running forward quite frantically.

Still, in the same moment, I saw Magwitch start up, lean across his captor, and tug the cloak from the neck of the shrinking sitter in the galley just enough to reveal a small bit of his face and cause him to jerk away from threat of exposure to the sun. Still in the same moment, I saw that the face disclosed was the vampiric profile of the other convict of long ago. Compeyson! Still, in the same moment, I heard a great cry on board the steamer, and a loud splash in the water, and felt the boat sink from under me.

It was but for an instant that I seemed to struggle with a thousand flashes of light. That instant past, I was taken on board the galley. Herbert was there, and Startop was there, but our boat was gone, and the two convicts were gone.

What with the cries aboard the steamer, and the furious blowing off of her steam, and her driving on, and our driving on, I could not at first distinguish sky from water or shore from shore, but the crew of the galley righted her with great speed, and, pulling certain swift strong strokes ahead, lay upon their oars, every man looking silently and eagerly at the water astern.

Presently a dark object was seen in it, bearing towards us on the tide. No man spoke, but the steersman held up his hand, and all softly backed water, and kept the boat straight and true before it. As it came nearer, I saw it to be Magwitch, swimming, but struggling to stay afloat. At some point, he must have turned wolf, for he had lost his clothes and remained covered ever so slightly in a downy fuzz. His nose was still in a state of shrinking back from a snout. He was taken on board, wrapped in a cloak, and instantly manacled with silver at the wrists and ankles.

The galley was kept steady, and the silent, eager look-out at the water was resumed, waiting to see if the other convict, Compeyson, would come up. Water was no certain death for a vampire, I knew, but coming up in the sun without the safety of his cloak to the block the rays would be. If he were injured, might he simply hold himself under water as if drowned?

The Rotterdam steamer now came up, and apparently not understanding what had happened, came on at speed. By the time she had been hailed and stopped, both steamers were drifting away from us, and we were rising and falling in a troubled wake of water. The lookout was kept long after all was still again and the two steamers were gone, but everybody knew that it was hopeless now.

At length we gave it up, and pulled under the shore towards the tavern we had lately left, where we were received with no little surprise. Here I was able to get some comforts for Magwitch—Provis no longer—who had received some very severe injury in the chest, and a deep cut in the head.

He told me that he believed himself to have gone under the keel of the steamer, and to have been struck on the head in rising. In wolf form, he couldn't be sure how it happened but he felt certain he'd had a bit of Compeyson's flesh in his teeth for the vile taste that remained in his mouth. The pain of being struck in the head must have brought him back to himself from the wild.

The injury to his chest (which rendered his breathing extremely painful) he thought he had received against the side of the galley. He added that he did not pretend to say what he might or might not have done to Compeyson, but that, in the moment of his laying his hand on his cloak to identify him, that villain had staggered up and staggered back, desperate to avoid being exposed to searing sunlight and certain painful death, and they had both gone overboard together, when the sudden wrenching of him (Magwitch) out of our boat, and the endeavour of his captor to keep him in it, had capsized us. He told me in a whisper that they had gone down fiercely locked in each other's arms, and that there had been a struggle under water, and that he had disengaged himself, struck out, and swum away.

I never had any reason to doubt the exact truth of what he thus told me. The officer who steered the galley gave the same account of their going overboard. When I asked this officer's permission to get the prisoner some clothes by purchasing any spare garments I could get at the public house, he gave it readily, merely observing that he must take charge of everything his prisoner had about him. So the pocketbook, which had once been in my hands, passed into the officer's. He further gave me leave to accompany the prisoner to London, but declined to accord that grace to my two friends.

The Jack at the Ship was instructed where the drowned man had gone down, and undertook to search for the body in the places where it was likeliest to come ashore. I didn't expect him to recover Compeyson. At best, he'd been beheaded in the fall under the steamboat and lived no more to destroy lives of human or wolf. At worst, he survived, floating out to sea unconscious, where he would most likely turn up on some foreign shore to terrorize new victims. It didn't much matter what became of him now. Magwitch was caught. The damage was done.

We remained at the public house until the tide turned, and then Magwitch was carried down to the galley and put on board. Herbert and Startop were to get to London by land as soon as they could. We had a doleful parting, and when I took my place by Magwitch's side, I felt that that was my place henceforth while he lived.

For now, my repugnance to him had all melted away. In the hunted, wounded, shackled creature who held my hand in his, I only saw a werewolf who had meant to be my benefactor, and who had felt affectionately, gratefully, and generously towards me with great constancy through a series of years. I only saw in him a much better man than I had been to Joe. As much as I resisted, he had become a part of my pack.

His breathing became more difficult and painful as the night drew on, and often he could not repress a groan. I tried to rest him on the arm I could use, in any easy position. It was dreadful to think that he was badly hurt, for the silver would keep him from growing strong to heal, but he would not die, though death perhaps would be a welcome alternative. That there were, still living, people enough who were able and willing to identify him, I could not doubt. That he would be leniently treated, I could not hope. He who had been presented in the worst light at his trial, who had since broken containment and had been tried again, who had returned from transportation under a life sentence, and who had occasioned the death of the man who was the cause of his arrest.

As we returned towards the setting sun we had yesterday left behind us, and as the stream of our hopes seemed all running back, I told him how grieved I was to think that he had come home for my sake.

"Dear boy," he answered, "I'm quite content to take my chance. I've seen my boy, and he can be a gentleman without me."

No. I had thought about that, while we had been there side by side. Apart from any inclinations of my own, I understood Wemmick's insistence on the importance of securing portable property now at last. I foresaw that, being convicted, his possessions would be forfeited to the Crown.

"Lookee here, dear boy," he said. "It's best as a gentleman should not be knowed to belong to me now. Only come to see me as if you come by chance alonger Wemmick. Sit where I can see you when I am swore to, for the last o' many times, and I don't ask no more."

"I will never stir from your side," I said, "when I am suffered to be near you. Please God, I will be as true to you as you have been to me!"

I felt his hand tremble as it held mine, and he turned his face away as he lay in the bottom of the boat, and I heard that old sound in his throat—softened now, like all the rest of him. It was a good thing that he had touched this point, for it put into my mind what I might not otherwise have thought of until too late—that he need never know how his hopes of enriching me had perished.

CHAPTER 51

THE NEXT DAY, MAGWITCH was taken to the Police Court and would have been immediately committed for trial, but that it was necessary to send down for an old officer of the containment ship from which he had once escaped to speak to his identity. Nobody doubted it but Compeyson, who had meant to depose to it, was tumbling on the tides, presumed dead, and it happened that there was not at that time any containment officer in London who could give the required evidence.

I had gone direct to Mr. Jaggers at his private house on my arrival overnight to retain his assistance, and Mr. Jaggers on the prisoner's behalf would admit nothing. There was no hope, Jaggers informed me, if the officer came forward. The case would be over in five minutes, and that no power on earth could prevent its going against us.

There appeared to be reason for supposing that the "drowned" informer had hoped for a reward and had obtained some accurate knowledge of Magwitch's affairs. When his body was found, and indeed it was, many miles from the scene of his death, and headless so that he was only recognizable by the contents of his pockets, notes were still legible, folded in a case he carried. Among these were the name of a banking-house in New South Wales, where a sum of money was, and the designation of certain lands of considerable value.

After three days' delay, during which the crown prosecution stood over for the production of the witness from the containment ship, the witness came, and completed the easy case. He was committed to take his trial at the next Sessions, which would come on in a month.

It was at this dark time of my life that Herbert returned home

one evening, a good deal cast down. "My dear Lowell, I fear I shall
soon have to leave you."

His partner having prepared me for that, I was less surprised than
he thought.

"We shall lose a fine opportunity if I put off going to Cairo,
and I am very much afraid I must go, Lowell, when you most
need me."

"Herbert, I shall always need you, but my need is no greater now
than at another time."

"You will be so lonely."

"I have not leisure to think of that," I said. "You know that I am
always with him to the full extent of the time allowed, and that I
should be with him all day long, if I could. And when I come away
from him, you know that my thoughts are with him."

The dreadful condition to which he was brought was so appalling, to both of us, that we could not refer to it in plainer
words.

"My dear fellow," said Herbert, "let the near prospect of our
separation—for, it is very near—be my justification for troubling
you about yourself. Have you thought of your future?"

"No, for I have been afraid to think of any future."

"But yours cannot be dismissed; indeed, my dear Lowell, it must
not be dismissed. I wish you would enter on it now, as far as a few
friendly words go, with me. In this branch house of ours, Lowell,
we must have a—"

I saw that his delicacy was avoiding the right word, so I said, "A
counselor?"

"A counselor. And I hope it is not at all unlikely that he may
expand (as a counselor of your acquaintance has expanded) into
a partner. Now, Lowell—in short, my dear boy, will you come
to me?"

There was something charmingly cordial and engaging in the
manner in which after saying "Now, Lowell," as if it were the grave
beginning of a portentous business exordium, he had suddenly

given up that tone, stretched out his honest hand, and spoken like a schoolboy.

"Clara and I have talked about it again and again," Herbert pursued, "and the dear little thing begged me only this evening, with tears in her eyes, to say to you that, if you will live with us when we come together, she will do her best to make you happy, and to convince her husband's friend that he is her friend, too. We should get on so well, Lowell!"

I thanked her heartily, and I thanked him heartily, but said I could not yet make sure of joining him as he so kindly offered. Firstly, my mind was too preoccupied to be able to take in the subject clearly. Secondly—Yes! Secondly, there was a vague something lingering in my thoughts that will come out very near the end of this slight narrative.

"But if you thought, Herbert, that you could, without doing any injury to your business, leave the question open for a little while—"

"For any while," cried Herbert. "Six months, a year!"

"Not so long as that," said I. "Two or three months at most."

Herbert was highly delighted when we shook hands on this arrangement, and said he could now take courage to tell me that he believed he must go away at the end of the week.

"And Clara?" said I.

"The dear little thing," returned Herbert, "holds dutifully to her father as long as he lasts, but he won't last long. Mrs. Whimple confides to me that he is certainly going."

"Not to say an unfeeling thing," I said. "He cannot do better than go."

"I am afraid that must be admitted," Herbert said. "And then I shall come back for the dear little thing, and the dear little thing and I will walk quietly into the nearest church."

On the Saturday in that same week, I took my leave of Herbert—full of bright hope, but sad and sorry to leave me—as he sat on one of the seaport mail coaches. I went into a coffee-house to write a little note to Clara, telling her he had gone off, sending his love to her over and over again, and then went to my lonely home—if it deserved the name, for it was now no home to me, and I had no home anywhere.

On the stairs I encountered Wemmick. I had not seen him alone since the disastrous issue of the attempted flight.

"Regarding the late Compeyson," said Wemmick, "I kept my ears open until I heard that he was absent, and I thought that would be the best time for making the attempt. I can only suppose now that it was a part of his policy to habitually deceive his own crew. You don't blame me, I hope, Mr. Pip? I am sure I tried to serve you, with all my heart."

"I am as sure of that, Wemmick, as you can be, and I thank you most earnestly for all your interest and friendship."

"What do you think of my meaning to take a holiday on Monday, Mr. Pip?" he asked.

"Why, I suppose you have not done such a thing these twelve months."

"These twelve years, more likely," Wemmick said. "Yes. I'm going to take a holiday. More than that, I'm going to take a walk. More than that, I'm going to ask you to take a walk with me."

I was about to excuse myself as being but a bad companion just then, when Wemmick anticipated me.

"I know your engagements," he said. "And I know you are out of sorts, Mr. Pip. But if you could oblige me, I should take it as a kindness. It ain't a long walk, and it's an early one. Say it might occupy you (including breakfast on the walk) from eight to twelve. Couldn't you stretch a point and manage it?"

He had done so much for me at various times, that this was very little to do for him. At his particular request, I appointed to call for him at the Castle at half-past eight on Monday morning, and so we parted for the time.

Punctual to my appointment, I rang at the Castle gate on the Monday morning, and was received by Wemmick himself, who struck me as looking tighter than usual, and having a sleeker hat on. When we were walking out, I was considerably surprised to see Wemmick take up a fishing rod and put it over his shoulder.

"Why, we are not going fishing!" I said.

"No," returned Wemmick, "but I like to walk with one."

I thought this odd; however, I said nothing, and we set off. We went towards Camberwell Green, and when we were thereabouts, Wemmick said suddenly, "Halloa! Here's a church!"

There was nothing very surprising in that; but again, I was rather surprised when he said, as if he were animated by a brilliant idea, "Let's go in!"

We went in, Wemmick leaving his fishing rod in the porch, and looked all round. In the meantime, Wemmick was diving into his coat-pockets, and getting something out of paper there.

"Halloa!" he said. "Here's a couple of pair of gloves! Let's put 'em on!"

As the gloves were white kid gloves, I now began to have my strong suspicions. They were strengthened into certainty when I beheld the Aged enter at a side door, escorting a lady.

"Halloa!" said Wemmick. "Here's Miss Skiffins! Let's have a wedding."

That discreet damsel was attired as usual, except that she was now engaged in magically changing the color of her green kid gloves to white. Next, she magically assisted the Aged's hands—poof—into a pair of gloves. The clerk and clergyman then appearing, we were ranged in order at those fatal rails. I heard Wemmick say to himself, as he took something out of his waistcoat-pocket before the service began, "Halloa! Here's a ring!"

I acted in the capacity of backer, or best man, to the bridegroom, while a little limp pew-opener made a feint of being the bosom friend of Miss Skiffins. The responsibility of giving the lady away devolved upon the Aged.

Soon, it was completely done and when we were going out of church, Wemmick took the cover off the font, and put his white gloves in it, and put the cover on again. Mrs. Wemmick employed her magic to change her white gloves back to green.

"Now, Mr. Pip," said Wemmick, triumphantly shouldering the fishing rod as we came out, "let me ask you whether anybody would suppose this to be a wedding party!"

Breakfast had been ordered at a pleasant little tavern, a mile or so away upon the rising ground beyond the green. We had an excellent breakfast. I drank to the new couple, drank to the Aged, drank to the Castle, saluted the bride at parting, and made myself as agreeable as I could.

Wemmick came down to the door with me, and I again shook hands with him, and wished him joy.

"Thankee!" said Wemmick, rubbing his hands. "She's such a manager of fowls, you have no idea. You shall have some eggs, and judge for yourself. I say, Mr. Pip!" calling me back, and speaking low. "This is altogether a Walworth sentiment, please."

"I understand. Not to be mentioned in Little Britain," said I.

Wemmick nodded. "Mr. Jaggers may as well not know of it. He might think my brain was softening, or something of the kind."

CHAPTER 52

DURING THE WHOLE INTERVAL between Magwitch's committal for trial and the coming round of the Sessions, he lay in containment very ill, in great pain, with two broken ribs. One of the ribs had probably punctured a lung, and his breathing suffered greatly. It was a consequence of his hurt that he spoke so low as to be scarcely audible; therefore he spoke very little and was ever ready to listen to me. It became the first duty of my life to say to him, and read to him, what I knew he ought to hear.

Being far too ill to remain in the containment prison, he was removed, after the first day or so, into a special section of the infirmary meant for Scapegraces. This gave me opportunities of being with him that I could not otherwise have had.

Although I saw him every day, it was for only a short time each day. The regularly recurring spaces of our separation were long enough to record on his face any slight changes that occurred in his physical state. I do not recollect that I once saw any change in it for the better. He wasted, and became slowly weaker and worse, day by day, from the day when the containment door closed upon him.

The kind of submission or resignation that he showed was that of an old wolf at the mercy of a new master. I sometimes derived an impression, from his manner or from a whispered word or two which escaped him, that he pondered over the question whether he might have been a better man under better circumstances, circumstances that eluded him as a Scapegrace scrapping out a living on the run, turning wolf at inconvenient times, and facing blame for unfortunate circumstances that were occasionally, but not always, of his own doing. But he never justified himself by a hint tending that way, or tried to bend the past out of its eternal shape.

It happened on two or three occasions in my presence that his desperate reputation was alluded to by one or other of the people in attendance on him. A smile crossed his face then, and he turned his eyes on me with a trustful look, as if he were confident that I had seen some small redeeming touch in him, even so long ago as when I was a little child. As to all the rest, he was humble and contrite, and I never knew him to complain.

When the Sessions came round, Mr. Jaggers caused an application to be made for the postponement of his trial until the following Sessions. It was obviously made with the assurance that he could not live so long, and was refused. The trial came on at once, and, when he was put to the bar, he was seated in a chair. No objection was made to my getting close to the dock, on the outside of it, and holding the hand that he stretched forth to me.

The trial was very short and very clear. Such things as could be said for him were said—how he had taken to industrious habits, and had thriven lawfully and reputably. But nothing could unsay the fact that he had returned, and was there in presence of the judge and jury. It was impossible to try him for that, and do otherwise than find him guilty.

At that time, it was the custom (as I learnt from my terrible experience of that Sessions) to devote a concluding day to the passing of sentences, and to make a finishing effect with the sentence of Death. But for the indelible picture that my remembrance now holds before me, I could scarcely believe, even as I write these words, that I saw two-and-thirty Scapegraces put before the judge to receive that sentence together. Foremost among the two-and-thirty was he; seated, that he might get breath enough to keep life in him.

The whole scene replays for me with the vivid colours of the moment, down to the drops of April rain on the windows of the court, glittering in the rays of April sun. Penned in the dock, as I again stood outside it at the corner with his hand in mine, were the two-and-thirty Scapegraces, some defiant, some stricken with terror, some sobbing and weeping, some covering their faces, some staring gloomily about. There had been shrieks from among the women convicts, but they had been stilled, and a hush had succeeded.

The sheriffs with their great chains and nosegays, other civic gewgaws and monsters, criers, ushers, a great gallery full of people—a large theatrical audience—looked on, as the two-and-thirty and the judge were solemnly confronted. Then the judge addressed them. Among the wretched creatures before him whom he must single out for special address was one who almost from his infancy had been an offender against the laws; who, after repeated imprisonments and punishments, had been at length sentenced to exile for a term of years; and who, under circumstances of great violence and daring, had made his escape and been re-sentenced to exile for life. That miserable werewolf would seem for a time to have become tamed, when far removed from the scenes of his old offences. But in a fatal moment, yielding to the wild inner beast, he had quitted his haven of rest and repentance, and had come back to the country where he was proscribed.

Being here presently denounced, he had for a time succeeded in evading the officers of justice, but being at length seized while in the act of flight, he had resisted them, and had most savagely caused the death of his denouncer, to whom his whole career was known. The appointed punishment for his return to the land that had cast him out, being Death, and his case being this aggravated case, he must prepare himself to die by slow hanging from a solid silver chain, followed by a shot to the heart of a single silver bullet, and drawing and quartering with burial in an unmarked grave.

Rising for a moment, a distinct speck of face in this way of light, the prisoner said, "My lord, I have received my sentence of Death from the Almighty, but I bow to yours," and sat down again.

There was some hushing, and the judge went on with what he had to say to the rest. Then they were all formally doomed, and some of them were supported out, and some of them sauntered out with a haggard look of bravery, and a few nodded to the gallery, and two or three shook hands. He went last of all, because of having to be helped from his chair, and to go very slowly.

It was the thought of his great and constant pain that made me wish he could die quickly and find an end to it, but live he would, with no strength to heal while he remained in containment with silver chains around him to keep him weak. I began that night to write out a petition to the Home Secretary of State, setting forth my knowledge of him, and how it was that he had come back for my sake, and petitioning on behalf of the rights of Scapegraces that laws be reconsidered to promote equality and freedom for all. I wrote it as fervently and pathetically as I could; and when I had finished it and sent it in, I wrote out other petitions to such men in authority as I hoped were the most merciful, and drew up one to the Crown itself to examine the laws with regards to rights of Scapegraces and unfair accusations and imprisonments based on our condition alone. I would have exempted vampires from my petition as the scheming, foul creatures they were, but it wouldn't do to judge or vilify one sort of being in calling for equal rights for all. Even laws wouldn't stop a slayer like Estella from her calling of removing the scourge from the earth.

For several days and nights after he was sentenced I took no rest except when I fell asleep in my chair, but was wholly absorbed in these appeals. In this unreasonable restlessness and pain of mind I would roam the streets of an evening, wandering by those offices and houses where I had left the petitions.

The daily visits I could make him were shortened now, and he was more strictly kept. Seeing, or fancying, that I was suspected of an intention of carrying poison to him, I asked to be searched before I sat down at his bedside, and told the officer who was always there, that I was willing to do anything that would assure him of the singleness of my designs. Nobody was hard with him or with me. There was duty to be done, and it was done, but not harshly. The officer always gave me the assurance that he was worse, and some other sick Scapegraces in the room, and some other Scapegraces who attended on them as sick nurses always joined in the same report.

As the days went on, I noticed more and more that he would lie placidly looking at the white ceiling, with an absence of light in his face until some word of mine brightened it for an instant, and then it would subside again. Sometimes he was almost or quite unable to speak, then he would answer me with slight pressures on my hand, and I grew to understand his meaning very well.

The number of the days had risen to ten, when I saw a greater change in him than I had seen yet. His eyes were turned towards the door, and lighted up as I entered.

"Dear boy," he said, as I sat down by his bed. "I thought you was late. But I knowed you couldn't be that."

"It is just the time," I said. "I waited for it at the gate."

"You always waits at the gate. Don't you, dear boy?"

"Yes. Not to lose a moment of the time."

"Thank'ee, dear boy, thank'ee. God bless you! You've never deserted me, dear boy."

I pressed his hand in silence, for I could not forget that I had once meant to desert him.

"And what's the best of all," he said, "you've been more comfortable alonger me, since I was under a dark cloud, than when the sun shone. That's best of all."

He lay on his back, breathing with great difficulty. Do what he would, and love me though he did, the light left his face ever and again, and a film came over the placid look at the white ceiling.

"Are you in much pain today?"

"I don't complain of none, dear boy."

"You never do complain."

He had spoken his last words. He smiled, and I understood his touch to mean that he wished to lift my hand, and lay it on his breast. I laid it there, and he smiled again, and put both his hands upon it.

"I saw an angel today, dear boy," he said. "She smiled at me and gave me to know that peace awaits."

There are no angels here, I meant to say, but the allotted time ran out, while we were thus. Perhaps it was best that I didn't shatter his illusions if he was having a beautiful dream. Looking round, I found the governor of the containment prison standing near me, and he whispered, "You needn't go yet."

It was unusual for the governor himself to show up and I suspected there was a reason for it.

I thanked him gratefully, and asked, "Might we speak for just a moment?"

He nodded and we stepped aside, out of Magwitch's hearing.

"He has taken a turn for the worse," I said, not knowing what to make of it. I never expected him to heal well or quickly, but his deterioration surprised me.

"This was beside his cot," the governor explained, holding out a silver dagger. "He must have got hold of it through fellow prisoners. We found him bleeding, the damage self-inflicted."

"Through his heart," I nodded, understanding. "The pain became too much to bear."

So much pain. It was all he had ever known, and now physical as well as emotional pain had taken a toll and become unbearable. But the dagger looked familiar, like one of Estella's. My heart raced. How could she have known?

"We bandaged him to try and stop the bleeding, but I'm afraid we were too late. He will not last."

"Might I speak to him, if he can hear me?"

The governor stepped aside, and beckoned the officer away. The change, though it was made without noise, drew back the film from the placid look at the white ceiling, and he looked most affectionately at me.

"Dear Magwitch, I must tell you now, at last. You understand what I say?"

A gentle pressure on my hand.

"You had a child once, whom you loved and lost."

A stronger pressure on my hand.

"She lived, and found powerful friends. She is living now. She is a lady and very beautiful. And I love her!"

With a last faint effort, which would have been powerless but for my yielding to it and assisting it, he raised my hand to his lips. Then, he gently let it sink upon his breast again, with his own hands lying on it. The placid look at the white ceiling came back, and passed away, and his head dropped quietly on his breast.

I knew there were no better words that I could say beside his bed, than "O Lord, be merciful to him a werewolf!"

CHAPTER 53

NOW THAT I WAS left wholly to myself, I gave notice of my intention to quit the chambers in the Temple as soon as my tenancy could legally determine, and in the meanwhile to underlet them. At once I advertised the chambers as available, for I was in debt, and began to be seriously alarmed by the state of my affairs. I ought rather to write that I *should* have been alarmed if I'd had energy and concentration beyond the fact that I was falling very ill. The late stress upon me had enabled me to put off illness, but not to put it away. I knew that it was coming on me now, and I knew very little else, and was even careless as to that.

For a day or two, I lay on the sofa, or on the floor—anywhere, according as I happened to sink down—with a heavy head and aching limbs, and no purpose, and no power to fight my changing body. The phases of the moon ceased to matter. I drifted in and out of wolfishness along with my delirium.

Whether I really had been down in Garden Court in the dead of the night, I did not know. Whether I had two or three times come to myself on the staircase with great terror, not knowing how I had got out of bed; whether I had found myself in the middle of a chicken coop, feathers sticking to the blood dribbling from my lips; whether I had visited the bokor and ripped the heads from all the just-turned Recommissioneds with my sharp claws alone; whether I had been in a scuffle with a mighty bear twice my size at the edge of the wood; whether I had been inexpressibly harassed by the distracted talking, growling, and baying of some one, and had half suspected those sounds to be of my own making; these were things that I tried to settle with myself and get into some order, as I lay that morning on my bed. But the vapour of a limekiln would come between me and them, disordering them all, and it was through the vapour at last that I saw two men looking at me.

"What do you want?" I asked, starting. "I don't know you."

"Well, sir," returned one of them, bending down and touching me on the shoulder, "this is a matter that you'll soon arrange, I dare say, but you're arrested."

"What is the debt?"

"Hundred and twenty-three pound, fifteen, six. Jeweller's account, I think."

"What is to be done?" I never had an answer, for I felt my bones melding one into another, twisting, turning, distorting, and I was wolf again before I could employ any of my methods to hold off or control the change.

I ran wild through the streets of London, through woods and fields. All of it blended in my feverish mind. I had a vague recollection of struggles, with animals, with people. Was I in the field sinking my teeth into the tender neck of a squirming hare? In the woods, running between trees and splashing into a shallow pond to get away from hunters? Was I running down alleyways, cornering vampires and gnashing my teeth? At last, I came to myself with a sense of fighting someone off, and then suddenly realizing that he meant to do me good, I sank exhausted in his arms, and suffered him to lay me down. I had an idea that it was Joe, and then I knew I was still delirious, and I would lose myself again.

After I had turned the worst point of my illness, I began to notice that while all its other features changed, this one consistent feature did not change. Whoever came about me still settled down into Joe. I opened my eyes in the night, and I saw, in the great chair at the bedside, Joe. I opened my eyes in the day, and, sitting on the window-seat, smoking his pipe in the shaded open window, still I saw Joe. I asked for a cooling drink, and the dear hand that gave it me was Joe's. I sank back on my pillow after drinking, and the face that looked so hopefully and tenderly upon me was the face of Joe.

At last, one day, I took courage, and said, "Is it Joe?"

And the dear old home-voice answered, "Which it air, old chap."

"Oh, Joe, you break my heart! Look angry at me, Joe. Strike me, Joe. Tell me of my ingratitude. Don't be so good to me!"

For Joe had actually laid his head down on the pillow at my side, and put his arm round my neck, in his joy that I knew him.

"Which dear old Pip, old chap," said Joe, "you and me was ever friends. And when you're well enough to go out for a ride—what larks!"

After which, Joe withdrew to the window, and stood with his back towards me, wiping his eyes. And as my extreme weakness prevented me from getting up and going to him, I lay there, penitently whispering, "Oh God bless him! Oh God bless this gentle Christian man!"

Joe's eyes were red when I next found him beside me, but I was holding his hand, and we both felt happy.

"How long, dear Joe?"

"Which you meantersay, Pip, how long have your illness lasted, dear old chap?"

"Yes, Joe."

"It's the end of May, Pip. Tomorrow is the first of June."

"And have you been here all that time, dear Joe?"

"Pretty nigh, old chap. For, as I says to Biddy when the news of your being ill were brought by letter, which it were," said Joe, "that how you might be amongst strangers, and that how you and me having been ever friends, a wisit at such a moment might not prove unacceptabobble. And Biddy, her word were, 'Go to him, without loss of time.'"

There Joe cut himself short, and informed me that I was to be talked to in great moderation, and that I was to take a little nourishment at stated frequent times, whether I felt inclined for it or not, and that I was to submit myself to all his orders. So I kissed his hand, and lay quiet, while he proceeded to write a note to Biddy, with my love in it.

Evidently Biddy had taught Joe to write. As I lay in bed looking

at him, it made me, in my weak state, cry again with pleasure to see
the pride with which he set about his letter. My bedstead, divested
of its curtains, had been removed, with me upon it, into the sitting-room, as the airiest and largest, and the carpet had been taken
away, and the room kept always fresh and wholesome night and day.
At my own writing-table, pushed into a corner and cumbered with
little bottles, Joe now sat down to his great work, first choosing a
pen from the pen-tray as if it were a chest of large tools, and tuck-
ing up his sleeves as if he were going to wield a crow-bar or sledge-
hammer. On the whole, he got on very well indeed. When he had
signed his name, he got up and hovered about the table, trying the
effect of his performance from various points of view, as it lay there,
with unbounded satisfaction.

Not to make Joe uneasy by talking too much, even if I had been
able to talk much, I deferred asking him about Miss Havisham until
next day. He shook his head when I then asked him if she had recovered.

"Why you see, old chap," said Joe, in a tone of remonstrance, and
by way of getting at it by degrees, "I wouldn't go so far as to say that,
for that's a deal to say, but she ain't—"

"Living, Joe?"

"That's nigher where it is," said Joe. "She ain't living."

"What happened, Joe? In the very end?" For I knew what Joe
could not, that a natural death was not for Miss Havisham.

"Arter you was took ill, pretty much about what you might call
(if you was put to it) a week," Joe said. "Strange, it is. She—they
say she got up from the table just as fit as if nothing had ever ailed
her. She jumped up and said she was done with all gloom. She
said she would find her heart again, wherever she had left it, and
she went tearing around her house in search of it. She threw her
wedding clothes right in the fire, they say! She sent for the tailor
to order new clothes, and until then she put on a frock from her
trooso trunk, which was a crimson velvet gown, so they say. And, in
that crimson gown, she ran straight for the front door, all the while

going on about how she meant to dance under the sun. 'That will teach him,' she supposedly said. 'All these years, I had it all wrong. Death won't teach him. It's life! Life will be my best revenge!' And she ran right out into the sun and—"

"And what, Joe?" I asked, though I knew. I knew what happened to Miss Havisham under the sun.

"And poof, that's what. She went off like a rocket in a blast of fire, a shower of sparks, and a hail of ash. Astonishing, they say it was. And that's all. That's the last anyone has seen of Miss 'avisham."

"I'm sorry to hear it. Have you heard what becomes of her property?"

"Well, old chap," said Joe, "it do appear that she had settled the most of it, which I meantersay tied it up, on Miss Estella. But she had wrote out a little coddleshell in her own hand a day or two afore the accident, leaving four thousand to Mr. Matthew Pocket. And why, do you suppose, above all things, Pip, she left that four thousand unto him? 'Because of Pip's account of him, the said Matthew.' I am told by Biddy that air the writing," said Joe, repeating the legal turn as if it did him infinite good, "'account of him the said Matthew.' And four thousand, Pip!"

I asked Joe whether he had heard if any of the other relations had any legacies?

"Miss Sarah," said Joe, "she have twenty-five pound perannium fur to buy pills, on account of being bilious. Miss Georgiana, she have twenty pound down. Mrs.—what's the name of them wild beasts with humps, old chap?"

"Camels?" said I, wondering why he could possibly want to know.

Joe nodded. "Mrs. Camels," by which I presently understood he meant Camilla, "she have five pound fur to buy rushlights to put her in spirits when she wake up in the night."

The accuracy of these recitals was sufficiently obvious to me, giving me great confidence in Joe's information.

"And now," said Joe, "you ain't that strong yet, old chap, that you can take in more nor one additional shovelful today."

The one additional shovelful involved an incident at Pumblechook's.

"An accident in the training of new Recommissioneds," Joe said.

"Training?" I asked. "I thought he just made them and sent them out to buyers."

"Since he took on the idea to sell them as domestic servants, he gives them a bit of training in what to do fur waiting on fine families they mean to serve arter he sends them out. Remember, Pip, when he warned us not to feed your sister."

"After her recommissioning, Joe. Of course."

"What happens is it makes them turn on those who makes them, feeding them does." Joe was clearly unaware of the fact that Biddy had told me what had happened at the end for my sister. "Turn on Pumblechook, is what I mean to say. About five of them Recommissioneds got into some wittles at Pumblechook's, and they turned powerful angry, Pip. Powerful. They cornered Pumblechook. Pendleton's boy, he's the other bokor in town, says they would have torn him limb from limb if not fur—"

"If not for what, Joe? What stopped them?"

"If not fur the young lady showing up when she did. A young lady happened to be passing and hearing Pumblechook's screams, she went in to help him. Pendleton's boy said she engaged them in battle, ripped their heads off one by one, and sent green goo flying everywhere. Pumblechook says no, it did not happen that way, but that some of the Recommissioneds was having adjustment difficulties and he would have had things under his control. But he was surely bruised and battered, he was. Now business is not so good for old Pumblechook, Pip, arter word got around."

"I imagine not." My mind was on the young woman. I had no doubt that it had been Estella. I wondered what Mr. Drummle would have had to say of his wife's heroic actions, or if he was even aware—but it was no affair of mine.

I was slow to gain strength, but I did become less weak, and Joe stayed with me, and I fancied I was little Pip again. Joe would sit and talk to me in the old confidence, and with the old simplicity, so that I would half believe that all my life since the days of the old kitchen was one of the mental troubles of the fever that was gone. He did everything for me except the household work, for which he had engaged a very decent woman, after paying off the laundress on his first arrival.

"Which I do assure you, Pip," he would often say, in explanation of that liberty, "I found her a tapping the spare bed, like a cask of beer, and drawing off the feathers in a bucket, for sale. Which she would have tapped yourn next, and draw'd it off with you a laying on it, and was then a carrying away the coals gradiwally in the soup-tureen and wegetable-dishes, and the wine and spirits in your Wellington boots."

We looked forward to the day when I should go out for a ride, as we had once looked forward to the day of my apprenticeship. And when the day came, and an open carriage was got into the lane, Joe wrapped me up, took me in his arms, carried me down to it, and put me in, as if I were still the small helpless creature to whom he had so abundantly given of the wealth of his great nature.

And Joe got in beside me, and we drove away together into the country, where the rich summer growth was already on the trees and on the grass, and sweet summer scents filled all the air. But when I heard the Sunday bells, and looked around a little more upon the outspread beauty, I felt that I was not nearly thankful enough—that I was too weak yet to be even that—and I laid my head on Joe's shoulder, as I had laid it long ago when he had taken me to the fair or where not, and it was too much for my young senses.

More composure came to me after a while, and we talked as we used to talk, lying on the grass at the old battery. There was no change whatever in Joe. Exactly what he had been in my eyes then, he was in my eyes still, just as simply faithful, and as simply right.

When we got back again, and he lifted me out, and carried me— so easily!—across the court and up the stairs, I thought of that eventful Christmas Day when he had carried me over the marshes.

We had not yet made any allusion to my change of fortune, nor did I know how much of my late history he was acquainted with. I was so doubtful of myself now, and put so much trust in him, that I could not satisfy myself whether I ought to refer to it when he did not.

"Have you heard, Joe," I asked him that evening, upon further consideration, as he smoked his pipe at the window, "who my patron was?"

"I heerd," returned Joe, "as it were not Miss Havisham, old chap."

"Did you hear who it was, Joe?"

"Well! I heerd as it were a person what sent the person what giv' you the bank-notes at the Jolly Bargemen, Pip."

"So it was."

"Astonishing!" said Joe, in the placidest way.

"Did you hear that he was dead, Joe?" I presently asked, with increasing diffidence.

"Which? Him as sent the bank-notes, Pip?"

"Yes. He was a werewolf, like me."

"I think," said Joe, after meditating a long time, and looking rather evasively at the window-seat, "as I did hear tell that how he were something or another in a general way in that direction."

"Did you hear anything of his circumstances, Joe?"

"Not partickler, Pip."

"If you would like to hear, Joe—" I was beginning, when Joe got up and came to my sofa.

"Lookee here, old chap," said Joe, bending over me. "Ever the best of friends. Ain't us, Pip?"

I was ashamed to answer him.

"Wery good, then," said Joe, as if I had answered. "That's all right. That's agreed upon. Then why go into subjects, old chap, which as betwixt two sech must be forever onnecessary? There's subjects enough as betwixt two sech, without onnecessary ones. You mustn't go a overdoing on it, but you must have your supper and your wine and water, and you must be put betwixt the sheets."

The delicacy with which Joe dismissed this theme made a deep impression on my mind. But whether Joe knew how poor I was, and how my great expectations had all dissolved, like our own marsh mists before the sun, I could not understand.

Another thing in Joe that I could not understand when it first began to develop itself was this: As I became stronger and better, Joe became a little less easy with me. In my weakness and entire dependence on him, the dear fellow had fallen into the old tone, and called me by the old names, the dear "old Pip, old chap" that now were music in my ears. I, too, had fallen into the old ways, only happy and thankful that he let me. But, imperceptibly, Joe's hold upon them began to slacken. I soon began to understand that the cause of it was in me, and that the fault of it was all mine.

Ah! Had I given Joe no reason to doubt my constancy, and to think that in prosperity I should grow cold to him and cast him off? Had I given Joe's innocent heart no cause to feel instinctively that as I got stronger, his hold upon me would be weaker, and that he had better loosen it in time and let me go, before I plucked myself away?

It was on the third or fourth occasion of my going out walking in the Temple Gardens leaning on Joe's arm, that I saw this change in him very plainly.

"See, Joe! I can walk quite strongly. Now, you shall see me walk back by myself."

"Which do not overdo it, Pip," said Joe. "But I shall be happy fur to see you able, sir."

The last word grated on me, but how could I remonstrate! I walked no further than the gate of the gardens, and then pretended to be weaker than I was, and asked Joe for his arm. Joe gave it me, but was thoughtful.

It was a thoughtful evening with both of us. But, before we went to bed, I had resolved that I would wait over tomorrow—tomorrow being Sunday—and would begin my new course with the new week. On Monday morning I would speak to Joe about my change of circumstances. I would tell him what I had in my thoughts and why I had not decided to go out to Herbert, and then the change would be conquered forever.

We had a quiet day on the Sunday, and we rode out into the country, and then walked in the fields.

"I feel thankful that I have been ill, Joe," I said.

"Dear old Pip, old chap, you're a'most come round, sir."

"It has been a memorable time for me, Joe."

"Likeways for myself, sir," Joe returned.

"We have had a time together, Joe, that I can never forget. There were days once, I know, that I did for a while forget; but I never shall forget these."

"Pip," said Joe, appearing a little hurried and troubled, "there has been larks. And, dear sir, what have been betwixt us—have been."

Before moonrise, I started having the familiar feeling that a change was coming on. I informed Joe of my impending transformation that he might help me with the necessary precautions of feeding me well and locking me in my room. As I settled in, Joe came in to check on me, as he had done all through my recovery. He asked me if I felt sure that I was strong enough to make the change and be back to myself by morning?

"Yes, dear Joe, quite."

"And are always a getting stronger, old chap?"

"Yes, dear Joe, steadily."

Joe patted the coverlet on my shoulder with his great good hand, and said, in what I thought a husky voice, "Goodnight!"

When I got up in the morning, refreshed and stronger yet, I was full of my resolution to tell Joe all, without delay. I would tell him before breakfast. I would dress at once and go to his room and surprise him. I went to his room, and he was not there. Not only was he not there, but his box was gone.

I hurried then to the breakfast-table, and on it found a letter. These were its brief contents:

Not wishful to intrude I have departured fur you are well again dear Pip and will do better without JO.

P.S. Ever the best of friends.

Enclosed in the letter was a receipt for the debt and costs on which I had been arrested. Down to that moment, I had vainly supposed that my creditor had withdrawn, or suspended proceedings until I should be quite recovered. The truth was here, that Joe had paid it, and the receipt was in his name.

What remained for me now but to follow him to the dear old forge, and there to have out my disclosure to him, and my penitent remonstrance with him, and there to relieve my mind and heart of that which had begun as a vague something lingering in my thoughts, and had formed into a settled purpose?

The purpose was, that I would go to Biddy, that I would show her how humbled and repentant I came back, that I would tell her how I had lost all I once hoped for, that I would remind her of our old confidences in my first unhappy time.

Then I would say to her, "Biddy, I think you once liked me very well, when my errant heart, even while it strayed away from you, was quieter and better with you than it ever has been since. You never minded my going wolfish, and I hope you won't mind it much again, as I can control it much better now than I used to, and it needn't be a bother to us except for once a month. If you can like me only half as well once more, if you can take me with all my faults and transformations, if you can receive me like a forgiven pup (and indeed I am as sorry, Biddy, and have as much need of a hushing voice and a soothing hand), I hope I am a little worthier of you than I was—not much, but a little. And, Biddy, it shall rest with you to say whether I shall work at the forge with Joe, or whether I shall try for any different occupation down in this country, or whether we shall go away to a distant place where an opportunity awaits me which I set aside, when it was offered, until I knew your answer.

And now, dear Biddy, if you can tell me that you will go through the world with me, you will surely make it a better world for me, and me a better man for it, and I will try hard to make it a better world for you."

Such was my purpose. After three days more of recovery, I went down to the old place to put it in execution. And how I sped in it is all I have left to tell.

CHAPTER 54

THE NEWS OF MY changing fortunes reached my native place and its neighbourhood before I got there. I found the Blue Boar in possession of the intelligence, and I found that it made a great change in the Boar's demeanour. Whereas the Boar had cultivated my good opinion with warm assiduity when I was coming into property, the Boar was exceedingly cool on the subject now that I was going out of property.

It was evening when I arrived, much fatigued by the journey I had so often made so easily. The Boar could not put me into my usual bedroom, which was engaged (probably by some one who had expectations), and could only assign me a very indifferent chamber among the pigeons and post-chaises up the yard. But I had as sound a sleep in that lodging as in the most superior accommodation the Boar could have given me, and the quality of my dreams was about the same as in the best bedroom.

Early in the morning, while my breakfast was getting ready, I strolled round by Satis House. There were printed bills on the gate and on bits of carpet hanging out of the windows, announcing a sale by auction of the household furniture and effects, next week.

The house itself was to be sold as old building materials, and pulled down. LOT 1 was marked in whitewashed knock-knee letters on the brew house; LOT 2 on that part of the main building which had been so long shut up. Stepping in for a moment at the open gate, and looking around me with the uncomfortable air of a stranger who had no business there, I saw the auctioneer's clerk walking on the casks and telling them off for the information of a catalogue-compiler, pen in hand, who made a temporary desk of the target I used to be brave enough to stand before and catch or dodge whatever Estella threw at me.

The June weather was delicious. The sky was blue, the larks soaring high over the green corn. As I left Satis House and headed to the house and forge that I still thought of as home, I thought all that countryside more beautiful and peaceful by far than I had ever known it to be yet. Many pleasant pictures of the life that I would lead there, and of the change for the better that would come over my character when I had a guiding spirit at my side whose simple faith and clear home wisdom I had proved, beguiled my way.

The schoolhouse where Biddy was mistress I had never seen, but the little roundabout lane by which I entered the village took me past it. I was disappointed to find that the day was a holiday. No children were there, and Biddy's house was closed. Some hopeful notion of seeing her, busily engaged in her daily duties, before she saw me, had been in my mind and was defeated.

But the forge was a very short distance off, and I went towards it under the sweet green limes, listening for the clink of Joe's hammer. Long after I ought to have heard it, and long after I had fancied I heard it and found it but a fancy, all was still. The limes were there, and the white thorns were there, and the chestnut trees were there, and their leaves rustled harmoniously when I stopped to listen, but the clink of Joe's hammer was not in the midsummer wind.

Almost fearing, without knowing why, to come in view of the

forge, I saw it at last, and saw that it was closed. No gleam of fire, no glittering shower of sparks, no roar of bellows, all shut up, and still.

But the house was not deserted, and the best parlour seemed to be in use, for there were white curtains fluttering in its window, and the window was open and gay with flowers. I went softly towards it, meaning to peep over the flowers, when Joe and Biddy stood before me, arm in arm.

At first Biddy gave a cry, as if she thought it was my apparition, but in another moment she was in my embrace. I wept to see her, and she wept to see me. I, because she looked so fresh and pleasant. She, because I looked so worn and white.

"But, dear Biddy, how smart you are!"

"Yes, dear Pip."

"And, Joe, how smart you are!"

"Yes, dear old Pip, old chap."

I looked at both of them, from one to the other, and then—

"It's my wedding-day!" cried Biddy, in a burst of happiness, "and I am married to Joe!"

They had taken me into the kitchen, and I had laid my head down on the old deal table. Biddy held one of my hands to her lips, and Joe's restoring touch was on my shoulder.

"Which he warn't strong enough, my dear, fur to be surprised," said Joe.

And Biddy said, "I ought to have thought of it, dear Joe, but I was too happy."

They were both so overjoyed to see me, so proud to see me, so touched by my coming to them, so delighted that I should have come by accident to make their day complete!

My first thought was one of great thankfulness that I had never breathed this last baffled hope to Joe. How often, while he was with me in my illness, had it risen to my lips! How irrevocable would have been his knowledge of it, if he had remained with me but another hour! But how much better this way, after all, for dear Joe and sweet Biddy to have each other. And best for Biddy, perhaps, to have a husband who wouldn't go wolfish under a full moon or give her the trouble of whelping a litter of pups instead of cherubic babes.

"Dear Biddy," I said. "You have the best husband in the whole world, and if you could have seen him by my bed you would have— But no, you couldn't love him better than you do."

"No, I couldn't indeed," said Biddy.

"And, dear Joe, you have the best wife in the whole world, and she will make you as happy as you deserve to be, you dear, good, noble Joe!"

Joe looked at me with a quivering lip, and fairly put his sleeve before his eyes.

"And Joe and Biddy both, as you have been to church today, and are in charity and love with all mankind, receive my humble thanks for all you have done for me, and all I have so ill repaid! And when I say that I am going away within the hour, for I am soon going abroad, and that I shall never rest until I have worked for the money with which you have kept me out of containment prison, and have sent it to you, don't think, dear Joe and Biddy, that if I could repay it a thousand times over, I suppose I could cancel a farthing of the debt I owe you, or that I would do so if I could!"

They were both melted by these words, and both entreated me to say no more.

"But I must say more. Dear Joe, I hope you will have children to love, and that some little fellow will sit in this chimney-corner of a winter night, who may remind you of another little fellow gone out of it forever, without the trouble of locking him in under a full moon. Don't tell him, Joe, that I was thankless. Don't tell him, Biddy, that I was ungenerous and unjust. Only tell him that I honoured you both, because you were both so good and true, and that, as your child, I said it would be natural to him to grow up a much better man than I did."

"I ain't a going," said Joe, from behind his sleeve, "to tell him nothink o' that natur, Pip. Nor Biddy ain't. Nor yet no one ain't."

"And now, though I know you have already done it in your own kind hearts, pray tell me, both, that you forgive me! Pray let me hear you say the words, that I may carry the sound of them away with me, and then I shall be able to believe that you can trust me, and think better of me, in the time to come!"

"Oh dear old Pip, old chap," said Joe. "God knows as I forgive you, if I have anythink to forgive!"

"Amen! And God knows I do!" echoed Biddy.

"Now let me go up and look at my old little room, and rest there a few minutes by myself. And then, when I have eaten and drunk with you, go with me as far as the finger-post, dear Joe and Biddy, before we say goodbye!"

Soon after that day, I sold all I had, and put aside as much as I could for a composition with my creditors—who gave me ample time to pay them in full—and I went out and joined Herbert. Within a month, I had quitted England, and within two months I was a counselor with the Office of Werewolf Affairs at Clavenger House for the Benefit and Education of Scapegraces. My responsibilities soon increased as Herbert had gone away to marry Clara, and I was left in sole charge of the Eastern Branch until he brought her back.

Many a year went round before I was a partner in the House, but I lived happily with Herbert and his wife, and lived frugally, and paid my debts, and maintained a constant correspondence with Biddy and Joe. It was not until I became third in the Firm that Clavenger betrayed me to Herbert. He then declared that the secret of Herbert's partnership had been long enough upon his conscience, and he must tell it. So he told it, and Herbert was as much moved as amazed, and the dear fellow and I were not the worse friends for the long concealment.

I must not leave it to be supposed that we were ever a great house, or that we made mints of money. We were not in a grand way of business, but we had a good name, worked for the good of all, did very well to bring attention to difficulties faced by Scapegraces the world over, and to end the prejudices we faced. We owed so much to Herbert's ever cheerful industry and readiness, that I often wondered how I had conceived that old idea of his ineptitude, until I was one day enlightened by the reflection that perhaps the ineptitude had never been in him at all, but had been in me.

CHAPTER 55

FOR EIGHT YEARS, I had not seen Joe nor Biddy when, upon an evening in December, an hour or two after dark, I laid my hand softly on the latch of the old kitchen door. I touched it so softly that I was not heard, and looked in unseen. There, smoking his pipe in the old place by the kitchen firelight, as hale and as strong as ever, though a little grey, sat Joe. There, fenced into the corner with Joe's leg, and sitting on my own little stool looking at the fire, was—I again!

"We giv' him the name of Pip for your sake, dear old chap," said Joe, delighted, when I took another stool by the child's side (but I did not rumple his hair), "and we hoped he might grow a little bit like you, and we think he do." With the exception, I was given to understand, that the dear lad was not at all wolfish.

I took him out for a walk next morning, and we talked immensely, understanding one another to perfection. And I took him down to the churchyard, and set him on a tombstone there, and he showed me from that elevation which stone was sacred to the memory of Philip Pirrip, late of this Parish, and Also Georgiana, Wife of the Above.

"Biddy," said I, when I talked with her after dinner, as her little girl lay sleeping in her lap, "you must give Pip to me one of these days, or lend him, at all events."

"No, no," said Biddy, gently. "You must marry."

"So Herbert and Clara say, but I don't think I shall, Biddy. I have so settled down in their home, that it's not at all likely. I am already quite an old bachelor."

Biddy looked down at her child, and put its little hand to her lips, and then put the good matronly hand with which she had touched it into mine. There was something in the action, and in the light pressure of Biddy's wedding-ring, that had a very pretty eloquence in it.

"Dear Pip," said Biddy. "You are sure you don't fret for her?"

"Oh no—I think not, Biddy."

"Tell me as an old, old friend. Have you quite forgotten her?

"My dear Biddy, I have forgotten nothing in my life that ever had a foremost place there, and little that ever had any place there. But that poor dream, as I once used to call it, has all gone by, Biddy—all gone by!"

Nevertheless, I knew, while I said those words, that I secretly intended to revisit the site of the old house that evening, alone, for her sake. Yes, even so. For Estella's sake.

I had heard of her as something of a legend, ridding the country of vampire scourge, but not usually of werewolves. No, she'd never harmed a werewolf save for possibly one, her husband. While he lived, he had reportedly used her with great cruelty, and had become quite renowned as a compound of pride, avarice, brutality, and meanness. And I had heard of the death of her husband, from an accident consequent on his ill-treatment of a horse. His jerking hard on the bit had somehow caused a silver star decoration of the bridle to shoot into his heart. I had no doubt that it was of Estella's doing, no matter how "accidental" a tragedy it seemed. Many a time, I had watched her fling her Chinese throwing stars at targets with deadly focus. This release had befallen her some two years before; for anything I knew, she was married again.

The early dinner hour at Joe's left me abundance of time, without hurrying my talk with Biddy, to walk over to the old spot before dark. But, what with loitering on the way to look at old objects and to think of old times, the day had quite declined when I came to the place.

There was no house now, no brewery, no building whatever left, but the wall of the old garden. The cleared space had been enclosed with a rough fence, and looking over it, I saw that some of the old ivy had struck root anew, and was growing green on low quiet mounds of ruin. A gate in the fence standing ajar, I pushed it open, and went in.

A cold silvery mist had veiled the afternoon, and the moon was not yet up to scatter it. But, the stars were shining beyond the mist, and the moon was coming, and the evening was not dark. I could trace out where every part of the old house had been, and where the brewery had been, and where the gates, and where the casks. I had done so, and was looking along the desolate garden walk, when I beheld a solitary figure in it.

The figure showed itself aware of me as I advanced. It had been moving towards me, but it stood still. As I drew nearer, I saw it to be the figure of a woman. As I drew nearer yet, it was about to turn away, when it stopped, and let me come up with it. Then, it faltered, as if much surprised, and uttered my name, and I cried out—

"Estella!"

"I am greatly changed. I wonder you know me."

The freshness of her beauty was indeed gone, but its indescribable majesty and charm remained. She had aged, true, but she was perhaps even more alluring with the changes of time. What I had never seen before in her was the saddened, softened light of the once proud eyes. What I had never felt before was the friendly touch of the once insensible hand.

We sat down on a bench that was near, and I said, "After so many years, it is strange that we should thus meet again, Estella, here where our first meeting was! Do you often come back?"

"I have never been here since."

"Nor I."

The moon began to rise, and I thought of the placid look at the white ceiling, which had passed away, and I thought of the pressure on my hand when I had spoken the last words he had heard on earth.

Estella was the next to break the silence that ensued between us.

"I have very often hoped and intended to come back, but have been prevented by many circumstances. Poor, poor old place!"

The silvery mist was touched with the first rays of the moonlight, and the same rays touched the tears that dropped from her eyes. Not knowing that I saw them, and setting herself to get the better of them, she said quietly, "Were you wondering, as you walked along, how it came to be left in this condition?"

"Yes, Estella."

"The ground belongs to me. It is the only possession I have not relinquished. Everything else has gone from me, little by little, but I have kept this. It was the subject of the only determined resistance I made in all the wretched years."

"Is it to be built on?"

"At last, it is. I came here to take leave of it before its change. And you," she said, in a voice of touching interest to a wanderer— "you live abroad still?"

"Still."

"And do such noble work, promoting a better world for us all."

"I'm not sure it is as noble as it is necessary. We've made progress, but there is still much to be done."

"For most Scapegraces, yes. But I hope you don't accomplish much to benefit vampires," she said.

"I trust you to make that part of my job unnecessary," I said. "There are not many of their kind left in England, I understand. Bravo to you, for your hard work to that end."

"Oh," she said. "I have help now. There's a whole active brigade of slayers here and throughout Europe, and more in training under Mrs. Brandley. Vampires only. I made Mrs. Brandley promise that we would make it our objective to rid the world of vampires, and leave other Scapegraces alone. Vampires are the only ones who become so by choice and seek to spread their venom maliciously."

"I'm glad to hear it. We're making great strides in promoting the good in Scapegraces and would accomplish all the more without the murderous and underhanded actions of vampires always setting us back."

"I have often thought of you," said Estella.

"Have you?"

"Of late, very often. There was a long hard time when I kept far from me the remembrance of what I had thrown away when I was quite ignorant of its worth. But since my duty has not been incompatible with the admission of that remembrance, I have given it a place in my heart."

"You have always held your place in my heart," I answered.

And we were silent again until she spoke.

"I little thought," said Estella, "that I should take leave of you in taking leave of this spot. I am very glad to do so."

"Glad to part again, Estella? To me, parting is a painful thing. To me, the remembrance of our last parting has been ever mournful and painful."

"But you said to me," returned Estella, very earnestly, "'God bless you, God forgive you!' And if you could say that to me then, you will not hesitate to say that to me now—now, when suffering has been stronger than all other teaching, and has taught me to understand what your heart used to be. I have been tried and tested, but—I hope—into a better shape. Be as considerate and good to me as you were, and tell me we are friends."

"We are friends," said I, rising and bending over her, as she rose from the bench.

"And will continue friends apart," said Estella.

"We will continue friends," I said. "Always. You saved my life. But tell me. How did you know him?"

She blushed and cast her eyes down. The effect was rather stirring, for I had rarely known her to blush. She did not need clarification as to whom I meant. "After what you said to me, when I killed that vampire holding you captive."

"Orlick," I affirmed.

"One of our kind, you'd said, so emphatically. I started to wonder at that time what you could possibly mean. I sought out a certain party of our acquaintance who worked, at one time, for both of our interests. He made some revelations to me without, of course, actually revealing anything."

"Jaggers." I nodded.

"I meant to stay away. What did a father mean to me then? A married woman, having grown up without a father, and never missing one as far as she knew? And with him in such miserable condition, sentenced to death. Curiosity got the better of me when I'd heard—or rather pieced together—all you had done for him. I knew he had to be worthy of you, for you to go to all the trouble. Though, God knows, there was a time you would have done it all for me and I was far from worthy."

"Don't say so. You always were, to me."

"I can't imagine why, but yes. Somehow, I was worthy to you, and I am grateful for your good opinion when I was so far from deserving of it. I must tell you it was quite a shock to discover that I had werewolf blood in my veins, with all the time I'd taken plotting to destroy your kind. At the same time, it suddenly made sense to me. I loved you, Pip, never more than when I watched you turn wolf and attack that other wolfish boy. The sight of both of you fighting—It was a sight to stir the blood. I knew you were for me, then, Pip. I knew we were meant to be together, and yet I wouldn't let that happen."

"I know, Estella. It had to be this way."

"I wish it hadn't. I wish I had seen that I could be warm, loving, and true. I needed to strike out and try on my own. I thought Drummle was the kind of man who wouldn't care what I got up to without him. I imagined we would marry and he would fall back into his independent pursuits so I could do the same, but he was—well, he wasn't what I expected at all, and that's over now. When I went to see my father, Pip, I felt my heart melt. All those years that I'd struggled to build up an icy resistance to any emotion just heated through in seconds. He was in so much pain. I did all I could for him, and I'm not sorry. He thought I was an angel and he begged me for mercy. How could I not deliver it for him?"

"How could you not," I agreed. "You did the right thing, Estella. You proved you had a heart. He told me he had seen an angel. I told him he had a daughter, and that I loved her. That I love her. And do you know? Presently, we have a scourge of vampires in Cairo."

"Vampires? In Cairo?" She smiled, and there was everything sweet and warm and nothing arch or icy in it. "Someone will have to see to their extinction."

I took her hand in mine, and we went out of the ruined place. And, as the morning mists had risen long ago when I first left the forge, so the evening mists were rising now, and in all the broad expanse of tranquil light they showed to me, I saw no shadow of another parting from her.

GRAVE EXPECTATIONS

CHARLES DICKENS AND SHERRI BROWNING ERWIN

INTRODUCTION

In this reimagining of Charles Dickens's classic, *Great Expectations*, Pip is an orphaned young werewolf living with his ill-tempered sister and her gentle husband, the blacksmith Joe Gargery. One fateful night, visiting his parents' grave under the full moon, Pip encounters a frightening stranger—another werewolf and a convict no less. Too afraid to do anything other than obey the stranger's instruction, Pip helps this convict and sets in motion of chain of events that will forever change the course of his life.

Pip is sent to reside with Miss Havisham, a vampire who was sired and left on her wedding day by the one she loved. She has adopted Estella and raised her as a vampire slayer, to seek revenge on the supernatural creatures that she blames for her ruin. Pip, in awe of Estella's beauty, falls instantly in love with her despite the fact that she has been trained to hate all "Scapegraces." When an anonymous benefactor sends Pip to London to become a gentleman, he believes it is his chance to win Estella's hand. The question that lies ahead is whether Pip will be able to overcome his wolfish ways and turn his once grave expectations for himself into great ones.

TOPICS AND QUESTIONS FOR DISCUSSION

1. In Pip's world, the term "Scapegraces" is used to define "those of a supernatural sort" (p. 11). What do you think

this term implies about the way that creatures like werewolves and vampires were viewed in this society?

2. On page 12, Pip wonders, "Was it a crime to merely be different?" While being a werewolf is simply a condition inherited at birth, vampires prey on the living to increase their population, and yet are "considered civilized and welcome to mix in society." Is one creature more monstrous than the other? Do both werewolves and vampires have the capacity for good and evil?

3. After being invited to Miss Havisham's and then later learning of his anonymous benefactor, Pip often feels ashamed of his roots, and of Joe's commonness even more so than his own Scapegrace status. Yet Joe never seems to exhibit any embarrassment over Pip's wolfishness. What does this say about each of their characters? What influences the focus of Pip's shame?

4. When Mrs. Joe dies (the first time), Pip finds what he knows to be evidence of Magwitch's crime, but he still does not accuse him. Why do you think Pip believes that Magwitch is innocent of this crime when the main piece of evidence points directly to him?

5. Throughout most of the story, Estella is cold-hearted and shows no affection for Pip despite his unwavering love for her. Why should he love someone who could possibly end up killing him in her crusade against Scapegraces? What makes him fall in love with her in the first place? Why do you think Pip continues to pursue someone who will never return his feelings?

6. Pip and Herbert have a very special friendship. Do you think this brotherly love grew out of the wolfish need to be part of a pack? Or something more human?

7. While Miss Havisham is herself a vampire, she has trained Estella in the ways of vampire slaying. Pip wonders "if Miss Havisham weren't really wishing to be staked by Estella one day in raising her to such an art." (p. 235) Do you agree? Do you think Miss Havisham's eventual outcome either supports or refutes this opinion? Why does Estella never stake her, if indeed her mission is to kill vampires?

8. Pip is horrified when he finds out the Magwitch has been his anonymous benefactor all along. Why do you think this revelation is so abhorrent to Pip, when he seems so willing to not only protect Magwitch and keep him safe, but to also protect his feelings by not revealing his disappointment?

9. On page 284, Pip explains to Miss Havisham that there are certain Scapegraces who "showed more humanity than the humans." Discuss which of the Scapegraces behave with the utmost humanity, and which of the human characters exhibit what could be categorized as monstrous behavior?

10. How does the discovery of Estella's parentage change things for Pip? Does it change your opinion of her?

11. Why is it so easy for Joe and Biddy to forgive Pip after he had neglected them for so many years? Should Joe have been angry that Pip spent so much time visiting Magwitch after he was captured, when he never kept up his visits to Joe like he had promised?

12. Though Estella is able to eventually see the goodness in werewolves, she never changes her opinion of vampires. Why do you think she can pardon and accept most Scapegraces and still seek vengeance against vampires?

ENHANCE YOUR BOOK CLUB

1. *Grave Expectations* is a reimagining of Charles Dickens's classic *Great Expectations*. Have you read *Great Expectations* before? If so, how did the supernatural version compare to the classic? What remained the same in this new version of the story? What changed? If not, choose *Great Expectations* for your next book club pick.

2. *Grave Expectations* is a literary mash-up—where a fictional classic is retold in present day or with mythical substitutions. Examples include *Pride and Prejudice and Zombies* or the movie *Clueless*, which was essentially Jane Austen's *Emma* set in Beverly Hills during the 1990s. Try creating a literary mash-up of your own with your book club. Pick a favorite classic and retell the story as though it took place in the present day or with some supernatural characters. The more imaginative, the better!

3. Legends of werewolves and vampires have been carried down through the centuries. How does their depiction in this work compare with your preconceived notions of such supernatural creatures?